TRYSMOON

Book Three: Hunted

By
Brian K. Fuller

TRYSMOON
BOOK THREE: HUNTED

Edited by Jessica Robbins JessiLynRobbins@gmail.com

briankfullerbooks.com
facebook.com/briankfullerbooks

ISBN-13: 978-1502806291
ISBN-10: 1502806290

For the Wind River Mountains:
A great place to get lost.

CHAPTER 49 - THUNDER AND RAIN

"We will ride for as long as we can," Maewen announced to the somber party gathered at the head of the bridge over Mora Lake. "We ride quickly, so keep together."

Grumbling was the only reply as her audience cinched saddles and stuffed what few supplies they had left into saddle bags. Despite their casualties, they came up one horse shy, and the Chalaine offered to ride double with Fenna. Dason protested, complaining that her horse would need speed if they fell into a fight, but the Chalaine silenced him with an order, and he helped her sit in front of the new Lady of Blackshire.

Finally someone obeys one of my commands, the Chalaine thought bitterly.

Fenna's pale, empty face darkly complemented Geoff's shamed, sobered countenance. Geoff was so out of character he seemed a different person altogether as he stowed his writing materials in his cloak and climbed up on a bay horse that reflected his lowering mood.

"We will almost surely need to leave the horses behind

at some point," Maewen continued, "and slaughter them for food. If the Uyumaak are against us in numbers, then we will need to tread paths too difficult for four legs. If I should fall, you must head toward the rising sun. At all costs, avoid getting trapped against the shard edge." She turned toward Chertanne and Padra Athan, who stood side by side improvising a way to tie the Pontiff's Staff onto Chertanne's horse. "I would ask both of you to reconsider leaving Gen behind. He knows wilderness lore and is the best fighter we have."

"Absolutely not!" Padra Athan refused sternly. "How can you even request such a thing, considering what he did last night?"

"How could I not," Maewen returned evenly, "considering what awaits us for the next month and a half? You will rue this decision."

She turned her horse and spurred it forward across the bridge. The Chalaine looked at her mother, who returned a meaningful glance. She would have Gen freed, whatever the cost. Her mother loved him better than anyone, and Padra Athan and Chertanne would find out what the former First Mother of Rhugoth was capable of.

The Chalaine kicked her legs, and her black stallion, Roarer, cantered forward. The morning dawned chill with a hint of autumn in it. The clear sky above them awaited a mass of roiling gray clouds to the east that churned toward them at an alarming rate. She didn't need anyone to tell her that it wasn't natural. While she was not Maewen or Gen when it came to the wild and the weather, the storm felt wrong even at a distance, and as the bridge over Lake Mora faced east and west, their departure from the Holy city took them straight toward the oncoming disturbance.

The Uyumaak attack and the casualties of the wedding night had reduced the once-mighty caravan to twenty-four souls. Three Dark Guard, their apprentices, Jaron, Dason, Cadaen, and five of Chertanne's personal guard were all that remained of the soldiers. The Chalaine rejoiced that the majority were Rhugothian. If for no other reason, Chertanne would hold his tongue and his hand while surrounded by those who by law were his subjects but by heart were hers. Jaron, she knew, would kill Chertanne without a second thought if he so much as treated her with disrespect, and she didn't doubt that others in the party would do the same. It was Gen's legacy.

They reached the end of the bridge and rode for the tall gate cut into the one of the high hills that surrounded the lake. The wind howled through the gap, plastering her veil to her face. Maewen rode on, glancing worriedly at the sky. Distant booms rumbled ominously in the wind, and, after they had ridden only a mile, lightning flicked across the edges of the mass of clouds now roiling above them. Maewen held up and signaled for everyone to gather around her.

"We must find shelter!" she screamed in the mounting wind. "There are several buildings along the path ahead of us! Keep a tight rein on your horses!"

Even as she finished, lightning struck a tree nearby, thunder booming so loudly that the Chalaine let her reins drop to cover her head. Her horse reared with fear and she and Fenna tumbled out of the saddle and onto the hard stones of the road in a heap. The Chalaine landed awkwardly on her right side, pain from her wrist lancing up her arm.

She extricated herself from Fenna and stood with Dason's help, Geoff nearby to lend his wife his hand. Tears stung the Chalaine's eyes as she supported her hurt wrist with her good hand. Her horse sprinted back toward the gap along with three other horses, Dason's and Geoff's among them. Her mother swore, handing her reins to Cadaen as she dismounted to aid her ailing daughter. The rain descended in pelting sheets.

"Come! Run or ride!" Maewen commanded.

Jaron lifted the injured Chalaine onto his horse, Mirelle sitting behind to help steady her daughter, and a fearful Geoff hoisted Fenna onto Mirelle's horse. By the time they found a small circular building shaped and constructed in the same fashion as those in Elde Luri Mora, the rain had thoroughly soaked everyone.

The soldiers tied the horses to tree branches as everyone else hurried inside. Lightning cracked and thunder rolled all about them, the ferocious downpour drumming up a deafening roar on the ceiling of the building. As with the Hall in Elde Luri Mora, a small circular skylight was cut into the top of the dome. In the center of the room was a fire pit surrounded by an elevated bench carved out of the floor, a place for gathering and talking. A spectacular painting of the city of Elde Luri Mora stretched around the walls and was so lifelike that it almost seemed to be a window looking on the city. The circular border of the fire pit was carved to resemble flames shooting up from the ground, and carved animals and vines filigreed the benches.

"Her Ladyship is hurt," Dason announced loudly, helping the Chalaine onto the bench. "Can you do something for her, Padra? Maewen?"

"My talents do not lie with healing, I am afraid," Padra Athan apologized. Maewen jogged over, face worried. Pushing the wet hair out of her face, she knelt before the Chalaine and pulled up the young woman's sleeve. As Maewen prodded her forearm, the Chalaine yelped in pain.

"It is not a bad break," Maewen reported, "but it will hurt you a great deal when you move. I will splint it and prepare a sling. I have some herbs I can stew for the pain. Do you want them?"

The Chalaine nodded. Her arm throbbed, and the pain scarcely let her think of anything else.

"I have enough for a few days," Maewen continued, "which should get you through the worst of it." She turned to the assembly of onlookers. "Don't just stand there! Find some wood for a fire before it is all too wet to burn! And find the horses that ran off!"

The Dark Guard dashed out of the building and into the rain. Maewen left and returned quickly with two straight sticks, and, as Jaron oversaw the fire, the half-elf gently splinted the break.

How can Gen ignore such pain? the Chalaine thought in her anguish, remembering him at the betrothal standing with an arm shattered far worse than hers and not seeming the least bit strained. Every time Maewen put any pressure on her arm at all she felt like screaming.

Dason retrieved two bedrolls and created a comfortable bed on the floor near the back of the structure. Mirelle led her to it and sat beside her, Fenna joining them. Before long, an acrid odor filled the room, and in dismay, the Chalaine realized the bitter smell was a prelude to what Maewen would force her to drink.

"A poor piece of luck, Highness," Dason sympathized.

"This is not cards, Dason. Luck had nothing to do with it," the Chalaine disagreed. "I let go of the reins and lost control of the animal. The thunder unnerved me. It was so close. I need more control."

"Highness," Dason said tenderly, "it is hardly your fault. The horse should have. . ."

"Enough, Dason," the Chalaine interrupted. "Being the Chalaine does not mean I am exempt from errors in judgment. I will pay for this and learn the lesson. Do not trouble yourself about it."

Dason opened his mouth to protest, but Mirelle stared him down and he snapped it shut.

The stewing required over an hour. Chertanne inquired after her briefly and Jaron brought her some dried meat and water. The rain and thunder continued unabated, the storm stalling in place above them. The only comfort they had was that the enemy could not reach them. Maewen guessed they could travel for at least a day under Elde Luri Mora's protection against Mikkik's creatures.

By the time Maewen arrived with her draught, weariness had sapped the Chalaine of her vitality. She had scarcely slept the night before, and the pain in her arm throbbed incessantly. The potion tasted as bitter as it smelled, but after several minutes the pain faded, dwindling to a shadow of its former strength. Maewen emptied one of her waterskins and poured the rest of the brew inside it.

"Take a little when the pain comes on," she instructed, laying it beside the Chalaine. "Drink sparingly. It will make you drowsy. I let you have a generous portion to start to help you rest."

The Chalaine nodded her understanding and laid her head in her mother's lap.

"There is one other thing," Maewen said, glancing to ensure that Chertanne was nowhere nearby. Once convinced, she reached into a pouch at her side and removed three necklaces, each with a pyramid-shaped stone. "Before I left him, Gen gave them to me and told me to have you wear them."

"What are they?" the Chalaine asked, taking them with her good hand. "What do they do?"

"I do not fully know," Maewen whispered. "He only mentioned that he wore them during his training and that they would help you. He also said to keep them secret, especially from the Aughmerians."

Mirelle helped the Chalaine sit up and put them on quickly, and they clinked as they knocked against the Ial Stone that already hung about her neck. She wondered what they could be, but knowing that Gen had thought of her at the last brought a small contentment to her, and she found herself missing him again.

The steady roar of the rain and the soporific in the medicine eventually lured her to sleep. She immediately fell into a dream, finding herself standing in a large Cathedral.

The Chapel was beautiful, rivaling the Great Hall of her home. Expertly crafted white marble columns, darkly stained benches, and high windows greeted her, and the statues lining the walls peered unendingly over the empty pews as if to inspire obedience and reverence in any that sat beneath their gaze.

The Chalaine walked forward tentatively, gasping at the magnificent stained glass window embedded in the ceiling, a picture of Eldaloth coloring everything around the altar. Turning her gaze back to the front, she noticed three doors to the rear of the choir loft, one in the center and two to either side. A quick glance to the rear of the building showed her nothing but a blank wall where the front door should have been.

Her raspy footsteps echoed through the empty building, and she wondered where it could be or if it was real at all. It was certainly nowhere near Elde Luri Mora, since sunshine shone through the windows from a cloudless sky.

"Hello?" the Chalaine called out, voice echoing through the vast spaces. Although she couldn't say why, *someone*, she knew, was supposed to greet her here. But no one came or answered her calls.

Something this finely constructed must be in a city of some size, or perhaps in Mur Eldaloth, she thought. Unfortunately, the windows were much too high to look out of, and after wandering around alone for what felt like an hour, the grand Cathedral felt like a prison.

As far as she could tell, the sun had not budged, the light slanting through the windows at the same angles it had when she first found herself inside the structure. The passing of time, which seemed instantaneous and inconsistent in most of her dreams, crawled along too authentically within the confines of the Cathedral. She wondered if the stones Gen had given her were connected with what she was experiencing.

But what does this Church have to do with Gen?

At last, she resolved to climb the steps to the choir loft and inspect the doors. They were constructed of the same dark, tightly grained wood of the benches. Within carved ovals on the door faces, an artisan had carefully chiseled likenesses—on two doors were the faces of men and on the rightmost door an elf. Each of the figures was different, and she thought the runes inscribed about the apex of the oval probably told their names, though she didn't recognize the runes and couldn't read them.

She decided to try the leftmost door, the oval depicting a man with short hair and a longbow. Of the three, he had the kindest aspect, though why it should matter she couldn't guess. The door opened silently, and she only opened it a crack before peering cautiously inside. Her eyes widened at what she saw.

A marble bier bore the body of the man whose face was carved into the door. He wore a black uniform very like what the Dark Guard wore, his sword and bow embraced within his arms. Candles affixed to the floor in mounds of wax encircled the bier, but their flames were motionless, frozen in time. The room itself was small, well-lit, and unadorned, though a placard was affixed to the bier in the language she could not read. The Chalaine thought he must have been part of the fighting order of the Church, but something about the profile of his pale gray face seemed familiar somehow and she entered to get a better look at him.

The candlelight on the floor cast his face into shadow, so she stooped down, careful of her dress, and pried one of the candles out of the wax. As soon as she grasped it, it sputtered to life, flickering and dancing in her hand. Craning forward, she held the candle out over the corpse's face to get a better look. There was a resemblance to someone she knew in his mien that she couldn't place, but as she tried to sort out who, hot wax dripped and burned her hand and she let go of the candle. It fell onto the man's chest and sputtered out. Delicately, she reached down to remove it, and as she touched his chest, his eyes snapped open. She screamed, startling backward and falling to the floor.

She woke.

"Are you well?" Maewen asked, coming to her side as her mother forced her to lay back down.

"Just a dream," she explained. "I am sorry." Then she saw it. The man on the bier reminded her of Maewen, though she certainly possessed a fiercer aspect. The two shared the same deep, knowing eyes.

"The potion often leads to dreaming. They are usually not unpleasant, however."

The Chalaine closed her eyes and tried to slow her pounding heart. "It was not unpleasant. Merely surprising. Do not be troubled."

She tried to relax and return to her slumber, but nervousness kept it at bay despite the dullness of the day. Time passed slowly with a great deal of talk in low voices. Padra Athan inquired after her welfare before turning to Maewen who sat against a wall nearby fletching. Athan crouched down before the ranger and she regarded him coldly.

"I was wondering," Athan said, "what you think the Uyumaak's strategy to find us will be, if indeed they are arrayed against us as we fear."

Maewen sheathed her knife and wiped the wood shavings from her legs. "I think it is certain they are there and waiting for us, though in what numbers, I cannot say. This rain, however, is quite deliberate. Soft, wet ground slows our movement, especially in ascent. The horses will leave such plain tracks that even a child could follow them for miles without difficulty. Even walking after today's deluge would do little to help us pass unnoticed.

"Most distressing, however, is that the storm is almost assuredly conjured through magic, which means they have a powerful Mage. We have you and Chertanne, but if we face Joranne, which is certainly possible, then I doubt the two of you can match her.

"Their strategy will be simple. Its effectiveness and our chance of overcoming it hinge solely upon their numbers and our ability to be stealthy. They know we must leave Elde Luri Mora and head north, but from where, they do not know. They will patrol an east-west line, searching for sign of us. Once they find it, they will come, and quickly. If their numbers are few, we may get enough of an advance to help us get to places where tracking will be more difficult for them. If they can thickly patrol that east-west line, then our chances slim considerably.

"The rain's only virtue for us is that after the ground absorbs the water, we will be able to travel more quietly—provided that whoever is causing the storm cannot keep it up indefinitely. We will leave a clear mark wherever we go, however."

"So what is your plan?" the Padra asked, mouth curled down in worry beneath his hooked nose. Chertanne wandered up behind, arms crossed.

"If they are smart," Maewen said, "they will expect us to travel the shortest route, given the state of our supplies. The shortest course is northwest. I plan to do the opposite. Before we leave the protection of Elde Luri Mora, we will strike east. We'll have to ford the river, but if we can get across, we will ride hard due north into the lower foothills. While we will be more visible, the easy terrain will allow us to put the speed of the horses to good use and get some distance on our pursuers. Before the Shattering, deer swarmed those hills, which, if still true, would go a long way toward solving our food problems. There is also plenty of water in that direction."

"How much longer will it add to our trip?" Chertanne asked, expression betraying his fear of the answer.

"At least two weeks, but with this route, we should be

able to keep the horses for most of the journey. It does take us close to Dunnach Falls Bridge again, though I doubt they left any force there."

"Have the Uyumaak any weaknesses we might exploit?" Athan inquired hopefully.

"Few," Maewen replied, twirling an arrow in her hand. "In most respects, the Uyumaak are our superiors. The Hunters are faster than us and have a superior sense of smell. The Warriors are stronger. The Bashers tougher. The Archers more accurate. All of them have scales that change color, so they can hide more easily, and they see better in the dark than humans do."

"A discouraging list," Athan frowned. "Where are they weak?—if you would answer my original question."

Maewen stood. "I was getting to that. They do not have language and must communicate by tapping rhythms on their chests, sticks, rocks, or whatever is available. Thus, to be coordinated they must at least partially reveal their position. They also must be led. If the Chukka and the Shaman in the group are killed, the Uyumaak tend to fight among themselves. So, you see, my decision to use Gen to help me try to assassinate the Shaman was not all folly.

"They also hoard and value shiny objects. I escaped an Uyumaak attack once by throwing bronze pieces on the ground behind me as I ran. Unfortunately, I don't believe anyone has any such treasures, unless you can conjure some up, Ha'Ulrich. Lastly, if you can kill the Hunters, they will be 'blind' in most respects and easy to evade, as they exclusively rely on the Hunters to track their quarry. We have little chance of pulling that off, unfortunately. They are likely patrolling Elde Luri Mora's borders in numbers."

"There doesn't seem much there to take advantage of," Chertanne interjected darkly.

"You are correct," Maewen agreed. "The speed and endurance of the horses are our only advantage, which is why I would prefer to keep them as long as we can."

14

"I will try to turn some of the dirt into gold," Chertanne offered, "if it will help."

"It might, but it need not be gold. The Uyumaak have no need of money and appraise the worth of an object by its luster only. Now, if you will excuse me. I need to search for some herbs while I have the luxury of doing so."

"But it's pouring!" Chertanne blurted out in disbelief.

"The rain concerns me not," Maewen said and left.

Maewen's dire description of their chances set the Chalaine's heart to beating, and she sipped her grog to help clam herself. The half-elf returned as night fell, soaked to the bone but not showing the least bit of inconvenience. The rain tapered off as full dark approached, the sound of dripping amplified as the roar of the downpour dissipated. Dinner consisted of tough strips of meat and bread that were alternately stale and soggy where the rain had soaked into saddlebags.

"We have about two more weeks of meals like this one," Maewen announced to the group. "After that, we need to find game, roots, and what berries might be left. Do not eat anything unfamiliar without asking me first. Tighten your belts and eat as sparingly as you can bear."

The Chalaine had little appetite to start with and pocketed most of what her mother handed her. Maewen's potion worked well for the pain, though the Chalaine had difficulty accustoming herself to the sling and splint. In the hours leading up to the meal, Chertanne managed to transmute the dirt around the doorway into four shiny disks the color of silver for use against the Uyumaak. He was enormously pleased with his success, though the task drained his strength and he fell asleep directly after dinner.

The Chalaine shook her head at his thunderous snoring. How could Chertanne possibly face down Mikkik? His abilities seemed only good for cheap parlor tricks or to create and destroy trinkets. She fervently hoped his skill and strength would improve vastly before she had to rely on his protection from anything.

Athan staggering into a wall, eyes wide and face in shock, silenced the room. He fended off attempts to see to his welfare, requiring several moments to steady himself, breath labored and hand clenched about his robes. Chertanne snorted awake at the commotion.

"What is it?" Maewen importuned, face concerned.

"It is the former Pontiff," the besieged Padra finally divulged. "He is dead. It is a great loss, for us all."

"Is your ward still intact," Chertanne asked urgently.

"Yes."

"Do you think Gen killed him?" Chertanne pressed.

"No," Athan said. "No. His time was come."

Chertanne was disappointed. The Chalaine felt a brief surge of hope, and her mother's face betrayed the same emotion. Even if the ward were up, with the Pontiff dead Gen might find some other way to get out of the building.

"Now, leave me be," Athan said, voice slightly strangled. "I need time to mourn . . . and to think."

"Everyone sleep," Maewen ordered. "We leave before sunup tomorrow."

Athan lay awake for hours reeling under the dying Pontiff's news. Mikkik was indeed clever. Gen had poisoned the Chalaine and her entire nation against the Ha'Ulrich without doing one thing anyone could fault him for. Their trip across the Shroud Lake shard demonstrated beyond doubt that the web of prophecy was slight and fragile, ripe for destruction. Gen's near devastating blow the night of the marriage confirmed the blindness of their eyes and the futility of their efforts to protect the holy couple. The time for tough measures had come.

While Athan wondered how deep Gen's complicity in Mikkik's plan went, the answer was little more than a curiosity. While Chertanne had promised he would not harm Gen, Athan had not. Scholars might debate ends and means, but with the world in jeopardy, such concerns faded into the realm of the pedantic and irrelevant. Padra Athan did not fear the secular or spiritual consequences of the tough decisions he had made and would make to ensure the birth of the Holy Child. Gen had already ruined the unity of the two most powerful nations on Ki'Hal, and if he should perchance escape the ward before death, he would no doubt spend every waking moment seeking Chertanne's life.

The greatest damage, Athan knew, was the plain disgust the Chalaine felt for Chertanne. The relationship so crucial to the final scenes of the prophecy had degraded to complete animosity by both parties, and Athan saw no clear way to repair it. The way the Chalaine and the Ha'Ulrich insulted and ignored each other frightened him beyond words. If he could reconcile the two—and he would try it against all odds—then Eldaloth could not help but reward a patient, stalwart servant.

The Padra rolled off of his bedroll and stood. Maewen, standing at the front door, glanced over her shoulder at the movement and then wandered out into the night. Athan shook his head. Gen's allies ruled their party and would hold the balance of power until they could portal off the shard. Luckily, Athan knew the art of tacit instruction as well as anyone.

Standing, he crossed to where Chertanne slept. "Your Grace," Athan whispered as he shook Chertanne gently, trying not to disturb anyone else. He glanced back to the door, hoping Maewen would not reappear. Dason or Cadaen was likely awake somewhere, but that could not be helped. The rest of the dark room was alive with the sound of muted and deep breathing, though the Padra couldn't ascertain if everyone was asleep.

After the former Pontiff's devastating final message, Padra Athan knew he had to inform Chertanne of what he knew without anyone else's knowledge or suspicion. Chertanne's eyes slowly opened and widened, the whites barely visible in the weak light. Padra Athan leaned close.

"Holiness," Athan whispered, "follow me out the back. Be quiet. Wake no one."

Chertanne wrestled his blanket off himself and stood more noisily than Athan wanted, but once they passed outside, damp grass soft beneath their bare feet, they listened for any sign that anyone had awakened. Once Padra Athan was reasonably assured of their secrecy, he whispered into Chertanne's ear.

"Before the Pontiff died, he sent a message for me to relay to you and to all Ki'Hal. You must keep this to yourself until you are within safe places and surrounded by people that you trust. He did not indicate how he knew, but he revealed to me that Gen is the Ilch!"

Chertanne's face transformed from misunderstanding, to shock, to near glee. "We must let everyone know immediately!" he whispered excitedly. "This will finally put an end to his interference! Furthermore, we should send someone back to kill him outright! At last, I have him!"

"No, your Grace," Padra Athan pleaded. "You must not say a word of this to anyone! If you so much as suggest the idea in that room, you will have a sword at your throat before you can let the last word fall!"

"But surely they should know," Chertanne argued, "for their own protection, if nothing else!"

"Do you think they'll believe you?" Padra Athan returned heatedly. "I'm not sure *I* believe it! It does explain why he tried to kill you and perhaps why he was so sickly in Elde Luri Mora, but beyond that, the notion that Gen is the Ilch is preposterous! Only the Pontiff's declaration that it is so makes me trust that it is."

"Why should you doubt?" Chertanne countered. "He fought my will at every turn. He set people against me who should follow and obey me. I would say he's done Ilch's work."

"Your reasoning is sound, your Grace, but for everyone else, there will be a lot of pieces that will not fit! Mikkik's greatest fear is that you and the Chalaine should have a child. Gen could have destroyed the prophecy at his convenience at any time in the last year. You and the Chalaine were both within easy reach of his sword. Instead, he has risked his life for her, and I, for one, am not ready to say or could prove that any of his deeds were faked or disingenuous."

"Yes, but. . ."

"Hear reason, Chertanne!" Padra Athan's voice intensified. "You hate Gen. Every Rhugothian noble and aristocrat knows it. If you go in there and start spouting accusations, they will only see it as further evidence of your jealous disdain and turn against you. They honor Gen and revere his actions and his bravery. Anything you say, especially without obvious, demonstrable proof, will be seen as spiteful slander!"

"You are the proof! The late Pontiff is the proof!"

"No!" Padra Athan, disagreed, voice calming. "I . . . I have not been as kind or respectful to Gen as the Rhugothians think I should be—for my own reasons. They think I dislike him, and if I stand with you in this claim, I hope you can see what would come of it."

Chertanne's face twisted into a dissatisfied snarl and he hit the nearby wall with the meaty part of his fist. "Why did you even bother telling me if I can do nothing with the information?"

"Because we must prepare some measures for your protection and the Chalaine's. Ilch or no, Gen will see you dead if he can. You must leave Gen for me to deal with and ask no questions. Do not talk of him, even to people you trust, or get lured into any conversations about him by those loyal to him. Avoid any private conversations with Mirelle at all costs. She is dangerous."

"Anything else?"

"Yes. While we travel tomorrow, I want you to talk to the Chalaine about how you were brought up, the people who taught you, the restrictions placed upon you, the things you enjoyed and those you didn't."

As Athan expected, Chertanne frowned. "Why? I don't think there is a woman alive that hates me as much as she does."

"That *is* why. Just do it and do not respond in kind if she baits or insults you. It is time for control."

Chertanne grunted, clearly dissatisfied, and Athan's stomach clenched with renewed worry. The Ha'Ulrich did accept, however, even if grudgingly.

"Now get some sleep," Athan ordered. "I have other matters to take care of."

Chertanne stumbled off to bed and fell asleep more quickly than Athan liked. He thought the man would be sufficiently worried about their circumstances that it would disturb him enough to fend off sleep for at least an hour.

As silently as he could, Athan woke a slumbering Aughmerian soldier. As with Chertanne, he led him out the back of the building.

"What is your name?" Athan asked him quietly.

"Wendeman, your Grace."

"Wendeman, I need to lay a task to you. This is for you alone and you should speak of it to no one else. Can you do this?"

"Yes, Padra."

"Good. Listen carefully. I am afraid that in our haste this morning, we may have left something behind that could be potentially dangerous to our mission. I would like you to return to Elde Luri Mora and scout the area. If you find a potential threat still alive, you will need to destroy it immediately. Do you understand?"

"Yes, I would do so gladly, but. . ."

Athan understood his worry. "If there is anything behind us, it will be weak and little able to defend itself. You shouldn't have much trouble, especially if you keep your distance and use a bow. If anything is there, of course, I will establish a connection with your mind. Should you need to inspect the Hall of Three Moons, you need but think the wish and I will drop the ward so you may enter. Once finished, return immediately. Do not report to me. I will know how you fared through the link to your mind. If anyone asks, I ordered you to scout about. Lord Khairn truthfully knows nothing of this and you will aver to such if asked."

"I understand."

"Now I will establish the link." Athan palmed the soldier's head, incanting softly for a brief moment. "Now go. Stay out of sight, especially from Maewen."

Wendeman left, slowly picking his way through the wet forest to the rear of the building. Athan bit his lip, hoping against hope the half-elf had occupied herself elsewhere. Wendeman was no match for her skills.

Reentering the building, Athan noticed Dason sitting wide awake by the sleeping Chalaine, eyes toward the front of the building, where, Athan noted thankfully, Maewen stood staring into the night. The Padra reclined on his uncomfortable bed, and, unlike the slumbering Chertanne, remained awake through the night listening to the thunder roll overhead.

CHAPTER 50 - WHISPERS AND SECRETS

"I can't see a thing," Volney whispered as he and Gerand peered through the open entrance of the Hall of Three Moons into an absolute blackness. Cloud cover obscured the light of the moons, and the fireflies that had illuminated the ceremony the night before did not appear to sense their plight or deem it important enough to return. "What do we do?"

"We wait," Gerand said, stepping to the left of the entryway and secreting himself inside the dense wall of flowering bushes that lined the building. Volney pulled his cloak about himself and hunched down next to his companion, boots squishing in the mud.

After arranging the branches to minimize their uncomfortable poking, Volney whispered, "If you don't mind me saying so, Prince Kildan, you seem to be quite angry about this assignment. I thought you should be happy to aid your prestigious countryman, whatever his mistakes. At the very least, it is an honor to serve the First Mother."

Gerand's tone reflected his unhappy feelings. "Maewen asked us to do this, not the First Mother."

"You know better, Gerand. Maewen acts on the First Mother's instructions. Surely you do not regard what we are doing as dishonorable?"

"Dishonorable? He nearly killed the Ha'Ulrich! Do you understand what that means? I dislike Chertanne as much as any decent person, but whether we like it or not, the world must have him. If Gen would have succeeded, this whole trip and the lives sacrificed to get us here would be for naught! This world nearly met its end at Gen's hands last night."

"I understand, but there's something else at stake here, isn't there? Something is eating at you."

Gerand sighed. "I think by accepting this assignment, I will, at last, have sealed the dishonor of my family."

"Why?"

"I'll tell you a little family secret, Volney. You remember when Dason lost the Protectorship?"

"Certainly."

"My father has not written to Dason since then, and the letters I received before this journey were nothing but admonitions to be circumspect in my behavior lest I further disgrace the family name. Dason was my father's pride, and I continually strove to match him in skill and honor. Once Dason fell from his position, my father looked to me to restore our good name among Rhugothians and to staunch the gossip in the courts at home. What will happen when the news spreads that I deserted the Ha'Ulrich and the Chalaine to aid the man who tried to assassinate the Savior of the World?"

Volney frowned. "Then why accept this assignment at all, Gerand? You could have declined and Kimdan would have taken your place."

"I have asked myself that very question repeatedly for the last two hours," Gerand answered. "I might ask you the same. You cannot be ignorant of the potential consequences for you or your family."

"I did this because I think the First Mother and the Chalaine wish to see Gen safe. I know Chertanne is my King, but I feel no attachment to him as I do to them. And Gerand, while Gen endangered Ki'Hal, can you not see that Chertanne not only wished for but planned out and invited the confrontation? He hoped Gen would attack him so he could demonstrate his power, a folly that almost turned to his own ruin. If Chertanne were any other person, every decent man would pledge their support to Gen now."

"And therein lies my difficulty," Gerand said earnestly. "Chertanne isn't just another man, and Gen has never given him any consideration for his station or his mighty purpose in the prophecy! He impudently and repeatedly crossed the most important man in the world. That is recklessness. If Chertanne wrote the invitation to a confrontation, then Gen addressed and sealed it."

"I can see your point, Gerand, but I am going to ask you a question, and I want you to answer it truthfully."

"As I answer all questions."

"Of course," Volney snorted. "The first night we were on duty and Gen challenged Chertanne for the Chalaine's honor, how did you feel when he won?"

"That's not fair."

"Oh, yes it is!" said Volney. "It is the very crux of the matter! I'll tell you how you felt. Your whole soul rejoiced! Joy, pride, and satisfaction coursed through your veins! You felt honored to be his countryman. You counted yourself blessed to keep company with and wear the same uniform as such a man. You chided yourself for not taking the initiative in the matter before he did. You cursed your brother, Dason, for his weakness in not supporting him. Tell me it wasn't so."

Gerand rubbed his eyes. "You know I cannot."

"Then how can you fault that same man, Ki'Hal notwithstanding, for confronting personal and despicable attacks from even the Ha'Ulrich himself? Should he have sought Chertanne's life? No. But for pity's sake, you must see that save for the Ha'Ulrich's calling, Gen was entirely justified! That is enough for me. Chertanne's destiny is holy, but his cause has yet to be just."

Gerand kept whatever he felt to himself, and they settled in to wait until morning light. Following Maewen's instructions, they had loaded their armor and their portion of food onto one of the horses and led it back to the holy city. They staked the horse behind the Hall of Three Moons and had tried to cross into the building, only to be met with a severe shock from Athan's ward that addled their minds and set them on the verge of vomiting. They had called Gen's name several times with no reply and then resigned themselves to watch, for the half-elven tracker feared that Chertanne or Athan would attempt to end Gen's life.

The wind blew more frequently as the night deepened, and booms of thunder in the west portended more rain to come. Gerand and Volney backed further into the bushes until they encountered the outer wall of the building and sat on a small, rounded ledge at its base. Trees and bushes bent and swayed in the wind, boughs and limbs creaking and bending in sudden gusts.

"Do you think anyone will come?" Gerand quietly asked.

"Not really," Volney yawned.

"You are wrong. Get low and be quiet."

They slipped from the ledge and crouched among the pink and white blossoms, pushing them softly aside to gain a vantage point on the walk leading up to the entrance of the Hall. At first, Volney thought Gerand was mistaken; save for the weather, all was preternaturally still. But after several minutes of trying to tame his pounding heart, he heard and then saw a man approaching. His drawn sword glinted dully in the weak light, but despite the night's obfuscation, they recognized him as one of the Aughmerian soldiers.

The soldier ascended the steps warily. In his surprise, Volney's fingers slipped from the branch he had lowered and it snapped upward noisily. Gerand dug his fingers into Volney's arm with one hand and placed the other on his own sword hilt. The Aughmerian stopped and squinted into the dark in their direction. Volney stiffened as a wind kicked up, noisily disturbing the trees nearby. The soldier surveyed the area around him for several long moments.

"Curse this darkness," he muttered before planting his feet in front of the arched entryway and bowing his head. After a few moments, he stepped forward tentatively, sword pointing ahead of him, until he at last passed inside.

"The ward is down!" Volney whispered excitedly. "We have to get in there!"

"Take off your boots," Gerand commanded, sitting on the wet ground and working at his own.

"What?!"

"Just do it! Quickly!"

Gerand led Volney out of the bushes and to the edge of the entryway. Water soaked into their woolen stockings, but as they neared the entry, Volney understood Gerand's reasoning. The Aughmerian's booted footsteps echoed loudly through the empty chamber.

Gerand pulled him back from the door. "Hug the edge of the entryway and pass inside quickly. We will be silhouetted against it momentarily. If he is looking this way, he may see us. Go!"

Without further explanation, Gerand slipped inside. Volney followed him, hugging the cold entry stones as he rounded the corner. Gerand touched Volney's shoulder once inside to signal where he was. The darkness in the Hall was complete. For several seconds they listened to the soldier wandering aimlessly to and fro about the Hall, boot steps echoing through the dome. The blackness foiled an easy search, evincing a great deal of foul language from the searcher. All torches and lanterns had been lost in the giant's attack, and the wet weather spoiled their ability to create new ones.

During one of the Aughmerian's tirades, Gerand whispered, "Last I remember the Pontiff trapped him near the dais on this side, though he could have moved anywhere by now. Put your hand on the wall and let's follow it. We should find the entrance to one of the side chambers before too long."

Their socks allowed for silent walking, though both men struggled to keep their scabbards from banging into the wall. The sound of footsteps nearing their position brought them both to a standstill.

"Where are you, Gen?" the soldier called, feigning concern. "I am here to help you!" He approached a spot just behind where Gerand and Volney stood frozen and afraid to breathe. "Those side chambers were around here somewhere," the soldier mumbled to himself.

Silently, Gerand pulled Volney away from the wall and out toward the middle of the chamber. To their left, the soldier passed by, scraping his sword along the wall to guide himself. The rustling of curtains signaled his entry into the nearest chamber. Volney exhaled, wondering how long it had been since he last took breath.

A soft glow in front of his face startled him. A firefly. In the profound darkness, the weak light illuminated Gerand's face briefly. Volney cursed their luck. When they wanted light, the insects wouldn't come. Now that they needed darkness, they appeared. But as they stood stock still, the firefly moved away and hovered ten feet from them. Gerand followed. Foot by foot it flew ahead of them, leading them across the expanse of the Hall.

Glow. Darkness. Glow. They were near the thrones. Darkness. Volney kept his hand on Gerand's shoulder as they inched forward. Glow. Darkness. Glow. A waxy, pale face, eyes open, stared unblinking toward the Hall's entrance. Darkness.

"Is he dead?" Volney asked quietly.

Glow. The eyes slowly turned toward them. Darkness.

"Gen," Gerand whispered. "It's Gerand and Volney. Stay still. We'll get you out of here." Darkness.

"Where's that firefly now?" Volney muttered.

"Hey!" someone shouted. Volney gulped air, and went for his sword. "I'm tired of hunting in the dark! I am here to help you! All I need is a word and I can find you!"

Volney relaxed the grip on his hilt, and he and Gerand waited and listened, crouching by Gen. Legs cramped as the Aughmerian wandered seemingly at random around the dark room. At length, the footsteps faded toward the side chambers on the opposite side of the Hall.

"Grab Gen's feet!" Gerand ordered. "We go now or not at all." Volney felt around, hand knocking against Gen's boots and socks which lay discarded by his feet. *He'll need those,* he thought. Gathering them, he placed them on Gen's chest.

He leaned close. "Can you hold these?" There was no response.

"Try shoving them under his shirt," Gerand suggested. "Hurry!" Volney worked quickly, but the awkward task proved difficult despite its apparent simplicity.

"What about his sword?"

"Forget it, Volney. We'll find another."

With effort, they hoisted Gen's flaccid body and half carried, half dragged him toward the entrance.

"I tire of this!" the Aughmerian's voice abruptly split the silence, sending Volney's heart to pounding. "You must help me find you!" They stopped, but as they bent to lay Gen gently on the ground, their scabbards clacked against the stones. "There you are! I am coming!"

Gerand and Volney drew steel, the echo multiplying the sound.

"No, no! I am here to help!" the voice was nervous, and Gerand grinned—the Aughmerian had no stomach for facing Gen, however sick he may be. "I can't see a thing. Let's meet by the door."

"Me first," Gerand growled in his best Gen imitation.

"All right, I'll walk over nice and slow. You go ahead of me."

Replacing their swords in unison and hoisting Gen, they ambled as quickly as they could toward the entrance, but when they were ten feet from the opening, the gig was up.

"Mikkik's Beard!" the soldier exclaimed.

Gerand carefully set Gen down and pulled his sword. "Drag him out, Volney!"

Volney pulled Gen out into the night as Gerand disappeared into the darkness, moving to the side to mask his location. Volney dragged Gen off to the side of the walk and took up position in front of the door in case the Aughmerian bolted.

Inside, the soldier had gone quiet.

He knows he is at a disadvantage, Gerand thought. *If he can hide and stay alive, he can return to camp and report.*

While ill at ease in the inky dark, Gerand thrilled at a chance to sink his blade into an Aughmerian; the list of his friends lost in Shadan Khairn's invasion was long. He crouched and attuned his ears to the sounds around him, noticing Volney's silhouette against the entrance.

Stand away from the door, idiot, Gerand remonstrated. *What if he has a bow?* After several agonizing minutes of absolute silence, Gerand stood. *We'll just guard the door and wait for morning. This is insane.*

Glow. Darkness. Gerand stepped quietly toward the soft yellow light. Glow. Darkness. Glow. Darkness. To the right across the Hall it led him until it hovered in front of the thick curtains covering the side chamber where Gen had rested before the wedding. Gerand did not want to charge into the room, but as he watched, the firefly's light dropped from eye level to chest level. Gerand lunged, blade passing through the curtain and plunging into the Aughmerian's chest. The soldier slumped to the floor with only the intake of an unfinished scream to mark his passing. Glow. Blood ran under the curtain. Darkness.

"He's down!" Gerand went through the curtain, and after fumbling around, removed the soldier's sword and scabbard for Gen. That done, he sprinted for the door, feet pattering across the smooth tiles, damp blossoms sticking to his socks.

"Stop! Gerand! Stop!" Volney yelled. Gerand pulled up short, heart sinking. Volney stood well away from the entrance now.

"Is it. . . ?"

"Yes, the moment you yelled. 'He's down!'"

"Mikkik's Beard!"

Athan marched inside the building, face burning with such lively anger that the groggy travelers immediately stopped packing and eating. "How could you do this, Mirelle?" he yelled, planting his feet in front of her. "We need those two to get home!"

"What do you mean by confronting me in this state?" Mirelle answered, face annoyed as she turned from a conversation she was having with Maewen. "What is it that you think I have done?"

"Don't play games, Mirelle!" Athan raged. "This is not the time! We are in grave danger and need every sword available."

"I still don't comprehend your meaning."

"Gerand and Volney! You ordered them back to help Gen!"

Mirelle folded her arms. "I most certainly did not."

"And you expect me to believe that?"

"If you want to believe the truth. You seem to forget

that Gerand and Volney were Gen's best friends while he served in Rhugoth and were no doubt deeply concerned for his welfare. Besides, they are no longer mine to command."

"They are mine to command," Chertanne asserted, joining them. A clump of blond hair jutted away from his head and his eyes rested on the puffy bags beneath them. "And I gave no such order. They have committed treason in this abandonment and will be punished for it when they are caught."

"Yes, Athan, *he* is the commander of everyone here," Mirelle said with a dash of mockery. "And, hmm, let me count now . . . and . . . my goodness! We are missing an Aughmerian soldier as well! Now I wonder where he might have wandered off to? Surely he wasn't a friend of Gen's as Gerand and Volney were? Do you happen to know where that soldier is? Padra? Your Eminence?"

Chertanne scrunched his brow and started counting the soldiers.

Padra Athan ground his teeth. "Mirelle, it is imperative that Gen not be set free! He attempted to kill the Ha'Ulrich and is a threat to the redemption of Ki'Hal! You must see both the justice and the reason in holding him there!"

"Padra, why are you explaining this to me? Perhaps you should mount your horse, ride to Elde Luri Mora, and give your sermon to Gerand and Volney. Besides, you haven't let your ward down, have you?"

"Of course not," Athan growled. "But. . ."

"Then why the fuss? It seems we have nothing to worry about from Gen."

Athan brought his hand to his face, covering his mouth and his chin as he debated with himself. A room full of silent people awaited the outcome of the spat.

"May I have a private word with you, Mirelle?" Padra Athan requested.

"Of course, Padra. Cadaen, stay here for a moment. I will return shortly."

Cadaen nodded, leveling one of his warning stares at the Churchman.

Mirelle and Athan left the building through the rear entrance, walking a short distance into the woods. Musty, cool air assaulted their noses, and the sky still closed itself against the morning sun. It had rained in spurts throughout the night, letting up near dawn. Water dripped from branch and leaf, and the ground squished unsteadily beneath their feet. Padra Athan stared off into the forest, hand on a damp trunk, carefully thinking how to formulate his words. Mirelle folded her arms across her chest, warming herself as she waited in the early autumn chill.

The Padra, thoughts collected, lifted his eyes to meet Mirelle's. Hers were ice blue, set in a stubborn, confident stare. Athan had never met her equal, in beauty or in exercise of will. A purpose, some mission she clung to with religious tenacity lurked behind those eyes and lent her iron. If he were ever to the control the woman, the Padra knew he needed to find what propped her up and put it into his own grasp.

"Mirelle, I need to tell you something. You will not believe it, but you must listen to me. It is the truth. Just before the old Pontiff died, he relayed a message to me that was most distressing and shocking. After we left the Hall of Three Moons following the ceremony, the Pontiff examined Gen. Now do not get angry when I say this. It is not baseless speculation. Chertanne and I did not collude to invent this fact as a wild rumor to discredit Gen. Hear me, Mirelle. The man Gen, the one you let into your house and appointed to guard the Chalaine, is the very Ilch."

"Yes, he is."

Padra Athan reeled, mouth unhinging for several seconds. "Wh-what!? You know? Merciful Eldaloth, Mirelle! How long have you known this? Did Chertanne tell you last night?"

"No. I've known since night of the betrothal, the one

that succeeded, I mean."

"How!?"

"Do keep your voice down, Padra. Ethris confirmed it the night the Chalaine tried to heal Gen of the demon's poison."

"You will be executed for this, the both of you!"

"We will deny everything."

Athan stabbed a finger at her. "Our magic can force the truth from you."

"Ethris has already made a provision for us against such an eventuality. Of course, any attempt to perform such an interrogation would be viewed with much disfavor. If only you and Chertanne hadn't tried so hard to discredit Gen in the first place, maybe you could accuse him now with some success. I am afraid you've quite worn out your credit with Rhugothian and Tolnorian nobility."

"Mirelle, I thought you were a sensible woman! How could you gamble your daughter's life like this? Indeed, how could you gamble the safety of Ki'Hal?"

"Gamble?" Mirelle stepped close, eyes firm. "The real gamble stands inside that building dumbly counting his soldiers! I have ample proof that Gen has rejected his calling as the Ilch and now serves the interest of my daughter and the world. I have yet to see one shred of evidence that Chertanne is either competent or serves any interest but his own.

"Think about it, Athan. The only two questions Chertanne ever answers with any authority are 'Do you hate Gen?' and 'Would you like another ale, your Grace?' He can't lead. He can't fight. He loves nothing. As a Magician you know better than I do that he has no will to work magic of any potency. I'll ride with Gen to the battlefield at doomsday. You go with Chertanne. We'll see who is dead when the first arrows fly."

"Where is your faith, Mirelle?" Athan countered. "The prophecy says Chertanne is to be Eldaloth's instrument in fighting Mikkik! Are you saying that you don't believe that anymore? Are you saying that Eldaloth will not use his power to bolster and protect Chertanne in that hour?"

"Padra, what I am saying is that I don't believe in Chertanne. It is enough that I let my daughter marry that boor so that he could father the Child. Even so, every time I see the Chalaine I feel like falling to my knees and begging forgiveness for ever letting her take an oath to bind herself to that man. It is my dearest wish to give the Chalaine what compensation and relief that a mother can from such a dismal life."

"Does the Chalaine know about, Gen?"

"No."

"She will, Mirelle. It will be known. Someday, everyone will know. I will see it done."

Much to Athan's annoyance, Mirelle laughed out loud. "Very amusing, Athan. I do pity you. You are duty bound to return to the kingdoms and convince the people that Gen is the Ilch and that Chertanne is their competent, holy leader. I'm not sure which task will be more difficult. Perhaps you should practice by persuading people that white is black and a rat is a greyhound. At least you and Chertanne have had the good sense not to make such revelations to our little party. Go ahead and tell the world, if you think you'll fare any better there than you would here.

"Nothing to say, Athan? Well, while we're being forthright, I must inform you that your attempt on my life and Gen's life the day we left Mikmir has not gone unnoticed by me. I confess it took me some time to sort out, but I did at last."

"I ordered no such thing!"

The First Mother grinned. "Of course not, just like I didn't order Gerand and Volney to help Gen. Well, I think you are far too angry for further discussion now. I wish you the best of luck training your new Pontiff."

Mirelle strode back inside, face pleasant, to a room full of questioning glances. Athan did not return until everything was packed and everyone mounted. He did not speak another word that day.

Chapter 51 - The Gate of Three Dreams

Gerand watched helplessly through the warded entry as Volney paced around the Hall of Three Moons over and over again. Unlike his unrelenting comrade in arms, Gerand had given up the search. They had inspected every inch of the smooth, white structure, hoping for any hint of a place where Gerand might slip through Athan's ward and escape. He and Volney had come up empty every time they had searched since daybreak. The building's narrow windows defied defenestration and the warded main entrance was the only opening into or out of the structure.

Gerand shook his head as Volney came around for another pass. It was time to get the big hearted Rhugothian to leave him behind. The Chalaine and the First Mother needed Gen. They loved him. They relied on him. His escape would give them courage, even if he couldn't be with them.

"Volney," Gerand called. "Come here."

His friend approached, face resolute but eyes showing panic. "There must be a way!"

"It's hopeless, Volney," Gerand said, trying to drill the point home to the determined young man. "My only chance of escape is if Athan decides to drop the ward or is killed. Since I killed the Aughmerian soldier, Athan cannot know that Gen is free and his ward now useless. I should have thought about that before I ran the man through. But what's done is done."

"You couldn't have foreseen this," Volney said.

"I could have, but I didn't. Get Gen on that horse and get moving. Now. You need to keep as close to Lady Khairn's party as possible. With just the two of you, you can ride. You've got to leave me here. Go."

Volney turned away, face fixed in a sad scowl of frustration. Gen lay just a few feet away. While otherwise lethargic, the Chalaine's fallen Protector had managed to don his socks and boots at some point during the night. Otherwise, he mimicked a corpse in demeanor and movement, and only the weak rise and fall of his chest from drawing breath and the sweat beading on his forehead from a persistent fever offered proof that he yet lived.

Volney paced around, hands on his hips, eyes roving everywhere as if searching for a solution in the trees and the sky.

"Volney," Gerand said, tone firm, "there is no decision here. You do not stand before two paths needing to decide which to take. Go. Now!"

"Shut up, Gerand. I'm trying to think."

Gerand shook his head in disgust and wandered back into the Hall of Three Moons. While it was daytime, gray cloud cover prevented the light from possessing any strength. The Hall felt like entering a room where someone lies sick and near death, a place where everyone holds their breath and fears to speak loudly for fear of disturbing the afflicted.

The wilted blossoms clung to his socks as he walked. He ran his hand through his dark hair, frustration burning off into acceptance. When he had learned of the Aughmerian invasion, he had waking dreams of victory and defeat. He either returned conqueror or died in the midst of some manly charge to rescue a beleaguered company or to break through impenetrable defenses. At the very least, he died with his boots on with a slew of enemies dead at his feet. Now he faced the most helpless, inglorious end he could imagine—starving to death alone and miles from home. In his socks.

Pushing these thoughts aside he tried to formulate some argument that would get Volney on the horse riding north. The appeal to duty had not worked, so he would try to seed a false hope inside his stubborn companion.

If I can convince Volney that escape is possible given time, Gerand thought, *he may feel more comfortable leaving, even if in his heart he does not believe my words.*

As he paced, arranging his thoughts into a persuasive argument, his eye caught Gen's sword lying on the floor several feet away from where the Pontiff had trapped his countryman. Gerand stooped and grabbed it. It was an ordinary weapon, save for its blade upon which an eagle with spread wings had been engraved on both sides so faintly that only close inspection would reveal it. The bird's demeanor was fierce, beak open and claws extended. Something about the design tickled Gerand's memory.

He walked back to the opening where Gerand still paced around the patio. "Volney! I found Gen's sword. There is an engraving on it that is familiar, but I can't place it. Here. Take a look and then put it back in Gen's scabbard." Gerand put the sword on the ground and slid it through the ward. "When you're done, throw me my boots. I'm rather tired of pulling blossoms off my socks."

Gerand wasn't sure that Volney heard his last request. He had retrieved the sword, and, after examining the blade, Volney's jaw dropped and he sputtered parts of words before coherency returned.

"I . . . I cannot believe he has this! It's unfathomable! The First Mother must have . . . but . . . I am unworthy to touch it!"

Volney dropped the sword as if it had cut him and backed away from it.

"What?" Gerand yelled loudly enough to break through Volney's stupor.

Volney pointed at the sword. "That . . . *that* is the sword of Aldradan Mikmir! No one was supposed to touch it until his return! Oh! If anyone knew Gen had it, the First Mother would be in a great deal of trouble!"

"Incredible!" Gerand said. "The First Mother must truly admire Gen to give him such a prestigious gift. Pass it back through so I can get another look at it."

"No!" Volney objected. "You have always nagged me about matters of propriety, and this, my friend, is far and away ten times as serious a matter as anything you have ever scolded me for."

"So what are you going to do, just let it sit there and rust? At least return it to Gen if you won't give it to me."

"This blade does not rust."

"That wasn't my point. We just can't leave it sitting there for anyone to pick up."

"I've got to think."

"Well," Gerand said, "while you are thinking, pass my boots through. My waterskin would be nice, too. I might as well starve as slowly as possible."

Volney retrieved the boots from the hedge and threw them toward the entrance. As they were passing through the opening, they stopped as if hitting an invisible wall, bouncing back onto the patio. He tried again with the same result.

"One moment," Gerand said, fetching the Aughmerian blade he had intended to give to Gen. He repeated what he had done with Aldradan's blade, but the soldier's sword stopped abruptly just as the boots had.

"I'm sorry, Gerand," Volney apologized at these failures. "I wish it hadn't. . ."

"Volney, you idiot, pass me Aldradan's sword."

"What?"

"Pass . . . me . . . Mikmir's . . . sword!"

Volney's eyes widened. "Of course! The blade could do wondrous things in the stories. They say that Aldradan could not be kept from going anywhere he wanted. There was this battle at. . ."

"Pass me the sword!"

"Oh, right. Of course!" Volney sent the blade skidding across the stones and Gerand eagerly grabbed it, standing and holding it before him. He breathed in and walked forward slowly.

"Maybe you should get a run at it," Volney suggested.

Gerand ignored him, maintaining a stately pace. As he approached the arched opening, he could feel the sickness coming, but just as he was about to despair, something pushed the discomfort out and away from him, the nauseous stirring in his stomach disappearing. Emboldened, he strode forward, crossing the threshold to join his friend on the patio.

"Amazing!" Gerand rejoiced, laughing for joy. "Gen had the power to leave this place the whole time and probably never knew it. Get the horse, and let's get out of here."

Volney whooped and set off toward the tree where their brown stallion munched on a tuft of grass. Gerand examined Gen while Volney fastened the saddle and saddlebags. Their swordmate was little better than a corpse, breath shallow and face slick with sweat. Gerand shook his head and buckled Aldradan's sword about his own waist.

Volney approached with the horse. "I think we should just tie the sword to the horse and . . . Hey! Unbuckle that sword from your hip! You can't use that! You're insulting my entire nation!"

Gerand rolled his eyes. "Volney, there is propriety and

then there is survival. Like my father told me, 'When the enemy is at the gates, don't put cushions in the catapults.'"

"What is that supposed to mean?"

"Simply that you use your resources to their best advantage when there is danger about. This sword is the best weapon we have. To not use it under these circumstances would be folly."

"All right," Volney said. "But I'm the Rhugothian, so it would be more appropriate if I carried it, I think."

Gerand shook his head. Volney just didn't get it. "But the sword was given to Gen—who is my countryman—so it is only fitting that I carry it for him—until he is able to take it up again, of course. Besides—and no offense—I am the better swordsman."

"Says who?"

During the ensuing argument, Gerand and Volney hoisted Gen over the horse and Gerand kept the sword. They left the deserted city, Gen draped awkwardly over the horse. Gerand was glad to be underway, thankful for a spark of hope after a morning of despair. The sun finally broke through the clouds as they crossed the bridge over Mora Lake.

"Eldaloth favors us today," Gerand said, thankful for the light.

Volney nodded in agreement. "I think we'd better make a litter for Gen. He doesn't appear too comfortable. You should try the sword on some branches, Gerand. They say it could cut through armor like . . . er . . . one of several comparisons not springing to mind."

"Use *this* sword to chop at a tree? Talk about dishonoring Aldradan and *your* nation, Volney! Here we have the blade that cut down Goras the Dire, hewed two hundred Uyumaak necks at Aumat, and felled Kudat the giant. Aldradan lifted it high to gather his armies, with it tapped the shoulders of aspiring knights to elevate them to service, and set it upon his knees while dispensing King's justice to rogues and fiends. Now you'd have me attack a pine tree with it? I can't believe you would even suggest such a thing!"

The Chalaine rode, thoughts inward, as the forested terrain around her slid by. The sun had emerged the day after she broke her wrist, and while at first the sunshine inspired a general cheer, Maewen smothered the good feeling before it could fester into anything hopeful.

"They soak the ground the day before," she said, "and now they let the sun shine so we will be more visible as we travel."

As a consequence, the half-elf led them off the road and into the wild earlier than she had intended. While she did not know where the protection of Elde Luri Mora faded, she wanted to make the point of their departure from the road as unpredictable as possible. It was now midday the day after they turned off the road. The woods provided ample cover for them and any enemies that wanted to spy on them. No one talked save under the direst need.

The Chalaine thought of Gen constantly. Dason always flickered in and out of her peripheral vision now, and as good a man as he was, she needed Gen's company. She missed his wisdom, his devotion, and his strength, but most of all she found herself longing for his irreverent sense of humor. His carefree smiles and conversation in the canyon had cast all her worries into objects of ridicule that she could manage or dismiss. With him gone, the shadows of her fears stretched long and wide across her heart.

And the biggest of those shadows is cast by Chertanne, she thought, smiling wanly at the joke she knew Gen would make of such a statement.

Chertanne spent his time near Padra Athan, the two

frequently leaning close, heads together in some private counsel. From time to time her husband would look over his shoulder to throw her an odd, pained look. While her mother would not reveal the details of her conversation with Athan outside the building near Elde Luri Mora, the Padra was obviously deeply offended or troubled by what she said. For her part, Mirelle remained as poised and calm as ever.

As the Chalaine did twenty times a day, she slipped her hand inside her cloak and into the pocket where she kept Gen's *animon*, the stone the Millim Eri had given her. Its warmth provided comforting testimony that her Protector still lived. Her mother had disclosed to her earlier that day that she thought Gen had very likely escaped, though she would not give her reasons for this hope.

Beside her rode Fenna, face cast in an unrelenting scowl. Geoff rode behind his wife as if dragged by a chain, the feather that had once seemed so indomitable now drooping unceremoniously off to the side. Fenna wouldn't look at him, speak to him, or acknowledge the many little kindnesses he extended to her during the day. Of all the caravan, Geoff was the only person the Chalaine pitied more than herself.

While she knew she should think more kindly of Fenna, the Chalaine wanted to slap her every time she bemoaned her forced marriage to Geoff. Geoff doted on her, and before their wedding Fenna had preferred the bard's company over any other, including Gen's, though she would never admit to it. The Chalaine considered her former handmaiden's treatment of Geoff as undeservedly punitive and hoped Fenna would mend her ways before the bard went mad.

The Chalaine sighed, ducking a low branch as they wound through the thick trunks of tall trees. The forest floor was clear of detritus and rolled gently around small rills. The leaves had just started to turn, edges hinting at yellows and reds to come. The thick canopy of high branches admitted spotty light to pepper the ground, and the Chalaine judged the place pleasant enough, though the gloom in her heart stripped her of any enjoyment of the scene.

Maewen, who ran as often as she rode, strode to her side. "How is your wrist, Lady Khairn?" she asked.

"Please call me Chalaine, if you will. The wrist is quite fine. I hardly feel it anymore."

"I am surprised," Maewen returned. "It should have taken far longer to heal. Perhaps I misjudged the damage done."

"Perhaps. At least it is one piece of good fortune." While the quick healing of her wound was unexpected, the Chalaine also felt unusually fit. While those around her groaned or slumped with weariness, she awoke each day stronger and more alert than the one before.

"Maewen?" the Chalaine asked, noticing the half-elf preparing to run ahead.

"Yes, Chalaine?"

"Can I ask you a question?"

"Certainly."

"Have you ever heard of someone named Samian?"

Maewen's head snapped around, eyes wide.

"Yes. Where have you heard this name?"

"Since I've worn the stone necklaces Gen had you give me, I see this man every night. He is in some magnificent Cathedral. Gen taught me enough of the old tongue that I know that he is speaking it. But besides exchanging names, we have understood little of each other. It is strange. It is a dream, but it is far too lucid and real to be just something from my own head. What do you know of him?"

Maewen turned her head away, but the Chalaine thought she caught some tender emotion on her face before the half-elf could hide it. "He was a human leader during the First Mikkikian War. He lived among the elves, took one to

44

wife, and had a child by her."

"Here, let's try something," the Chalaine suggested, removing the necklaces. "Wear them tonight and see if he comes to you when you sleep. Maybe you can figure out what he is saying. He seems quite urgent about something, and I think he's even said your name a couple of times."

The Chalaine expected protest to her offer but got none, Maewen grabbing the stones and donning them immediately. "Thank you, Chalaine. I will see what I can make of it."

Maewen loped off to the front of the party as a hill steeper than most rose before them. The half-elf led them to the east of it along a small creek that proceeded from a still forest pool. As they stopped to water the horses, the Chalaine noticed Athan saying something to Chertanne, who looked at her and then rode to her side. She exhaled roughly. Since leaving Elde Luri Mora the Chalaine had counted herself blessed for never finding herself in her husband's company.

"Lady Khairn," he greeted her nervously. The Chalaine wondered if he had ever had a meaningful conversation with a woman in his life.

"Lord Khairn," she returned politely.

"What were you and Maewen speaking about earlier?"

"Nothing of consequence. She was just checking on the condition of my wrist."

"Oh." He patted his horse and looked around.

This is the part where you ask me about my wrist, too, you dolt, she thought.

He raised his head and regarded her briefly. "I shall have the horse put down for throwing you once we return. So, how were you brought up?"

The Chalaine almost laughed at the ham-handed question—Athan at work. "Well, I lived mostly confined in my Chambers. I was tutored in reading and history by the best available scholars, and every day I was asked to recite the prophecy and listen as a wide variety of Churchmen outlined my duty to remind me of the frightful consequences that must occur as a result of any deviation from an absolutely moral life. I only left the Chambers or the castle complex to heal people in the city. And you? I imagine your lifestyle and instruction were quite different from mine."

Chertanne nodded. "At first they confined me to Ironkeep, but when I grew older, the Churchmen, scholars, and Warlords had a weeklong debate about whether I should be allowed out more often. The Churchmen wanted to keep me safe, the Warlords wanted me visible, and the scholars were divided. I was so tired of being cooped up by that time that I informed them I would leave when I pleased, and the argument ended.

"The Churchmen tried to force me to recite the prophecy every day, as well, but I refused one day. The Prelate, Coriander, I believe, was so angry with me. Oh, at first he tried gentle entreaties to get me to recite it, then humor, and finally a stern lecture. When I still refused, he grew enraged and started yelling at me and threatening me with all manner of ridiculous punishments. After I had him killed for his disrespect, the Church seemed more willing to let me set my own direction."

"How old were you then?" the Chalaine pressed, horrified.

"Thirteen."

"And at thirteen they let you dispense with such justice?"

"Yes. All my tutors felt I should learn to act independently as soon as possible."

"And how old were you when you took your first concubine?"

"Fifteen."

"And who was the first?"

"I don't remember. The five principal Warlords of

Aughmere gifted me their eldest daughters on my birthday. So I received five at once. Such a gifting of women is not unusual for a Shadan or for one who will likely win that position."

"I see," the Chalaine said as calmly as she could. "But normally such a 'gifting' would occur after the first wife is taken, correct?"

"Yes."

"So was the Church furious at your break from tradition? They reject the practice of wives and concubines."

"Honestly," Chertanne returned, "I didn't hear one word about it. I suppose one might call it the 'Coriander Effect.'" He laughed loudly enough to draw attention to himself. "No, the Warlords taught me early that the Church would try to convert me from an Aughmerian into something more palatable to other nations. I, of course, thwarted such efforts as quickly as possible. After all, Eldaloth had me born Aughmerian for a reason."

To the Chalaine's relief, Maewen signaled them forward. As if reading from a script, Chertanne bid her farewell. "Thank you, Lady Khairn. It was a pleasure talking to you. I hope it will be oft repeated." The Chalaine inclined her head as he rode off to where Athan awaited him.

While the conversation helped her understand him better, his last statement raised questions within her. Why did Eldaloth have the Ha'Ulrich born Aughmerian? Was it a matter of blood or chance? From where she stood, there wasn't any reasoning in it at all. When the Church had first announced that the Ha'Ulrich was Aughmerian, neither Tolnor nor Rhugoth took it well. The people solaced themselves, however, by convincing themselves that an Aughmerian Ha'Ulrich would be a mighty man of war, just what was needed to counter Mikkik's forthcoming assault. Even better, his father was the most renowned fighter and warrior of their age.

Her conversation with Gen about the uncertainty of prophecy now rang more true to her than ever. Doom came to the world before she had ever seen or known Chertanne or Gen. Chertanne was selfish and weak, and she desperately loved the man whose destiny it was to destroy her. The only thing she could think to bitterly laugh at amid the wrack of prophecy was that she imagined Mikkik would be just as confused as anyone when he won the coming war without the Ilch's help and practically without trying. All Mikkik need do now to recapture Ki'Hal was show up.

The Chalaine wiped away tears she didn't realize she was crying. *How did it all go so wrong?*

Maewen led them northeast along a slender stream couched in a small depression brimming with ferns and low leafy plants with small white flowers. The soft gurgling of the water calmed the Chalaine's nerves. Gradually, the density of the trees lessened and their size increased. Maewen mounted her horse and led the group forward at a brisk pace through the easy terrain.

As daylight faded, they encountered a path of paved stones that forked beneath two towering oak trees spreading toward each other to form a natural arch. One fork disappeared south into the forest from which they now emerged, the other veering southeast. The path appeared to stretch north and south as a single road in an empty plain until it bifurcated where they stood. Maewen called for a dismount. As there were no tents, few provisions, and no fire, situating their camp required nothing more than caring for the horses and finding somewhere devoid of roots and rocks to lie down.

The Chalaine fished a hard roll from her saddle bags after checking the *animon* again. Fenna approached and threw herself down grumpily at her side. The Chalaine steeled herself for another dose of Fenna's self-pity, but thankfully, the young woman seemed content to smolder while gnawing on a particularly tough morsel of dried meat. Geoff approached, his book, quill, and ink in hand. Fenna turned away, evincing a hurt look from her husband. He controlled his face and strode by them without a word to seek out Maewen, who managed to not appear more annoyed and concerned than usual.

"Maewen," Geoff entreated her, "may I beg you to tell us more about this place . . . for the record?" Maewen regarded him coldly. The Chalaine quickly stood, Dason following her as she came to Geoff's side.

"I, too, am curious," the Chalaine added. "The trees are so beautiful and the breeze so pleasant that this place must have been something out of the common way."

At the Chalaine's request, Maewen acquiesced, Geoff flopping open his book and thrusting his quill into the ink bottle.

"We camp beneath the Gate of Three Dreams, for it was said that no matter what path was chosen from here, there awaited a delight in beauty that would linger forever in the dreams of the traveler. The path to the southeast joins the southern fork of the Dunnach River where scented trees line the bank of the wide, clear river. There moose drink the cool water and bear feed on silver fish that leap from the depths.

"The path to the south plunges into the heart of the Muliel Forest where giant firs thrust into the sky with such height and with branches bristling so thick with plump needles that they cast the wanderer into an eternal evening at noonday. Feathered ferns and wide leaved water plants wet the boots and cloaks of those that pass with dew that continually falls to soft, damp earth.

"Our road lies northward. Here the path runs out into an open plain of waving green grass where once mighty herds of elk and deer ran with abandon, hooves striking up a thunder in the air. Low clouds thread through the jagged peaks of the Far Reach Mountains to the west, falling as they pass under the fire of the sunset sky to cover the land in a soft haze that thickens in the night into a blanket of fog."

Maewen turned to peer into the north where the haze gathered. "I can only hope that some of those herds remain. We need food."

The half-elf's turn toward the practical broke the spell created by her descriptions, Geoff scribbling with inhuman speed across the pages to capture her words.

"I long to venture these paths again," Maewen continued, "and if you should mourn anything, it is that you will tread only one way and likely never see the others."

"Marvelous, Maewen," Geoff complimented her, face happy for the first time since his forced marriage. "I think your eloquent descriptions will inspire caravan loads of people to journey here after the Unification."

Maewen frowned. "Then please strike what I said from your record. Such a crowd would surely ruin the place."

She stalked off to scout around before darkness and mist obscured her view completely.

"I don't think she'll ever like me again." Geoff said glumly after closing his book and arranging his other implements within his cloak.

"Maewen or Fenna?" the Chalaine inquired softly.

"Fenna."

"Give her time, Geoff. She was very fond of you before the unfortunate events on the wedding night. Fenna is stubborn and can be petulant when hurt. Be patient. The storm will blow itself out."

"Thank you, Chalaine. I know it is hard for her losing a man such as Gen. If she loved him, then loving me will not be easy. Gen and I are as different as a peacock and a falcon."

"True," the Chalaine agreed. "But honestly, I believe she is better suited to you than him."

"Do you mean it?"

"I do, and I know her as well as any."

"Your words bring me comfort," Geoff said, "but I wish I could do something to speed the storm's passing. Every day I live with her scorn is a day boiling in agony."

"Well," the Chalaine said, squeezing his arm as she turned to go, "you are a bard, and if sweet words—and sincere ones—are a way to a woman's heart, then you are eminently qualified to negotiate the trail, however thorny it may be at the moment."

Fenna looked away quickly as the Chalaine returned. A chill washed over the party as breezes blown in from the plain to the north pushed them deeper into their cloaks. Fenna's eyes flashed angrily as the Chalaine reclined on her bedroll.

"How can you speak with him?" she whispered angrily, trying to keep Dason from overhearing.

"Why shouldn't I? Has he done something wrong?"

Fenna folded her arms. "An honorable man would have died rather than accept a forced marriage to a woman who doesn't love him. If Gen and Geoff's places were reversed, I would not be married now."

The Chalaine shook her head. "No. You seem to forget that Gen's life was in the balance. Think, Fenna! By marrying you, Geoff was attempting to save an honorable man, and however you feel about him, his feelings for you are obvious. Why should he die when his life could secure so much good, even amid woe?"

"Well I thought you at least would understand what it is like to be forced to marry someone you don't love, but I suppose there is one difference between us—you have never really loved anyone else. Your heart has never been uprooted from where it was content and joyful and asked to thrive in a cold, foreign country. When you have felt an attachment as I have, then maybe you will understand what it is like to have it torn away!"

The Chalaine could bear no more, choking back a

hundred explanations and chastisements Fenna had no power to understand or profit from. Without a word she rose, strolling slowly around the trees until those majestic views which were said to inspire dreams faded into fog and shadow.

CHAPTER 52 – HUNTED

Stirring in the camp snapped the Chalaine out of a blissfully dreamless sleep just before Dason stooped to wake her, and when she woke, she needed no explanation for the hurried movements. Somewhere in the forest behind them the Uyumaak thumped their chests and beat sticks against trunks, familiar sounds introduced to her during the last days of the doomed caravan. The rhythmic pattering struck fear into her heart, and she nearly forgot to collect her bedroll before moving to the horse that Kimdan finished saddling as she approached.

Dawn struggled to make its presence known. Fog clumped thickly about them, blinding their eyes, dampening their cloaks, and matting their hair. Mirelle grabbed her daughter's hand briefly as she walked by, Cadaen seeing to her horse. Chertanne was already astride his mount, head darting about at every sound. The Chalaine checked the *animon* as she waited for the rest of the company to mount. Gen yet lived. What comfort this brought was short-lived.

"We ride fast," Maewen informed them, signaling for everyone to come close. "They have our trail and likely know exactly where we are going. It will be easy to get separated in this fog. Keep to the path. If you do lose your way, ride in widening circles until you find the road. Keep the sun and the mountains to your left. The fog should clear by midmorning. Ride hard!"

They started slowly until they were sure everyone was on the trail. After a quick glance over her shoulder, Maewen spurred to a gallop, dark hair streaming behind her. The Chalaine rode just behind the half-elf and Chertanne, the soldiers bringing up the rear. While Maewen had described the fog as a blanket, it was a ragged one, clarity and blinding obscurity alternating in irregular succession. They rode single file down a road as wide as a man is high, pushing the horses to the limit to gain time and distance.

Maewen reined the party in as they ascended a slight rise into a clearing in the fog. She rode around, counting to make sure no one had drifted away. The Chalaine patted her horse as steam shot from its nostrils. The thumping Uyumaak still dogged them, sounding uncomfortably close.

Maewen frowned. "We should have put some distance between us with that run. They have elements out here on this plain. We need to get somewhere high and more defensible. The fog works to their advantage—they can smell us but we can't see them. Stay close. We will leave the road."

Again they streaked forward, pounding hard down the stone path before them, the sun breaking above the horizon to their right, casting diffuse light through the mist. The Chalaine's heart pounded, wetness matting her veil to her face and hampering her vision as she struggled to keep Maewen in view. A sinking dread took hold of her.

We're not going to get off this shard.

Thumping behind her and to the right startled her by its nearness.

"They are a hundred yards behind us!" Maewen yelled. "Break left now!" As one, the horses plunged off of the road, mud and grass flipping off their swift hooves. The Chalaine hung onto the reins as they ascended a steep hill she hadn't seen, the riders in front of her fading in and out of the fog. Abruptly they emerged into the weak morning sunshine, cresting a hill with a narrow top of knee-high, thick-bladed grass just starting to brown. Before her stretched a sea of misty white interrupted by islands of hilltops jutting up into the clear.

"Look!" Dason yelled, pointing below them. Eddies swirled in the fog below as Uyumaak, practically invisible save for the disturbance in the mist, raced toward the hill.

"Everyone that can fight dismount and put the horses in a tight group behind us," Maewen ordered.

"Wouldn't we be at an advantage, mounted?" Dason asked.

"We need to protect the horses. Uyumaak are not noble. The horses give us an advantage and they will kill them before they kill you. Do it."

"Jaron!" Mirelle yelled. "You stay with my daughter." Jaron nodded, moving his horse to the Chalaine's side and taking the reins from her.

"Uyumaak can spook horses," he explained.

The Chalaine trembled. Her mother, Geoff, and Fenna joined her as the fighters jumped from their horses and pushed them back. The soldiers, Maewen in the middle, formed a line at the edge of the hill. The half-elf drew her bow, pulling an arrow to her cheek. Chertanne rode away from the line, heading for the Chalaine's tightly knotted group before Athan intercepted him.

"Your Grace," he pleaded, "we need your magic!"

Chertanne, already pale, turned an even whiter hue. "I . . . I am not. . ."

"Chertanne!" the Chalaine yelled, anger welling up within her. "Get in the fight, for all of our sakes! This is what you were born for!"

"The moon is not full!" he yelled defensively. "My magic is yet weak! I will be of no use!"

Athan appeared ready to present some argument, but

Maewen's bow singing and a yell from the men at the line prompted him to abandon his entreaty and rush forward to help with his own magic. Chertanne sidled up to Geoff, not meeting anyone's eye for fear of what he would find there.

The soldiers shifted their weight and gripped and regripped their swords. Maewen shot three times before shouldering her bow and drawing her knives. The defenders stepped back as a band of Uyumaak Hunters slammed into the line as one. Long limbed and lanky, they soundlessly pressed the attack, their many eyes darting among several targets. The Chalaine startled at their long claws and frightening speed. The men fought off lightning slashes and chopped at the bony arms, holding the charge at bay. Sharp Uyumaak nails shrieked along plated armor and tore clothing and flesh.

Athan, riding behind the battle, incanted. One of the Uyumaak turned from its human opponent and attacked the other Hunters. The confusion afforded the advantage to a nearby Dark Guard who quickly finished off the creatures and gave aid to the Aughmerian soldiers. Sharp swords hacked away arms and impaled the bodies of the silent enemy. Two of the attackers finally broke and ran, Maewen finishing them with her bow.

"How many?" Athan asked, after the battle was over.

"Eighteen," Maewen calculated, grabbing her horse. "If there are two companies out there, they should have numbered twenty-two. We are missing four, though they may have returned to give news of our position. It is time to be a little unpredictable. Let's check the wounded and get moving."

What wounds there were received a hasty, rough bandaging of shredded cloak, and in short order Maewen led them off the hill and back into the fog, veering west toward the mountains. She kept the pace even, saving the strength of the horses against the need to flee.

As the half-elf had said, the rising sun coaxed away the

fog by midmorning and added greatly to the relief of the party. The land spread green about them, rolling and inviting, as pleasant a morning as any traveler could ask to favor her for a journey. The Far Reach Mountains rose a hazy gray-green before them, steep, grassy foothills gashed with gullies crouching at their base.

They rode in silence until midday, crossing several gurgling streams as Maewen gradually turned north to avoid the uneven terrain of the foothills. As they halted for lunch, Maewen explained that she hoped she would find more animals nearer the mountains, for as yet the mighty herds she had described the night before had not materialized.

She said, "The gullies and washes also provide us a quick way into the mountains and more defensible places where we can find better concealment. With the Hunters mostly destroyed, we should be able to stay ahead of the main body of Uyumaak . . . unless there are more in front of us."

The rest of the afternoon saw nothing of animals, Uyumaak, or conversation. The territory simultaneously fascinated and worried them. As travelers, their eyes and hearts anticipated what views awaited just behind the next rise, around the next bend, or just behind a jut of rock; as prey, they feared the same. Once evening approached, the haze and fog returned to accumulate in the low places as Maewen searched the high ones for a defensible place to encamp.

As the sky turned a deep purple and the fog threatened to overtake them, the Chalaine noticed a grin cross Maewen's face. "This way," the tracker yelled before turning her horse and galloping up a hill.

As they approached, a ruined wall of loose river rock crowning the hill appeared to her veiled vision, the party passing inside through a narrow breach. While the wall barely rose to the level of her waist, Maewen was clearly pleased with her find.

After Captain Tolbrook helped the Chalaine from her

saddle, Maewen approached and led her to the other side of the animal where they could converse in private. The half-elf lifted the three stone necklaces from off her neck and assisted the Chalaine in donning them again. The Chalaine regarded her in the warm evening light, finding a brightened, even lively, cast to Maewen's eyes.

"I cannot thank you enough, Chalaine, for lending me these. While in such a camp as this, I do not feel at liberty to tell you a very private tale, but you should know that Samian is my father. This is, indeed, a wise gift to you from Gen, and if you see him again, you should give him your gratitude. But you had best do it before I see him, for I will most likely kill him for keeping this a secret from me."

The Chalaine asked, "What do the stones do?" the Chalaine asked. "What am I to do with your father when I dream? I cannot even understand him! I'm sure he will tire of me soon."

"I do not know all, but the stones will lend you breath, strengthen your frame, and help you heal. As for my father, he is a warrior but a gentle man. He could return to the sleep of Erelinda, but after I communicated to him our circumstances, he is anxious to help you. Some teaching can be done without words."

Geoff ended their conversation, approaching tentatively, book in hand. "There you are, Maewen."

"I suppose you are in search of information about this wall."

"Yes. I know that a wall might be a bit dull, but if it is the residue of some lost civilization, then it may be worthy of note."

"Lost is certainly an appropriate word in this case. I will tell anyone who is interested more when I return. I want to scout around before full dark and full fog."

Maewen sped away after asking Kimdan to care for her horse, and after the horses were properly unburdened, brushed, and staked out, they dined on a meager meal of bread and dried meat whose flavor had long since bored the tongue into apathy. To their delight, the fog did not rise to envelop them, allowing a hazy view of the moons. Stars and shards gradually bloomed into view as the sun loosened its bright grip upon sky, cooling a gentle zephyr as refreshing and clear as a mountain pool.

Maewen returned shortly, Geoff dogging her, and the Chalaine crossed quickly to them along with others she had informed of Maewen's promise of information. Before ten words were out, the entire camp had gathered around her save Jaron and Tolbrook, who kept vigil at the wall.

"The place we have stumbled upon is nothing more than a corral for animals used by the dwarves long ago. They trained dogs to harry sheep, goats, and even elk into these hilltop enclosures, shearing or slaughtering them at need."

"Would the dwarves come this far out of their mountain strongholds?" Geoff asked. "I thought they lived mostly on wild mountain game."

"They preferred the mountains, but they loved meat. There simply wasn't enough game to be had to satisfy their appetite for it. They were poor hunters due to their general lack of stealth or general tendency toward boisterous behavior, however you wish to view it. They were a thunder in the mountains, and the animals learned to run at the sound of them. Hence, they built these hilltop corrals, defensible and above the fog.

"The mountains nearby housed several different but related clans, the Ghozan, the Shaek-Khur, and Jhorak-Khur, to name a few. The dwarven kings lived several days north of here in a mighty mountain they named Khore-Thaka-Tnahk. We will see it if we are given the luxury of following our present course."

"Were all the dwarves killed in the Shattering?" Mirelle inquired during a pause.

"The dwarves disappeared at some undetermined point

before the Shattering. As the time called Middle Peace drew to a close, the intrigues of Mikkik undermined the strength of the kingdoms of man, war and civil war ripening Ki'Hal for destruction. Elves and dwarves, on account of their long lives and deeper wisdom, did not fall victim as easily to Mikkik's schemes, but they were few in number. They needed the race of man to beat Mikkik back as they had done before. Both elves and dwarves sent ambassadors, advisers, and embassies to try to piece together a unity among the human kingdoms, but the schisms were too deep and too bitter to remortar.

"It was the dwarves who first noticed the approach of Mikkik's vast army streaming across this very plain. The elves and dwarves determined they would stand together with whatever human forces they could convince of their report. The plan was laid, but with little confidence of success. The elves and several thousand humans set a line of defense around Emerald Lake, hoping to control the numbers of creatures Mikkik could bring to bear by throwing up defenses at a narrow constriction in the valley between the Ironheart and Wardwall Mountains.

"Mikkik's army approached, but the promised aid from the dwarves never arrived, neither did a promised contingent of Rhugothian men from Echo Hold. Since Khore-Thaka-Tnahk and Echo Hold are in close proximity to each other, it was simply assumed that Mikkik's army had overtaken and destroyed them both. The following years and the Shattering permitted no time or means for investigation of the matter.

When I explored this shard last summer, I had hoped to find signs of them, but the size of the shard only allowed me to find Elde Luri Mora and return. I have a hard time believing such a race as they—hearty, vigorous, and fierce—met with total annihilation. At Unification I sincerely hope to encounter a group of them marching to our aid. Elves and dwarves were very different, but I would rather have a contingent of dwarves than elves at my side in a close fight."

"Why?" Chertanne asked. "Seems they would be too short to be effective."

Maewen disagreed fervently. "The dwarves were short, yes, but stronger than men, possessing more endurance than elves, and they were more relentless than either one. Uyumaak hated dwarves more than any other enemy. When both sides reached the unspoken point of exhaustion and called a cessation in the fighting to recuperate, the dwarves would not let the enemy rest, harrying them unendingly. While it may seem glorious or satisfying to decapitate an enemy or run a sword through its heart, it is just as effective to smash its knees with a warhammer or disembowel it with a sharp battle ax."

"There is something out there!" Jaron yelled. Drawn steel rang through the night as soldiers pulled weapons and ran to where Jaron stood. The Chalaine found herself guided back toward the horses by a firm hand from Dason, Cadaen performing the same service for her mother. Fenna, Geoff, Chertanne and one of his soldiers joined them shortly thereafter. The Chalaine gritted her teeth at the Ha'Ulrich's lack of iron.

Ahead of them Jaron pointed into the fog below. "Something yellow rose up out of the fog just for an instant. It was round and wet, about the size of a waterskin. It looked like, well. . ."

"An eye," Maewen finished for him, unlimbering her bow. "Throgs."

"What in Mikkik's name are Throgs?" Jaron asked.

"Quiet. I will explain later," she remonstrated. "Just kill anything coming up that hill."

The night took on a hollow, haunted feeling as they waited in the dark, every sense attuned to the sounds of the breeze waving through the grass and the nervous movements of horses and men. Just when Maewen would relax her bow, some rustling not quite natural would snap it up again. A reek carried on the wind that reminded them of rotting meat in a hot summer market and wrinkled their noses, eliciting quiet oaths from those at the wall.

Then they all saw what Jaron spied many minutes before.

An oblong orb, wet and yellow in the moonlight, drifted up from the fog, its round, black iris focusing on them. Maewen fired, but the eye plunged back into the fog and her arrow flew harmlessly into the night.

"What is that thing?" Jaron asked again in a hushed tone.

"It's an eye," she explained. "It floats up from the head of the Throg."

The sound of a rock falling from the top of the wall and thudding to the ground spun heads in that direction, but nothing presented itself in the ample moonlight.

"It may be moving around, and there may be more than one," Maewen announced quietly. "They know we are here. They should leave."

The last she spoke to the swirling fog ahead of them as if trying to convince whatever concealed itself inside to depart. Another rock fell near the same place as the last.

"Are they toying with us?" Jaron speculated to himself as they fixed their gaze to that spot, a rustling noise behind the wall in that area drawing Maewen's arrow point in that direction. As she moved left, the men moved out of her line of sight and followed her closely. The horses nickered and stamped nervously as the uncomfortable smell of decay befouled their nostrils.

"What is this?" Jaron demanded of Maewen. Then Geoff yelled in pain and two of the horses reared and screamed, pulling at their stakes. Eyes darted about frantically. Standing in the moonlight ten paces from the Chalaine was what in shape most resembled a dog, but one that would be found curled on the hearth of Mikkik's fire.

In size it was a mastiff, in form a greyhound, in color sable. Coarse, wiry hair jutted from its body in uneven patches. Several small, spider-like eyes glinted like flint in the weak light, ringing an abnormally large head. Where a snout would have been was a hole from which three fleshy tubules had shot forth, one embedding itself on Geoff's leg and two others attaching to the flanks of the horses. Blood pulled from its victims pulsed along the tubules, swelling the creature's belly.

Fenna stood frozen at her husband's side. Dason leapt past her and brought his sword down on the tubule leeching blood from the bard, severing it. The tubule slurped back into the mouth of the Throg, the other two returning with it as the horses bolted into the night. The Throg turned to go, the large floating eye descending to fit inside a cavity of its head as it sprinted for the wall. Maewen shot, but a rearing horse took the arrow instead.

"There are more!" Jaron yelled.

Panicking horses pulled up stakes, bucked, and bolted, scattering the party and throwing the hilltop into chaos.

"To the center!" Maewen yelled, everyone endeavoring to obey in the midst of flying hooves. Four more Throgs jumped the wall and regarded the party for a moment before chasing the horses into the night and disappearing with them.

"Geoff is hurt!" Fenna finally yelled, kneeling at his side. The Chalaine rushed over with Maewen, the remainder watching the wall for more signs of the beasts. Geoff lay pale and unmoving, insensible eyes fixed on the heavens. Two feet of the tubule still attached to his leg drained blood onto the ground. Maewen reached down and yanked it out, a hunk of flesh coming with it, while the Chalaine worked to heal the handsome bard. After several seconds, comprehension returned to his eyes and his face colored. He seemed about to talk, but Fenna hushed him with her finger.

For the next hour every ear extended into the dark only to be assaulted at random intervals with the agony of dying horses. Nearly an hour of complete silence passed before anyone had the stomach to speak, and it was Jaron.

"Now do you want to explain what those were, Maewen?"

"As I said," she returned bitterly, "those are Throgs. Mikkik invented those late in the second war as a way to track down anyone gone into hiding. They can communicate with the mind of a Chukka to whom they are bound. As you saw, the eye they possess allows them to spy silently and at distance, and they drain the blood of animals for sustenance. They are intelligent, but not hearty. Under better circumstances, we could have killed them easily. They don't often chance coming near an armed party. They were hungry."

"So you are saying that the Uyumaak know where we are?" Athan asked, his high-pitched voice almost at a whine.

"Yes," Maewen answered, a calm counterpoint to the terror breeding around her. "But the worst blow to us is the loss of the horses. Once we killed the Hunters, we had the advantage. Without the horses, it falls to the Uyumaak again."

"It is obvious that this entire trip was badly planned and horribly mismanaged!" Chertanne spat. "Regent Ogbith must have been bereft of reason when he approved this! Only an idiot would not have foreseen the Uyumaak threat! We needed five times the numbers and much better intelligence. Blood sucking dogs? Mikkik's breath! I didn't hear the Regent mention those!"

The Chalaine, feelings raw, could listen no longer. "The only thing he didn't foresee was that the Ha'Ulrich would be the most useless coward ever to walk Ki'Hal! For Eldaloth's sake, Chertanne, you were in all the planning meetings for nearly a year. Did you think to voice your concerns then, or were all the details just too boring for you to pay attention to? Perhaps you spent your time trying to determine which concubine to visit or decide on a brothel where you hadn't sufficiently sowed your seed! Regent Ogbith treated me like a daughter and I loved him. Don't ever take his name on your lips again unless it is to praise his memory. He was ten times the man you are!"

Chertanne slapped her, pain erupting on her cheek.

"Chertanne!" Athan yelled, running forward.

"I will not be. . ." Chertanne managed before Jaron dropped him with a thunderous punch to the face. The Ha'Ulrich crumpled to the ground, dazed and bleeding from a cut under his eye. The two remaining Aughmerian soldiers drew their swords, Jaron meeting their challenge. Before a fight could erupt, Athan interposed.

"Weapons away! Put them away!" he ordered, eyes frantic. "Can't you see that this serves no one?"

After several tense moments, both sides scabbarded their swords and Athan dropped to a knee, pressing part of his cloak to Chertanne's cut while helping him sit. When the Ha'Ulrich's eyes did focus, they burned with anger and shame.

"As I was saying," he continued, standing with Athan's help, "I will not be talked to in that manner by anyone, especially not my wife."

Jaron's gagging tore the Chalaine's attention away from her husband. Her Protector had grabbed his throat, unable to breathe.

Chertanne said, "You see, my magic may not be powerful enough to do great things, but men can be killed by simple ones." The Ha'Ulrich breathed heavily, face registering exhaustion from the effort required to cast the spell. "I suggest you hold your tongue, Chalaine, or this will happen again, only to those more dear!"

Jaron fell to the grass, face turning purple.

"What have you done?" the Chalaine demanded, Jaron

spasming. "Undo it, Chertanne! Now!"

Chertanne turned away, Athan helping him toward his horse while talking quickly to him in low tones.

Maewen ran forward, pulling her knife. "Get his hands away from his throat!" she ordered. Kimdan and Dason pulled them away with difficulty, Jaron thrashing and desperately trying to wrench his arms away from his companions. Cadaen and another Dark Guard immobilized his legs. "Come close, Chalaine," Maewen said, "and be ready to heal him. We may have a chance to save him."

As the Chalaine knelt near Dason, grasping Jaron's forearm, Maewen cut into Jaron's throat, slicing it along its length. Jaron convulsed in pain, momentarily stopping the procedure. Once Jaron was subdued, she continued by wedging open the windpipe with the tip of her knife until she found the obstruction Chertanne had created by transmuting the air inside it.

Working quickly, Maewen removed a smooth stone from Jaron's airway. "Now, Chalaine."

The Chalaine concentrated, sending her thoughts to the injured throat and healing it from the inside out. When done, the Chalaine opened her eyes and sat to rest herself. Jaron took several moments to relax, rubbing his throat where Maewen had sliced him open. Chertanne watched from a distance, Athan lecturing him animatedly.

Jaron stood. "I wish Gen would have killed him. I should have helped. He always did see clearly."

Mirelle stepped forward and grabbed the front of Jaron's tunic.

"Listen to me," she hissed. "I know Chertanne is unbearable, but you must subdue your feelings. Bury them, Jaron. The Chalaine will suffer indignities, but she must stay alive, and I need you alive to see that accomplished. If Eldaloth is with us, we can hope her sufferings will be short. Please control yourself. We have already lost Gen and cannot afford to lose you."

"I am sorry, First Mother. I will try. But this I swear: when he lays a hand on the Chalaine, I will mete out worse to him. What stings her will bruise him. If she bleeds, he will gush. If a bone of hers is cracked, one of his will be broken. If she falls by some blow of his, then he will fall into his grave by one of mine."

"I hope it will not come to that," Mirelle soothed, rubbing his arm. "Padra Athan, no doubt, is busily chastening Chertanne on the matter now, and I think Athan is the only one Chertanne is listening to. Just exercise caution and act for our greater good! Now if you and Dason would step away for a moment, I need to have a private word with my daughter."

The Chalaine stepped aside with her mother, the Dark Guard surrounding them at a discrete distance. Mirelle took her daughter's hand and pulled it to her heart, thinking several moments.

"I am sorry, Mother," the Chalaine apologized. "I know what you are going to say, and I will keep quiet. I have been so upset, angry, and now terrified. I have been saying and thinking the most awful things."

"No, daughter," Mirelle counseled, voice stern. "Silence is not enough now. I told you after your wedding that you would need to let me deal with Chertanne and Athan, and you have to let me do it. I know it will be hard, but you must act the part of the submissive wife, for now. You must take Chertanne's side, even against your conscience. You must be obedient. And yes, you must keep your tongue. I know this is repugnant. I know it. But for the salvation of all, and for the salvation of a few now, you must suffer. It should not be so, but there is no helping it until we are in safer times and places. I promise you there will be amends for you some day."

"I can see that this must be, Mother. I doubt even you could know what pains it will give me."

Mirelle embraced her. "I can only imagine, but you have

a mother's promise that it will not last forever. My daughter will be as happy as she once was. I will not rest until she is."

"There is something you should know," the Chalaine offered after several moments. "When I was in the canyon, I could heal Gen without any effort. If I touched him, he healed instantly."

Mirelle put her at arm's length. "Chalaine!" she exclaimed before quieting her own voice. "Chalaine! You know what that means, don't you?"

"He loves me." The Chalaine tried to decipher Mirelle's mood. It hovered between awed shock and feverish excitement.

"Did he see you unveiled?"

"He did. It was an accident. But the proofs of his love were there before he saw me."

"He saw you unveiled? Did he. . ."

"No. It was the strangest thing. I could see the desire rise in his eyes, but just as he took a step toward me, he shrugged it off as if emerging from a wild dream. He wouldn't say how he could resist me, but I walked for days with him without a veil and he never acted the least bit affected by me other than incessantly nagging me to wear it again."

Mirelle raised her hand to her mouth, speechless while she considered her daughter's news. "Eldaloth help us all if Athan or Chertanne ever found out! You bury that secret deep, Chalaine. You shouldn't have told me, though I am glad that you did. This is incredible, dangerous, and wonderful."

"But what are you feeling, Mother?"

"I am happy for you, Chalaine, and I forbid you to be sullen any more. You won the love of one of the best men to walk this world without him having seen your face. Even if you never saw him again, the fact that he loved you should teach you something about yourself. I know you are diffident, but think of Gen and ask yourself what kind of woman he would love, and I mean truly love. That is who you are. If only every woman could have such a sure sign of a love not dependent on desire!"

"I confess," the Chalaine said, "there were times I wished the desire was there. I would really like to know what it is like to be kissed by a man who feels for me as he does. You kissed him, after all."

Mirelle's voice turned sad. "He told you about that, then? His heart wasn't in it, unfortunately. Apparently, it belonged to you. Don't think his passion for you wasn't there within him, though. You know him well enough to know that he would never give into it. To think that I ever thought he loved Fenna. Oh, Chalaine, I hope he still lives."

"He does."

"You know this?"

"I think so," she answered, not ready to reveal the *animon* or what it meant. "I think I will know when he is dead. I will feel it."

"It could be a bond formed between you by the same affinity that allows you to heal him. If he is still alive, then he very likely has escaped Elde Luri Mora. This is good news. All is not lost. You have given me much to think about, and, in turn, you think about what I said."

"I will."

Mirelle kissed her forehead. "Goodnight, daughter."

The Chalaine spread her damp blanket and lay down with her arms wrapped around her. She felt the faint warmth of Gen's *animon* against her side, the night's terror feeding her longing for him. She had always had many occasions to act other than she felt, and she wondered why it was now, when pretending was most needed, that she could no longer do it. The role fate asked her to play had changed from her first imaginings of her duty, its nature more alien and unnatural than it ever had been. She was a novice actress asked to deliver the most difficult lines of a dramatic play to an audience that was, at best, disinterested in anything she said or felt.

But the challenge of her evolving role could not explain away all her inability to perform it. She had changed, too, and Gen's hands were the ones wet from shaping her clay. He taught her to see her calling and herself as two different entities, and whenever he talked with her, she sensed she had worth outside of her role as the Chalaine. He taught her to despise abject submission and degrading self-abnegation. Most of all, his companionship in the canyon showed her she was interesting beyond her beauty and calling, that she was worthy of the love of an honorable, powerful man.

What would you do to see him again? She asked herself. *Anything,* came the reply. *Then do it. Act the part. Endure it well.* Comfort followed resolution, and she cleared her mind, preparing herself for what awaited her in dream.

A horse's dying scream, the first for hours, carried faintly on the breeze and startled her from her half-sleep.

"That's all of them," she heard Jaron whisper from behind her.

"You've been counting?" Cadaen asked in turn.

"You haven't?"

"I didn't see much point," her Mother's Protector confessed. "When I saw those creatures chase them out, I gave them up completely. Damnedest horrible things I have ever seen."

"You've the right of it there. We are in grave danger, my friend. Whatever his insolence and disrespect, Chertanne was right about one thing—we were not prepared for this. Only the hand of God will get us home."

The Chalaine shuddered. Gen had not taught her courage, and she could no longer lean on his.

CHAPTER 53 - THE MASTER OF ECHO HOLD

Gerand gripped the reins of the horse, walking in front of it while Volney sat behind Gen in the saddle to keep him from falling off. Two days after they had passed through the gates of Elde Luri Mora on their way north, the smooth, even road that led their steps to the holy city had sunk completely beneath the earth, the city bidding farewell to its visitors and declining to invite more. A pleasant, grassy track remained in its stead, awaiting seed, sun, and time to clog it with tree and bush.

They progressed little the first two days from Elde Luri Mora with Gen tied semiconscious to the horse and the other two afoot. By the third day, Gerand guessed that the warding protection of Elde Luri Mora would no longer avail them, and they left the road whenever the rocky, mountainous terrain permitted to hide from unfriendly eyes.

Gerand's heart eased as Gen gradually improved. The farther they pushed north the third day, the more his pale skin regained its color and tone. His eyes opened more frequently, and his posture straightened from its pain-induced constriction. He talked only once to inform them that the Chalaine was well north and east of them and that catching up with them would be impossible if they followed her party's exact route.

"Our best chance," he suggested weakly, "is to go north and intercept them when they turn west."

The fourth day saw them passing through a tight valley between two pine covered mountains, the trail paralleling a deep stream bordered by a thick mass of shoulder high bushes that covered the entire valley floor with long, thin leaves. The sound of deer and moose crashing through the undergrowth brought their hands to weapons for fear of an Uyumaak ambush.

By midday Gen hopped down from the saddle and walked for the rest of the afternoon. The look on the Chalaine's former Protector's face worried Gerand. Gen often hid his emotions, but he was clearly anguished now. Volney tried conversation with him, but Gen was not amenable. Gerand judged it best to steer clear.

As night approached, they encountered a massive, flat-topped boulder that afforded them a view downstream and a defensible place to sleep. After tying the horse to a tree near the stream and a mound of thick grass, they climbed the gray stone, its sides roughened by pale green lichen, wind, and water. The mountains on the east and west blocked their view of the sunset, shadows and skies quickly deepening to black. The soft trickle of water and light woodland breezes relaxed tense muscles as they ate their poor fare.

Gerand rose as they finished their meal and crossed to Gen, unbuckling Aldradan's sword. "Here, Gen. I think you're fit enough to use it."

Gen took it wordlessly, lying back with the sword across his chest and falling directly asleep. Volney cast a worried look at Gerand who shrugged and said, "I'll take first watch."

Gerand awoke Volney some hours later and slept little. A bitter chill descended on the valley near dawn, pulling Gerand permanently from sleep. He stretched to try to dispel the cold, noting a light frost that had settled on the leaves and grass.

Gen had relieved Volney from his watch and now sat at the edge of the rock to watch the indistinct movements of large animals wandering slowly and concealed through the bushes and trees. During one of his sleepless bouts during the night, Gerand found Gen silently practicing sword forms, no doubt limbering his body and strengthening muscles weak from disuse. While he looked much better than he had four days ago, the indisposition he had suffered darkened his face and hollowed his cheeks.

Gerand stood and Gen nodded to him, coming to his feet.

Gen nudged Volney with his boot. "Let's go."

"But it's still dark," Volney grumbled, one eye looking heavenward through the barest of slits.

"The valley walls hold back the day, but it is broken," Gen prodded, beginning his descent down the rock. "Long days and short nights are what we need now if we are to catch the Chalaine's party and have enough food."

Gerand helped Volney up. They collected their belongings and descended the rock, numb fingers aching as they gripped the cold, rough stone. They ate on the trail, the path switchbacking down a series of wooded ridges that sloped down to an open plain. Near midday, they stopped where the trees parted to show them a fertile grassland stretching north, a low line of hills forming its eastern edge. The plain, bathed in the warm morning sun, stretched west for several miles from the hills, ending in an abyss at the shard's edge.

"We should cover some good distance down there," Gerand speculated.

"There could be Uyumaak out there," Volney inserted

less enthusiastically. "They must have left at least a company of them to cover the road."

"No," Gen disagreed. "If they were going to attack, they would have done so in the valley we just left. They have the Chalaine's trail and have marched north and east in pursuit. We should be at our ease for at least a week."

"And how is the Chalaine?" Gerand asked, hoping to keep Gen talking. "What do you feel?"

"She is well."

"Will you let us know of any change in her condition?" Gerand asked.

"Of course."

Volney patted Gen on the shoulder. "I am certainly glad to have you back. I'm sure the Chalaine misses you. I think she was very fond of you. The First Mother, too."

Gen's dark look took Gerand aback.

"Listen, both of you," Gen said, stopping them under the shade of an ancient pine. "If we can intercept the Chalaine's party, we will shadow it for as long as we can but not approach. If we can get through the Portal and back to Rhugoth, you must split from me and seek what fortune you can. I thank you for coming for me, though I would rather you had stayed with the Chalaine and let me die. I have failed the Chalaine badly." He paused, mastering some emotion. "You should despise me, and so should she."

"You are too hard on yourself!" Volney exclaimed.

"No, Volney. Gerand understands, and you will too, in time. I have but one purpose for my life, and that is to see the Chalaine safe and happy if I can. Because I tried to kill Chertanne, I will be an outlaw forever, hunted and on the run. The two of you may share a similar fate. You owe me no allegiance, but swear this to me, that no matter what circumstances you find yourselves in, you will never cease to work for the Chalaine's cause, and I do not just mean her physical protection, to which you are already sworn. I mean her comfort, her pleasure, her happiness. I doubt either of you know the tenth of her suffering, some, now, of my infliction. Swear that you will aid me in relieving it, even if I fall."

Gerand did understand Gen's pain, but understood Volney's point, as well. Something was off about Gen's emotions, something Gerand couldn't quite place. He was ashamed, but not necessarily of losing the Protectorship. Regardless, Gerand would support him.

"I swear it," Gerand promised, Volney following suit.

Gen thanked them and pressed on, eyes calm and step falling more lightly now. Gerand's mind was packed full of questions he hadn't the courage to ask their severe swordmate. After he and Volney had taken their oaths, Gen kept well ahead of them on the trail and did not seek company. What conversation he offered tended only to the practical, all matters of emotion, conjecture, and opinion vouchsafed quietly within himself.

During the next several days they found evidence of the departed Uyumaak as they hiked quickly across the open plain. The damp ash of old cook fires, crumbling feces, and abundant tracks all indicated a hasty movement to the east to intercept the Chalaine and her companions. As a consequence, Gerand worried little about any immediate encounter with the Uyumaak, and with Gen's blessing they traded stealth for speed.

The nights upon the plain grew colder, and what food they had did little to assuage their hunger, though Gerand noted that Volney was the only one who complained openly. Only the horse fed well on the abundant grasses of the field.

"I believe they have lost or abandoned the horses," Gen informed the others near midday three days out on the plain.

"How can you tell that?" Volney asked.

Gerand answered for Gen. "Their rate of travel."

"Yes," Gen confirmed. "They have turned northwest

and are moving very slowly. I think their enemies or harsh terrain dictate their path now. They do not travel in a straight line, and they stop frequently."

"We must hurry to catch them," Volney said, face scrunched in worry. "I know that Chertanne swore he would kill you, and he would likely do the same to us, but they could not but welcome our presence if their circumstances are dire."

"We will help as we can," Gerand assured him, patting him on the back.

"And there is another problem," Gen added. "I think they are on the opposite side of the Dunnach River canyon. If we cannot cross at Dunnach Falls Bridge, then we will have to turn West on Echo Hold Road and meet them back where the caravan first ascended into the mountains. We will likely outstrip them, but if they don't hurry out of the mountains, the weather will be a more threatening danger than the Uyumaak."

As if to mark his point, for the next two days their view of the steadily nearing Far Reach Mountains was obscured by bouts of cold rain falling from low clouds to feed the yellowing grasses at their feet. Moisture soaked into their clothes, boots, and hair, everything a sopping, dripping mess. When the sun finally splashed upon the left side of their faces one late afternoon, they stopped and stripped what they comfortably could to let the articles dry in the weak warmth.

The next day they started their grueling ascent into the mountains. Damp pines thickened as they hiked the foothills through gullies and depressions. They were forced to slaughter the horse for meat, divvying up the remainder of the scanty supplies among them. While difficult, the trail rewarded them for their efforts. The maples and aspens blossomed in bright yellow clumps amid a field of dark evergreens, though many had cast over half of their foliage to the ground. Cloudy mountain streams, swelled temporarily by the autumn rain, complicated fording in several spots, forcing them to lose time hunting for shallower waters or bridges formed by deadfall.

By late afternoon, they ascended a steep ridge, hoping for a view of the Echo Road which their northward tack would force them to cross. Clouds, a deep blue-gray, adorned the sky in patternless clumps, a stiff wind pushing them northwest. The trees thinned as harder rock near the top of the ridge denied the roots an easy purchase into the earth, scraggly bushes and grasses thrusting up unhealthily from shallow cracks dotting the pale brown rock.

Gen stopped, raising his hand to signal his companions to hold up. He dropped quickly to the ground. Gerand and Volney followed suit, crawling to catch up with Gen.

"I heard thumping on the wind," Gen reported quietly. "Let's approach the ridge cautiously and low."

Gerand was grateful that Gen increasingly took command, thankful to see his sure, experienced manner taking hold again. The three of them got on their bellies and worked their way gradually upward. Volney noisily sucked air through his teeth, and Gerand shot him a cautionary look.

Volney grimaced, picking a large sliver out of his hand. Gerand resumed his climb. He recognized the necessity for stealth, but his knees and elbows complained at the bruising they received as they clambered over the hard stone. At the top of the ridge, a convenient group of boulders allowed them to walk at a crouch and peer at the scene below them.

The convergence of three ridges formed a roughly circular meadow. A lazy river ran on the eastern edge of the glade, a broken, uneven road running along its banks. In places, the road disappeared completely, overtaken by water and tall grass. Another road branched from that one, running west, dodging out of sight behind the trees on the far side of the clearing. To their dismay, nearly two hundred Uyumaak encamped about the intersection. They milled about aimlessly, an obscenity squirming in a womb of alpine beauty.

"The road branching west leads to Echo Hold," Gen explained, leaning back against the rock. "If we can't find a way around, we will have to fight our way through."

"But that's two hundred Uyumaak!" Volney exclaimed. "I know you have Aldradan's sword, Gen, but. . ."

"Calm yourself, Volney," Gen admonished curtly. "And speak quietly. They hear much better than you think. I hope we can be clever enough to avoid such a confrontation. This ridge intersects with the one at the far side, and on the other side of that is the road. It may be possible to climb over the ridge and get onto the road behind them. We may have to deal with a patrol or two, but the mountain road will be much more defensible than this open field. If either of you have a better idea, I am open to suggestion."

No suggestions forthcoming, Gen led them carefully back down the incline until they were hidden from the view of the creatures in the bowl on the other side. Rather than risk stepping on loose rocks or branches due to speed, Gen set a careful pace toward the ridge intersecting perpendicularly to the one they followed. The rushing water and wind provided excellent cover, and Gen wanted the aid of evening shadows before they started their ascent.

"It's too steep," Volney complained when they arrived at the perilous slope adorned with stunted, half-green pines leaning at wild angles. The gnarled trees stretched knotted branches into the wind.

Gerand put his hand on Volney's shoulder. The tall Rhugothian looked sick. "It will be challenging," Gerand affirmed, "but I think we can do it. Be careful not to break any of those branches. It will sound like thunder splitting the air."

By the time Gerand finished his sentence Gen had started the difficult traverse, using the abundant cracks and gnarled tree trunks to propel himself upward. Gerand followed his example, Volney coming awkwardly after. Every pebble knocked loose and every twig snapped from a dangling branch, brought a displeased look from Gen. Near the top, they were exposed to the bowl below, but as they pulled Volney up the rest of the way, they exhaled in relief—they had not been detected. The Uyumaak milled about as purposelessly as before.

They rested for a moment out of sight behind a thick, squat cedar. The opposite side of the ridge proved more daunting than they hoped. A sheer drop greeted them, the road running along a tree-lined lane that, on its far side, dropped even farther into a canyon hazy and shadowy in the weakening light.

"How do we get down to the road from here?" Gerand asked, peering over the edge to search for handholds.

Gen pointed to a stately pine growing close to the edge a few yards up the ridge. "We use the tree. It will be noisy, but it must be half a league from the main body. As long as we are reasonably silent, we should get down undetected."

What looked and sounded easy at a distance proved difficult once they surveyed the tree up close and faced the task. No branch thick enough to support their weight stretched near the perilous drop off at their toes. They stared at the closest limb for several moments as if willing it to thicken and grow closer.

Gen breathed out, eyes focused on the tree. "Follow me. It will hurt, but it's the only way."

Gerand shook his head. This was foolhardy. He opened his mouth to say as much when Gen leapt from the edge into the mass of coarse needles and branches. The top of the tree swayed as if hit by a hearty gust of wind. Bark and detritus rained down through the boughs, but in short order Gen worked himself to the ground, a mass of scratches covering his arms and sticky pine gum besmirching his clothes.

"Oh, look, that was easy," Volney said, voice heavy with

sarcasm.

"You'd better go next," Gerand prodded him, "while the example is still fresh."

Volney looked like he would be sick, but after screwing up his face, he issued a determined grunt and heaved his massive frame into the air. The tree got the worst of the impact, a branch snapping under his weight and echoing loudly through the air. Gerand swore, shaking his head as his lumbering friend wove himself downward through the branches like a sack of rocks. Uyumaak drums pounded a frantic new rhythm. Gerand executed the leap before Volney hit the ground.

No one needed to be told to run. The road lay in interconnected gray bricks before them, wide enough for a carriage or wagon to comfortably travel without fear of the edge. A thick stone balustrade provided a barrier between the road and the precipice, though wind and rain had eroded the support from underneath it, sending sections tumbling into the canyon in years past. The brick, too, proved uneven. Depressions and loose, upthrust sections sought out their boot tips in the approaching dark, sending the young men stumbling. Behind, the sound of claws scrabbling on the brick neared.

"Go on ahead," Gen ordered. "I will slow them down."

"We should fight together!" Gerand protested.

"I'm not going to fight!" Gen answered, drawing his sword and felling one of the large trees along the lane with a single stroke so that it fell onto the roadway with a tremendous crash, effectively blocking the path. "I'll down a few more. Now go!"

The sprint up the incline strained burning muscles already weary from travel. Despite urgency, the arrival of dark forced Gerand and Volney to slow their pace.

"Let's stop a moment and wait for Gen," Volney suggested.

"I concur," Gerand said. He leaned against the canyon

wall breathing hard, hands on hips. They walked in circles to keep loose, spitting bitter bile over the balustrade and into the abyss. The wind had died, a thin mist gathering as a damp chill set in.

After several moments, Gen arrived, resheathing his sword. "That should slow them down for a while. Let's move. I don't think we will have any sleep tonight. Look for any good places to hide as we go."

They continued their march upward as the night deepened. The air thinned. Gerand struggled to catch his breath, need and sheer will pulling each leg up and placing it before the other. His companions fared little better. They needed rest and a decent meal.

The road worsened as they climbed higher. Complete sections of brick went missing or were kicked aside into rough piles. Larger sections of the roadway had fallen into the canyon, forcing them to scoot along the edge of the canyon wall on what little ground remained.

At length, they arrived at a section completely fallen through. Two sturdy planks laid side by side spanned the fifteen foot gap. Gen walked across unconcernedly.

Gerand stopped and stared down. Certain death waited in the unfathomable dark drop. His shaky legs needed a little rest before attempting the crossing. Volney backed away from the precipice as if it were a poisonous viper.

"Just walk across at a nice even pace," Gen advised. "The longer you think about it, the scarier it will become. It's just like walking down the middle of a passageway."

"Except for the plummeting-to-your-death part," Volney whined.

Summoning his courage and stretching his legs, Gerand struck out, crossing the abyss with only a little wobble at the end. Volney's unsteady attempt, however, sent Gerand's heart into his throat. Volney shook from head to toe, stepping forward slowly with eyes riveted to the board as if looking for a rusty nail that he might step on. His arms flailed at his sides, flapping this way and that as his body leaned precariously in every direction. As soon as he could, Gen extended his hand and pulled him over.

"My family lives on a plain," Volney explained defensively.

"Should we pull the planks over?" Gerand asked. "The Hunters could make the jump, but none of the other Uyumaak could cross until they found a replacement."

Gen opened his mouth, but before he could speak a green light bathed them all in an eerie luminescence. Hands went to weapons, but they could only faintly make out a figure sitting on the balustrade holding a recently unshuttered lantern fueled by a translucent green glob.

"Leave my pretty planks where they are, if you please," a man's voice instructed them. "I went through such work to put them there."

"Show yourself," Gen ordered. "Are you friend or foe?"

"Relax my young gentlemen. I assure you that I have no love for the Uyumaak. But you need not fear them if you hurry along with me. I have a safe place to stay. Indeed, some have said it is the safest place ever built by the hands of men. As for my name, you may know me as the Master of Echo Hold, at present."

Gerand didn't like this stranger's carefree tone. "Is it close?"

"Yes, young one. Come. There are Uyumaak charging up the road from the other direction as well. If we do not make the drawbridge, we shall have an unpleasant time of it. Just follow the lamp."

He stood from where he sat on the balustrade and started up the hill at a quick, soldierly march. He was tall and powerfully built, a thick mane of hair falling a little past his shoulders. He sang as he walked. The song, while cheerful in lyric, he sung in a melancholy fashion, as if the Master of Echo Hold regretted the words:

My light it beckons,
My light it calls.
It shines and warms
On whom it falls.

Come now, travelers,
Come and rest
Within my light,
A welcome guest.

For where it shines
All cares will flee,
The restful glow
Of eternity!

Away your burden;
Cast shoes from feet,
Let eyelids fall,
And summon sleep.

Gerand felt ill at ease, sharing worried looks with his companions. The farther along they traveled, the more the bones of long-dead Uyumaak littered the road. Their new companion took no heed of them, pulverizing the brittle remnants of their enemies with powerful steps from heavy boots. Gen and his friends tried with little success to avoid them, the snapping sounds destroying all stealth.

"This abominable racket will get us killed!" Volney complained.

The man ahead of them chuckled. "Quite the opposite, sir. The Uyumaak cannot bear to hear the cracking of their own bones. Didn't you know? Besides, knowing your position can hardly help them now. Another turn around the bend and you will see your rest for this evening. All these years have not lessened my wonder at its majesty."

The last bit of canyon wall gave way as they curved around a steep protrusion. Before them sat Echo Hold, a mighty fortress of men bathed in moonlight. The castle was built upon an upthrust of rock that rose from the canyon floor to the level of the road hundreds of feet up. The rock was large enough for the castle, a small city, and a large terraced area for farming.

The castle was built of a dingy white stone, and while the walls were not tall, rising only twenty-five feet, they were so thick as to defy any penetration. The keep rose higher than the walls, soaring upward into the moonlit night. Such was the elevation that low clouds floated beneath the level of the castle, giving it the strange sensation of movement.

The gap from the canyon road to the outcropping of rock on which the castle stood stretched over one hundred feet, a drawbridge spanning the distance. Two more of the green lanterns hung against opposite sides of a gate built into the wall that was wide enough to admit two carriages side by side. Their would-be host did not stop to let them admire the scene but kept up his steady pace amongst the piles of bones.

"Who killed all these Uyumaak?" Gerand asked. The Master of Echo Hold turned his head to the side briefly, revealing a noble profile and a closely cropped beard.

"I have killed them. Seems they would learn to avoid this place, but I never tire of teaching the lesson, however thick-headed the students. Come. It appears we may have some trouble after all."

Squinting beyond the lantern, Gerand could discern three Uyumaak Hunters loitering along the road near the bridge, tentatively examining their surroundings and the lamps upon the walls across the ravine. Gerand stiffened as the Hunters turned from the bridge and approached the stranger and his lamp at an easy pace.

"Stay still," the man commanded them, halting himself.

"They only have eyes for the lantern."

The Uyumaak approached, twitching eyes riveted to the ghoulish light. The scales on their skin turned to match the colors within the circle of the lantern's glow. Gerand fingered his sword hilt. The man appeared perfectly at ease as the creatures approached, their clawed hands reaching reverently for the light. Just as a Hunter touched the lamp, the man shuttered it. Gerand found himself blinded by the sudden absence of light, and he and his companions drew swords at the sound of scuffle. But before his eyes could adjust, the light broke forth anew. The three Uyumaak lay dead upon the ground, eyes wide, without a visible mark of violence upon them.

"The light attracts them," their leader explained, voice fresh and energetic. "Such foolish creatures, really."

"Why do you hang lanterns by the gate, then?" Gerand asked. "What if they came in numbers? Are the walls guarded?"

"You have not heard what I said or understood what you just witnessed. The Uyumaak only have eyes for the lanterns. They are quite insensible when entranced. As for guarding the walls, I am quite alone here. I am happy now to have you as guests so that I can, at last, report the discharge of my obligations. Come forward. We shall enter, and I will retract the bridge so that you can slumber without worry tonight. I am sure your road has been long and toilsome."

The bridge was also made of stone. It was not lowered from the wall, but appeared to retract horizontally into a space beneath the castle. The grounds around and within the castle grew wild with weeds and thorny shrubs poking through even more piles of bones at the base of the wall. Their host removed the lanterns and signaled for them to follow him through the gate and into the tunnel that ran beneath the wall. He again hummed his song to himself. Gerand's skin crawled.

CHAPTER 54 – BONES

Gen glanced back at his companions, their worried faces mirroring his own misgivings about their host. But they were all exhausted. They needed rest and protection, and while Gen had confidence in his own skill and that of his friends, the Uyumaak were too many. They would chance a night in Echo Hold.

Bones littered the length of the tunnel through which the stranger led them, mice and rats scurrying away from the light and the heavy feet of men marching forward. Fetid dust reeked of age and decay. As they entered the main courtyard, the wind dissipated the smell, though bones lay about in prodigious numbers. The Master of Echo Hold led them along a path of ground down bones until they crossed into the streets of a deserted city that surrounded the inner keep and the tower that sprang from it into the sky.

As with gate into the castle, the gate into the keep was flung open as if the resident invited an attack rather than feared one. Another green lantern hung by the heavily fortified door into the keep.

"This place is impregnable," Gerand commented. "I remember reading that farther back there are places to farm and raise animals. Good weather permitting, the fortress could sustain nearly two thousand inhabitants indefinitely."

"It's as safe a place as anyone could hope for," Volney added, "if the gates are shut. The Uyumaak certainly managed to get in here in numbers at some point."

Gen nodded. Their host certainly had a knack with the creatures, particularly with killing them.

"I will shut the gates tonight, young friend," their host assured them as he waited for them to cross the threshold into the dank interior of the keep. When he slammed the door shut and barred it behind them, Gen thought he might have preferred it open, after all. He wasn't sure if the Uyumaak were being locked out or they were being locked in.

The floor of the keep was paved with white tiles embedded with circular purple and gold patterns. The walls held shredded hints of fine tapestries and long-rusted sconces, but all that wasn't stone had faded beyond recognition. Thankfully, while the hall was narrow and uncomfortably dark, no bones crunched underfoot, and their boots kicked up no dust. The hall terminated in another narrow door that opened into a room glowing orange from the coals of a recent fire. The warm light was a welcome change from the lurid green of the lanterns, and they filed into the room eagerly.

A long stone table big enough to seat ten stretched along the center of the room, and it took Gen a moment to realize that the skull of an Uyumaak had been placed on the table in front of each chair. Even the chairs themselves had been fashioned from bones, an especially complex one gracing the head of the table near the fire.

The Master of Echo Hold made a gesture toward the table. "Come, young companions, and sit. Oh, I see you are put off by my table decorations. I do apologize. It does get a little lonely at the table, as Bibbs doesn't like to come near it. Here, let me make things a bit more pleasant."

With a broad sweep of his arm the Master of Echo Hold

circled the table and knocked the skulls to the ground, sending them bouncing and cracking all over the room.

"I would have you know," he said when finished, "that I had named them all. So I do feel a bit guilty dashing them to the floor, but more lively guests await, and they must go lower. Bibbs!"

Gen, Gerand, and Volney, stood rooted in their places. Gen wondered where their host's oddities would end, feeling more discomfited by the moment. The Master of Echo Hold clearly wasn't in his right mind.

An unarmored Uyumaak Basher bumbled in from a side entrance. Gen drew steel, his friends following his example. The Basher cowered at their display of arms, covering its eight eyes with a quivering hand.

Their host laughed. "Put your weapons away, gentlemen. This is Bibbs. He has served me for several years, at least. Bashers are the best servants. They are just bright enough to do what you say but not clever enough to scheme."

As weapons slowly returned to scabbards, the Basher relaxed, and master and thrall communicated with each other, the former in Common, the latter by slapping its chest. After a few moments, Bibbs turned and left.

The Master of Echo hold turned toward them again. "I was quite stunned to find that the Uyumaak understood the tongues of men, elves, and dwarves. In my boredom, I took the time to learn its language, though it is complex and they have no teachers among them. As you can imagine, the first thing I learned to understand was their beat pattern for, 'please don't kill me.'" At this the Master of Echo Hold guffawed, slapping his hand on the table and ignoring the troubled stares of his guests. "Of course, I have uncovered many mysteries in my solitude and boredom. If you are very good, I will share some of them with you. But while we wait for Bibbs to conjure up a meal, I must make a confession, and since you are the first human faces I have seen since the Shattering, I can at last lay my conscience bare and perhaps find some solace. Please sit."

"How is it possible that you've been alive since the Shattering?" Gen asked cautiously as he took his place at the table. The bony chair was a little knobby against his back.

Their host leaned back, eyes distant. "That is part of the story. From your conversation, I know you have heard of this place in legend or history. Likely, that history questions its fate. Echo Hold was built by a collaboration of the human kingdoms during the Middle Peace, and—as you have so aptly noted—it is as impenetrable as a Basher's skull. In its glory it was a nation unto itself, nearly five thousand men and their families living within the walls— only the best of men and the finest of fighters. A Knight General ruled over the fort with a council of eight Knight Captains. Knight General Oakenstone was a good man, seasoned and sensible, and I felt honored to serve as his High Captain on the Council.

"As well you know, the Middle Peace ended as Mikkik sowed corruption and betrayal to break apart alliances and dull the honor and hope of all good things. Echo Hold was no exception, though Oakenstone's vigilance and swift justice secured our safety for a time. Mikkik threw armies at this place only to have them slaughtered by the thousands. Soon, he ignored us and sent his strength to drive the armies of men, dwarves, and elves to the west. We sallied forth from time to time, confident in our security, and harried the enemy, but we never wandered far from our gates.

"Messengers arrived from the dwarves that dwelt in the underground mountain halls not far from here. They brought word that they had called forward all that remained of their men and boys that could fight and equipped them with the best armor and weapons from their mighty forges. They proposed that we join with them, a force ten thousand strong, to fall upon Mikkik's rear and turn the tide of the war. Oakenstone rejoiced at this opportunity and heartily agreed, as did the rest of the Knight Captains. I, of course, voiced the same publicly. But inwardly, a doubt grew, spreading its enervating vines in my heart.

"Was it cowardice? You would be right to ask. I think not. It is not my nature. I can only say that this place had grown upon me. My wife, young, inviting, and tender-eyed lived here, and whenever I rode back through these gates after a raid or a short march, my feet felt married to the ground beneath them and my heart a part of these stones. The thought of riding half a continent away inexplicably terrified me, not because I feared death or battle, but because anywhere but this place, I thought, could only be alien and forlorn."

"But despite these misgivings, I still honored my duty and supported Oakenstone in his preparations. But doubts shoved aside and not confronted are but cracks into which evil can pour its poison and sicken us, and before we are aware, we are gripped in a feverish madness of emotion that overcomes all sense or pledged commitment. And when I was in this fever, a servant of Mikkik found me.

"Like a god he was, but without the brilliancy, and he made no pretense at presenting himself as holy or even as my friend. It was a Mikkik Dun, and after unhinging my joints with some spell, he forced into my head a vision of what the dark one planned and the doom that awaited the Knights of Echo Hold were we to leave the safety of our walls. Numberless columns of dark creatures streamed through the canyon below and overthrew all in their path. He offered a way to save myself and my men. I took it.

"And then he changed me by some power, and he gave me the means to kill Oakenstone without suspicion. To my eternal shame, I did it. To all appearances, Oakenstone had simply gone to bed and never awakened. You cannot imagine the sorrow, but the funeral and mourning provided a convenient excuse to delay our departure. I then cited the need to scout around the area to be sure that no ambush would befall us, and thus we waited more.

"The dwarves grew impatient and sent me missive after missive, begging that we make haste, to honor Oakenstone's pledge, but still I delayed. At last, a ragged dwarven messenger, haunted and harrowed, arrived at our gates, claiming that some horror had flooded their halls and mines, killing his people in droves. He begged for our assistance, and I would not give it. And in that cowardice, the members of the Council overthrew and imprisoned me. Immediately they marched to their aid. They never returned. Not one. Only women and children remained here afterward, and of course, I remained in my cell. My wife abandoned me, ashamed, and I did not bother to explain my actions.

"But that is the tale of my sin and my guilt, and after you have eaten, you shall see my penance and witness to it. Perhaps, then, this prolonged existence can find its end. I have been cursed, and that curse will not allow me to die. I do not know if it can be undone, but I hope that by showing you my work of restitution, I might receive some reprieve and find peace again."

"You are Sir Tornus, then," Gen stated, "if I remember my history."

"That is correct," Tornus replied, eyes distant. "That name stood for honor and bravery once. Part of my penance is that you will teach my history so that I can no longer be held in such esteem. I am a murderer. I betrayed the dwarves. Following a certain line of reasoning, I betrayed the world. Ah, but here is dinner!"

Gen's mind spun, but a meal delievered by the sulking Bibbs set his mouth to watering. A rich venison stew with spiced bread filled the famished corners of his belly. They ate until sated while Tornus, who didn't bother with the feast, regarded them carefully.

Once it was clear that they had finished, he stood. "If

you are satisfied, I ask you to come with me so I can show you what poor atonement I have attempted for my mistakes. Come."

Tornus guided them through a side door and several dim passageways until they walked into a courtyard softly lit by the moons. As with other areas they had seen, bones clumped about in uneven heaps upon the paving stones. Outside the keep, the city of Echo Hold stretched before them along dark, abandoned streets. Sturdy, two level buildings of stone slid mournfully by as they followed Tornus through the maze of lonely avenues toward an unknown destination. At last they emerged into an open plain separated from the city by a waist-high wall.

"Beyond this," Tornus explained, "is where all the agriculture needed to sustain Echo Hold in the event of a siege took place. The orchards have grown wild and the fields returned to weed, but here was the only place big enough to accomplish my task."

He led the young men through a broken wooden gate and headed into the quiet field of dry, raspy grass. All about them sat stones placed at regular intervals, forming long rows to their left and right.

"These are grave markers," Tornus announced. "I went into the dwarven halls and found all the dead and carried them here for burial, each warrior with his weapon and each mother with her children. A staggering task, to be sure, but a debt that I owed them for my part in their destruction. Did you know that their bones, like their weapons, do not age or rot? But no matter. What I want to show you awaits us ahead."

Gen glanced back at his stunned companions. Staggering hardly sufficed to describe the enormity of the task. The rows of graves ran interminably in all directions, disappearing into the dark. As they proceeded, the burial sites were newer and less choked with grass and weed until soon fresh mounds of dirt indicated recent work. A polite cough from Tornus tore their attention away from the graves to an enormous pit dug into the earth.

"This," he said, pointing into the abyss, "is what killed them. All of them. It destroyed the armies sent forth and then turned and slithered into their mines and caves and halls and poisoned the rest. After the Shattering, the host of them just stopped and lay where they were. They did not rot, and, while lifeless, they still feel warm to the touch. I gathered every one I could find and threw them here."

Gen peered into the pit, trying to understand what it was he was seeing. It took several moments before he could discern that the moonlight softly glinted off the bodies of an uncountable number of black-scaled and unmoving snakes.

"If you are wondering," Tornus said, "there are sixteen thousand, three hundred and thirty-three of them down there. I cannot be sure I discovered them all. There are simply too many cracks and crannies in the dwarven halls."

"I can't tell what they are," Volney said, nonplussed.

"They are snakes," Gerand informed him. Volney edged away from the pit, blood retreating from his face just as quickly.

"Black-toothed vipers, to be exact," Tornus corrected. "They are only as long as a man's arm or leg, typically, but just imagine if thousands of them slithered into a column of soldiers marching through high grass. Their teeth can puncture boot leather, and the poison reduces muscle to barely coagulated slime in moments. While I rue my decision not to march with the dwarves, leaving them unprotected, I cannot fathom what we could have done had we been there. Only Mages would have had some recourse, but I doubt even they would have lasted for long."

A voice intruded into Gen's mind. *"I await thy bidding, my master. I am Ghama Dhron, one of the four fell servants of Mikkik."*

The voice spoke in the ancient evil tongue, and Gen jumped back and drew his sword, only to find his companions and Tornus regarding him as if he had gone mad.

"What startled you, young master?" Tornus asked, face curious.

Gen's mind raced. "I thought I saw something move," he lied.

"Oh! You have good eyes in the dark. They have been a bit twitchy since the light of Trys rejoined the sky."

"What?!" Gerand and Volney exclaimed.

"Do not fear, friends! They have done nothing, as yet, amounting to purposeful movement. One will twitch or spasm now and again. I suppose that if we waited until Trys bloomed full in the sky, we might have a problem, but I plan on burning the lot of them as soon as I can pile enough tinder and wood into the hole. Nevertheless, I can see you are uncomfortable, and it is most discourteous of me to have taken up so much of your evening in this fashion when clearly you need your rest. Come, let us retire to the keep."

"Speak the word, master, and I will follow. I do the bidding of he who holds the power of my making."

Gen shook his head to clear it, and while he could no longer hear the words, he sensed a presence in the back of his mind, full of hunger and malice, awaiting his call. The feeling remained strong even after they crossed into the safe confines of the keep.

Tornus wound his way back to the hall where they had taken dinner, all the plates and bones now cleared away.

"Stay and rest a moment by the fire," Tornus encouraged them graciously. "I will go command Bibbs to prepare a room with three beds for you. When you are ready to rest, use the stairs by the main entrance. It will be the first door on your left. Now, I must bid you good evening."

"Thank you for your hospitality, sir," Gerand said in parting.

Tornus turned, expression strange. "There is no need for thanks. The company you provide is certainly worth more than anything you have received at my hand. Sleep well."

Gen waited until the echoes of their host's steps had long faded down the empty corridors before calling for Volney and Gerand to come close so they could talk quietly.

"I feel a great deal more than uneasy about this Tornus," Gen began. "Something doesn't seem right about him."

"Doesn't seem right?" Volney interjected. "He's bloody mad! Imagine, stuck here for centuries with nothing but a Basher and wagonload of guilt to keep you company! For pity's sake, he dragged every dwarf carcass in this mountain range and buried them here!"

"I do not think he is mad," Gerand contradicted. "Loneliness and time have warped him, but he is willful and perfectly in control of himself."

"His own narrative of events holds the key," Gen added. "He said the Mikkik Dun changed him somehow to keep him alive for all these years and taught him some secret of murder. That is the most disturbing. He made a covenant with dark powers, though his forthright confession and heroic efforts at atonement certainly cast him in a more favorable light."

"But what of those lamps?" Gerand asked. "Those Uyumaak he killed—and killed in an instant—had not one mark upon them! How was that done? Not to mention the piles of bones everywhere."

"Perhaps the way he killed the Uyumaak is part of the secret he gleaned from the Mikkik Dun," Gen speculated. "Remember how no one could tell that Oakenstone had been killed? We take watches tonight and leave early tomorrow even if a company or two of Uyumaak encamp at the gates."

"Agreed," Gerand and Volney said in unison.

Gen stretched and placed his hand on his sword hilt. "We now know the answers to some questions historians have asked since the Shattering. Hopefully we can live to share them."

They left the hall, only the sounds of their own footsteps and the crackling and popping of the dying fire accompanying them. They found the stairs where they had first entered the keep, the door locked and barred. Bibbs had ensconced torches along the staircase and the hallway it intersected at the top. The door to their quarters stood open invitingly, a lamp inside casting a wan yellow glow that spilled into the hallway.

The room was spacious with a high ceiling and thin round columns decoratively placed down the middle. Two arched windows flanked the fireplace mantel, wood old and brittle. Gen speculated that the room had served as a meeting hall or an officer's mess. A single fireplace stood in the center of the long room, the three beds clustered close to it, though nothing burned within.

"I suppose all the blankets and mattresses have gone to rot," Volney observed dourly. "The mention of a bed had me hoping for a little more than a wooden plank a few inches off the floor."

Gen closed the door and joined his companions, spreading their travel stained blankets on the ancient furniture. "I will take first watch. I will trim the lantern but leave it burning for as long as it has oil."

"I'll take second watch," Gerand volunteered.

Despite the lack of comfort, Gen's friends drifted off to sleep quickly, and Gen breathed out and tried to relax his mind and body. Since escaping Elde Luri Mora and regaining his health, he felt, as Sir Tornus did, that he had a restitution to make for his mistakes, mistakes with potentially disastrous consequences for the world. And perhaps, as their host also thought, nothing he could offer as expiation met the cost of the severity of the crime. While he could never pledge any allegiance to Chertanne, the enormity of his mistake in trying to kill the Ha'Ulrich weighed upon him.

Pride and madness, he thought.

But there was more. He had yet to admit to himself that he loved the Chalaine in a way that he should not, for he found nothing unwholesome in his feelings with which he could convict himself. If he wanted her unjustly or wantonly, surely the self-reproach would come more easily.

Only her pain and disappointment in his love stung him, and with whatever life he had allotted to him, he was determined to prove to her that to trust him had been no mistake, that his heart was true, and his motives pure. He would serve her without any hope of reciprocation or reward, though he recognized that his stupidity had rendered his ability to protect or aid her feeble, indeed.

The hours passed slowly. The sound of Bibbs shuffling down the hall and extinguishing the torches provided the only break in the uneasy monotony of the passing time. Gen threw open the shutters to get a better look at the sky to check how much time had passed, the weak light and view of the sky calming his nerves. A soft, cool wind helped alleviate the oppressive feeling he'd felt since entering the keep, and the uncomfortable bed now beckoned to him.

Only an hour more.

CHAPTER 55 - GHAMA DHRON

Gen awoke Gerand for his watch in the dead of night. A chill had stolen over the room as the night deepened high in the mountains. After stretching and rewrapping his cloak about himself, Gerand slipped on his boots and went to the open window to refresh his eyes. Moonlight streamed through the opening, a slanted column of moonlight casting the shadow of Gen's companion across the room.

Remembering their strange circumstances set Gen's blood to churning, grogginess fleeing as anxiety and a need to depart in haste took hold. Were it not for the scant illumination from the moons, the room would be lost in utter darkness. The ancient bed creaked wildly as Gen settled on it, and, despite the toils of the day, sleep would not come.

Time crawled by as he stared at the cracked ceiling, ears primed for any sound besides that of his companions' breathing, every moment passing lending him hope that the night would pass uneventfully and the protecting sun rise to free him from the nagging fear that gripped him in the presence of their host.

So it was that when he first heard soft, steady footsteps in the hallway, he could not tell if it were real or a product of an imagination ripened by fear. The voice of experience and the nearing footfalls pulled him off his bed, Gerand casting a worried glance at him. A quick shake pulled Volney from his slumber. They struggled with their boots and strapped on their weapons. Anxiously and in silence they waited, hearing someone tread back and forth just outside the room like a sentry for nearly fifteen minutes. At length, the pacing stopped and the door swung inward. They drew their swords, staring at the vague shape outlined the door frame.

"Who goes there?" Gerand demanded.

"Forgive me, young master," the voice of Sir Tornus spoke. "I had only come to check to make sure my guests slept well." He entered and closed the door. "Bibbs can, from time to time, be mischievous. But I see that you are ready for a fight. A shame on my house that my guests cannot find rest after such a tiresome day."

Gerand relaxed, noting that Tornus held a shuttered lamp at his side, but no weapon. An awkward pause kept nerves raw. Unexpectedly, Tornus's voice, sad and agonized, broke the silence.

"How can I do this?" he moaned, face angled toward the ceiling. "I suppose I hoped too much that my penance would bring release. Too many crimes. Too much to forgive. There is no escape, and I am so hungry! The Uyumaak do not satisfy. What are three more among so many? I must feed this one last time and leave this place." More sobs filled the room. "I am sorry, my young friends."

"Take him!" Gen yelled, but as they moved to advance, Tornus threw open the shutters of his lamp and a pale blue light bloomed in the room. In that instant, Gerand and Volney stopped, eyes wide and faces slack, swords clattering to the ground. Tears ran down the haunted face of their host, red rimmed eyes widening with surprise at Gen's unabated advance. Gen chopped sideways with his sword, the blade passing through Sir Torunus's neck. The man made no move to avoid the attack.

Gen's shock followed as he watched the skin behind the blade adhere and heal the instant the blade had passed through, Tornus's expression turning melancholy. Gen stepped back defensively.

"Believe me," Sir Tornus said, "I wish that had worked as much as you do. I've thrown myself off parapets and cliffs, stood in bonfires, crushed myself under avalanches of snow and rock, and spent months lying in the lake. Nothing will do. I've no pleasures but to feast on the spirits of the living, and one as strong-willed as you must satisfy!"

With frightening speed, supple fingers darted for Gen's neck. Gen sliced at the incoming strike, but the blade simply gave his attacker a newly severed sleeve of his shirt, leaving the arm undamaged and the hand latched around Gen's throat in a crushing grip. Tornus's eyes flashed with a spectral light and hungry anticipation, but Gen felt nothing, his attacker's expression turning to disappointment and curiosity.

Gen kicked the ancient knight in the midsection, sending him staggering back into the stone wall with terrific force. The lamp skittered to the ground as it leapt from Tornus's grip. Gen sheathed his useless sword and dashed for the lamp, but Tornus recovered quickly and collided with him, sending both men skidding across the floor.

"Well, my young friend," Tornus hissed as he stood, "I have often wondered what I had become, but you . . . what are you? You've no soul to feast on! Are you my damnation come at last? Come, get the lamp if you can, but beware, I just need an instant to consume one of your drooling companions!"

Hand-to-hand they struggled, Gen employing the elven fighting art of Kuri-tan, thinking he could gain the upper hand on his opponent, but Tornus was even more immune to pain than Gen was, quick hits and distracting slaps as useless as his sword had been against the demon at the

Chalaine's betrothal.

"You are fast, young one." Tornus grinned maliciously. "But enough of the girlish elven fighting!"

Tornus dashed toward Gerand and Volney, Gen leaping onto his foe's back and covering his eyes, throwing his weight down. Tornus stumbled and then purposefully dropped backward, slamming them both into a bed. The ancient frame broke, Gen's breath exploding from his lungs as his back hit the cold floor, his enemy's crushing weight driving him down.

Gen rolled and flung Tornus away from his friends and into a nearby column. As he tried to stand, the blanket tangled around his arms and shoulders, Tornus taking advantage by delivering a crushing punch to his face that sent him to the ground, head spinning. Gen fought for his concentration and his balance, thrashing against the blanket and trying to stay between Tornus and his friends. Just as Gen tossed the blanket away, Tornus rushed him, encircling him in a powerful embrace. Grinning, Sir Tornus reared his head back and butted his forehead into Gen's face. Gen took the strike on his cheek, ignoring the dull pain and using his weight to pull Tornus down. The knight let go before they fell, Gen landing hard on his backside.

Tornus dashed toward Gerand, Gen realizing that he could not catch Tornus in time. The light shining through the window reminded him of his power, and with a thought he dissolved half of Tornus's boot heel at a slant, a technique he had read about in one of Ethris's texts. Even that simple effort winded him, but it had the desired effect. As soon as their host set his hurried foot down, the ankle twisted and broke, sending him to the hard ground, dust exploding from the floor.

Thinking quickly, Gen sprinted forward and grabbed Tornus's leg and dragged him toward the lamp, feeling the man's ankle knitting back together under his fingers. Tornus clawed and scratched at the ground, finally grabbing the leg of one of the beds. With another spell, Gen weakened the leg so that it broke off in Tornus's hand, and, with muscles roping in strain, he pulled Tornus' body over the lamp and fell on top of him, ramming his elbow into Tornus's neck and breaking it. The blue light extinguished.

Gerand and Volney's slack faces regained their tightness and comprehension, and, grabbing their weapons, they rushed to Gen's side. Already Tornus's neck was healing, and Gen pinned a thrashing Tornus to the ground.

"Get out!" Gen yelled to the others. "Get out now! Wait for me outside the door. Swords are useless! Go!"

Reluctantly, his companions left. Gen had Tornus flipped onto his stomach, and taking his hair, bashed Tornus's face into the ground three times as hard as he could muster before extricating himself from the knight and bolting for the door. Tornus regained his feet with impossible speed, but his warped boot heel sent him flailing into the wall, lending Gen just enough time to get out and pull the door closed. Tornus arrived seconds later, and the two men strove with each other, each pulling at the door handle with every ounce of his strength.

"Get out of here! I will find you!" Gen yelled to his friends.

"We can't leave you!" Gerand protested.

"You can and will! You cannot defeat this foe! Run!"

Gen put enough terror into his voice that the hint of it in his entreaty persuaded his companions to obey. Gen held to the handle, planting his feet against the wall and pulling. Inch by inch the door crept inward, Tornus's strength fueled by his need to escape and feed.

"How long can you keep this up?" Sir Tornus said, voice strained. "Let me out. Let me out, and I will let you leave this place. I only want your companions. They will sate me."

An idea popped into Gen's mind, and he knew what he had to do. Gathering himself, he yanked backward with everything he had left, the door slamming shut. Envisioning the inside of the room, he used Trysmagic to create a lip of stone on the floor just in front of the door. Exhausted, he fell away against the wall on the opposite side, limbs listless and energy spent.

"What in Mikkik's name?" Tornus thundered. Cursing, he pulled at the door several times before pounding his fists upon it. "You're a Mage! Let me out of here! This won't keep me long!" Silence prevailed for a few moments, and then Tornus laughed. "Why, the moons are lovely this evening. I think I'll go to the window for a better look."

Gen swore. Legs wobbly, he half jogged, half walked down the corridor, hand on the wall to steady himself. "Don't go outside!" Gen yelled. Gerand and Volney ran back up the stairs toward him. Gen sat down and probed the bruises on his face, mind racing.

"What happened?" Volney asked.

"I think he went out the window."

"That is good information and all, but I mean, *what* happened in there? One minute we're talking to Tornus, and the next thing I know you're wrestling with him on the floor."

"He had a lamp like the ones he showed us for the Uyumaak, but this one was for men, apparently. I was able to resist the spell. He is a Craver, one of Mikkik's most awful creations, invented sometime near the Shattering. Nearly impossible to kill. I'll explain later. I think he is heading back in here."

"Can we gather our supplies?" Gerand asked.

"No. He's barred the door somehow," Gen lied, not wanting to explain why the door could no longer be opened and not possessing the strength to undo his spell. "We have to find a place to hide. I think the door into the keep is the only one, and there are no windows on the first floor."

"If we can find a place to hide, perhaps we can wait until he comes in, hide until he passes, and then make a run for it," Gerand suggested. "Do you think we can outrun him?"

Gen shook his head. "For a while, but Cravers are relentless and tireless when they want to feed. If he's shut the gates or pulled in the drawbridge, then we could be in a great deal of trouble."

"I've been thinking about that," Gerand said. "I think he can manage the gates by himself, though it would take time. The platform across the canyon, however, is too heavy and needs the services of many horses to pull in and out."

"That is some comfort," Gen commented, legs feeling stout enough to stand and walk. "For now, let's head down the hallway and see what we can find."

"Don't forget that Bibbs is bumbling around here somewhere," Volney reminded them. They had proceeded down the hall several paces when Gerand stopped dead in his tracks, a smile spreading across his face.

"What?" Gen whispered.

"The one room he will not think we are in is the one he barred shut."

"Right," Gen replied, "but we can't get in."

"We can. You have Aldradan Mikmir's sword. It can cut through anything! We can cut out a section of the door at the bottom, go inside, replace it, and with any luck, he won't even notice it."

Gen smiled in return. How could he have forgotten the virtues of the sword? They ran quietly back to the door. "Let me see if he spiked it somehow," Gen said, lying prone and jamming the sword into the crack beneath the door, breaking apart the rock he had created earlier. "I looks like he jammed some rock underneath it or something. Try it now."

As they went to open it, they heard pounding on the outer door, Sir Tornus yelling for Bibbs to unlock it.

"If we can beat Bibbs to it, Sir Tornus would be locked outside," Volney suggested.

Gen pulled them in and shut the door. "It isn't worth

the risk. Volney, jam some of the rock back underneath the door, if you can. Gerand, see how far of a drop it is to the ground. I'll get our gear packed back up."

In a few moments, the squeal of the keep door opening suspended Volney's efforts, and he Gen and Gerand neared the window.

"It is about twenty feet to the ground," Gerand reported. "Does anyone have rope?"

No one did.

"I'm home!" Tornus yelled from out in the hall. "There is only one way out of this keep! Well, only one way that doesn't hurt a great deal, and that is through this hallway. So I think I will wander around a bit and see what I can find! A little hide-and-seek, perhaps." They held their breath as Tornus briefly pushed their door, Volney's wedges holding long enough to satisfy the Craver that the way was barred.

Gen slid his sword quietly from its scabbard. With precise cuts he whittled away a bit of the stone floor so that Gerand could hold it up while he cut a small circle around it. Once complete, Gerand lifted the section of flooring up and they peered downward. The hole opened up into the kitchen. In the low firelight, they could make out low tables with unidentifiable pieces of meat lying in pools of blood. Quietly, Gen cut more sections of the floor away while Volney and Gerand carefully laid the pieces aside. Once the hole was wide enough, they dropped into the room.

The kitchen smelled of flesh and rot, a large pot reeking of some cooling substance that appeared uncomfortably like what they had eaten for dinner. Even worse, bits and pieces of Uyumaak lay scattered carelessly about the floor. Gen pulled his disgusted friends toward the back of the kitchen until he found what he thought was an outer wall.

Gen raised his sword. "I am going to cut through this wall. It will be noisy, but fast. We run for the gate. Get ready."

With quick strokes, Gen cut a triangular exit into the wall, the blade passing easily through the thick stones. They pushed their shoulders into the cut out section to heave it outward, the sound of stone grinding on stone echoing through the keep. Somewhere, Bibbs was slapping the walls in warning to his master.

"You should have cut a smaller section!" Gerand exclaimed as the chunk of wall moved inch by inch outward. Several seconds later the stones and mortar crashed to the paving stones outside, and they leaped out into the night. Gen led them back toward where he remembered the gate to be. Stealth was impossible, the litter of bones beneath their feet filling the air with cracks and snaps that echoed about the empty streets. Although exhausted, they knew they could not stop—Tornus knew exactly where they would run.

As they neared the courtyard, Gen suddenly pulled up. "Do you hear that?"

"More Uyumaak," Gerand stated flatly. "I'll bet those lanterns of his are still out front."

Cautiously they approached the courtyard, hugging the sides of a building. Gen chanced a look out into the square and pulled back quickly. "The gates are open, but I think that entire division of Uyumaak soldiers we spied in the glade are milling about out there. I cannot see that any of the lamps are lit. They are searching about at their leisure."

"What do we do?" Volney asked nervously.

"We think and we. . ." Gen started to reply.

"What is that?" Gerand hissed, cutting off Gen's comment. A yellowish orb floated just above them for a few moments before dashing away back into the courtyard.

"Run!" Gen ordered just as the sound of Uyumaak speech reverberated through the streets, the sound of their pursuing feet adding to the din. Gerand and Volney followed Gen as they darted down deserted avenues, turning unpredictably at corners and fleeing down alleys to throw off the Hunters. Echoes confused their senses as the scrabbling and scuffing of boots and clawed feet reverberated.

"In here!" Gen ordered quietly. They slipped into a dark building with rock walls and floor, the door and furniture long since turned to dust. "Get down away from the window and don't move. Don't breathe if you can help it."

Moments later, a large body of Uyumaak passed outside. Gen held his breath, hoping they would pass on. They stopped, snuffling and thumping to each other in the night. Abruptly, the entire company fell silent. Beads of sweat pooled on their foreheads as they crouched in the dark, unable to hear anything of their motionless pursuers.

A voice outside incanted. "Hideya Uk!"

"They've brought a Chukka," Gen whispered. White light streamed through the window of the room where they sat, brightening until a blinding luminescent sphere passed through the opening and flashed with the intensity of the sun before winking out.

"I can't see!" Volney said frantically.

"Stay against the back wall!" Gen's words barely left his lips when his ears told him that four Uyumaak, probably Warriors, had pushed through the doorway. Gen's night vision was washed out by the light. Relying on his training, he shut his eyes and listened for the sounds of footfalls and breathing.

Remembering his surroundings, he stepped forward and sliced downward. The sword of Aldradan Mikmir cut through the Uyumaak as Gen laid about him with every ounce of speed he could muster. Two died, cloven in two, before the other two could recover. The Warriors wielded great clubs, and Gen ducked a high swing he heard coming an instant before the devastating blow pounded the wall and sent chips of rock skittering across the floor. A quick upthrust to the gut finished the creature, and Gen spun to impale the last in the back as it leveled a strike against

Gerand.

They had no time to think as more Uyumaak charged the door. Remembering something he had read in his Trysmagic books, Gen used his power to create a small patch of razor-sharp spikes at the threshold of the door. Two Hunters had entered before his spell, but the next two fell down in agony as they crossed, tripping up their companions while Gen dispatched with the first.

"Aywejha!" the dark elf outside screamed.

Gen knew the Elvish word. It meant *wall*, but once his eyes finally adjusted to the dark, he couldn't see the result of the spell. Quickly he butchered the Hunters that had run afoul of the spikes. The floor was slick and treacherous with blood and bodies.

"I think I can see," Gerand whispered, "but my sight does little good in this blackness."

"The Chukka is out there, alone I think," Gen said. "Let's run. Kill him quickly. Step on the bodies near the door. The floor is a mess."

They ducked the window and ran for the door as one, slamming into an invisible barrier and falling about into the gore. Cursing, they stood, peering through the doorway to find the Chukka slapping his chest, summoning reinforcements.

"Wait here," Gen said, extending Aldradan's sword before him and passing through the invisible barrier. He sprinted at the surprised Chukka who stood alone in the street. The dark elf's hood was around his shoulders, long dark hair falling loosely down his back. Raising his hands, he started to incant until Gen created a small stone in its mouth. The obstacle threw off the spell, the Mage spitting the stone out just as Gen beheaded him.

"Come on." Gen waved to his companions, feeling exhausted. Magic took its toll.

"But which way?" Volney asked, terrified.

"Any way is a guess," Gen wheezed, trying to catch his

breath. "We need to work our way back to the gates, but the buildings make it difficult to get my bearings."

The sound of running Hunters to their left chose path to the right for them, and they loped away into the darkness along the paved streets. Empty rows of blank windows and doorways whirred by as they ran away from their persistent enemies.

"I see a clearing ahead," Gen informed Gerand and Volney. "Let's see if we can figure out where we are."

To Gen's dismay, the clearing was the edge of the city, the long lines of graves dug and filled by Tornus stretching before them on the other side of the low wall.

"I can't run anymore," Volney admitted, nursing an aching side.

"Over the fence!" Gen ordered them. "Lay down at the base and cover yourselves with your cloaks. Let's render their eyes useless, although we cannot help their noses."

The overgrown field on the other side of the rock wall provided excellent cover as they rested and listened for signs of their pursuers. Gen fought to control his labored breathing, mind racing. They were trapped on the wrong end of the upthrust rock, gate back to the road hopelessly out of reach.

Again the malevolent voice intruded into Gen's mind. *"I am at your command. I serve those with the power of my making. Long have I waited."*

The voice, solicitous and urgent, carried with it a taint of violent intent, an avalanche eagerly awaiting a yell to send it in a destructive course down the mountain.

"I am Ghama Dhron. I am sixteen thousand strong. I can bring you aid."

Gen shivered, the creature's dark language reminding him of the demon that crushed him during the Chalaine's betrothal. He ignored the call, shoving the offers of assistance out of his mind until the scratch and thump of a large number of Uyumaak on the other side of the wall set his heart pounding. Lying on his back, he leaned up to chance a look, finding the field swarming with the yellow eyes of the Throgs. Several memories of the disgusting beasts surfaced from Samian's memories. He had taken great pleasure in sticking arrows in the floating eyes.

"The Uyumaak are many. They are made from the same power as I. My poison will not harm them, and their skins are too thick for my bite. Command me and I will take the bodies of the dwarves laid in this field and drive your foes into the abyss."

Snuffling on the other side of the wall turned to thumping.

"They are upon us!" Gen yelled, leaping to his feet. As one, nine Hunters leaped over the wall and toward their prey, one remaining to summon the rest of horde. The eyes of the Throgs raced to where the battle was joined as a host of Warriors and Bashers emerged from alleyways into the moonlit field.

They fought desperately against the first wave of Hunters, sustaining many shallow cuts as they retreated slowly backward against uneven ground.

Gerand wiped sweat from his brow after the last Hunter fell. "What are those floating yellow orbs, Gen?"

"Throg eyes," Gen answered. "I'll tell you about them later."

"No need. We're dead," Volney said.

"Then let's make a heroes stand!" Gerand yelled. "And let them find a pile of Uyumaak at my feet!"

Gen swallowed hard as no fewer than twenty Warriors and a handful of Hunters hopped the wall. The Uyumaak bolted at them, circular mouths contracting and expanding as if already imagining their meal. More approached from the city. Gen had no choice. He extended his thoughts outward to the ethereal force. *"Come!"* he commanded, not sure what to expect.

At once, a mighty keening wail tore through the field, a sound of dark relief and delight, the pleased expression of a murderous convict set loose from his prison into a field of unsuspecting blood. The Uyumaak drew back, momentarily unnerved, and Volney and Gerand stood rooted, wide-eyed with horror.

"This way!" Gen commanded, leading them in the direction of the pit that Tornus showed them earlier that night. They did not travel far between the graves and weeds before a mass of sleek, dark serpents boiled into the field like dark water, groups stopping to burrow into Tornus's shallow graves. One by one, dwarven skeletons wrapped in snakes rose from the ground, one snake poking its head through an eye hole while others wrapped themselves around the bones, adhering them together and striding forward. Dwarven weapons as bright as the day they were crafted glinted in the light of the moons, serpentine hands gripping them with purpose.

The Uyumaak did not wait until the snake-animated skeletons formed a column five hundred strong before deserting the field at a dead run for the confines of the city.

"What is your wish, master? Shall I pursue?"

"Yes. Clear the way for us," Gen replied in thought.

"I thank you, master. Ghama Dhron will not fail you."

The counterfeit dwarven army sprinted away in pursuit, leaving the field quiet, save for the whistle of the wind through the weeds by the disturbed graves. Gerand and Volney looked around, faces troubled.

"A lot of strange things have happened tonight," Volney finally said. "But Holy Eldaloth! That is the most disgusting, horrifying thing I have ever beheld!"

"The chill in my spine is permanent," Gerand added. "Gen, do you have any idea what just happened? Because, despite the fact that we have just been delivered, I don't think the sound of my clapping for joy would overcome the thunder of my knees knocking."

"I do not have an explanation," Gen answered. It was mostly true. "It is a creature of dreadful evil and violence, but for some reason it helps us. We must accept the gift. I don't think we have a choice."

They walked toward the city tentatively, weapons at the ready. Uyumaak lay dead along their path, cut apart and scattered. Rarely did they find the body of a snake torn by an Uyumaak claw or smashed by a club, but the the Uyumaak and their Chukka masters could not hold against the puissant force of the dark army. When they arrived at the courtyard, the serpent-animated dwarves stood in ranks. Three of the skeletal warriors held a struggling Tornus fast.

"Do not approach him," Gen warned.

"I am quite content to stay where I am," Volney asserted as Gen strode forward between the ranks of the creatures, the hissing and sleek black bodies testing his courage.

"This one we could not kill. He is a Craver."

"Throw him in the pit," Gen ordered, *"into which he threw you and cover it with the rocks he used as grave markers. Then follow us onto the mountain road. Bring as many of the green lanterns as you can, but shutter them. I will give you further instructions once we are on the road."*

"Your will."

Sir Tornus glared at him, face alight with discovery. "You can command this abomination!" he yelled as he was dragged away, army following to aid in the task of his final incarceration. "I know what you are! Do they? Do you want to tell them or should I?"

"Silence him," Gen ordered.

Two snakes wrapped themselves around Tornus's mouth and nose, turning his epithets into muffled grunts of frustration.

"Let's go," Gen said to his companions, who waited until the snake-dwarves had cleared away completely before joining him.

"Gen," Gerand said nervously, "I hate to ask this, but can you communicate with that . . . thing?"

Gen nodded his head in reply.

"How?" Volney blurted out, face shocked.

"It uses Mynmagic to speak directly to the mind. It uses the corrupted tongue, just as the demon that sprang from the Burka pattern. I do not trust it, but it seems eager to help us for the time being."

"You mean. . ." Volney started.

"It's coming with us," Gen finished.

"Are you mad?" Gerand objected. "That monstrosity could turn on us and destroy us at a whim! It is evil! Can you command it to stay behind?"

"I think doing so would anger it. It is evil, but it appears indiscriminate. Remember that it just annihilated hundreds of Uyumaak and is now burying a Craver. It thirsts for violence and cares little for right or wrong, our side or their side. I have a feeling that we and the Chalaine's party will need aid before this is over. The Chukka are fools if they have not secured the beachhead against us, and Ghama Dhron is—at this point—willing to do as I say, for what reason I cannot fathom."

"Ghama Dhron?" his companions said in unison.

"Its name. It means 'Wrath of Poison' in the dark tongue."

"I don't like this," Gerand stated frankly.

"Neither do I," Gen agreed honestly. "I will keep it at a distance, if I can."

They crossed over the extended bridge, the early morning wind drying the sweat on their bodies and chilling them. They turned right onto the road, which started a slow, switchbacked descent through whispering pines.

"We have the mystery of Echo Hold solved," Volney commented at last. "But what of the Craver? Why didn't you kill it with your sword when you had the chance?"

"He could not be killed. His wounds healed the instant I delivered them. Do you remember nothing from when you were in thrall to the lantern?"

"Not a single thing," Volney answered.

"'They only have eyes for the lantern,'" Gerand quoted. "And how did you manage to escape that?"

Gen could not help but notice a note of suspicion creeping into his companions' voices.

"As with the wail of demons, it seems that the effect of the lantern can be overcome by sheer will."

Gen knew this did not satisfactorily explain what had happened. When Tornus had opened the lantern, it held no attraction for him. That, combined with the Craver's inability to consume him led to some disturbing conclusions.

"As for the other question, Mikkik created Cravers. . ."

"There are more than one?" Volney interrupted worriedly.

"There were. Mikkik created Cravers to feed on the souls of living creatures. While no one knows for sure, it is rumored that creating them requires some kind of sacrifice. They do not eat. They do no sleep. And they can only be killed in two ways: a Trysmagician has to unmake them entirely, converting them into a different substance all at once, or they have to be starved."

"But you said they don't eat," Gerand pointed out.

"They consume the essence of the living. It is a powerful need, and they must feed to survive."

"That's why he kept those lanterns out!" Gerand deduced.

"Exactly. Legend says they had to be kept from consuming for one year and a day. Of course, trapping one without being consumed is difficult, especially without magic."

"So if Tornus really wanted to die, why didn't he just starve himself to death?" Volney asked.

"The process of starving for over a year with food plentiful nearby probably proved too difficult. He wanted to be ended quickly. I don't know whether to pity or curse him."

Volney humphed. "I think I'll choose the curse option. He is one of the most—if not *the* most—notorious traitor in the history of Ki'Hal."

"Until me," Gen deadpanned, ending all conversation.

"I am near, master. What do you wish?" Ghama Dhron asked.

"Send half ahead and leave half behind. Kill any Uyumaak you find, but leave alive all else."

"Your will."

"Stand back off of the road," Gen told Gerand and Volney, who obeyed without question. In minutes, two hundred and fifty snake soldiers marched eerily by, weapons resting on bony shoulders. One flicked his ax at a tree as it passed, a cloven squirrel falling to the ground. They waited until they lost sight of the ghastly company around a switchback before following.

"I'll say one thing for this evening," Gerand said, voice upset. "It has been instructive. I think the only thing left to happen is for Mikkik himself to hike up the path and dance a jig. You'll let us know if he's coming, won't you Gen?"

116

CHAPTER 56 - THE SAVIOR OF ALL

Maewen permitted them little rest, awakening the company long before dawn and spurring them to pack more quickly. For the first time in her life, the Chalaine shouldered her own burden despite numerous offers to relieve her of it. She felt the need to prove she could stand on her own legs, and the virtue of Gen's Training Stones infused her with an unusual vigor and a confidence in her own strength.

Samian had started his instruction immediately after Maewen had returned the stones, and the Chalaine already felt she could buckle, draw, and resheathe a sword with her eyes closed and hopping on one leg. While she had no pretensions that she would ever acquire the skill of Dason or Gen, she took a smug satisfaction in knowing more of the sword than her husband.

"Gather to me quickly," Maewen ordered. "I have argued with myself all night about which course to take, and I choose the riskier one in terms of the way but safer in terms of Uyumaak. I am going to take you over the mountains and hopefully into the Dunnach River Valley and from thence across the plain to the lake. The wind and water in the mountains will hinder our enemy's sense of smell, and, without a wide plain, it will be difficult for them to come at us in numbers or use their archers effectively. The dangers, of course, are the weather and the raw wilderness we must traverse.

"I will be plain. There is no trail. I have never traveled this way, before the Shattering or after. It will be cold and arduous, and a misstep in the wild can be deadly. If anyone sprains an ankle or breaks a leg, they will be left behind, Chertanne and the Chalaine excepted, of course. If any feel to disagree, do so now, but this is the course I think best."

"What is the other option?" the Ha'Ulrich asked grumpily.

"The other way is to travel along the edge of the foothills but stay on the plain. The way is longer, but the travel would be faster. We would also be more visible and the Uyumaak able to approach us with superior numbers."

After no one voiced any objections, Maewen removed her two knives from their sheaths. "We will be traveling in the dark and fog for the next few hours. If you have a weapon, keep it at the ready. Your vision will do you little good, and you must rely on your other senses to keep you safe. The Chalaine, Chertanne, Mirelle, Fenna, and Geoff walk in the center of the party. I will lead, and Dason, bring up the rear. Walk close together and raise a quiet shout if you are separated. Let's get into the mountains."

They left the ringed hill through the same opening they had entered, turning west and plunging into an almost impossible dark. The Chalaine followed Chertanne more by sound than sight, her husband's stumbling and cursing warning her of obstacles in the path. By the time the first hint of light blushed the sky, she doubted they had covered a mile. The putrid stench of Throgs sometimes invaded their nostrils but quickly faded, inciting muffled curses. The Chalaine drove out thoughts of snaky tubules launching from the dark to leech blood from her leg, but images of Geoff pale on the ground stoked her fears until morning flooded the sky.

For the next several days, they climbed steadily and slowly, and—despite Maewen's ample skill—they found themselves backtracking to find better routes or alternatives to dead ends. Only the foul reek of the Throgs and the intermittent appearance of a yellow eye just out of bowshot bespoke the enemy's presence.

Maewen's analysis, as usual, left little opportunity for hope or comfort. "The Uyumaak likely know the mountains better than we. It could be they have elements ahead and are content to let us stumble along until we encounter one of their fortifications."

To the Chalaine's satisfaction and relief, after Geoff's near fatal encounter with a Throg, Fenna had doted on the dispirited bard, seeing to his comfort and cheering him with light conversation and little compliments. Both she and her husband tired quickly, breathing heavily and trudging slowly at the slightest incline, and as Maewen led them deeper into the mountains, the grade of their path increased in steepness and difficulty. Whatever their struggles, no one huffed and blew or complained more than the sunburned Ha'Ulrich, who found opportunity to curse nearly everything on the trail when he wasn't busy sucking wind.

His comments ranged from the annoying to the ridiculous. "I swear, it's as if someone placed these rocks here for me to trip on!" "I thought this was the top?" "Surely Mikkik created these bugs." "I think moving more slowly is in order, for everyone's safety. This reckless sprint into the mountains is folly enough as it is."

Maewen eventually gave up trying to convince the Ha'Ulrich to keep quiet, though Chertanne's complaints gradually subsided into barely vocalized mumbling.

For her part, the Chalaine found little difficulty in their ascent, thanking Gen for the stones she knew imbued her with a greater fortitude than most of her party. She used what surplus of strength she had to aid her mother, who, while uncomplaining, wore her exhaustion openly in spite of every attempt to hide it. Cadaen appeared ready to carry her at any moment, and between his help and her daughter's, Mirelle kept pace.

As Maewen promised, the nights in the mountains chilled them almost beyond toleration. As a concession, she allowed fires, saying that the Throgs ensured that the Uyumaak knew of their whereabouts, fire or no, though she chose camps that would keep archers from using the light to pick at them in the dark. Geoff spent the evenings writing in his book, Fenna snuggled next to him. The Chalaine huddled with her mother, and Dason always sat uncomfortably close on the other side of her, whispering compliments and hopeful prognostications, however lightly the Chalaine treated them.

A full week into mountains they hiked through a lightly forested ridge just below the snowline.

"We should have an easier time of it now," Maewen comforted them. "We will descend as directly as we can toward the Dunnach."

"I cannot see the river," Chertanne said, peering into the valley below them.

"It is at least two ridges over, perhaps three," Maewen explained. "We aren't done ascending completely."

Chertanne's face fell. "At least the weather is holding."

"It isn't," Maewen contradicted.

"What do you mean?" Athan inquired.

"Look to the northeast," the half-elf invited them, casually whittling at a new arrow. "There is a slight haze at the trailing edge of a storm. Didn't you feel the wind change?"

"Will it be bad?" Athan prodded.

"Yes, but brief, as well. We will need better shelter than we have found previously."

"And when were you planning on informing us about this storm?" Chertanne grumped.

"I figured it would become rather obvious to you in a few hours."

"I am the leader of the caravan!" Chertanne asserted. "Please inform me immediately of any changes of this kind."

"As you wish. You may also want to know that a company of Uyumaak will likely overtake us by nightfall, probably around the same time as the storm. What do you command?"

Chertanne's eyes widened and then darted about. "What do you suggest?"

"I suggest we find better shelter than we have found previously, by which I mean more defensible to weather and enemies."

"Make it so," Chertanne commanded lamely.

Maewen brushed the wood shavings from her legs and sheathed her knife. "Let's march."

As early afternoon set in, Maewen's predictions came true. A dark mass of cold gray clouds sped across the sky directly toward them, and for the first time in days they heard the percussive thumping of the Uyumaak. More disconcerting was the troubled, frustrated look on Maewen's face. Increasingly, she ordered halts as she wandered about in search of some place to hole up for the night, returning with a scowl.

As evening fell, the wind rose in gusts and the clouds threw a blanket across the sun. "Stay here," Maewen commanded, running ahead and returning after several minutes. "I have found a cave just ahead. If we hurry, we can reach it before the weather turns dangerous."

They descended down the ridge a bit farther before the Chalaine could spot the cave through her obscuring veil. A wall of brown rock ran along a steep incline to their right. Between the sparse but ancient trees the Chalaine could just make out a dark hole worn into the rock-face by water and wind.

The ascent took effort and time, shards of loose rock beguiling their feet and sending nearly everyone to all fours to keep from slipping down the hill. By the time they reached the base of the rock wall, the storm whipped snowflakes around their faces with fury.

The entrance to the cave rose shoulder high and stretched several feet wide, the bulk of the cave lying below the entrance after a slight descent. The interior, to their amazement, was quite commodious, and the change from cold exposure to relative warmth and protection prompted a wave of relief.

"Won't the Uyumaak trap us in here?" Athan asked worriedly.

"Unlikely," Maewen answered. "If you didn't notice, we haven't heard them speaking for nearly two hours. If there is a brain among them, they are doing what we are right now. We will leave as soon as we can to keep the advantage of distance, though the difficult approach to the cave and the cover of the trees actually make this an excellent place to stand, if needed."

"Can we light a fire?" Chertanne asked.

"A small one, but we have no wood," Maewen answered. "I doubt anyone wants to retrieve any."

"You two," Chertanne ordered his two of his personal guards. "Fetch us firewood."

"Yes, Ha'Ulrich."

By the time they returned, they shook with cold and carried a paltry amount of wood and tinder.

"Is that all you could find?" Chertanne complained, displeased.

"Forgive us, Lord Khairn," they begged, "but that is all we could gather before our hands were too numb to gather more."

"Warm your hands and return for more."

It required three trips before the obedient soldiers gathered enough fuel for the fire to satisfy their Lord. Once the small flame sprang to life, the Chalaine invited them to enjoy its warmth first, for which they thanked her. While the smoke rose gradually out of the hole, the cave filled with a smoky haze that burned their eyes. The relaxing warmth far outweighed these inconveniences, and soon they all lay back against the cave walls and listened to the wind howl outside.

"If we had some meat, I would almost be content," Chertanne announced. His two soldiers cast terrified looks at each other, but to their relief their Lord did not command them out into the bitter dark in search of game.

The Chalaine regarded her husband, wondering at his new-found assertiveness. Athan sat nearby lost in thought, face careworn and drawn. The Chalaine could not like the man, but she could appreciate the burden he had shouldered. Counseling and shaping Chertanne was a daunting task, as doomed, she thought, as the foolish potter who threw a slab of granite on his wheel only to find his hands worn away well before the stone.

Night fell completely some while later, driven snow spraying into cave when the wind kicked up. A scrabbling outside pulled them from their pleasant rest, setting everyone at edge. Weapons quietly slid from discarded sheaths as the sound persisted, nearing. Something ascended the incline toward their camp, disturbing the gravel and rocks on the hill. Breathing shallowed and eyes sharpened, all attention riveted on the opening to the cave just above them. The scrabbling stopped, and several tense moments passed, imaginations spawning everything from a stray deer to an Uyumaak Hunter in the cave entrance.

The Chalaine, hearing muttering nearby, turned toward the sound, finding Athan incanting something under his breath. At first she thought he might be warding the cave against entry, but as she watched, Chertanne, who hugged the cave wall, face pale, grew more composed, color returning. A bold determination took hold of his features, and he scooted toward the edge of the cave where Maewen, Tolbrook, and Jaron awaited in readiness.

Slowly, the sickly yellow eye of a Throg drifted in, facing the cave wall. As it rotated downward, Maewen switched her knives to a throwing grip, but before she could launch her attack, the glistening eye fell from the sky as if the invisible force that infused it with buoyancy and motion had suddenly dropped it. It clanked once as it hit the rocks, its second bounce shattering it like glass, little shards clinking as they descended to the floor. Chertanne, face exultant, sunk to the ground exhausted.

"I did it!" he said quietly. "I changed it to glass! Did you see, Athan?"

"Well done, Lord Khairn!" Athan congratulated him heartily. "You see? I told you we would have need of your power before this journey is over! Do you see what you can accomplish?"

"Yes, but I am so tired!"

"It is often so with new Magicians, Milord. The ability to use magic is like a muscle that strengthens as it is used. You will grow in ability day by day and will soon have the ability to change twenty such eyes without so much as a thought."

The Chalaine found her mother casting her a meaningful glance. The Chalaine rolled her eyes up into her head and quietly exhaled. "That was well done, Chertanne," she said as sincerely as possible. "Such use of your power is exactly what we need in our dire circumstances."

To her surprise, Chertanne's brow furrowed. "I do not need you to tell me what is needed," he rejoined testily. "I have a mind about me."

"She wished to compliment you, your Highness," Athan interjected, trying to recover the glow of the moment.

"Compliments and scorn are what women use to shape men into what they want them to be. I will achieve greatness, and I will do it without anyone's assistance or interference."

"Then how am I to express appreciation or gratitude? If I say nothing, then you might think me insensible or uncaring of your accomplishments." The Chalaine tried to say this as meekly as possible, but from Chertanne's expression, it appeared the obvious frustration in her voice had revealed her artifice.

"Your mistake, Lady Khairn, is assuming that I need your appreciation or your gratitude. I do not. Therefore I will view any such expressions as useless or as distasteful attempts to manipulate me."

"As you wish," the Chalaine returned, inclining her head, noticing Mirelle staring Jaron away from his sword hilt. The Chalaine felt annoyed at Chertanne's arrogant independence, though she viewed Chertanne's insistence that she never compliment him as an unintended act of beneficence that would preclude her from actually needing to vocalize several lies she had at hand to get her through her marriage.

"Let us rest now, Highness," Athan encouraged his charge. "Mikkik's servant is blinded, and we will all rest more easily now."

Chertanne returned to his place near the fire and immediately dozed off. The Chalaine lay awake for nearly an hour, watching her companions drift off one by one. Fenna lay asleep, her head on Geoff' shoulder and her arm on his chest, and the Chalaine smiled, remembering the night in the canyon when she slept in just the same fashion with Gen. By now, her addiction to the warmth of the *animon* had grown proportionate to her insecurity, and she hoped that the cold weather would keep the others from wondering why she thrust her hand into her pocket from sunup to sundown.

They left the protection of the cave just as the sun paled the morning sky. The storm had blown through quickly, leaving the heavens clear and the sun bright in their eyes as they gradually turned west. The snow, while not deep, had drifted, though a short descent took them out of the snow onto a wet, grassy track.

Maewen led them down off of the mountain into a pleasant glade running with gurgling water as she scouted for a place to ascend the next line of high hills. The Uyumaak signals did not torment them that morning, but every snap of a twig set eyes to darting and hands flinching toward weapons.

At their midday rest, Maewen returned back along the trail to scout for any sign of their pursuers while the company ate and prepared for another uphill trudge. The Chalaine was sitting upon a fallen log absentmindedly gnawing on a leathery scrap of dried fruit when she found Geoff approaching her. The Chalaine smiled. A little bit of the energy of his step had returned, no doubt springing from a more confident heart.

"Highness." He bowed. "May I?"

"Please," she said, signaling for him to sit next to her.

"I haven't had the chance to thank you for healing the Throg's bite, so I do so now. Yours, by far, has proved the most useful magic on our adventure."

"You are most welcome, and I am happy to see you better in body and spirit."

He grinned. "Yes, my soul seems to be finding its way back to a bit of the rejoicing it once knew. I think it will not sing as proudly as before, but innocence cannot but give way to wisdom, and I have lost something in this venture that I cannot quite place, but perhaps it will come to me when I have a little more peace and solitude to reflect upon it."

"I feel it, too. If you do find words for it, then share them."

"I will, Highness."

"I am also gratified to see that Fenna has lost her temperamental prejudice against you."

Geoff sighed, but not altogether unhappily. "It is a bit

strange that she loved Gen for his force of arms and she only found her love for me when I demonstrated the complete opposite."

The Chalaine laughed. "As I recall, it was Gen's devastating injury against the demon that boosted her affections for him. So it is a similar case."

"Then to keep her faithful, I will have to make sure that none of the men in Blackshire attempt anything that might incapacitate them, lest sympathy for their plight spin her affections in another direction."

The Chalaine chuckled. "I think our dear Fenna is done spinning. I hope to come visit you when this is over. With you two the Lord and Lady of Blackshire, I cannot imagine there will be a merrier place for a heart ready to forget Throgs, Uyumaak, and other . . . unpleasantness."

"You will always be most welcome," Geoff said, now lowering his voice to a whisper. "As will a certain disenfranchised young gentleman. If you come together, we shall throw a party such as you will never forget."

"Thank you," the Chalaine returned, emotion rising. "You are a good man. Do not worry for us. Think on Fenna, treat her well, and you will never want for anything in matters of the heart. I cannot promise you that there will not be future vexations, but I think they will be short in comparison to the last one."

"Maewen!" Jaron yelled.

All eyes followed his voice. Along the swollen stream bank Maewen sprinted, bloody daggers in her hands. "Get up!" she yelled. "We must leave!" As they hefted their packs, a single Hunter broke from the trees, charging Maewen with frightening speed. If it noticed the rest of the party, it did not acknowledge it, eyes riveted on its prey. Hands fumbled for bows as the Uyumaak closed on the half-elf.

"It's going to catch her!" Geoff said, exclaiming what everyone left unspoken. Just as the first bows raised to take aim on the creature, Chertanne stepped forward, eyes fixed and face serene. The Chalaine looked to Athan whose eyes had closed as he worked his fortifying magic, saying the spell quietly. Without expression, Chertanne concentrated, and just as Maewen turned to face the Hunter, it grabbed its throat and fell to the ground, spasming as it struggled to pull air through a clogged airway. Maewen finished it quickly.

"Let's move," Chertanne commanded to everyone's surprise. "The Dark Guard to the rear. Dason, stay with the Chalaine. Maewen, lead us forward. My guard, to me."

Shocked but silent, the party complied and moved as quickly as they could, Maewen scanning about for a way up and over the next rise. After a brutal, swift climb, sides pinched in pain and breath came in ragged gasps. Maewen called a halt on a gentle slope shadowed by lofty pines. They leaned against trees and rocks to regain their strength, all ears nervously attuned to the noises around them. Maewen returned down the line to find the Chalaine, Athan leaving Chertanne to follow her.

"Chalaine," Maewen gasped, face pained, "I will not be so proud this time." A gash in her side bled enough to soak her shirt, cloak, and the hand she had used to cover the wound while they walked. "Do you have the strength for it?"

"Of course."

"What happened back there?" Athan asked the half-elven ranger while the Chalaine concentrated.

"I found a group of them. Just three Hunters and a handful of Warriors. No more than a scouting party. I killed two of the Hunters and a couple of the Warriors."

"I thought you had learned your lesson about attacking Uyumaak by yourself after your misadventure with Gen," Athan remonstrated.

"I will keep my own counsel on when to fight and when to withdraw. If Gen were here, they would all be dead and we could move with more security."

"As it is," Athan said, "they know exactly where we are. If you had left them alone they might be ignorant of our whereabouts."

"Keep to your books, Padra," Maewen chastised, face relaxing as the Chalaine's magic mended her side. "They had our trail. Without the Hunters, they are blind. They will be able to follow us for a time, but I can lose them before nightfall. But I warn you, they are merely pushing us somewhere. We should have had more trouble with them. Thank you, Chalaine."

Maewen returned to the head of the party and started their ascent again, though at a much more relaxed pace.

"Can magic turn a coward into a conqueror?" the Chalaine asked the nearby Athan quietly, hoping to avoid the prying ears of Dason, who followed behind her at a few paces.

"No, but it can help one emerge," he answered with equal discretion.

"Do you think your magic enough to see him through his confrontation with Mikkik?" the Chalaine asked, striving to keep a mocking tone out of her voice.

"I know you have little faith in him," Athan said, "but what I do is no different than what any father might do to a young son facing new dangers and experiences. When I was barely as tall as my father's waist, a neighboring farmer came into possession of a bull mastiff to help protect his flock against winter wolves. I was terrified of the beast and refused to walk to town to do the little errands my father always sent me on.

"So one day my father carried me in his arms and, despite my wailing protestations, walked me past the giant dog. Eventually—by which I mean some weeks—I only needed his hand as the dog rubbed against us and barked. In time, I felt comfortable if he only watched over me. Before the year was out, the mastiff and I became the fondest of friends. So you see, by holding Chertanne's hand a little, by helping him experience success, his confidence may grow so that he can master his fears and start to lead a little."

"There is little time."

"I know, but I will try. I thank you for trying to help with your compliment last evening. It helped, whatever his reaction. You may try to talk to him about how he uses his magic. If you don't seem to be manipulating him, he may be more amenable to your conversation. Now I must continue my instruction, if you'll excuse me."

Athan returned to his charge, speaking with him intermittently as they hiked.

Three days later they caught their first view of the Dunnach River Canyon from atop a high ridge. From their lofty standpoint, it kinked through the forest, a gray crack that seemed as if a giant had plunged its hands into the valley and ripped it apart. The distant roar of the rocky river and the proximity of familiar—if unpleasantly remembered—places provided a sense of orientation and progress that buoyed them.

"By my estimation," Maewen informed them, "we are about two days from the meadow where the Uyumaak massacred the caravan. We will stay out of view of the canyon and the road on the other side of this ridge, but we must have care, now. The bulk of the Uyumaak once encamped somewhere near here, and I doubt not that we have just as many before us as behind. I will scout more frequently now, and we must move more cautiously."

Cautiously, as Maewen made perfectly plain in the following minutes, meant no talking and required expending some effort not to step on every brittle stick and pine cone that littered the ground in abundance. The Chalaine found she had little difficulty doing so, though the rest of her party, Maewen excluded, raised enough of a ruckus to permanently affix a frown on Maewen's face.

They stopped early that evening, Maewen informing them that she would scout ahead farther than usual and would not return until near midnight.

"Don't attack a camp full of Uyumaak, Maewen," Athan cautioned her. "Our survival is more important than any pleasure or revenge you may want to exact."

The tracker did not acknowledge his words and ran into the night, leaving her company in a dense, rocky thicket that provided shelter and protection from prying eyes.

No one slept or spoke much until she returned. When she did, she said, "It is as I feared. There is a Portal a few miles from here, and several companies of Uyumaak are nearby. I would guess that the Portal is where they resupply and reinforce. They densely patrol a line from the shard's edge to the canyon wall. I suspect that if the rearward element hunting us gets word ahead, we will find ourselves in a thick of the creatures within two hours."

Hearts sank in unison, a silence ensuing as they all waited for Maewen to proffer some clever way out of the situation.

"What do we do?" Chertanne finally said, voice weak and unsteady.

"You are in command, Ha'Ulrich," Maewen returned. "What is your will?"

"My will? My will is to be off of this accursed shard as soon as possible! I suppose that since you're finally asking me for an idea that you've run out of them. We're all dead, aren't we?"

"Have courage, Milord," Athan soothed. "We have resources yet. Tonight I will place a ward of turning on our camp to keep us safe. It will cost me strength, but that cannot be helped. What we need is time to think about what can be done. The morning light will, no doubt, lend our minds a bit more clarity than our present worry can permit."

But after a night of bitter cold shivering, the dawn only

saw them wrenched with worry and agitation. They decided not to make way for fresh panic, conservatively choosing to keep on with the unrelenting, stale panic they had lived with for weeks.

Maewen left before full light to scout ahead again, and in the cramped quarters of their stony enclosure, it took a supreme effort from everyone to keep from shouting in annoyance at every bump, discomfort, and misstep. All annoyances quickly passed when the sounds of Uyumaak drums reached their ears, though at a distance. Maewen arrived soon after.

"They have grouped and are moving. I expect them soon. Anyone that has a bow and can shoot it with some accuracy, join me on top of the rocks when I give the order. Those with weapons or magic, stay inside the stone circle until I tell you to leave and form a line of defense. If you leave cover too soon, you risk getting cut down by the Uyumaak archers. The rest should stay inside the cover of the stones."

The day rose clear and cold, and they stood tensely listening to the rise and fall of the drums. Maewen lay atop one of the rocks silently surveying the tree-dotted ridge top around them.

"I wish they would bloody come," Jaron grumbled impatiently.

But as they waited, the drums gradually faded again until they could not hear them. Longer they waited, and after nearly an hour of hearing nothing but pleasant birdsong and wind, Maewen hopped down and left, returning a while later with a puzzled expression.

"I don't understand it, but the main body of Uyumaak has moved south and east of here. I can't be sure where they are going or why, but it is good fortune for us."

"Is the way ahead clear?" Athan asked.

"Not entirely, though the defenses are much thinner. Their shaman remains at the Portal gate, but only about fifteen Uyumaak, mostly Hunters, linger nearby."

"We can kill that many," Jaron affirmed, "but it won't be easy."

"It's not their numbers I fear," Maewen said. "It is their drums. If they are able to signal to their brothers that we are passing through or engaging them, they will chase us and catch us with ease."

"Then we wait until the cover of night and try to slip by," Athan suggested.

"You forget," Maewen reminded him, "that the Uyumaak see well in the dark and smell all the better. We've hardly a better chance of slipping them now than in the dead of night, though it will improve the odds some."

"We need a diversion to pull them in the wrong direction," Jaron piped in, "although whoever does the diverting will likely die for it."

Chertanne stepped forward and opened his hand, revealing a number of shiny discs. "I've been making these to practice my magic. I believe, Maewen, you said that these attracted them."

Padra Athan smiled proudly.

Maewen nodded. "That is good. Make as many more as you can. The question is how we can get these into a position where they will start fighting over them without compromising ourselves."

"Perhaps I can help" Athan spoke up after a pause. "If I can get close enough to see one of them, I can use my magic to direct it to go wherever we choose.   Maewen could place the discs away from the main body, I could guide an Uyumaak there and direct it to return and dump them on the ground."

Maewen considered for a few moments. "It is the best we have, but rather than drop them on the ground, have the creature show his companions and then run in another direction away from the Portal. For now, rest. We will be traveling through the night."

The Chalaine tried to sleep, but she found her busy thoughts and general lack of exhaustion prevented her from doing so. The hours limped slowly by, Chertanne creating four more of the shiny, coin-like objects during the day before Athan insisted that he conserve his strength and rest.

Near evening Maewen left to scout once again, returning just before full dark. "Everyone, follow me and keep as quiet as you can. One loud noise will ruin us all."

No one needed the additional encouragement as they slunk into the night, the bright moons providing just enough light to keep them from committing the gravest of blunders. After nearly two hours of slow going, Maewen silently raised her hand to halt the party, waving Padra Athan forward. The two disappeared into a line of whispering, long-needled pines swaying just ahead of them.

Since the Uyumaak did not talk or shout, the commencement of the scuffle manifested itself in thumps and the crack of rocks dislodged by hurried feet and the crunch of gravel beneath squirming bodies.

Maewen signaled them forward from the edge of the trees, and they jogged forward as the sounds of Uyumaak fighting moved slowly away. Padra Athan stood inconspicuously behind a tree, joining Chertanne as they pushed forward into a large clearing. Stumps still remained where the Uyumaak had cleared space in the trees. Feces, ashes, and several slashed Uyumaak bodies littered the ground as they picked their way between roots determined to trip them.

As they neared the opposite edge, a blue light cascaded through the clearing, the stumps casting long shadows. All eyes turned the source, finding the familiar sheen of a Portal some fifty yards to the north.

"Hurry! We run!" Maewen commanded.

The Chalaine picked her way through the difficult tangle of roots and detritus with surprising ease, leaving her companions and guards behind and finding herself second after Maewen to enter the relative safety of the tree line on the other side.

"You run well," Maewen complimented her. "Those stones are more beneficial than I thought."

As the rest of the party straggled forward, the first shadowy silhouettes appeared in the Portal. Only Maewen's restraining hand kept the Chalaine from darting out to help her mother. As soon as they all managed to get inside the dark of the trees, they spent several moments catching their breath and watching what would unfold behind them.

The Portal only remained open for a few minutes before it winked out.

"I count a full company of Uyumaak," Maewen reported. "Walk away into the wood quietly. If they pick up our scent, we may have a fight yet."

But before they turned to go, the Chukka thumped to his subordinates, and the Uyumaak company dashed away in the direction the Chalaine's party had come from.

"What could possibly have been so important that finding us became the second priority?" Maewen mused out loud. "Well, let us use our good fortune to our advantage. Stick together. Getting lost in a forest during the day is easy. At night, it is nearly unavoidable."

Chapter 57 - Lights in the Mist

Maewen waited until the mist of the lake had crawled inland and obscured the open grassland before she sneaked into the twilight of evening for another glance at the stalemate they had faced for three days. They encamped in a weedy, though spacious, copse of trees that grew a mile from the slope that descended to the beachhead.

Their rejoicing at having come so far and nearing what they hoped were friendly fortifications was dashed instantly at the half-elf's first report—Uyumaak had control of the beach and the hastily built fort and enjoyed the security of numbers and position. The only way off the shard lay as far out of reach as the moons in the sky. Once Maewen confirmed repeatedly that she, despite her experience, could not conjure up a way past the barricade, conversation in the party lapsed into laconic grumbling and terse complaints.

Maewen could find no fault with their collective surliness. What bread remained had the texture and density of rock, and the dried fruit had gradually turned black and leathery. Of the two, the fruit claimed favor, for the length of time required to chew it at least afforded the illusion of a larger meal. Adding to this, daylight no longer brought relief from the cold, and during their second night, an inch of snow fell that did not melt away from the blond grass until well past midday. Shoulders hunched habitually beneath tattered cloaks, and sore muscles cramped from the cold and lack of exercise.

As she stepped to the edge of the tree line, Maewen breathed in the smell of the lake, damp and bitter, tinged with the more unpleasant smell of scaled hides and bubbling cook pots. The fog dampened the steady pounding of Uyumaak drums, but as she jogged out into the field, she noted that the character of the beats differed from what she had grown accustomed to in her previous forays. An increased frequency and subtle shift in the rhythm signaled a change, and—while she did not know how to interpret the language—reporting even the minutest difference in their circumstances to the party would provide her human companions at least a day's worth of pointless speculation to help pass the time until rescue or death.

Stealthily, she pushed forward, keeping low among the tall grass and scattered bushes, which dampened her leggings with the watery residue of the mist. Proximity to the pounding beat of Uyumaak speech confirmed her initial perception—a note of agitation resounded within the menacing cadence. Carefully, she wound her way to a mound to the left and above the beach, scooting forward on her belly until she could glimpse the Uyumaak encampment.

The virtue of her elven blood allowed her eyes to penetrate the weak light and swirling mist. At first she saw nothing that would account for the change she had discerned earlier. As before, the Uyumaak surrounded both sides of the wall, half facing out toward potential threats from the lake, the remainder watching the hill and waiting for an attack or wild attempt to circumvent their lines to gain the freedom of the water.

But even should the weary travelers gain such freedom, the Uyumaak had burned all the boats, a fact Maewen had not yet worked up the courage to tell the ragged survivors of the caravan. Given time and means, they could probably construct a rude raft, but the thought of them awkwardly hoisting such a craft onto their shoulders and charging the Uyumaak lines like beggars with a battering ram brought a grin to her face despite the decided lack of levity in their situation. The probability of the Uyumaak archers butchering them before they paddled to knee-deep waters returned her expression to its usual sobriety.

A gentle breeze momentarily cleared a portion of the hill that descended to the wooden wall, and in the brief moment of clarity she saw what she was looking for. A ragged line of Hunters, Bashers, Archers, and Warriors descended in a file to an audience of their fellow creatures, who ogled them and slapped their chests in a staccato commentary. The idea that their enemies were receiving reinforcements momentarily gripped her heart with terror and frustration until a few minutes of additional vigilance revealed something more favorable.

While little more than faint shadows even to her eyes, the way many of the creatures walked or carried themselves was off somehow, and it took her only a few moments of puzzling to discern that several of the Uyumaak limped while others held injured arms close to weary bodies rather than swinging them as they normally would when walking. This was not a reinforcement; this was a retreat.

Maewen slid backward and turned over, letting the obscuring fog envelop her in its dampness until full darkness had fallen. What did they leave behind them that could put large numbers of Uyumaak to flight? Had Ethris and Shadan Khairn survived the battle of Dunnach Falls with a large enough remnant of his army to push the Uyumaak toward the shore? Had the soldiers that once occupied the walls regrouped somewhere behind them?

Both possibilities struck her as wrong. The Uyumaak had nearly decimated the soldiers at Dunnach Falls before she had run out of the meadow that day, and the soldiers that had once occupied the fortifications at the beach had no doubt been trapped on the wrong side of their own protection and been slaughtered, although they all hoped that some few had escaped in boats back toward the Portal to deliver warning.

Shivering, she rose and picked her way through the field back to the quiet, cold camp where she related her news to the huddled group. They raised the same possibilities that she had to herself, dismissing them and reintroducing them with desperate 'buts' and 'what-ifs.' Frustration and irritability ended the conversation nearly an hour later, and everyone settled in amongst the boles for another uncomfortable sleep.

"Injured Uyumaak are, at the very least, a good omen," Geoff announced before lying next to Fenna. Maewen hoped he was right and meandered around the camp until everyone was asleep. As night deepened, she walked toward Jaron and Cadaen, who took the first watch. The men guarded their charges silently, arms crossed against the cold, just inside the edge of the copse. Mirelle slept close by with her daughter, and Maewen took great care not to wake them. Their Protectors sensed Maewen approach.

"Have you heard anything unusual?" she whispered.

"I think I can make out movement in the dark, though it is distant," Jaron replied.

"Have care tonight," Maewen advised. "If there are still stragglers fleeing a battle, our little hideaway may seem as attractive to them as to us, though I would hope the smell of their own food would lend them enough iron to march the rest of the way to their camp."

"We had discussed the same," Cadaen replied.

"Good. I will let Chertanne's guard know as well."

Maewen turned and started back toward the heart of the

camp when a bird trilled loudly in the distance. At its call, she stopped immediately and turned her head toward the sound. Again it broke the night. A smile crept across her face. When it sang the third time, she answered in kind— the call of the Silver Loon from the forests of her home. Only one person living would know the sound or how to make it so well. She turned around.

"I am going to scout a bit more," she explained to Jaron and Cadaen. "I will return shortly."

Neither appeared to think anything was amiss as she again disappeared into the night. She waited until she was well away from the camp before using the bird call again and waiting for its answer to guide her. For the first time in months, a genuine enthusiasm coursed through her veins. Wounded Uyumaak and Gen arriving on the same day could be no coincidence.

At last she saw them, Gen, Gerand, and Volney huddling against the lee side of a steep hill in a low thicket not a half-mile from Chertanne's camp. They stood as she approached and greeted her on the plain. The faces of the young men, bearded, gaunt, and gray in the night, matched those of her own party, and at her approach, only Gerand and Volney managed a grin. Gen's severe demeanor dampened Maewen's excitement at seeing him again. The lines on his face and the gravity of his eyes immediately refreshed to her mind the scenes played out at Elde Luri Mora, and at once she comprehended the weight of his predicament and his sorrow.

"Your coming brings great joy, Gen," Maewen greeted him in Elvish, despite his determined solemnity.

"I am glad to see you well. How fares the Chalaine and her party?" Gen asked, voice tired.

"They are frustrated and trapped. Health has favored us, but there is little else good to be said. The food runs short, and the Uyumaak bar the way home."

"We have been without food for two days ourselves,"

Gen reported. "The Uyumaak have killed all the game. We have help for the last. Where are you encamped?"

"Not far from here. A contingent of Uyumaak limped past our position this evening. I take it you are responsible, then?"

"Yes," Gen said, "but what aid we have brought is not . . . wholesome. It is a long tale. Tonight you will see green lights upon the hill that leads to the shore. Stay well away from them. In the morning, your prospects will be brighter, I think."

"As you wish. What do you plan to do?"

"I need to talk to Mirelle. Does she . . . does everyone know who I am?"

"What do you mean?" Maewen asked, eyebrows knitting together. She thought she caught a flash of hope in Gen's eye.

"Forget it. Do you think I could speak to her alone? I know Cadaen will be nearby, but it cannot be helped."

"It is possible, but not wise. If Athan were to trap you again, you would not escape his justice."

"See if he is asleep. If you can bring Mirelle a little apart from the camp, that would be best, but if not, I will risk venturing in. I will be brief. Once the night's business is done, we three will try to reach the Portal before the rest. If we get there before Athan, then perhaps we can pass through without any difficulties."

"Remain here," Maewen said. "I will return shortly."

Gerand and Volney approached Gen as Maewen loped away. "Well," Volney asked, "anything you would like to share with us?"

"They will wait while Ghama Dhron does his work," Gen said. "I am going to speak to the First Mother."

141

"That is insane, Gen!" Gerand protested. "You'll be caught!"

"It matters little anymore. The Chalaine will get off the shard now, and that is really all I can do for her anymore. You will soon know why. Stay here. If I do not come back—or even if I do—you are free to find your own path. Again I thank you for your help and remind you of your vow."

Maewen returned shortly and waved him after her. When visible between waves of mist, the night sky gleamed full of stars above them, the moons suffusing the fog with an ethereal glow. Uyumaak drums beat slowly and irregularly in the night, footsteps of half-elf and man crushing the damp grass the only other sound in the still night. Mirelle waited just outside the trees, Cadaen close behind. Her hood was off, and she fussed with her hair while casting glances into uncertain gloom.

Gen approached her quickly and knelt before her, head bowed. "Forgive me, Mirelle," Gen intoned sorrowfully. "I have done you and your daughter a great wrong."

"Get up, Gen," Mirelle commanded, grabbing his arm and pulling him upward.

"Milady, I. . ." His words were quelled by her lips on his, and his concentration wandered as she covered his face with kisses and tears.

"Please, Mirelle," Gen begged. "I have things I need to say."

"And I won't listen to one word until you have held me until I am warm again. I have been cold for so very long. Come, sit against this tree. Not another sound unless I command it."

Gen obeyed, Mirelle melting into the circle of his embrace. Her warmth and affection dulled his impatience and fear of discovery, and he relaxed, weeks of anxiety draining away. She laid her head on his chest, sporadically rising to kiss him. Eventually she quieted, and the

142

comfortable glow of her presence and the deep rhythm of her breathing lulled Gen toward a sleep he knew would finally be free of fearful visions. But as his eyes fluttered, he denied himself such a dangerous escape and he stirred, forcing himself awake.

"You are more prickly than the last time I slept on your shoulder," Mirelle reminisced dreamily, rubbing his beard with her hand. With effort she sat up and smiled at him. "I wish you loved me as you love my daughter."

Shame rose within him. "It was wrong of me to let my feelings for her get out of hand. It was unforgivable and foolish, at best."

"No, Gen," Mirelle whispered, leaning into him again. "I am glad of it. Every woman should know the love of a good man, and you have given her that gift. Your words and your consideration have strengthened her and edified her in ways only I would notice."

"But I am not that good man, Mirelle. I have come because I wanted to apologize for not listening to you and not obeying Lady Khairn."

"Do not call her that!"

"It is who she is, Mirelle."

"It is not, Gen. That is what she is called by anyone who does *not* know her. You know better than to ever associate her with that name."

"I am sorry. But I have something else I must tell you. It won't be easy for you, but I want you to hear it from me and not Athan. Mirelle, I am the Ilch."

Her soft laughter caught him off guard. "I know. Athan does as well, but he hasn't told anyone yet. I've known for as long as Ethris. He consulted me about it before letting you join the Protectorship. Please keep that fact to yourself. I have plans."

"And you still let me. . ." Gen blurted out incredulously.

"Yes, and I still let you guard my daughter. You had me in your power long before then. And, I am happy to say, that despite my blindness when it comes to your behavior, I was right about you."

"I don't know what to say."

"Good. Then shut up for a little while longer." She pushed him back against the tree, but he resisted.

"I really should go," Gen said, a sudden sadness washing over him. "I don't want to be trapped by Athan again."

Mirelle sighed disappointedly and rose. "Let me wake the Chalaine," she said, walking toward the camp. "I'm sure she would like to see you. She has worried a great deal."

Gen pulled her back. "No, Mirelle, please. I have hurt her enough and I cannot face her. I have disgraced myself and failed her."

"Please, Gen. That is nonsense!"

"It isn't. She hasn't told you all, I am sure. I cannot see her. It would be best that she forget me."

Mirelle's face wrinkled with worry. "I will respect your wishes, though I assure you that you do not comprehend her feelings for you at all."

She stepped forward and hugged him tenderly. "One last kiss for a friend?"

He obliged her momentarily and tore himself away before he could enjoy it. "Tell them not to come toward the lights," Gen said as he turned to go. "It will be a brighter day for you tomorrow."

Mirelle watched him leave, straining to see him in hopes that he would return and fill the emptiness she had lived with her entire life. Time slipped by, and something told her she would never again enjoy that voice or that embrace. There in the hollow night she felt as if a part of her died and slipped from her body to intermingle and slide away with the mist.   Wiping her eyes and gathering herself, she found Maewen waiting for her by the Chalaine.

"Did he tell you about the lights?" Maewen asked, tone guarded and eyes sympathetic.

"He did. Wake the others."

The Chalaine had rarely felt what she considered 'spitting' mad, but after her mother revealed to the party what Gen had told her, the Chalaine was furious that her former Protector had not spoken to her instead. She was the Queen, after all. When her mother pulled her aside privately shortly thereafter and told her that Gen flatly refused an opportunity to see and speak with her, the Chalaine nearly screamed in frustration despite their precarious circumstances. She had half a mind to command Maewen to find him and drag him back to her camp, but the sight of Athan nearby forced her into more sensible thinking.

"You should stay well back within the grove, Ladyship," Athan suggested. "If Gen does bring some force and a battle is joined, this is a natural place of hiding and retreat for friend and foe. Stay close to your Protectors."

I will make him pay for this, the Chalaine thought, ignoring Athan completely. No specific punishments leapt to mind, but she had ample time to exercise her creative powers. She dragged a protesting Dason and Jaron toward the edge of the copse that faced the Uyumaak at the wall. She wanted to watch, not cower. Everyone stood listening and peering into the dark from behind tree trunks save Chertanne, who had obeyed Athan's advice.

Several minutes passed in tense excitement, but as time wore on with nothing but darkness before them, her companions shifted and yawned.

"Something approaches," Maewen announced some

time later. "Stand ready."

In a few moments the Chalaine heard it. A large company passed well ahead of them in the dark, a discomfiting hissing noise accompanying their passage. At once, Uyumaak drums pounded a new and frantic rhythm, and the sound of their marching filled the night.

"Whoever Gen brought, there are a lot of them," Jaron commented. "I do not like the sound of their passing."

Athan gasped. "We are in grave peril! Merciful Eldaloth! What he brought with him has an ancient mind and an evil heart. We must flee this place at once!"

The sight of nine ghoulish lanterns unshuttering a hundred yards from their position tore all eyes away from the Padra and onto the field. Nine pools of green mist flickered before them as short figures bearing sharp axes and heavy hammers crossed between them and the light.

"Dwarves?" Maewen half announced and half asked.

"It is not the minds of dwarves that I sense," Athan said, voice quavering. "I recommend we retreat."

"No," the Chalaine piped in firmly, her ill mood lending her words a sharp tone of command. "Gen would not endanger us. We wait here."

Athan regarded her briefly. "Perhaps I should consult the Blessed One."

Yes, the Chalaine derided inwardly, *go convince your puppet to order us to leave.*

"The drumming and thumping has stopped," Maewen announced unnecessarily. "What is at work here?"

Their straining eyes could just make out the shapes of Uyumaak slowly and reverently approaching the luminescent mist. More approached, peeking around each other's shoulders at the lamps, a great horde of them ringing around the lights until only the faintest of glows could be discerned above the throng.

Chertanne approached. "Athan has apprised me of the danger, and I command everyone to. . ."

A thunderous crash of colliding bodies and weapons drowned out the rest of his order. Two mute parties strove with each other in the confused black. No screams of pain or rallying cries pierced the night, only the hissing of serpents and the thumping of overmatched Uyumaak. At first the lanterns provided some illumination, casting wild and frightening shadows into the air, but all too soon rushing feet kicked them over for corpses to fall on and smother. Full dark reclaimed the mist, amplifying the eerie sounds as they stared ahead in vain.

"Something is nearing," Maewen warned them, drawing her bow. "Probably deserters."

Those with weapons drew them.

"Ready your magic, Sire," Athan admonished his charge who withdrew farther behind a tree that shielded him. Maewen released two arrows into the dark before a line of Uyumaak warriors emerged from the mist, stumbling over each other in full retreat. Dason pushed the Chalaine behind him, but upon seeing armed men ahead of them, the Uyumaak turned and faced their pursuers, and what came after them in the dark stole the breath from every throat.

The terror the Chalaine felt at the sight of the Uyumaak paled in comparison to the horror of what Gen had brought to slaughter them. Dark, sleek vipers intertwined with dwarven bones, providing strength to long-dead limbs in a perverted, counterfeit resurrection. Snake heads poked from empty eye sockets, and the lithe bodies of other vipers provided the skeletons with musculature to walk and to grip wicked battle axes as bright as the day they rose from the forge. But more than this, the ire of a trapped malice exuded from the unholy warriors in palpable waves emanating from the tiny, wet eyes of the serpents that opened a window to the wicked intelligence that commanded them.

The snake-animated dwarves pushed the Uyumaak

backward toward the copse, hewing their enemies down brutally without finesse. Rarely, an Uyumaak would score a hit, and a serpent would fall to the ground, only to be replaced by a reinforcement slithering up the frame until the creature was again complete. The last Uyumaak fell not ten feet from the edge of the woods, an ax blade chopping into the space between its head and shoulder.

One of the monsters stepped forward and the vipers of its body turned their gaze upon the Chalaine's party. A snake slithered into the space where a dwarven tongue had once rested. "Are there more?" it hissed.

"Leave us be!" Athan yelled. "Back to the Abyss with you!" The Padra gestured, incanting a spell. Nothing happened as he moved his arms and chanted frantically.

"Pitiful fool," the snake mocked. "The only reason you are not meat for my children is that we are bound to obey the One. Do you want to know my mind? Then learn!" Athan screamed, spine arching as if someone had stabbed him in the small of the back, falling to the ground wrenched in agony. "Your mind is a puddle and mine an ocean. You have no room for the flood."

The creatures turned and ran toward the sound of distant battle, and Athan went limp. Maewen knelt by him, but he waved her back, managing to slump against a nearby tree. "What imagination could create such an abomination? What will could control it?"

The Chalaine had clutched a branch near her so tightly that her fingernails had sunk into the bark. Her mother stood nearby, face and eyes blank. Seeing her mother reminded her to be angry at Gen, though she wondered how he had come to ally himself with such a terror and if he was in danger in the mayhem in the dark. The only thing more unforgivable than not seeing her would be for him to die before she could properly chastise him for it.

The sounds of battle rose and fell, gradually fading in frequency and duration until the faintest rays of light

colored the horizon and all sound ceased. The absence of
Uyumaak drums, the party's constant companion for days,
was the most keenly and most welcomely missed. Figures
milled about half seen in the mist, but the weary survivors
of the caravan waited, not daring to step out and investigate
and having no desire to give thanks to the dark creatures to
whom they owed their liberty.

When the sun rose high enough to burn off the mist,
they stared with astonishment at the grassy slopes before
them. Not one corpse, amputated limb, or ruptured serpent
littered the field. All weapons, drums, and cookpots had
gone. Only the blood on the grass evidenced the battle of
the previous night or the presence of the Uyumaak the
weeks before, and even that seeped into the ground as
melting frost carried it to the earth.

Tentatively, Maewen led them from the copse and into a
day dawning cold and clear. They walked past the
fortifications and to the lakeshore. There they found sand
discolored with ash and the charred remains of the barges
that had brought them to where they now stood. They
scanned the water near the cliff edges in the hopes of
perhaps finding a barge that had strayed and caught on the
rocks, but no such luck attended them.

Fenna was first to voice the question, "What now?"

"I will try to communicate with the other Padras,"
Athan announced, "but I will need my privacy."

"I thought you couldn't do that across shards," Maewen
said.

"I am hoping a Padra will be stationed at the floating
dock. I will return to the trees. Do not follow. I should
return shortly."

"Shall I accompany you?" Chertanne asked hopefully.

"Not this time, your Grace. Please stay with your Queen
and see to her safety and comfort."

Athan shouldered his pack, striding purposefully up the hill. As he reached the top, he exhaled and turned, finding the others milling about the beach or reclining on the sand. Maewen had thrown in a fishing line, and Athan mentally prayed for her success. Freshly broiled fish, even something as inferior as carp, would brighten his mood considerably. But as for that, as he turned his back and found himself truly alone for the first time in weeks, his anxiety drained from him.

Peace.

Only in blessed solitude could he calculate the true weight of the grinding burden that guiding Chertanne had placed upon him. A necessary duty, but a difficult one. Chertanne's wants and selfish needs loomed so large that they blocked the young King's vision of the necessary and expedient. Miles of danger, carnage, and exhaustion had failed to aid a nobler character to develop. Athan's fellow Padras would certainly find Chertanne's nascent sobriety encouraging if any of them could distinguish it from his egregious cowardice. *Suffering does not ennoble man. It is the invitation to nobility,* Athan reminded himself.

And if molding Chertanne into a King were not trial enough, Athan had to instruct him how to appreciate and respect the most beautiful woman in the world. Of all the tasks that should come naturally to a young man, even if an Aughmerian! Of course, the Ilch had poisoned her opinion of him, and she had failed to show a properly submissive attitude until after facing the Throgs. But even then he sensed a firm will within her waiting to assert itself, no doubt at some disastrous moment for Chertanne and the world.

Pushing these thoughts aside, he entered the copse, unpleasant memories of the past several days returning. He continued on until he could no longer see the field or the lake, and, after casting a quick ward to turn away visitors, he opened his pack. Reaching deep inside, he pulled the Assassin's Glass out and unwrapped it from its cloth. Miles of travel had not broken or tarnished the artifact that he had pilfered from Regent Ogbith so many weeks ago.

Ethris thought himself so clever, Athan thought. *I suspect I thought of bringing it long before he did.*

When he had gone to the Church Archive to fetch it— only to find it missing—it took little reasoning to connect its disappearance with the reports of Ethris and Kaimas on the road together in Mur Eldaloth.

Turning the mirror toward him he nearly laughed at the weathered, unkempt face presented to him. The man in the mirror rubbed his tanned forehead and scratched at a beard he could not wait to shave off. He lost several moments contemplating his reflection, but the thought of cooked fish awaiting him on the shore prompted him to hurry. He stared intently into the magical device.

"Padra Nolan."

The mirror flashed blue for a few moments before resolving on the back of a balding head. Padra Nolan sat at his desk in a tent, a lantern providing him light as he read a letter in the predawn chill.

"Padra Nolan," Athan called softly, and the older man jumped and turned, nearly upsetting the lantern. His eyes cast about frantically before finding the small Portal hovering in the air.

"Padra Athan!" he exclaimed. "Eldaloth be praised! We had nearly despaired of you! Chertanne, does he live?"

"Yes, fortunately, as does the Chalaine, who is pregnant with the Holy Child. The First Mother and a handful of others also survived. All the Eldephaere we secreted on this mission died in an attack at Dunnach Falls."

"We heard of that event three weeks ago."

"How?"

"Ethris, Shadan Khairn, and a few soldiers escaped death that day, but were pursued by a large body of Uyumaak to the fortifications on the beach. They rowed away while soldiers bought them time."

Athan nodded. "All were apparently killed in that attack. The Uyumaak held the wall against us and burned the barges."

"We have been building boats as fast as we can," Padra Nolan reported. "We still don't have enough to shuttle enough soldiers to. . ."

"There is no need, now. The Uyumaak were killed."

"By what means?"

"That can wait. Just send whatever barges or boats you have prepared immediately. I have a job of the utmost secrecy to assign to you."

"Name it, your Grace."

"You will have questions about what I am to tell you. Do not ask them now, but suffice it to say that Gen betrayed the Ha'Ulrich during the marriage." Padra Nolan's mouth opened with questions threatening to spill out in a rush, but Athan stopped him short. "No questions for now. There is a lot to explain, but listen. Do you have any of the Eldephaere with you?"

"Yes, but. . ."

"Good. Gen is running fugitive somewhere on this shard with Gerand Kildan and Volney Torunne. I have reason to believe that they may be able to reach the Portal gate before us. I would like you to wait for him on the floating dock. Act relieved to see him, but when you get the chance, cast a stupor upon him, restrain the others, and then drug Gen so that he does not wake. Drug the others as well, if you feel it necessary. Keeping Gen unconscious, however, is of utmost importance. Do you understand?"

"Yes, but what do I do with them?"

"Sneak them back through the portal in a supply wagon as secretly as you can. Take them somewhere in the woods, and when I return I will explain everything. Keep the Eldephaere near them at all times."

"As you wish, your Grace. What if they do not come?"

"They will, eventually. If I know Gen, he will follow the Chalaine wherever she goes. For now, however, get the barges moving and make the preparations I have asked."

"It will be done, Padra."

Athan relaxed his concentration and the mirror resolved to a reflection of his face. After carefully concealing the Assassin's Glass in his pack, he started his hike back to the beach. Everything hinged on catching Gen. With that one feat he could protect Chertanne and control the First Mother. Best of all, he could eliminate the Ilch and foil Mikkik before the babe was ever born.

Volney breathed easily for the first time in days. Ghama Dhron's serpent-animated dwarven host turned away from them and marched toward a nearby wood. From their vantage point within a stand of scrub oak on the cliff, Volney, Gen, and Gerand spied the Ha'Ulrich's party resting on the beach.

Gerand regarded the Chalaine's party, face a mixture of emotions. Volney thought he understood, for he felt the same. He wished he could return to them and share in the relief of deliverance from a shard he hoped never to see again. The idea that they would return to Rhugoth as fugitives rather than heroes nearly crushed them both, and by Gen's somber looks, Volney thought him the worst afflicted.

Of course, Gen had risen higher and fallen further than either of them, and for that Volney could sympathize. The journey through the Shroud Lake shard had changed the complexion of prophecy, and they all wondered if the mistakes and missteps had somehow ruined the future events they had all worked and sacrificed for. For his part, Volney still placed the blame on Chertanne. Once he saw Maewen broiling fish on the beach, however, he wondered if he could beg the Ha'Ulrich's forgiveness.

Gen returned shortly after Ghama Dhron disappeared from sight. "It will make us a raft we can use to get us over the Lake," Gen reported, voice gruff and drained. "It will be ready soon, and Ghama Dhron will lower it and us to the lake. I've commanded it to kill any Uyumaak it finds after that."

"Do I even want to know how it will 'lower us down?'" Volney asked.

"Probably not," Gen replied.

Gerand turned away from his vigil of the beach and faced Gen. "How is it you can speak to that monstrosity?"

"I wish I knew," Gen answered. "It uses the same black speech as the demon used during the betrothal, only it speaks to the mind."

"And where does one learn the black speech in Tolnor?" Gerand pressed.

"I never learned it. At least not that I remember. I cannot account for it."

Conversation died as they lay on the ground and slept soundly. Ghama Dhron returned in the afternoon with a rickety raft roughly hewn by dwarven battle axes. It was little better than what peasant boys would lash together in an afternoon.

"Nice," Volney commented sarcastically. "And I thought the barges were bad. Here's hoping they believe us when we get to the Portal, if we don't drown first."

CHAPTER 58 - THE BARGAIN

The Chalaine stared out across the still, glassy lake. Compared to the days behind, the broiled fish and ragged lean-tos felt luxurious, even when a cold winter squall blasted in off the lake and lashed the wooden wall while they squatted shuddering around a weak fire on the lee side. Padra Athan promised rescue would arrive in a few days, though he fretted over how the recently constructed watercraft would fare in the brief but violent storm.

At last the conversation of their bedraggled group turned hopeful, full of home, familiar places, and beloved people. The Chalaine had long since abandoned any hope of spotting Gen before returning to Rhugoth, and she turned her attentions to praying for his safe return. As much as she wanted to see him, she hoped that he would forsake her and hide to save his own life. Her mind resolved to see her divine task done, for only its completion would bring to fruition the pleasant future scenes that occupied her thoughts.

Her mother persisted in as gloomy a state as the Chalaine could ever remember seeing her in. After nearly dying at Three Willows Inn, Mirelle had been fearful and even vulnerable, but after her visit with Gen two nights before, an abiding hopelessness held her captive. While perhaps a trick of months of hard travel, the former First Mother had aged, her empty eyes only doubling the effect of its appearance.

The Chalaine guessed her pain. The last few weeks had stripped one of the most powerful figures on Ki'Hal of her title, her throne, and her love, and while the Chalaine knew her mother yet had plans and work she wanted done, these provided no fire in her heart or animation to her features.

Not even the barges emerging from the mist in the late afternoon and the arrival of fresh food and warm blankets could jar Mirelle from her stupor. Only the arrival of Ethris, Captain Tolbrook, and Shadan Khairn a few minutes later stirred her from her shelter, and before Athan could trap the Mage, Mirelle had corralled him into a private area behind the wall to explain everything. The Chalaine noted the Shadan's questioning glances as he scanned the beach for his pupil. To the Chalaine's surprise, Torbrand ignored his own son and Athan and approached her, executing an uncharacteristic bow while Captain Tolbrook, Jaron, and Dason watched.

"Forgive my lack of niceties, Lady Khairn, but has Gen been killed?"

"No, Shadan," the Chalaine answered. "It is rather more complicated than that."

At first the Chalaine hesitated, wondering what and how much to tell him, but in the end decided that the unpredictable man was an ally where Gen was concerned. She told him of her former Protector's attack on Chertanne, his entrapment, and his eventual rescuing of their party and disappearance. Torbrand grinned as she finished.

"Thank you for your report, Highness." He smiled. "So he is a fugitive for trying to kill that fool son of mine. Running from Chertanne certainly sounds more appealing than running with him at the moment, so perhaps I shall try to kill him myself later on. Don't worry too much for Gen. He is a clever one. Good day, Highness. Oh, and since Chertanne is now High King, I am no longer Shadan. You may address me as Warlord, now, or General, if you prefer."

"I will," she replied. "Thank you, General."

Mirelle and Ethris returned some time later, Ethris clearly shaken. He threw a weak smile her way before walking over to consult with Athan. Her mother sat beside her and quizzed her about Torbrand's visit.

"He is a strange ally," Mirelle said, "but we will take him."

The Chalain leaned into her, wishing she could infuse her mother's heart with some liveliness or hope. "How did Ethris and Torbrand Khairn escape the battle?"

Mirelle indicated the Chalaine should follow her along the shore of the lake. "After felling the giant at Dunnach Falls, Ethris had completely exhausted himself. Captain Tolbrook hid himself and the Mage within the creature's mangled armor throughout the night and the next day until the army had moved on in pursuit of the main party.

"Torbrand and the Aughmerians held the road against the Uyumaak for nearly an hour until he and about twenty of his men fled into the hills. The Uyumaak pursued them and killed all but Torbrand and four others. The night provided enough cover for them to evade the rest. Ethris met up with them as they searched for any of the scattered mounts that might have survived.

"Fortunately, three of the animals still lived. Knowing the way to Elde Luri Mora would be unattainable with their small numbers, they resolved on returning immediately to the Portal gate to summon reinforcements. They rode hard to the beach landing. A few days from the lake, they found an army of Uyumaak marching in the same direction just ahead of them, apparently dispatched to secure the fortifications. They obviously succeeded, but not before

Ethris, owing to his craft, overtook and passed the marchers, galloping the last two miles at great peril.

"They secured a raft just as the Uyumaak fell in fury upon the wall. Ethris and Torbrand nearly worked the rowers to death, so you can imagine the disappointment to their urgency when they found that only an honor guard had been stationed at the Portal, the main body of soldiers quartered some miles away. But even worse, the lack of barges precluded shuttling any great numbers across the Lake anyway. In the interim, Ethris and the Shadan returned to the shard beachhead to learn the outcome of the battle, finding what we found a few days ago, an unapproachable beachhead swarming with Uyumaak archers that could cut them down before they rowed within fifty yards of the shore.

"They returned to oversee preparations and to plan. I certainly wouldn't have wanted to trade places with any of the craftsman set to constructing more barges. I'm sure Ethris and Torbrand were rather intense with their supervision. Of course, the Church of the One disgorged every member of its fighting orders and sent them to the gate, leveling all manner of accusations of incompetency at Rhugoth just as they did after the attack at the betrothal."

"Considering recent events," the Chalaine said, "they certainly have a case. We were too arrogant."

"True. We did not feel our danger then as we should have, or perhaps failed to perceive its nature."

"I am sorry about Gen, Mother," the Chalaine continued in a low voice after a brief pause. "I do not know what he told you, but it has apparently destroyed you."

Mirelle smiled bitterly. "You know, while I always loved him, I had intended him for you once Chertanne met his fate, which, by my calculations, will be several seconds into his encounter with Mikkik. Somewhere I lost sight of the altruistic blessing for my daughter and thought of myself instead. I nearly fell apart when he announced his ridiculous betrothal to Fenna." Here she sighed and lifted her eyes to the lake. "It is no matter to you, dear. At least you have his love. I think I could have won it, too, if he could have mastered his apparent fear of me."

"You were brutally forward."

Mirelle smiled again, eyes softening. "That I was. You can only imagine how vexing it is to find that you can easily procure any man in the world except the one you want. Do you think I appeared a bit desperate? I was aiming for playful and passionate. "

"Desperate? Hardly. Playful, yes, and to him probably not serious until you declared it with a rather frank kiss, which—from his reticence to talk about it—I infer that he enjoyed immensely."

"I've been meaning to ask you what occasioned him to tell you about that."

"I don't recall," the Chalaine lied, not wanting to recount the particulars of that conversation with anyone.

"I enjoyed that kiss as well, so please don't begrudge me a few weeks of sullen misery. In any case, do not worry over much for me. If any of us survive the next year, then I am sure I can find just as miserable a mate as you, and we can invite Gen over for tea and take turns at discomfiting our husbands by flirting wildly with him."

"Gen and Chertanne drinking tea together. Eldaloth will truly have transformed the world if that meeting ever takes place."

Their conversation ended after Padra Athan goaded Chertanne into a leadership role that consisted of telling everyone to embark for immediate departure.

The Chalaine swatted the sand off of her tattered dress. "I must attend to my husband. It is time to pretend again."

The oarsmen knelt as Chertanne perfunctorily extended his hand and guided her onto the barge. Athan and Torbrand boarded next, followed by Ethris, Jaron, Mirelle, and Cadaen.

"And so you thought of everything but clothes, then?" Athan complained to Torbrand.

"Believe it or not, your Grace," Torbrand said, "there are clothes for you all awaiting on the other side of the Portal. You can thank Padra Nolan for that kindness. In our hasty departure, we neglected to load them. We forgot the toilet buckets, too, so you will have to settle for a leather sack or the lake. Mikkik's beard, but we forgot the dancing women and the kegs of wine, too. I hope you can struggle by without them for a few more days."

"That's enough, Torbrand," Athan growled.

Two days of knocking elbows and stepping on feet while they slipped across the foggy lake on cramped barges failed to ameliorate anyone's mood. During the slow journey, Ethris used his magic to confirm the Chalaine's pregnancy. To hear Ethris say it somehow surprised her despite the sour stomach she had felt for weeks. A life not her own thrived within her, and before another year passed she would bear the title of *mother*. With all that had attended her conception and the anticipation of a glorious birth, she wondered at how it could all seem so unreal and, in her thoughts, secondary to more pressing concerns.

Their third night out, the floating dock resolved into view, and a great shout rose. A mass of cheering soldiers, torches and lanterns haloed in the dark, ushered the disheveled party through the Portal. At last Rhugothian soil greeted their weary feet. The afternoon sky, every bit as dank and gray as the lake's had been, provided nothing of cheer for the Chalaine despite the jubilation of the people—mostly soldiers—who rejoiced at their narrow escape from danger and ruin.

The boots of thousands of men had churned the snow

into mud, turning the frozen ground around the smoky bonfires into slippery quagmires. Athan eagerly jumped at every opportunity to herald the story of Chertanne's usage of magic to slay the Uyumaak that had threatened them in the mountains, promising that this was only one of many noble deeds to be told in the days ahead.

While the Chalaine could understand the need to bolster the people's confidence in their new King, she wondered just how many lies a Churchman could tell in good conscience to accomplish the task. No doubt by the time they arrived in Mikmir, Chertanne's single dead foe would multiply fivefold. Wickedly she thought she might just coax her own creativity out of hiding to fabricate some stories of her own bravery for everyone to believe, but decided she would just leave it to Athan, who appeared to have some skill in such things.

Dason, Jaron, Cadaen, and her mother all kept close by her, and from her mother's biting of her lower lip, the Chalaine divined that the same crisis that filled her mind filled her mother's. Already, several of the leaders and generals had posed questions about Gen's fate, and for some reason, Athan declined to comment. He and Padra Nolan gravitated from one brief meeting to the next, heads low and together, perhaps arriving at some consensus as how to handle the situation. Geoff appeared nervous as he performed a song for the revelers, Fenna behind him with her hands on his shoulders. Maewen had disappeared almost as soon as she had crossed through the Portal.

Most disturbing, however, was the continual presence of the Eldephaere, the emasculated soldiers of the Church who, anciently, had seen to the protection of the Chalaine before an indiscretion with the tenth Chalaine had thrown them into disgrace and out of the castle. They followed the new Queen's party wherever it moved, sable cloaks swirling around tall thin frames in the light wind. Their dark clothing contrasted with pale faces, haughty eyes regarding all with disdain, especially the retinue of Rhugothian soldiers that surrounded what was left of the Dark Guard. Of course, all now wore the colors of King Chertanne, a red field with a golden hawk clutching a fully waxed Trys in its talons.

Chertanne had barely set one foot through the Portal before Athan had shepherded him off to clad his charge in the kingly garb, though it hung loosely about the wearer. The royal tailor had stitched the clothing based on measurements taken before Chertanne had suffered weeks of privation, though as for that, the thinner features and weathered face aided the new King's appearance, subtracting some of the spoiled, soft aspect of his demeanor that had presented itself so plainly on first acquaintance. The Chalaine even thought he could pass for handsome should the trend continue, but from the way he thrust his fingers into every passing platter stacked with meat and bread, she thought his shirts would find themselves inflated with his girth soon enough.

Her own stomach could not chance anything so heavy as what was served. Whether from anxiety about Gen or the recurring nausea from her pregnancy, she felt she could take nothing more than the mulled cider she clutched in cold hands. As yet, no one had indicated she should wear anything other than the ragged black dress she had donned after tumbling with Gen over the falls, and the memory of those pleasant days served to distract her until a grave Padra Athan started toward her and her mother.

Athan said, "Your Ladyship, Mirelle, I would ask for a word with you apart from the camp. I have a tent set up in a little clearing away from the here so that we can talk with some privacy. You may bring whatever retinue you wish, but I would ask that we speak alone in the tent."

"We are not inclined to speak with you at the moment, Padra. No disrespect, intended, of course," Mirelle answered.

"It concerns a certain common acquaintance of ours. I think you know the one I mean. There are questions about him that must be answered, and I thought I would extend you the courtesy of providing some of what must be said before I bring it to light in a more public arena."

"Lead on, then," Mirelle agreed, face severe.

The Chalaine took her hand, wishing to give strength while seeking it herself. Athan led them away at a brisk pace, several of the Eldephaere flanking him. Nearly fifteen soldiers accompanied the Queen and her retinue down a rutted track of frozen mud that led much farther into the woods than the Chalaine had envisioned when Athan described it. After they had covered at least a half a mile, a bright circular tent glowing with an orange light beckoned to them in the darkening evening.

As they approached, several things caught the Chalaine's eye. A bald, plump man in a bloody apron stood to the side of the tent pounding nails into a small oblong box, and as they came nearer, he seemed shifty and nervous, increasing the rhythm of the hammer strokes. Two large sacks sat on the ground nearby, each guarded by a pair of Eldephaere. As they approached, the Chalaine thought she saw something move inside one of the sacks, and her heart started to pound as a horrible idea took root in her mind.

"I told you to have this mess out of here an hour ago, Captain," Athan yelled grumpily at an Eldephaere who stood at the door.

"Apologies, your Grace," he said smoothly, bowing. "We will return for the other after full dark."

The party stopped as the man with the hammer hoisted the box onto his shoulder, and the soldiers lifted the ungainly sacks, revealing for a certainty that people were inside. The Chalaine swallowed hard and stared at the tent, trying to get a peek inside the tent flap.

"Now," Athan said, "if you would leave your soldiers here and come with me inside, I have a brazier there and we can talk comfortably."

Cadaen, Jaron, and Dason protested nervously, but Mirelle, face drawn, waved them back wordlessly. Together the Chalaine and Mirelle followed Athan through the tent door, the Chalaine trying to control her trembling. The scene outside prepared her enough not to cry out. A table in the center of the tent supported an unconscious, wan Gen, left leg amputated at the knee. Blood covered the floor and pooled around the cauterized stump. Mirelle released her hand.

Athan turned toward them, and a livid Mirelle slapped him so hard that his eyes watered and he staggered. Without warning she flew at him in a rage, raining down blows upon him. She did not cry out as she waded into the stunned Churchman, tears and hair flying with fists in a primal fury.

The Chalaine, tears of her own running down her cheeks, used the distraction to cross to Gen, eyes drinking in his face as she placed her hand on his forehead. He sucked in a deep breath at her touch, his color returning. Inch by inch the leg beneath his knee regrew, all the way down to his toes until Gen was whole again. The black dot marking his prophetic identity darkened on the reformed instep. She marveled how such a difficult healing cost her nothing as she quickly replaced Gen's boot lying nearby to cover the mark, wondering why he hadn't wakened.

When she turned back to the scuffle, Athan and her mother had come to their feet, each with a hand to the other's throat. Athan bled from his nose, a mass of scratches lining his face.

"Mirelle," Athan gagged, "calm yourself and listen to me if you want him to live."

Cadaen burst through the door, sword drawn, followed by Dason and Jaron. Cadaen took one look at Athan and charged. Athan's eyes widened and he incanted, Cadaen falling limp to the floor. At his collapse, Mirelle relented and released her grip on the Padra. The Chalaine ordered her Protectors to stand down, drag Cadaen out of the tent, and leave them alone. Mirelle sat down hard on the floor and wept.

The Chalaine knelt by her mother and comforted her as Athan wiped his face and calmed his overwhelmed Eldephaere guards outside the tent. By the time he returned, Mirelle had stood, reaffixing her hair as best she could. The Chalaine crossed to Athan and healed his wounds while her mother composed herself.

The Chalaine felt angry, mind running through every scheme it could of how to free her beloved Protector, while every idea seemed sensible of its own futility. She focused on her mother, whose heart, like her own long ago, had finally broken.

"I will not apologize, Athan, if that's what you're waiting for," Mirelle finally said. "Say what you are going to say and be done with it."

"As you wish," he returned acerbically. "As you can see, I have apprehended the Ilch and his companions. I have had his leg amputated . . . and you have healed it. Well, no matter. It will be nice to have a spare in case the other one is misplaced. As you may have guessed, I intend to tell the world that Gen is the Ilch and that he attacked the Ha'Ulrich after the marriage ceremony."

The Chalaine noted that her mother seemed unaffected by the revelation of Gen's identity, and both Mirelle and Athan stared at the Chalaine as if expecting some reaction from her.

Mirelle spoke first. "You knew?"

"Yes."

"But . . . but . . . how? When?" Athan stammered.

"When we traveled alone in the canyon. The Millim Eri who turned him from his destiny found us and revealed to me who he was and presented me with the opportunity to kill him, if I would. My choice is obvious. I love him and would never let him come to harm if it were in my power to stop it."

Athan paced about the room, thunderstruck, requiring several minutes to collect himself. The Chalaine took the opportunity to ask her mother about when she knew, surprised to find how early her mother and Ethris had come to trust Gen despite the fate the prophecy declared for him.

Athan, at length, righted himself and sat in a chair near table where Gen lay. "I am shocked. Shocked! That Gen managed to win both your confidences independently of each other truly manifests the cleverness of Mikkik's creature."

"You will never convince anyone that Gen is the Ilch," the Chalaine said confidently.

This seemed to spark Athan from his wonderment. "Oh, yes I will," he glared, "and you will help me."

Mirelle laughed bitterly. "What could you possibly hold over our heads to induce us to hurt a man we both love?"

"I will hold the man himself," Athan returned. "I have a bargain to strike with you. I will not kill the Ilch, but hold him away secretly in Mur Eldaloth. We will tell the people that he attacked Cheranne in the throne room and escaped, which is true and was witnessed by many. You will agree to say that as the Ilch tried to return to Rhugoth, Chertanne confronted and killed him using Trysmagic. We will present his leg and prophetically marked foot as evidence. If you do not agree to publish this version of events, I will have the Ilch executed immediately."

"You are a liar, Athan," Mirelle said, shaking her head, "and a pathetic one. If you think for a moment that I believe you will let Gen live, regardless of what we promise or do not, then you must consider me a fool."

"Unfortunately, Mirelle, I don't have the time or the inclination to prove to you the good faith of my proposal. Take my offer or he dies; that is all. You rule nothing anymore and have no power now but to save his life or to let it fall."

"But I do," the Chalaine asserted to the startled Athan, who turned toward her, face concerned.

"You are the Queen, but I afraid that in matters of. . ."

"You mistake me, Padra. I hoped rather than expected my position to lend me any real influence in the world. What I speak of is my ability to guarantee your promise. I will know it when Gen dies. I am linked to him in a way you have no power to obscure or hinder. The instant he dies, I will feel it. If that happens, whether by your doing or the doing of another, I will use whatever influence I have at my command to destroy you, Chertanne, and this little charade you want to foist upon Ki'Hal. For the sake of the world, I will play 'Lady Khairn' and the obedient wife. I will carry this Child and try to help Chertanne rally the world to defend it. But neither my mother nor I will speak one word against Gen, ever. If we are forced to speak on the subject, then you will regret it."

"I cannot believe that you would sabotage the prophecy and endanger the world, no matter what you feel about him!"

"Then you suppose wrongly," she returned evenly. A strange calm had enveloped her, the way forward coming clear in her mind. "To be sure, I want to do my part to save Ki'Hal, but I will not act against my conscience or my heart any more than I already have in order to do so. When this world is whole again, I want the people I love to be left in it. I want Gen left in it. If you upset that plan, I will certainly have no care for upsetting yours."

Athan stared at her, eyes searching and mind racing.

"Ah, yes," Mirelle stepped in, clarity dawning on her face. "You are thinking that perhaps you can kill Gen now and secrete us in some location for 'our safety' to minimize the damage we can do. A bold plan, and it might work, if it weren't for that one person you know who is wholly loyal to me and powerful enough to smash you in an instant. And if he suspects you are maltreating us, he will see us rescued from your grasp. We understand the need for my daughter to support Chertanne and to be seen in concert with her husband for the morale of the people, but trust me when I say that neither of us will have any qualms about abandoning the King forever if you cross us. And in case you are in doubt, I have more friends than Ethris who are quite willing to do my bidding, whether I sit on a throne or not."

"The choice, I hope, is clear, Padra," the Chalaine continued, confidence building. "Keep Gen alive and well, and we will parade around with King Chertanne and help him build his army. Kill or hurt Gen, and we will part ways and let the drama unfold as it may. Too many people witnessed Gen's attempt to kill Chertanne for us to deny it, but we will not assert that he is the Ilch, nor will we be party to telling the lie that Chertanne somehow felled him, which is so outrageous that I couldn't say it without laughing out loud. Those are the conditions. Are we in agreement?" Athan's tongue seemed tacked to the top of his mouth and the Chalaine continued. "Well, no matter. No verbal acceptance is required. Things are as I have stated them. How you choose to act will be the hand that pens the history of Ki'Hal."

To irritate Athan as much to express their fondness, the women each anointed Gen's brow with a kiss before leaving the tent into the bitter night. The Chalaine wondered how much Dason, Jaron, and Cadaen had heard of the exchange, all of them wearing troubled expressions as they marched behind their charges.

Mirelle put her arm around her daughter and pulled her close and whispered, "I am proud of you. I do not think I've ever seen you exhibit such open courage! It was quite a gambit to try to convince Athan that you could sense Gen's death. I hope he really believes it."

"It is true, whether he believes it or not. I will carry out my promise if Athan kills him, and Ki'Hal can curse me if it will. I know I must seem terribly selfish."

"Perhaps, dear, but you will hardly find any objections from me. Even so, I must remind you now of your resolution to play your part and let me deal with the nasty particulars of keeping Gen alive and attending to other unpleasant matters. I will not consult with you or report to you so that you cannot be impeached or interrogated. You will have the harder task. It is time for you to be a wife and stand with your husband, whatever mortification it may cost you. Bend a little, dissemble when you must, but keep hope alive."

The Chalaine nodded in agreement and said no more as they traversed the lonely track back to the main encampment. The celebration rose as night fell, bonfires blazing and casting wild shadows in the wood as soldiers clapped and danced to the lively rhythms and songs of minstrels. In the Chalaine's present mood, it all smelled unpleasantly of sweaty men, smoke, and ale. As she passed the revelers, toasts were raised in her honor. Her mother goaded her into offering a weak response to the celebrants honoring her.

When they caught sight of Chertanne dancing near a fire surrounded by nobility, Mirelle left her daughter to attend to "urgent matters," disappearing into the night. The Chalaine braced herself and strode into the circle of Churchmen and dignitaries who were allowed the privilege of company with the Ha'Ulrich. She noted that several Regents were there, along with Warlords from Aughmere and Dukes from Tolnor.

Torbrand mingled with his Warlords. Disappointingly, though not unexpectedly, Chertanne had wasted no time wading into a nearby cask of ale, and, by the red on his nose and cheeks, the underside of his ample mug had seen more of the stars than the mud. Geoff awaited his Lord's pleasure nearby, while Fenna, happy and contented, sat nursing a mug of her own on her lap.

All save Chertanne bowed as the Chalaine crossed to her husband. He rose and grabbed her in a wild embrace.

"Minstrel!" he shouted. "A song for the Lady and me! It is time for dancing!"

For the second time in her life, the Chalaine danced with Chertanne, only this time her heart was so heavy that what resulted was little more than a lugubrious shifting about. Fortunately, Chertanne, who could not be parted from his ale even in dance, cavorted so wildly that he slipped and landed on his backside, ejecting the ale to run down a dour Churchman's cloak.

The company laughed at his antics, and the Chalaine took the opportunity to perform her best impression of concern for his wellbeing.

"Have you hurt yourself, my Lord?" she asked, crouching near him and grabbing his arm to help him to his feet. "Shall I fetch a Pureman?"

"Not unless he has a mug of ale in his hand!" Chertanne laughed hysterically at his own joke and handed the Chalaine his mug. "Go see if you can find him!"

Jaron hissed under his breath, and the Chalaine cast him a warning glance. If anything, retrieving ale exempted her from further dancing, which Chertanne now undertook alone. Fenna met her by the cask.

"It is so good to be home!" she brimmed excitedly. "I feel so much better now. The past few months seem like such a dark dream! Padra Athan said that Geoff and I are to ride to Blackshire come morning. I would like to have remained with you, but he said that you would be well taken care of."

"Padra Athan spoke with you and Geoff?"

"Yes, when he came for the book Geoff wrote. Geoff tried to convince the Padra to let him finish a few more things, but Athan was so insistent that Geoff gave way. I

170

suppose it won't matter much, anyway. Have you heard anything about Gen?"

"Nothing new, I'm afraid," the Chalaine replied, topping off the mug. "If I hear anything definite, I will write to you."

The Chalaine looked into the green eyes of her former handmaiden and felt tears coming to her own. As much of a trial that the young woman had proved to be in the preceding weeks, the Chalaine loved her dearly. Setting her husband's drink aside, she embraced Fenna for many long moments, thanking her for her years of devoted service.

"It was an honor to serve you, Chalaine," Fenna said in kind, wiping tears of her own. "Promise to write and to visit me whenever you can."

"I will."

Chertanne's impatience ended their discussion. "Have you found that Pureman yet, Lady Khairn? It turns out I need a bit more medicine after all!"

After another quick embrace, the Chalaine returned the mug to its owner, who drank deeply and with satisfaction. "Well done, my dear, I believe I shall keep you around a while longer."

Athan, face guarded, approached the assembly, and all mirth ceased. Chertanne returned to sit on an ample stump that served as a makeshift throne in the sylvan environs. The Chalaine followed and sat by him on the ground, wondering how long it would take Jaron's teeth to dissolve to powder from such frequent grinding. Athan shushed what little conversation persisted in their immediate party, though the raucous festivities continued unabated all around them.

"With Chertanne's permission, I would like to address several questions I am sure you all have had since our return. Firstly, the Chalaine is pregnant with the Holy Child. She has lain with Chertanne but once after the moon Trys broke into the sky. Thus we can confirm that the

Child was conceived according to the dictates of prophecy.

"Secondly, as some of you have no doubt heard, Gen attacked the Ha'Ulrich on the night of his wedding. I can confirm to you now that Gen is, indeed, the very Ilch." Gasps ran through the assembly, and Athan paused a moment to let the news sink in. "Chertanne killed him as he tried to sneak back into Rhugoth, and we will, starting tomorrow, show the mark of prophecy upon his severed foot as proof that the designs of Mikkik have been frustrated."

The Chalaine grasped the *animon* within her dress, comforted by its warmth.

"That's preposterous, Athan, even for you," Torbrand spoke up. While shock at this affront rippled among the dignitaries, Torbrand continued. "It is simply irrational, even for one as irrational as me. If the Ilch's purpose was to thwart the prophecy, he could have ordered Gen to kill the Chalaine and Chertanne months ago. And while it is true that he attacked Chertanne, it was *after* Chertanne and the Chalaine had conceived the Child and *after* my brilliant son stripped Gen of rank and title and gave the woman he was to marry to another man. If Gen were under Mikkik's orders, why would he have not killed Chertanne and the Chalaine outright, and why would he have waited until after they had conceived the Child? It is ridiculous."

While the Chalaine could not understand Torbrand's strange affection for Gen, she could only smile as his logic set tongues to murmuring and heads to nodding in assent. Chertanne even set his ale down for a moment.

"I cannot explain what Mikkik's plans might be, but even the Chalaine knows it to be true, don't you? Why don't you tell them how you were deceived?"

The Chalaine saw the challenge in Athan's eyes, defying her to keep to her word. *So you think the weak little Chalaine will not go through with her blustery words. You asked for this, Athan. Remember it.*

The Chalaine rose to her feet, and with the most believable conviction she had ever thrown behind any lie, said, "On the contrary! Gen is the most genuine person I have ever met! He attacked Lord Khairn because he had affronted Gen's good character beyond toleration, and Gen was honor bound to confront him to defend his good name. I would no more believe that Gen is the Ilch than I would believe that you are. Everyone here is well aware of Gen's unimpeachable moral character. It is a shame that you should foist such a dreadful slander on one who has done so much to aid the prophecy. Why, I doubt there is anyone alive that has helped it along more than he."

The Chalaine thought Athan endured her tirade admirably, despite the fact that her argument had clearly put the majority against him.

"Then I offer this as proof," he said, signaling to a group of Eldephaere who brought forth the box the Chalaine had noticed outside of Athan's tent. The group contracted around the box as the Church soldiers pried the lid open. There, on a mat of straw, lay Gen's freshly amputated leg, the mark of prophecy plain upon its instep.

"Will you deny, Chalaine, that this is the leg of your Protector?" Athan prompted.

"I cannot say. I have never seen his naked leg, and the last time I saw my Protector, he had both of his."

"Because you healed what we had done!"

"How could I have done that? You said he was dead. I cannot restore limbs to the dead. Besides, if I had seen Gen dead, I would be in my tent mourning, not celebrating here. I believe you have the wrong man. You may have captured and killed the Ilch, but it was not Gen."

I doubt he'll ask my opinion again.

Athan ordered the box away, the Chalaine noticing the slight trembling of his hands as he addressed an unconvinced audience. "It is Gen, the very one. Before he died, the Pontiff Belliarmus examined Gen personally and found it to be so. I will not contradict him. I certify that the leg you have just seen is Gen's."

"And what has the Ha'Ulrich to say?" said Ulodean Mail, an imposing Warlord of Aughmere. "His word is law, and I will follow."

Chertanne wrinkled his nose when he realized someone had addressed him specifically. He set his mug down and stood, hitching up his loose pants. "I, Chertanne Khairn, Lord of Ki'Hal declare Gen to be the very vermin Ilch, just as Athan has shown you. He set his foot against me from the beginning and tried to end my life, which no one save those affiliated with evil would undertake! He deceived the Chalaine, and she is yet confounded by that deception."

"I beg your pardon, My Lord," the Chalaine interrupted. "But I am in my right mind and suffer under no spell."

"Do not contradict me!" Chertanne growled, shoving her to the ground. The Chalaine landed hard, turning to see what Jaron would do and finding him arm extended and sword rammed through the left side of Chertanne's upper chest. No one moved, gaping in shocked disbelief as Chertanne crumpled and slid off the bloody blade. The thud of his body hitting the ground thawed frozen tongues and feet. Jaron dropped his blade and raised his hands as Chertanne's guard and the Eldephaere closed upon him. Athan sprung to Chertanne's side immediately, taking time only to yell for Jaron to be left alive.

The Chalaine stared in wonder and sadness at her Protector, who regarded her softly and with resignation. "I cannot live and see you treated like this, Highness. Not for the world. Gen is right. He was always right."

"Chalaine!" Athan screamed frantically. "Help him!"

The Chalaine picked herself up and wormed her way through the group of men clustered around their King. He lay on the ground unblinking and pale. Trembling, she grasped the limp hand and concentrated.

"I cannot help him," she reported to a sea of expectant

faces. "I cannot raise the dead."

Chapter 59 – Escape

Maewen doubted she had ever traveled in company with two people less like herself. While she found humans generally intolerable, some few, such as Gen, she could stomach. Torbrand Khairn and the retired General Harband each possessed such a penchant for violence and irreverence—exacerbated by a criminal self-assurance—that their own kind feared and shunned them. How could she, accustomed to solitude, patience, and long wisdom, endure their endless blather, pointless bragging, and manic emotion?

The First Mother had asked them to aid Maewen in a bid to free Gen, but every day the temptation to sneak away on her own in the night mounted. Both Torbrand and General Harband had been in Chertanne's camp the night Jaron killed Chertanne, and once Mirelle had informed Maewen of Gen's plight, Maewen had Ethris use the hair she had recovered from the floor in Elde Luri Mora to create a brand so that she could track Gen's whereabouts. The First Mother instructed her to search out Torbrand and the General and ask their assistance. Both accepted eagerly, and—while Maewen knew of Torbrand's obsession with Gen and Harband's devotion to the First Mother—

she suspected both wanted to help just for the opportunity to bash in a few heads.

The former Shadan and former Rhugothian General had an instant and unfortunate bond that drew out the worst qualities of the other. In the wild she could minimize the consequences of their impulsiveness; if she ever had to lead them into a city or an inn, she had little doubt they would invent some excuse to start an altercation within minutes, and she would be forced to disavow any knowledge of them.

At the very least, Torbrand's appearance would attract little attention, though handsome and striking. General Harman Harband (or Hardman, as he like to be called), could easily pass for the Ilch in any play that depicted the Apocraphon. His lean skeletal frame, though not in its prime, still moved with power. His face lacked any padding, weathered skin stretched taut against the skull. Small cavernous eyes peered from darkened sockets with a juvenile hunger, and light gray stubble capped his head. Most frightening, however, were sharpened foreteeth and fingernails, both the color of yellowing parchment, and the wicked spiked war club that hung from a thick, well-worn belt that held up tight black leather pants. He wore his long sleeved white shirt open nearly to his navel.

"I've got to hand it to you, lass," Hardman complimented her. "I thought for sure they would take him to Ironkeep, but there they are. A nifty bit of tracking to find them so precisely. Looks like they'll set up camp for the night."

She hadn't bothered explaining the branding Ethris had performed upon her, content to let the two rascals credit her tracking abilities. They hunched behind thick trees on a low hill some two hundred yards from the main road. An evening haze hung over a shallow valley which was starting to give way to farmland. Elsen, a town a couple of miles on, housed a Portal that led to the city of Tenswater, a Church

Protectorate shard rich with Portals. Nations had fought over control of the small shard so bitterly that the Church had intervened for the sake of peace, placing it under its jurisdiction. Most importantly to the caravan carrying Gen, the main Portal to the Church's headquarters, Mur Eldloth, lay within the city.

Hardman scratched his beard. "I wonder why they do not press on to Elsen? They can't be more than a mile or two out. The Church has a small fighting order there that could provide them more protection and, for us, more fun."

"The Church wants this little parade kept quiet," Torbrand answered. "Gen, according to them, is supposed to be the Ilch and, more importantly, is supposed to be dead. The more they avoid company and questions, the better. They are doing the right thing, strategically. Unfortunately, such a light caravan will provide little sport. I don't think there are more than thirty men down there."

Hardman grunted his agreement. "I'd hoped for at least fifty. Well, which flank do you want? We'll have this over before full dark."

"No!" Maewen objected, trying to keep her countenance. "I think you are forgetting something."

"Yes, of course!" Hardman exclaimed. "Thank you, elf. They have a Padra or two down there. Magic is so unfair and unsporting."

"That's not much of an issue," Torbrand piped in. "We wait till dark. Use bows to assassinate the Padras. They'll send a token force up the hill to investigate. We kill them and then clean up the rest. We'll be done before midnight."

"An excellent plan," Hardman concurred. "Let's eat."

"The Padras are not what I meant," Maewen interjected as they went for their packs. Both turned toward her with annoyed looks. "While the Padras and the soldiers are obstacles to consider, the main issue is the carriage."

"The carriage?" Hardman questioned. "Oh, you mean

that the carriage door will likely be locked. No worries. There isn't a door that Destiny can't break down."

"Destiny?" Torbrand asked quizzically.

"My club," Hardman explained a bit sheepishly.

"You named your club? I confess that I have been tempted to name a sword or two after some of my more unfriendly wives, but I never went through with it."

"It's a family tradition."

"I see."

"Gentlemen!" Maewen interrupted. "The lock on the carriage is not the problem. Your poor human eyes cannot see the protecting runes inscribed upon the sides and the door, but mine can. Remember, Lord Khairn, the many protections cast upon the Chalaine's wagon. It survived a solid knock from the helmet of the abomination and a tumble over a cliff. If that wagon is similarly protected, then Destiny will do us no good, and killing everyone will just leave us with a carriage we can't open."

"Then what do you suggest?" Torbrand asked. "We are a day from the Portal into Tenswater and then barely an hour to the Portal to Mur Eldaloth. I do not want to risk a trip to the Church's home shard. As long as we can drive the carriage, we should be able to get it back to Ethris and have him undo the magic."

Maewen said, "That, I would suggest, is our contingency plan, though I fear they may be able to magically track the wagon, as well. I have an alternative, but what I am about to propose will require such precise execution that we may need something to fall back on."

"Say on," Hardman prompted, curiosity piqued.

Maewen sat down. "Portal crossings have a single danger: if the Portal is closed before an object has completely passed through it, the object will be split in two. We need to be in position near the Portal Mage on the Elsen side as they drive the carriage through. It will be moving slowly enough that if the Portal is closed at the right moment, the inside will be exposed and the carriage rendered useless. We need to sever the very rear of the carriage, which will expose the insides and chop the rear wheels in half.

"While I cannot be certain, I am confident that they will do one of two things, go to a Church stronghold within Tenswater, or make a dash on foot for the Portal to Mur Eldaloth. In either case, Gen and his companions will be more accessible, and the city gives us more places to hide and a wealth of Portals to use for our escape. Two of us will go through the Portal ahead of the caravan. One will stay behind to interrupt the Portal Mage."

"How will they reopen the Portal if the Portal Mage is dead?" Hardman asked.

"I never said we would kill the Portal Mage," Maewen answered. "There is no need. We need only distract him momentarily, and I might add that if whoever stays behind to do the distracting does not appear to do so innocently, he will likely find himself in a great deal of trouble from the Church, or even worse, the Portal Guild. Our best chance to recover Gen will be directly after they remove him from the carriage. If the Padras have time to establish a ward, or if reinforcements arrive, this will be for naught."

Torbrand regarded her coolly, though a hint of excitement bloomed in his eyes. "Since you say '*he* will find himself in a great deal of trouble' may I infer that you will not be the one staying behind?"

"That is correct. The General and I will go through a few hours early to scout and to acquire weapons so they we can arm the young men once we have released them. You will stay behind. Like it or not, you are the least recognizable of our little party in these lands. I confess I have thought of no good way to deal with the Padras. We must not harm them if we can avoid it."

"So to summarize your plan," Hardman began, tone carrying a hint of mockery, "you want to slice open the

180

carriage in a Portal by distracting a Portal Mage and then engage in a pitched street battle with the Eldephaere in Tenswater while trying to avoid the magic of the Padras?"

"And don't forget avoiding the Tenswater militia," Torbrand added.

"Yes."

"That is the most insane, desperate plan I have ever heard!" Hardman exclaimed.

"I love it," Torbrand voted.

"I do too!" Hardman concurred.

"This one is even more foolhardy than the one she and Gen concocted to attack an entire Uyumaak company by themselves," Torbrand reminisced. "I am still angry you didn't invite me along."

"Elves must live so long that they bore of a straight fight," Hardman said. "One can hardly find that kind of creativity anymore, Maewen. You are to be congratulated. I would have to be pig drunk to come up with something like that. Torbrand, how are you going to distract the Portal Mage? Maybe you should dress up like a woman and. . ."

"I'm going to scout about," Maewen announced, though the men hardly noticed her departure as they schemed. By the time she returned, both had fallen dead asleep without bothering to set a watch. She woke them well before dawn, wanting to arrive at Elsen at sunup so she and Hardman could scout Tenswater.

The road, soft and damp in the late autumn, led by fields freshly harvested. Low stone walls marked field borders, small farmhouses puffing smoke into the chill air. Snow would come soon, and Maewen wanted to get into Rhugoth before the real cold and blinding winter squalls descended on Kingsblood Lake. Hardman and the Shadan rode with the expressions of children in a hay wagon on the way to the fair. The tracker ignored their brightness of spirit easily, a dread of their task settling in as Elsen, sleepy and small, emerged at the foot of a low line of hills. The thought of battling humans rather than Uyumaak discomfited her, and the magic of the Padras gnawed at the back of her mind, the one asset of the enemy all their strength at arms had no answer for.

"I would have thought the town would be a worthier size, considering where the Portal leads," Torbrand commented.

"Unfortunately," Hardman explained, "or fortunately, depending on your point of view, Tenswater can provide a greater variety of goods and services at a cheaper price than these little towns. The farmers are forced to cross into Tenswater to barter their goods at low return, actually impoverishing the town more than prospering it. Besides, there is little of interest to travelers passing this way. I'm sure the Portal Mage has seen nothing the size of the caravan behind us in a good while."

The road from the hill descended gradually, paved stones replacing dirt as they crossed through a low gate flanked by town militia sharply dressed in blue and gray. The three travelers kept cowls up and heads down as they sped through without a challenge. Despite its irrelevance, the citizens of Elsen demonstrated pride in their village, the roads and buildings clean, well-maintained, and inviting. Their horses' hooves echoed through the sleepy street, only a few shutters having opened an eye to the day.

The road led straight to the Portal, the boundaries marked by two slim pillars flared inward and toward each other at the top. A modest though comfortable house stood nearby, although the dark of the windows and the lack of smoke filtering through the chimney evidenced that the owner had yet to rise.

"I will part ways with you here," Torbrand announced. "I will breakfast and then start to work into a state in which I can aid our plan. While I will not take the part of a woman, I can certainly manage drunk and disorderly. After my little disruption, I will try to move through the Portal as quickly as I can, though you may have to spring me from a holding cell first."

"Good luck, my friend," Hardman saluted. "We shall see you soon." Torbrand rode back toward the center of town while Hardman rousted the Portal Mage with a few wood-splintering knocks on the door from Destiny. Maewen gritted her teeth, assuming a lesson on subtlety would find little to stick to in the head of the brutish General. The only advantage, Maewen surmised, was that when the scrawny, young Portal Mage did emerge from the door, he was so indisposed and intimidated that he simply opened the Portal without bothering to collect payment or force Hardman or herself to sign the customary ledger.

In moments they crossed through the shimmering blue field and into Tenswater, which was bathed in afternoon sunshine. As with the Rhughothian side, a small building stood nearby, the blue-robed Portal Mage sitting on his porch talking with two stoutly built men. He regarded them briefly as the Portal winked out, returning to his talk.

"Church soldiers out of uniform," Hardman commented about the two men once they had left earshot. "Both fighters and too clean to be mercenaries. I think they are giving the Portal Mage a little notice. My bet is they pass through the Portal before long to give my new friend on the other side the same information. If they are giving advanced notice, it could be that they have implemented some arrangement that will make our day a little more interesting."

Maewen nodded. Finally Hardman was saying something useful. "Let's scout their most likely track to the Portal to Mur Eldaloth first and then acquire the weapons. We've little time to get our bearings before the caravan reaches the Portal."

While Maewen eschewed the sights and sounds of cities, Tenswater she could tolerate for its unique qualities. As a Church Protectorate shard, an ever present guard diligently discouraged the accumulation of the filth, noise, and urchins that plagued other places of similar size. Strict regulations prohibited gambling, prostitution, and public insobriety, meaning that only good, clean commerce was allowed free rein.

Even more striking than its wholesome character, however, were the myriads of naturally occurring pools and fountains that dotted the level, grassy landscape. The water, clear and blue, showed hints of the limestone caverns from which it emerged. Trees grew strong and wide in the tracts of verdant grass. The buildings of the city, rather than running in long uninterrupted rows, clumped together in areas where the lack of pools had allowed builders to put down foundations. The abundance of water had forced the road pavers into a more artistic frame of mind, white stone paths and streets rarely running in a straight line for more than a few yards.

Maewen and Hardman's business, however, prevented them from dwelling on the pleasant scene. With a few quick questions to the local guard, they rode off in the direction of the Portal to Mur Eldaloth, finding it a short time later no more than a mile from the Elsen Portal. Unlike the tall shops with pointed roofs that shot into the air around them, the Church had constructed a circular granite fortress around the Portal to their holy city, a mass of guards patrolling a solid wall that rose twenty feet into the air around it. A portcullis, shut and guarded, stood between any passerby and the ornate Portal enclosure inside. A grand, semicircular wreath some fifteen feet in diameter spanned the Portal area, carved leaves of beaten gold reflecting dully in the late afternoon light.

"Well, Maewen, I think we would do well not to let the caravan get anywhere near this place. Honestly, I wish this city were a little more like Mikmir for our purposes. You could send a toddler from one side of this town to the other with a bag of gold and his innocence and he would get to the other side without endangering either. This may be harder than we thought."

To hear such a cautionary statement from one of the most reckless, foolhardy people she could imagine sent a chill up Maewen's spine, but she gathered her resolve and turned her horse back toward the Portal to Elsen and its nearby cluster of buildings. If the Church managed to get Gen into Elde Luri Mora, then no one would have a chance at recovering him. Tenswater was their only opportunity, and she would take it.

For the next hour they scouted the route to several Portals close to the one from Elsen that they could escape to once the job was done. They purchased plain but sturdy swords from a local merchant, who was surprised but pleased to have sold so many at once. Hardman removed his cloak and bundled the swords inside to carry them less conspicuously.

As evening settled in, lanterns flared to life and a chill rode upon a northern breeze. Hardman and Maewen tied the horses to a tree at a small park adjacent to the Portal to Elsen and snacked while they waited for their cue. The cold air emptied the streets, but the Portal Mage remained at his post, eying the two strangers across the way with curiosity and a little suspicion. Only the Portal flashing blue tore his eyes from them. Maewen and Hardman stood, moving quickly to the horses, but only a solitary figure astride a horse emerged before the Portal winked out.

"It's Torbrand," Maewen said. "This is not a good omen."

Hardman whistled and signaled their companion over. "What news?" Hardman asked. "What are you doing here?"

"Our little plan has run into a hitch," Torbrand reported, breath channeling the ale he had recently imbibed. "The Churchmen are clearing the street and shutting everyone indoors. They've posted a contingent of guards at the Portal. I had to be very persuasive to win my way here."

As he finished, the unmistakable sound of armored men marching sank Maewen's heart.

"We should have attacked them last night," Hardman muttered.

"Let's get clear of here," Torbrand suggested. "If we can get down a side street, we might be able to remain close enough to see what is happening. If we stay here, they will force us into the nearest building. Ride now!"

Maewen and Hardman mounted quickly and rode after Torbrand. They crossed the street into a smaller road to the side of the Portal Mage's house. To their right a file of at least fifty men in polished chainmail with white tabards marched toward the Portal in perfect cadence. As the three fled into the smaller avenue, they spotted a smaller contingent of soldiers rounding up groups of bewildered townsfolk and forcing them inside a nearby inn. Their leader, a muscular, clean-shaven warrior atop a bulky gray warhorse, signaled for the fleeing trio to stop.

"My apologies, citizens. You must dismount and go inside until we signal that the way is clear."

"We have business just beyond here," Torbrand explained casually. "May we not continue and enter there?"

"No," the warrior answered firmly. "Tie your horses to the rail and get inside. I won't ask again."

Maewen admired Torbrand's restraint as he worked up a relaxed, but annoyed sigh and complied. They tied their horses to the rail as quickly as they could under the close scrutiny of the Church soldier.

"Grab your gear and keep close," Torbrand whispered.

They took what they could carry and followed Torbrand to the inn door, a commanding tone and expression asserting itself over his former, carefree levity. "We'll have to hurry to have any chance of this at all. Keep close. We'll be making for the stairs."

Maewen turned up her nose as they crammed their way in to the packed common room of The Crooning Loon.

The stench of beer and the unnatural warmth and stink of cramped bodies, combined with a steady din, fermented the atmosphere into an uneasy agitation. Torbrand put his muscular frame to good use as he unapologetically and forcefully plowed through the throng, Hardman and Maewen following in his wake. The stairs provided a convenient place to sit due to the paucity of chairs and benches, but Torbrand simply stepped on whomever wouldn't move until they gained the second story.

Dim lanterns lined the hall where even more people loitered. The former Shadan paused but a moment to consider the doors around him, and then, victim chosen, strode forward and kicked it open without checking to see if it was unlocked already. Patrons screamed and shied away, Maewen gritting her teeth as she plunged into the room after Hardman, finding they had interrupted a plump merchant counting silver coins in a small, ornate box.

"Thieves!" he yelled, clutching the box to his breast like a treasured infant. "Thieves! Guard!"

Hardman's hand shot out and grabbed the man's pudgy cheeks in an iron grip while Torbrand yanked open the shutters. "We don't want your money, pig," Hardman hissed, eyes intense. "Shut your yap or I'll cut your tongue out and use it to polish my boots."

The terrified merchant scooted back on his bed, yanking a gray woolen blanket around himself with his freehand as if he hoped the cloth would ward him from the demon before him.

"Just as I hoped," Torbrand stated with satisfaction. Maewen went to the window and peered over his shoulder. Beneath the window, an eave sloped downward, terminating at a height just above the lowest part of the Portal Mage's roof. A five foot gap separated the two. "It will be a little tricky, but manageable."

Torbrand hoisted himself out the window. Carefully, he stood on the brittle wooden shingles, smiling wickedly as they jiggled, cracked, and slid underneath his feet. "Excellent," he muttered to no one in particular before crashing headlong down the eave and heaving himself over. Several shingles tumbled over the edge and into the alley, sound covered by the ruckus of marching men. He landed on his stomach with a thud that shook the Portal Mage's house.

Hardman's eyes raised speculatively. "I think I'll let you take the next go at it, lass. I need another example before I attempt that. I'll barricade the door and make sure this fellow stays quiet for a couple of hours . . . or so."

Maewen wasted no time, nimbly jumping the distance and landing lightly on her feet. She could only watch in horror as Hardman defenestrated and executed a desperate run and leap with all the grace and poise of a fat, delirious cow. He landed unceremoniously on his side, slipping backward. Torbrand spared him the indignity of falling into the alley with a deft grab of the hand.

Quietly they worked their way to the top of the roof and peered over. Light from the soldiers' torches illuminated the Portal enclosure, the company forming up on either side of the road.

"I count at least a hundred," Torbrand informed them. "I can't see any Puremen or Padras yet. There are at least ten men on horse. I don't think there is much we can do here, Maewen."

Maewen's mind raced down dead end after dead end. Her companions were right. They should have tried to rescue Gen the night before, though even that, she thought, would have ended in defeat. She turned on her back and lay facing the stars, trying to imagine the First Mother's disappointment at her failure. The Church had learned its lesson about caution from the disastrous caravan journey through Elde Luri Mora.

"I'm sorry Maewen," Hardman consoled her. "Perhaps tomorrow we can dress as pilgrims and get into Mur

Eldaloth. I doubt they'll let anyone through tonight. I suppose we'll have to find a different inn. I doubt they'll let us back into this one. It smelled bad, anyway."

A flash of blue signaled the Portal opening, and they crawled back up to the apex of the roof and peered over. A Padra came through first, followed by marching Church soldiers. At last, four black horses and the wagon pulled through, followed by another Padra and the remaining soldiers. Once they were through, the Portal winked out and the caravan stopped as the soldiers took their places, the fresh soldiers replacing their travel-weary brothers.

"So close," Maewen whispered to herself.

"May I join you for a moment?"

All three startled, nearly losing their balance on the slanted roof. A woman, dressed in black and veiled walked easily up the incline toward them. Her voice sounded aged, and her back was bent with time. The slightly acrid smell of old ash accompanied her as she walked past them and stood at the top of the roof, careless of the eyes that might see her silhouetted against the sky. Maewen cast warning glances at her companions, who already had hands on weapons.

"You will appreciate this, elf," the woman said. "Come watch. They will not see you." Despite the reassurance, they took pains to present the smallest profile to those below. The woman incanted and gesticulated. A cracking sound momentarily silenced the soldiers as the wagon tongue broke in two and fell. The Padra behind the wagon spurred forward, casting his eyes around. With another chant and a downward motion, the wagon quickly and quietly sank into the ground, the driver heaving himself to the side to avoid interment. When done, the road appeared as solid as it ever had, soldiers and Pardras gawking at it in disbelief.

"I want ten men digging in this spot right now!" the Padra shouted. "I want every Portal Mage in the city rounded up and taken to the the Bastion immediately. No one leaves this shard until that wagon is found. Double the city guard. Call up every soldier. Search every building! Go!"

The woman turned and casually walked down the roof. "My time is coming and I must go. Take care of Gen. He is your only hope."

"Where is the wagon?" Torbrand asked.

"Your elven tracker will find it," she answered. "Good night." She jumped from the roof and was gone.

"Was that who I think it was?" Hardman asked.

"Joranne," Maewen confirmed.

"Why would she help us?" Hardman followed, sounding perplexed. "From what I was told of Three Willow, she had tried to capture Gen for herself, but it appears if she is simply content to let us have him now when he is within her power."

"I do not know," Maewen responded. "Her mind is dark and twisted, her reasons her own."

"Can you find the wagon?" Torbrand asked, scooting downward toward the roof edge. "Will they survive being buried in the dirt?"

"I can find it. She is using a spell the elves perfected for traveling within the earth. They should be quite safe. We, on the other hand. . ."

Maewen let the thought trail off as they dropped into the alley and waited in the shadows as the mass of soldiers broke apart in groups and scattered.

"They will lock the entire city down," Torbrand stated. "It will be amusing to see what tale they offer as justification, and even more amusing to see how we will get off this shard."

Hardman asked, "How far away is the carriage, Maewen?"

"I cannot say for sure. Come. I think we can sneak by now." They turned away from the main street that led by the front of the inn, slipping to the rear of the structure and ducking down behind a low fence that bordered a tree-lined road.

"I can see two of the Church soldiers," Maewen announced, peering into the dark. "They seem at their ease."

"Only two?" Hardman complained.

Chapter 60 – Underground

"We're dead," Volney lamented, voice echoing in the impenetrable darkness. "We're dead and in the Abyss. What did I do to deserve this?"

"We're not in the Abyss," Gerand disagreed, voice exasperated. "For Eldaloth's sake, Volney, get a hold of yourself. This is no worse than the sacks they put us in before."

"I expected there would be a lot more pain and torture, perhaps with some fire or demons, but I think the dark will drive me barking mad."

"You already are," Gerand said. "Look, people go to the Abyss when they die and *if* they have been disposed to evil. We sank into the ground. Didn't you hear them shouting in surprise? This was some sort of magic. If we could get out of this accursed wagon, we might just find our way to light. If you listen carefully, you can hear the wind moaning from time to time. That means there is a way to the surface." Gerand yanked at the bars, kicked the lock, and then slumped down in frustration. "At any rate, since they can't drug Gen anymore, perhaps he'll wake up and have some sort of brilliant idea."

Since their disastrous encounter with Padra Nolan on

the floating dock, the Puremen who fed them their meals had always forced Gen to drink some foul-smelling liquid. Not once since their capture and entrapment within the carriage had Gen managed any sort of coherency, even if he managed to open his confused, bleary eyes. Gerand shook him, eliciting a brief moan.

"Why do you think they did that to him and not to us?" Volney wondered aloud. "Drug him, I mean."

"I don't know," Gerand admitted, leaning back against the wall. "I've asked myself that on occasion. I would say that they fear that he might use his intelligence, fame, or persuasiveness to find some way out of this rolling jail cell."

"And what are we, a couple of dog-brained morons?" asked Volney. "We're both in the upper classes! We're both educated and eloquent!"

"If that's the way you feel, if they find us, I'll ask them to drug you, too—for the sake of your pride and a little peace and quiet. We need to think."

When the wagon had passed through the ground and into the empty chamber, it fell several feet, splintering the wheels. The carriage rocked back and forth uneasily with their movements. The absolute, enveloping dark clouded their notion of the passage of time. They said little save to engage in inane conversation just to gain the reassurance that another person waited with them in the dark.

Gen began breathing more shallowly, turning restlessly and mumbling.

"I think he's coming out of it," Volney observed hopefully.

"And I think it's getting lighter out there," Gerand added.

After butting heads with Volney scrambling for the window slit, Gerand gripped the bars and peered out, noticing a faint orange glow. Periodically, the faint echo of whispered voices would reach their ears, or the staccato of a loose rock kicked about the stone walls.

"We're definitely in a cave," Gerand asserted.

"Have the Eldephaere have found us?"

"I don't think so. Whoever is coming treads lightly without a lot of armor. They are too quiet."

"And you two thunder mouths are not."

Maewen's voice sent a surge of hope through Gerand's veins, her torch blinding him as she rounded the corner of an underground passageway. Once his eyes settled, he saw that the carriage had fallen into a large, damp cave with stalactites and stalagmites sticking up like points of wet clay.

"I hope Ethris is with you," Gerand commented.

"He is not," Maewen reported. "I have Torbrand Khairn and. . ."

"General Harband!" Volney exclaimed. "I'd recognize him anywhere, after all the stories."

The General executed a small bow for his benefit.

"Recognition is not our friend right now," Torbrand cautioned seriously, "and neither is the door of that carriage, I assume."

"It took a Padra incanting some spell to open it," Gerand confirmed. "We're trapped, aren't we?"

"For the time being," Maewen said, face troubled. "Is Gen well?"

"They drugged him to keep him incapacitated. They usually administered a dose at night when the caravan stopped. They did not get around to that tonight, so perhaps he will wake soon. I don't know."

Maewen crouched on the ground and rummaged through her backpack. "Just a moment. Tell me, does he have both of his legs?"

Gerand and Volney both creased their brows. "Yes," they answered in unison.

"Then he truly is the most dangerous man alive. Put a pinch of this under his nose," she said, handing Gerand a small pouch she produced from her pack. "Just a pinch, mind you."

"I need a bit more light!" Gerand requested after fumbling in the dark for several seconds. Maewen strode forward and put the torch near the bars.

"What do you mean about Gen and the leg?" Volney inquired, perplexed.

"The Church has sent riders throughout Ki'Hal proclaiming that Gen was the Ilch, attacked Chertanne, and was then killed by him. They say they amputated Gen's leg and are carting it around to major cities in a grand procession. So you see, if Gen shows up not dead and with both legs attached, the Church has a major credibility problem."

"Gen? The Ilch? That's ludicrous!" Volney exclaimed. "Who would believe such a fable? And if Gen is such a liability, why haven't they killed him? He's been helpless in this wagon for days!"

"Information, perhaps," Shadan Khairn ventured. "That would assume, however, that they truly believe he is the Ilch. If they could spend time and search his mind, he might reveal some clues as to what Mikkik was up to. Of course, with Chertanne dead, I suppose the outcome of the prophecy is already set."

"Chertanne is dead!?" Gerand nearly smashed Volney's face into the bars as he shot from Gen's side. Volney's mouth hung silently open as his companion pushed him out of the way. "Who killed him?"

"Keep your voice down," Maewen hissed. "Jaron killed him. Few know that. Mirelle was able to sneak the news to us before she left for Aughmere."

In the wagon, Gen began to wheeze and cough.

Maewen looked behind her nervously. "I'll tell you all we know when Gen awakes. I dislike telling the same story twice. Return the pouch to me, please."

Gerand complied, returning to Gen's side, helping him struggle to a sitting position, clarity returning to his troubled, dark-rimmed eyes.

"Easy, Gen," Gerand cautioned.

Gen sat up and ran his fingers through his hair. "Where am I? The last thing I remember was greeting Padra Nolan on the dock."

"Gerand smiled, relieved to see Gen awake and coherent. "Well, my friend, we have quite a tale to tell you."

"It will have to wait," Maewen said, voice sharp. "Listen."

Ears strained, reaching out into the darkness, but it took nearly a minute for Maewen's human companions to hear the sound that alarmed her—above them, in the darkness, someone was pounding on stone.

"Unbelievable!" General Harband laughed. "They actually dug a hole all the way down here! They really are desperate. Well, Torbrand, ready for a fight?"

"Always, but I'm afraid I have an idea that may delay the pleasure, at least momentarily."

"What are you proposing?" Maewen asked.

"I'm proposing that we let them open the carriage door for us. The wagon is broken. I'm assuming they won't take the effort to fix it and haul it back up the hole. If I guess right, they will lower a token force of men down here to secure the area, and then send in a Padra to open the door. Once he is sure that Gen is sedated, they'll haul them out. With limited opponents and the element of surprise, this should be relatively easy, especially if we can eliminate the Padra early."

"The plan is sound, but I don't want to kill a Padra," Maewen said.

"I can incapacitate him without killing him," Gen offered. "If I can get close enough to him."

"They've been drugging you. . ." Gerand began

"Yes, I can taste the elm's draught on my lips."

"If you feign that you are near waking, perhaps the Padra will enter the carriage personally to administer the drug."

Torbrand loosened his sword in its scabbard. "It's set then. Maewen, you'll need to cover our tracks in this room so they won't suspect that anyone's been here. General, pass those swords inside so they can fight for us once the door is free. Gerand, Volney, when they start coming, yell for help and act as terrified and alone as possible. Gen striking the Padra will be the cue to advance. The cave entrance exits into a sewer a half mile from here. We will likely have to fight most of the way out. Soldiers will drop through the hole like rats fleeing a flood once we hit them. Go!"

Hardman shoved the swords through the bars and retreated back into the passage, Torbrand following. Maewen stayed behind for several minutes, using her cloak to smooth the dirt into as natural a state as she could before she turned the corner and extinguished her torch. Darkness fell again, Volney muttering uncomfortably under his breath.

Nearly an hour passed, the sound of the pick and then shovel resounding ever more clearly in the benighted cavern. "It appears our haste was unnecessary," Torbrand observed. "By the sound of it, there are three diggers at most." As he finished his sentence, a rumbling shook the cave, and all at once the ceiling above the carriage collapsed. A thunderous wave of rock, dirt, and diggers' bodies showered down to bounce off the carriage and onto the hard cave floor. Two of the diggers lay motionless while a third yelled in agony, clutching his legs.

Hardman snorted. "Morons."

Pale, flickering light from bonfires around the hole provided weak illumination to the scene below. On cue, Volney and Gerand yelled for help.

"We've found them!" someone shouted from above. "Lower Padra Seffire first."

"Mikkik's fury!" Torbrand swore quietly. "I miscalculated. They aren't expecting us down here, they're expecting a Magician. They had at least three Padras in the caravan. I expect we'll see all three shortly. You may have to reevaluate your reluctance to kill Padras, Maewen."

True to Torbrand's prediction, the soldiers above lowered Padra Seffire first, and as soon as his boots touched the ground, he incanted, a translucent sphere of dusty air encompassing the cavern. Maewen frowned and Torbrand shook his head in disappointment.

"Wouldn't have had much fun if it had gone according to plan," Hardman whispered consolingly. "Let's hope Gen is as clever as I've heard tell."

Two other Padras were lowered in immediately after Seffire, one attending to the fallen diggers. Maewen watched as Padra Seffire approached the bars, holding a brief conversation with the incarcerated. He approached the door, removing a flask from a cloak pocket.

"Here we go," Hardman said.

"Have you seen anyone else down here?" Padra Seffire asked Gerand. "Be quick, boy."

"No, Padra," Gerand answered as meekly as he could, which to Gen's ear came across as just a shade under stubborn haughtiness.

"And Gen still sleeps?"

"Yes, Padra. . ."

Gen interrupted Gerand by grumbling and stirring noisily.

"But I think he is near waking."

Seffire abandoned the bars and the conversation

immediately. "Orvis, Brace, we have to hurry. Get as many soldiers down here as you can." He incanted his spell and the lock popped. "You two get out," Seffire commanded after pulling open the door. Volney and Gerand hesitated, unsure what to do. Gen stirred again. "Get out!" Seffire yelled.

Gen steadied himself and kept up his restless act, moving his head back and forth and fluttering his eyelids. Volney and Gerand dismounted the carriage and the Padra incanted again, though Gen couldn't tell what the spell had done. Seffire's robes rustled as he ascended the carriage, his shadow returning the brief glow of light behind Gen's eyelids back to darkness. The acrid smell of the elm's draught filled the carriage as Seffire unstoppered a vial. Gen opened his eyes briefly and closed them again as if in a waking swoon.

Just a moment longer.

Seffire placed the vial on Gen's lips. Gen rocked backward and thrust forward with his legs, heels catching the Padra squarely in the chest. The top of the low door of the wagon smashed into the Padra's head as he shot backward, rotating his body forward while the momentum carried him outside. He was limp before he landed face first on the cave floor. The protective dome of air vanished.

"Seffire!" the other Padras shouted in unison. A deafening battle cry reverberated through the hall, General Harband yelling a knee-weakening command to attack. Gen moved toward the carriage entrance, muscles sluggish. He gathered the swords under his arm and thrust himself through the open door, weapons clanging as he unfurled the cloak and let them fall to the ground.

The other two Padras yelled for help from above as their eyes cast about in fear as they assessed the threat they faced in the dark. Volney and Gerand were as still as statues, the victims of some spell.

Forgoing a weapon, Gen dashed at the Padras. Using

Trysmagic, he eroded portions of the floor beneath their feet to throw them off balance and keep their minds far from their spells. With a precise punch to one and a kick to the other, they fell to the ground unconscious. Volney and Gerand snapped from their stupor, and Gen joined them, retrieving the weapons from the ground. Ropes from above cascaded down the hole.

"Let's go!" Torbrand yelled.

Maewen shot down the first two soldiers plunging down the rope before shouldering her bow and reigniting her torch. Hardman and Torbrand punished the first eager soldiers to shimmy down the ropes with a brutal assault. Once the young men joined Maewen, they dashed away from the hole, and the chase through the cramped cavern began. The cave floor alternated between damp, smooth rock and loose gravel, confounding boots and ankles as they struggled forward in the dark.

"I think we went faster walking," Hardman commented after Gerand slid and bashed his head into the wall. Gen straightened him up and helped him along, his own bare feet cut and bleeding. He realized the mark of prophecy on his instep would be visisble in better light.

Shouting echoed to them from the tunnel behind. The cave rarely widened enough to let more than two people walk side by side.

We could hold them here forever, Gen thought.

"We should find the sewer before long," Maewen reassured from the rear after they had hiked for several minutes, confirming what their noses already sensed. The sounds of pursuit came no closer, harsh, guttural oaths evidencing that their enemies also found the way treacherous.

Rank, dark fluid seeping along the walls and pooling on the floors signaled their proximity to their goal, and as they rounded a corner, the torch revealed a scattering of pale bricks knocked out of the sewer wall intermixed with rocks picked out of the cave to form a squat, wide opening.

Maewen stiffened. "Someone is approaching, more quickly than is natural."

"A flash skirmisher," Torbrand identified. "Into the sewer. We'll have more room to deal with him there. Looks like you didn't hit one of the Padras hard enough, Gen. Seffire was a fine piece of work, though. He probably won't remember what table manners are when he wakes up . . . if he wakes up."

Gen ushered Maewen forward and placed himself at the rear of the retreat, ducking through the low opening last. He remembered vividly the night Samian taught him about flash skirmishers. Magicians on both sides of the war used them, enhancing a warrior's or creature's natural speed and strength. The result was a fighter that could slash into an enemy camp to assassinate a general or into the front line of a defense to quickly weaken a point for a breakthrough charge.

While costly to Magician and warrior alike, flash skirmishers proved effective tools in killing large numbers quickly with few resources. If the skirmisher caught them in a cave where only one defender could be brought to bear, he would cut through the lot of them like a scythe on summer wheat.

"Get into the middle of the sludge," Torbrand ordered. "It will slow him."

However clean the streets of Tenswater, its sewer presented no improvement over any other. A dark, fetid water—if it could be called that—rose up to the height of their knees, garbage of all varieties carried slowly on a barely discernible current. The cold liquid chilled their legs as they sloshed forward.

"Stand behind us, Maewen," Gen ordered. "Keep the torch forward so we have light. Those knives will do you no good if the skirmisher has a sword." Maewen complied, but not before shooting him a look that said, "I know that."

Gen assessed his options. The spell he had used to trip up the Padras tired him, but he could manage more. A well-placed spell could put a speedy end to the skirmisher, but he could not risk anyone knowing of his magic. Discrete forms of Trysmagic that would delay or momentarily throw off an attacker would be of little use—skirmishers could recover too quickly. Creating an obstruction in the enemy's windpipe would scream magic, but perhaps disabling a weapon or damaging a leg might give them an edge.

The too-quick staccato of boots on the damp rocks tightened grips on swords and pinned eyes to the entrance into the sewer. Gen's mind raced, but not quickly enough as a blurred figured darted through the hole and into the sewer water, blackish green spray flinging up behind churning legs. While difficult to see, Gen could tell that the soldier wore the white of the Eldephaere, a long sword drawn and whipping back and forth.

There was no time to think. With a quick effort, Gen used his magic to weaken the sword metal where the hilt met the blade just as the skirmisher crossed the distance to face him. Gen timed his swing, the skirmisher easily blocking, but as he did the blade simply gave way and fell into the water. The skirmisher withdrew several paces and stopped momentarily to regard the hilt. The Church soldier was built like Gen, tall, lean, and fast. He regarded them briefly and sprinted forward with such speed that they could barely follow him.

On his first pass, he bashed Volney in the face with the heavy hilt. The young man fell backward into the water, blood spurting from his nose. Gerand stooped to help him up but received the same punishment as the skirmisher flew by in the opposite direction.

"Clump together!" Torbrand ordered. Gen complied, sidling up next to Hardman and Maewen. Gerand and Volney floated in the water unmoving. Gen swallowed hard. As the blur started at them again, they all struck out, but the skirmisher diverted to the right, flanking them. In a half a moment he had grabbed Maewen by the jerkin and slammed her into the slimy sewer wall. Her head cracked against the stones and she slumped down unconscious. Her torch sizzled out in the repulsive water, and absolute darkness fell. All sound and movement stopped momentarily.

"Mikkik's curse upon you!" Hardman yelled. Gen felt the general step away from them and heard tentative steps forward. "Can't see worth a bugger, Churchman? Can you? Well, I've the eyes of an owl and. . ." Rapid splashes, three solid thumps, and a heavy splash later, Gen knew Hardman had fallen. At worst, the skirmisher would have taken hold of Destiny.

Unwittingly, Gen realized, their attacker had afforded them the protection of darkness and an advantage to exploit. Closing his eyes, Gen concentrated his senses in the direction of the struggle, the quick breathing of their assailant plain above trickling of the water.

While committing a cardinal sin of sword fighting, Gen took the risk. Swinging both arms above his head, he flung the sword point first in the direction where he heard the rapid breaths. The soldier rewarded him with a painful grunt and the sound of footsteps staggering back away from them. To Gen's surprise, Torbrand thrust his sword into his former pupil's hand and hastily felt through his gear, removing a torch and flint.

With two sure strikes the torch flared to life, revealing the skirmisher leaning against the wall bandaging a bad cut to his lower-left abdomen. Even blurred, the pale of his face revealed his weakness, and Gen remembered the bane of flash skirmishers—quickened bodies moved, healed, and bled at an accelerated pace. Hardman lay slumped over a flotilla of garbage.

"If you would have aimed just a touch higher, this would all be over," Torbrand criticized as Gen returned his sword to him. Torbrand started toward the skirmisher, and Gen was looking to follow when he noticed that Volney and Gerand floated facedown in the water. As quickly as he could, he dragged them out of the sludge and to the slightly raised bank where Maewen lay bleeding from her scalp, face wan. To make matters worse, the sounds of soldiers approaching in the cave grew painfully close.

Gen looked up. *This has to end now.* Torbrand approached his quarry cautiously. The skirmisher made no move, standing stock still until Torbrand shot forward, slicing the fatigued soldier on the arm, blood running out in a steady stream. The former Shadan backed away, but the soldier sprang forward, landing a solid blow to Torbrand's midsection and ripping the sword from his hands.

Gen concentrated. While experienced Trysmagicians could alter the complex organs of the body directly, to do so required great will and great power. Gen chose the easier path, creating a thick, gooey substance in the empty airway. The celerity with which the skirmisher choked, turned purple, and died surprised Gen. Torbrand's face showed his surprise, but he did not dwell on it as the sound of hurried boots drew near.

"I'll heal Hardman," he said. "You see if you can get those two breathing and then find a sword." Gen had already thought the same thing. They could not heal or carry everyone before the first wave of soldiers found them, but they stood a better than average chance of beating them off.

Remembering Samian's training, Gen pumped his friends' chests and breathed into their mouths until they gagged and expelled the smelly water from their lungs and started to stir.

Gen wiped his mouth and set his mind to ignore the awful taste. He found a sword by the time the first soldiers piled through entrance wielding short swords and bucklers meant for fighting in close quarters. Seeing no immediate offense, the leader waited until twelve others joined him. By that time, a tired Torbrand had healed Hardman, who, by virtue of a leather strap, still had possession of Destiny.

Their foes formed a wedge, preparing to charge. Gen glanced at the hungry, anticipatory fire in his companions' eyes and then back to the Church warriors before them. Perhaps never before in Ki'Hal had a group of soldiers met with such misfortune.

"At last," Hardman growled, stretching his neck, "a straight fight."

The Eldepahere were well-trained but wildly outclassed. What Hardman did with brutal delight, Gen and Torbrand accomplished with determination and precision. In moments the three men swept away their resistance like dry leaves before the gale.

"Too easy," Hardman commented as they crossed to their injured companions.

"I will have to recover before I can heal Maewen," Torbrand informed them.

"I'll carry her." Gen tucked his sword into his belt and hefted the half-elf after donning her gear.

"Can you two walk without help?" Torbrand asked Volney and Gerand. The lack of response from the stunned young men was answer enough. Hardman and Torbrand pulled them to their feet, looping their arms over their shoulders.

"Now we find a place to hole up and heal," Torbrand said.

"Anywhere but here," Volney gagged.

CHAPTER 61 - IRON KEEP

The Chalaine, Mirelle, Dason, and Cadaen huddled under piles of blankets for warmth, as the weather had turned unexpectedly cold during the last two weeks of travel.

"It will only be a few more days, I suspect, Highness," Dason comforted the troubled Queen as the wagon crept along the snow-buried road. If possible, the conveyance chosen for them felt even more dark and cheerless than the carriage Regent Ogbith had designed for the journey to Elde Luri Mora.

The Chalaine regarded her Protector and thought she should feel grateful that Padra Athan had permitted any more of her personal guard to remain with her at all. Wrongly, Athan wrote off Gen's attack as a consequence of prophetic destiny and Jaron's as a result of Gen poisoning his mind against the Ha'Ulrich. Since both men had acted while in her Protectorship, she initially thought Athan would dismiss all the Dark Guard in favor of the Eldephaere, but then again, with Chertanne dead, the only person who had ever treated her with egregious disrespect could no longer trouble those loyal to her.

Since they rose that morning, the snow had fallen

steadily, the wind sometimes gusting and driving the chill powder through the slim, barred openings on the sides of the wagon. What time it was, the Chalaine could not guess, the sky an immutable gray from sunup to sundown. The snow had drifted up high on the boles of the trees which were thick along the side of the road, slowing the growing caravan in its progress. Athan saw to it that every man-at-arms who could survive a brutal winter march lined up to accompany their 'wounded' King and his anxious bride.

Out of the corner of her eye, the Chalaine caught Dason staring at her and she stood and crossed to the back of the wagon to escape his scrutiny. While appropriately noble and caring, the Chalaine noticed another emotion in his eyes—a hope and anticipation—that frightened her. So many emotions and confused thoughts strove within her that she wished Dason as dull and expressionless as Gen had been in his early days in her service. Her love for Gen easily eclipsed her girlish infatuation with the Prince of Tolnor, though she dreaded the thought of telling Dason outright that she felt nothing for him, at best. At the worst, her association with Gen had—in her own mind—transformed her handsome Protector into a babbling, fawning nuisance.

But gazing upon the snow-washed track behind her and the other dark wagon trailing theirs shoved these thoughts away, for within the other wagon lurked the instigator of all her twisted confusion. Chertanne was dead. After Jaron had killed him, Padra Athan had the Eldephaere immediately remove the new King from the festivities under the pretext of ministering to him. A while later the Padra had returned and told the mass of squelched revelers that their King lived but had sustained a serious wound that the Chalaine had healed to the best of her ability. For security's sake, the entire party left at once despite the late hour. The Eldephaere had executed Jaron by fire just before the caravan got underway, and the Chalaine could not bear to watch.

Once underway, Athan told them that his brethren had cast spells to maintain Chertanne's body fresh, hinting that there were still options, though the Chalaine saw none save choices between modes of interment. But Athan kept up the farce. Servants delivered three meals a day to the dead man, Church leaders consulted with him regularly, and the Chalaine had been permitted to visit her husband every other day to spend time to heal and condole her 'beloved' Lord. For her part, sitting with his corpse only agitated her. Never before had horror and absolute relief had such intimate intercourse in a human heart, though she chastised herself for the relief. Relief to be rid of Chertanne sprung from a selfish, short-sighted root; the horror, more justly, grew from the consequences of his demise that now stared the unsuspecting world in the face.

While no one, including Gen, thought Chertanne would have fared well against Mikkik, no one had any clue as to how the prophecy would get along without him, either. Even more confusing was the question of leadership. How long would Athan pretend that Chertanne still drew breath? Cynically, she realized that Chertanne's death bestowed a great deal of power upon Athan, for in the King's absence, the Padra commandeered all of his responsibilities, all under the guise of his being spokesman. Of course, Chertanne had acted as little more than the Padra's puppet when alive, and of the two, Athan was the stronger leader.

A shout rose, and the caravan stopped to rest and feed the horses at midday. The Chalaine hoped Dason was accurate in his assessment that the end of their trip approached. The long journey through Aughmere wearied her, and she hated the thought that innocent men perished in the cold to protect a dead man. While she had learned that Aughmere consisted mostly of dense wood, she was not prepared for the boxed in, blind feeling of traveling down a road so thick with trunk and branch that only a formidable, choked darkness waited beyond the edges of the road. In places, the trees hunched over the road for long stretches, creating dark sylvan tunnels as cold and forbidding as caves of stone.

While the original plans for the caravan had them passing through major cities and towns on their way back to Chertanne's stronghold in Ironkeep, Padra Athan ordered that Gen's leg and the accompanying narrative of the events in Elde Luri Mora travel the circuit instead. To the Churchman's consternation, General Khairn and Ethris had turned up missing the second night from the Portal gate, and no one had seen Maewen since before Chertanne's death. The Chalaine quizzed her mother about it, but Mirelle simply returned one of her smiles that told her it was safer not to inquire.

Athan passed nearby with two Puremen to deliver lunch to the corpse. She figured the Puremen who served it also ate it, perhaps using Chertanne's shroud as a napkin. She suspected those in the robes of servile Puremen walked a little too much like soldiers to be holy men, crediting her ability to perceive such a detail to Samian, who continued to instruct her in the ways of the sword in her sleep.

The Chalaine felt awkward about the training at first. Strutting around a dream Cathedral, sparring with a teacher she could rarely understand, and using a weapon she had only seen in the hands of men brought a blush of embarrassment to her face every night until her steps and strokes fell with more surety. As her confidence and skill grew—with an alacrity she found startling—she found her nightly instructions a great release, especially since in dream her stomach was not sour or expanding.

Once the horses were fed, the caravan proceeded forward, heavy flakes swirling in a whistling wind. Cuddling up to her mother, she fell into a deep sleep until Dason woke them all with a shout.

"We've arrived!"

They crowded around the bars to stare out, finding

nothing but a white plain surrounding them. The lack of trees allowed the bitter wind to ply its full biting power, and soldiers around them wrapped raw faces with whatever cloth they could find and walked with arms folded and faces to the ground.

"How can you tell we are there?" the Chalaine asked. Dason cocked his head to reply, but Cadaen butted in before him.

"The land around Ironkeep is kept free of trees for at least two miles in every direction, though I have heard they have extended that area under Shadan Khairn. With all that wood you could bring an army in from any direction, though it would be difficult going if the forest is as dense as it appears. It shouldn't be long now, Chalaine."

The Chalaine remained at the bars, surveying what she could in the obscuring snow. Before long, a regiment of horse soldiers added to their numbers. Inside an hour, people started to line the road, cheering the return of their King and undoubtedly wondering where he and his father were. The weather and the lack of anyone important to see likely rendered the event a little less festive than it was intended to be, and before long the caravan rolled through an immense gate and into Ironkeep proper.

"But there was no city! Is the entire city inside the wall?" Dason asked, astonished.

"There is no city, inside or out," Cadaen explained. "This place was chosen as the location to build Ironkeep because there are several Portals that converge in this general area. This is purely a military complex with some areas dedicated to Portal pass-through for trading purposes. The Shadan lives on the Ellenais shard, though I doubt Athan will let us winter there. There will be few creature comforts here, though we are the first non-Aughmerians to come within these walls in at least a hundred years. Not even ambassadors are permitted to enter here."

"Well, if I were to attack it, I would simply bring along

torches," Dason commented. "I thought Ironkeep would be primarily iron, but it appears mostly wood banded with iron. A good blaze would fell this place in a day."

"Each spring they treat every inch of every beam and plank with some substance so it won't burn," Cadaen explained, clearly fascinated by what he was seeing. "I hope they give us a chance to wander about when the weather clears up. We could use some good intelligence about this place."

But Cadaen's wish was not to be granted. To the Chalaine's dismay, Athan's graciousness ended as soon as they disembarked from the carriage and entered the dour, formidable hall. The Chalaine barely had time to gaze at the cavernous room before Cadaen and Dason collapsed to the floor as a result of some spell from any one of the multitudinous Churchmen thronged about them.

"Athan!" Mirelle barked. "Just what do you think you are doing?" The Eldephaere wasted no time dragging the unconscious men from the room.

"I am removing potential threats to the prophecy. While I do not have direct evidence that any of them have done anything that merits detention, the Dark Guard do not hold a high place in my trust at the moment. Captain Tolbrook and the others will join them as soon as they arrive, as well, and the rest of Rhugothian soldiers will be sent home as quickly as possible. Fear not, however. Your guards will be unharmed, though I'm sure I have affronted their honor rather gravely." The Chalaine gritted her teeth and bit back an acerbic accusation as Athan continued. "As for you, Mirelle, I am afraid that you, too, have garnered my mistrust, and therefore you will be confined to your quarters, under guard, for the duration of your stay."

"Word of this will get out, Athan, and there will be a price," Mirelle warned him.

"I am only doing this for your protection, of course. The road, as I recall, was particularly inhospitable to you, and your new King could hardly stand by and see his mother-in-law put in peril."

"And what of me," the Chalaine jumped in. "Are you going to lock me up, as well?"

"For now. At least until we can deal with the issue of Chertanne."

"*Deal with the issue?* He is dead!"

"Keep your voice down, Highness. There is hope yet."

The Chalaine couldn't fathom what trickery Athan possessed that could revive her dead husband, but she hugged her mother before soldiers escorted Mirelle out a side door, and the bulk of the Churchmen left to attend to other duties. Only Padra Athan and two Eldephaere remained behind. The Church soldiers were both tall, blond, grim, and exactly identical in their appearance.

"These two," Padra Athan announced, indicating the two stiffly bowing soldiers, "will be your new Protectors. They are loyal to the prophecy first and then to you, unlike some of your previous guards. Their names are Adrenne and Bradden, twin brothers of a devout woman who lost her husband recently in one of Joranne's explosions in Mikmir. They are your countrymen, so I thought them a good match for you. I have also arranged for a new handmaiden for you. She should be . . . Ah, yes, there she is."

The Chalaine turned toward the rear of the hall. An unveiled woman with raven black hair and dark eyes approached them, escorted by two veiled girls in plain brown dresses. The unveiled girl was confident in her bearing, though she approached the Padra tentatively after bowing to the Chalaine. Her eyes darted about quickly as if searching for someone.

"Lady Khairn, this is Mena, one of Torbrand's daughters. Where is your veil, Mena?" Padra Athan asked.

"I thought my father would be here. He commands me never to wear it in his presence. Is he nearby, your Grace?"

"I am afraid your father turned up missing a couple of weeks ago. You will wear your veil as is custom among your people."

Mena curtseyed. "Thank you, your Grace."

"Show the Chalaine to her chambers. She will be kept there for her safety for the next several days as we work out all the details to guarantee her security and that of the Ha'Ulrich."

Mena curtsied again. "This way, Highness. You will have my room, and I will take the one next to yours."

"I don't want to displace you," the Chalaine said as they left the entryway of the hall and proceeded down a dark hallway, the twins following at a discreet distance. "Whatever I am given after the last several months will be a luxury. A comfortable bed and a warm fire are all I will insist upon. If you'll forgive me, you seem a bit anxious. Is something wrong?"

"There are some people I was expecting . . . hoping . . . to see. They were a part of your Dark Guard, I believe. To own the truth, I wanted to see my husband."

"You have a husband among the Dark Guard?" the Chalaine asked incredulously.

"It was a particular arrangement of my father's." Mena blushed. "After he conquered Tolnor, I was given to Gerand Kildan as wife. Did he never mention it?"

"I am afraid not, though I had little conversation with him, as he wasn't one of my Protectors."

The tears welled up in Mena's eyes, and she turned away until she could force down the emotion. "Then Gen was right," she finally said. "Gerand must despise me as a matter of honor."

"And you've spoken to Gen?" *This woman is full of surprises.*

"He never mentioned me? I assumed since he is your Protector that he might have brought up his visit to the Ellenais shard."

"He didn't. He was very miserly with details about his past."

"And where is he, and the rest of your Dark Guard? I should think, from the stories, that Mikkik himself couldn't drag that man from your side. And where is your husband? He so coveted Torbrand's throne that I expected him to sleep in it for at least a week after returning."

The Chalaine smiled wanly and checked the *animon* in her pocket. "I have much to share with you, Mena, but perhaps when we are alone. I am afraid, however, that most of what I have to say is not pleasant or hopeful."

Mena nodded, face glum, and they proceeded through the hallways in silence.

While the Chalaine was grateful to be indoors, Ironkeep presented a sharp contrast to her home in Mikmir. Her mother's Hall reflected art, refinement, and beauty, whereas Ironkeep's theme centered around trophies and strength. The entirety of the structure was wood, and it felt like a sprawling lodge. Weapons of all varieties hung from the walls, intermixed with animal heads and various appendages of defeated enemies. Red carpets covered the floors in the public areas, while the natural wood of the floor was left bare in the living quarters save for a few plain rugs.

During the following week, the Chalaine found herself in company with her new handmaiden almost constantly, and she decided that she liked the young woman. Her feelings for Gerand revealed a tender, romantic heart, while her conversation demonstrated a maturity, intelligence, and self-command. The Chalaine told her what had happened during the journey to Elde Luri Mora, hiding her own feelings for Gen and his identity as the Ilch. In turn, Mena related Gen's visit to Ellenais to her, providing more insight into a time Gen rarely spoke of.

Mena told her a few days later that Padra Athan had spread the word about Gen in the immediate environs around Ironkeep, and the Chalaine vehemently denounced his actions as the most vile and baseless slander. Mena took her side of the story without question. Aughmerians, it seemed, held the Church and its leaders in low esteem and had long suspected them of all manner of trickery and political maneuvering.

True to his word, Athan, faking commands from Chertanne, ordered the Chalaine into seclusion. Only Mena was allowed traffic in and out of the Chalaine's chambers to serve her needs, though she proved adept at teasing information from guards and other servants about the keep and delivering it to the Chalaine. From what Mena could gather, Athan had ordered the entire Council of Padras to haste to Ironkeep, though bad weather and distance would delay their arrival for some time. Athan kept Mirelle under the same restrictions as her daughter, again, for the ostensible reason of keeping her safe.

But while the Chalaine at first found Athan's measures to be punitive, she realized that her own seclusion was part of a larger plan to keep the secret of Chertanne's death, for if the Chalaine were allowed to wander the halls of Ironkeep, then why wouldn't Chertanne be afforded the same privilege? And from what Mena told her, speculation about the absence of the High King mounted daily, while the nature of Aughmerian culture provided the Chalaine the cover of unimportance.

As the days rolled slowly by, the Chalaine busied herself with reading and playing games with Mena. Against all odds and deepening snow, the Padras trickled into the keep by ones and twos, and at the end of three weeks Mena reported that the entire Council had arrived and had met in seclusion for two days straight. The Chalaine could only imagine their consternation and bewilderment. What does one do with a dead Ha'Ulrich? The Chalaine could only think of two possible options. They could have faith that the baby growing in her slowly expanding belly would redeem them without the Ha'Ulrich's help, or they could find a suitable lookalike for Chertanne and let the charade begin in earnest.

The next day, one of her guards—Adrenne or Bradden, she couldn't tell which—knocked on the door and informed her that Athan had summoned her to meet with the Council in an hour.

So they have come to some decision, have they? she thought. While inwardly disdainful, excitement welled up within her at the prospect of knowing *anything* about how the next months would play out.

Athan had seen to it that properly noble attire was delivered to her shortly after her arrival, though to her dismay it was all white. She found the most ostentatious outfit of the lot and donned it quickly. Once ready, she followed between her two Protectors as one led the way and the other brought up the rear. Serving women, veiled and young, ogled her as she strode by, whispers blooming behind her.

Adrenne and Bradden led her back into the Great Hall and then up a flight of stairs to a large assembly area accessed through a pair of enormous doors that creaked wildly as they were opened. The room itself was unpleasant enough. Ironkeep had no glass for windows, so most of the shutters in the room were shut, the only light emanating from a roaring fire at one end of the room and a set of braziers glowing orange. A slight haze hovered about the room as she entered and walked steadily toward a long table on a plum-colored rug in the center of the room.

The Council rose at her approach, regarding her with curiosity. *I wonder if Athan has poisoned them against me or told them of our little 'bargain.'* Athan signaled for her to sit next to him at a finely appointed chair set at the corner of the head of the table where he presided. Books littered the table, along with parchment and quills, although from a quick glance it appeared they had all turned whatever notes they had been writing upside down to not attract her scrutiny.

Once she had seated herself, the screeching doors boomed shut, leaving her alone with the Council.

"We thank you for coming, High Queen," Athan said. "I trust your needs have been adequately met these past few weeks?"

"Yes, thank you."

Athan sat and the council followed suit. "Very well. Let's get to the matter at hand. So you know, we have warded this room against prying ears so that we may speak freely. I have spent the last two days informing the Council of every detail of our journey, including my feelings about Gen, your actions, and the actions of your mother. I have also informed them frankly about Chertanne's death, and we have spent the greater part of the last day discussing what options are available to remedy this."

"Remedy?" the Chalaine exclaimed. "We must tell the people the truth! I know it will cause panic, but you cannot hope to carry on this ruse indefinitely. I know you trust your Eldephaere and the Churchmen under your control to guard this secret, but it will get out, if it hasn't already."

"We agree," Athan answered. "Rumor and suspicion already ply their corrosive trade within Ironkeep, and with Ethris and Torbrand loose, I fear what weeds of dissent they may be sowing. Perhaps you know where they have run off to?"

"I am afraid not," she answered truthfully.

"I didn't think so. I will have to pay a visit to your mother for that, I suspect. At any rate, we have brought you here to inform you that we believe there is a way to restore your husband to life and set the prophecy back on course."

"What? No one has had power to raise the dead since Eldaloth! Do you think I could do it? If you do, you are mistaken!"

Athan stood and paced around the table. "There are a great many mysteries that were forbidden to be spoken after the death of Eldaloth, knowledge dark and evil that would only serve to foment corruption and strife if it were known. What I am going to tell you now only those who are accepted into this Council are permitted to know. We have had some debate about whether to tell you at all, but I believe it important that you understand so that you can help us. Before I do, I wish to have your word that you will not spread what I tell you to anyone beyond this room."

"As you wish."

"Very well. In public Church doctrine, we teach that Mikkik slew Eldaloth after killing Owena and Haldir, the gods over Myn and Duam. We do not preach the particulars of these murders under the guise of ignorance or the scantiness of the ancient record. In truth, however, we have precise information on how Mikkik planned and implemented these evil deeds, thanks to a dissenter in Mikkik's ranks who refused at the last to participate in Eldaloth's death."

"Aldemar," the Chalaine said quietly, but not quietly enough. The Padras near her gasped in shock.

"How do you know that name, Chalaine?" Athan said, eyes wide. "It is the deepest secret."

"I have spoken to him," she said. "I do not care to share the particulars at this time other than to say that he showed me the manner of Eldaloth's death."

"Fascinating! But you must tell us more! That he still lives and would show himself to you after all this time is extraordinary and may lend us some knowledge we can use."

"He did not choose to see me. Please ask me no more, for I will say nothing more of it."

"Will you at least share with us what he showed you?"

The Chalaine acquiesced and related the vision to them. Quills dashed over hastily shuffled parchments as she spoke. "What I sensed that he wished me to learn was the difference between the wholeness and virtue of Ki'Hal before Eldaloth's death in contrast to what it is now," the Chalaine continued. "He also wanted to impress upon me the horror of what Mikkik had done to a being who was kind, just, and divine. It is something I will not forget."

"Thank you, Highness, for this favor," Athan said, "and we urge you to reconsider telling us the rest, though I will not press you now. What you have seen is the key to the first secret. The world knows that there are three great powers: Trys, Myn, and Duam. What Mikkik knew was that there is a fourth: blood. After Aldemar forsook his master, he sank into despair. In an attempt to atone for what he had done, he wrote every detail of the magic worked by his master in pursuit of his twisted ambition. That book lies in the chest against the wall, there, under some of the strongest magical protections placed upon any object in this world.

"The second secret, and the one that most particularly is of concern to us, is that blood holds the power to both utterly destroy—what we would call annihilation—and to revive, or unite soul and body together again. Of course, Mikkik was interested in the former while we are concerned with the latter.

"The third secret Aldemar revealed was that the blood of the several races was not of equal strength. The blood of Gods held more power than that of the Millim Eri, the Millim Eri, more than the elves, the elves more than dwarves, the dwarves more than the race of men.

"Lastly was the principle of seven. To utterly destroy another being or to return a soul to the body requires the blood of seven willing victims of the same race or seventy of the next lower race in power of blood. Thus, Mikkik brought seventy of the Mikik Dun to the glade that day for his spell. It is Aldemar's dissension, we believe, that prevented Eldaloth from total annihilation that day."

"So will you petition for seven willing victims to die so that Chertanne might live? Perhaps the Eldephaere?" the

219

Chalaine asked, a knot forming in her stomach.

"Not precisely, for there is a complication. Chertanne, while in race a human, has unique blood that lends him the ability to manipulate Trysmagic. If we wish to revive him to his body with that ability, we have to find humans who also possess that gift. There is only one of those we know of, and you know well who that is."

"Gen." The Chalaine felt a sudden shiver.

"Precisely."

"But there is only one!" the Chalaine said. "You need seven! And not only that, you need a willing victim! I doubt Gen would qualify."

"We need the blood of seven, or in this case, one bled seven times. As for his willingness, I expect you to aid us there. You will heal him so that he may be bled, and you will speak with him to gain his consent."

She shook her head. "This is madness! You don't even know if this will work, do you? Did I not make my regard for Gen plain? How could I in good conscience ask him to submit to this?"

Athan strode straight for her chair, pulled it roughly around, and forced his gaze upon her.

"How can you not? I am not asking him to die. I need his blood. The rest of our bargain will remain as you stipulated it. The prophecy is teetering on the brink of failure, and if you care about this world at all, you *must* lend us your support! If the prophecy is true, then the Child in your belly will need its father to survive the coming battle, whenever it falls upon us.

"There is another complication, as well. Gen escaped from his captors two weeks ago. While I believe he will seek you out anyway, we must ensure that he will. I apologize, your Grace, for the need to do what we are about to. It grieves us, but he must hasten here. Every day Chertanne is absent only causes more unrest and doubt. We must have an end to this."

What thrill the Chalaine felt at learning of Gen's freedom evaporated at Athan's unexplained solution to drive him to her. "Are you saying you are to do something to me to goad him onward?"

"Yes, Chalaine. We know that the bond between you allows him to know where you are and what pains you may be suffering. While we could not let you suffer and endanger the Child, we have a way to let your body feel the pain but in way that you will not sense it. I'm sure that sounds strange, but you must trust me. I will not let harm come to Gen if you aid us in bringing him here to attempt to raise Chertanne."

She squirmed uncomfortably. "I doubt I have much choice, though I do not think it wise of you to let him think that you have harmed me. He will seek me out without your intervention. If you value your lives, leave me alone. Where did he escape?"

"At the Portal gate to Tenswater on his way Mur Eldaloth," Athan reported. "We were taking him there for detention and interrogation. The column fell prey to some powerful magic, no doubt worked by some of your mother's associates. The Council of Padras agreed that he would be a fool to attempt to come to you here, thus our recommendation to add some incentive to convince him to make the attempt. While I understand you objections to the plan, even you would admit that you cannot guarantee his arrival, and we must, therefore, create our own insurance."

Before she could object, Athan closed his eyes momentarily and incanted. At once, her mind seemed to disconnect from her body and float on a pleasant breeze outside of the dark room. Dimly, she recognized Padra Nolan standing and beginning his spell. Somewhere outside the euphoric haze of her mind, she was aware that every nerve of her body shot through with staggering pain. It lasted only a few seconds, and, almost as soon as it had started, it ended. Her capacities returned, and she stood, taking stock of herself.

"I object to being used in this way! How dare you work your magic upon me without my permission! And what of the Child?"

"I apologize for the necessity, Highness," Athan said unapologetically. "You must see that it is for the greater good. We took precautions not to harm the Child. You need not fear."

"I will not do this again," she stated firmly. "When Gen arrives, I must be permitted to talk with him alone if you wish me to convince him to go along with your plan. I don't wish to see any of you before that time."

She left the Council muttering and whispering behind her. She would not be their tool. Fuming, she made short work of the walk back to her quarters where a pacing Mena bit her lip in anticipation of her return.

"What news, Chalaine?" her handmaiden asked once the door was shut.

"Much. But first, I need to get a message to my mother. Can you do that?"

"It will be difficult, but I will try."

"Good."

CHAPTER 62 – TRAP

For two weeks they holed up in the sewer, healing, talking, and dodging the incessant patrols that hunted low and high for the escaped fugitives. Only Torbrand wandered above ground to gather news. The Church militia allowed no one onto or off of Tenswater, and grumpy soldiers searched and scoured every structure at any time of the day or night without warning.

After the fight, a diligent search of the sewers yielded another opening into a small cavern that afforded some relief from the choking stench and damp sewage. Torbrand nearly exhausted himself healing them all, but within hours they felt fit and anxious to move. Unfortunately, the continual presence of marching feet above and sloshing trackers below pinned them underground.

All save Maewen grew accustomed to the smell, and while she strove not to show it, their confinement below ground wore visibly upon her countenance. What light they had filtered in weakly through a small moss-covered street drain, and they did not have enough fresh water to wash away the black muck that stiffened their clothing and rotted their boots. Torbrand's near daily excursions brought fresh food, drink, and bedrolls, but the news remained stale:

Portals closed, soldiers everywhere.

Gen and his companions looked little better than street beggars, uneven beards and ungroomed hair roughening their appearance. White streaks shot through Gen's beard where hair sprouted from scars along his cheeks. The clothes they had worn through the hardships of Elde Luri Mora still hung from their bodies, tattered, stained, and rigid. Only their bearing and fit bodies betrayed that the wearers might be more than they appeared. Gen busied himself by trying to work himself back into shape after lying prone for days in a potion induced stupor.

"How long will they keep this up?" Volney whined after another evening patrol passed overhead. "If they haven't found us by now, surely they realize they won't."

"They will give up," Torbrand asserted from where he sat on the ground, back against the wall. "Thanks to Joranne, they will assume we have magical help, therefore it stands to reason that we could have used one of the Portals to get off the shard. They can't be sure they have rounded up every Portal Mage in the city."

Thunder boomed outside, and they looked at each other hopefully in the weak light. They had waited for rain for days.

"I'm first under the grate if it rains," Maewen pronounced forcefully, moving in the direction of the opening. The rest busied themselves claiming positions and moving their bedrolls away from the probable path of the deluge. To their delight, the rain fell, fresh water roiling down the opening. By the time the storm abated an hour later, they were all clean and cold, wrapping themselves in their bedrolls for warmth.

Sleep came quickly and pleasantly as darkness enveloped them. "A good omen," Volney yawned as he settled in. Gen hoped so. The feeling that he had let down everyone he cared about ran like a dark river through his heart, reminding him of Mikkik's persuasions when the demon's poison took him. *Were there not a hundred before? Will there not be thousands after?* He needed to get clear of the sewer, get his bearings again, and put himself to whatever good use he could.

Two more days passed before a herald on the street above announced that the Portals had reopened and that the watch had ended the lockdown of the city. The herald's message proffered no excuse, but the citizens of Tenswater asked few questions, rejoicing at the end of constant patrols and raids. To the six sewer-weary fugitives straining to hear the proclamation through the slender grate, the news was the key to open their proverbial cell, and after Torbrand procured decent clothing for the young men, they waited until full dark before ascending into the city again.

"We don't want to be caught wandering the streets at night," Torbrand informed them. "The militia take an unkind view of those with business in the dark. We'll sleep in the first inn we find and leave in the evening of the next day. Gen, Maewen, and Hardman will need to stay out of sight, as you are easily recognizable. Volney and Gerand will help me gather what we need to return to Mikmir."

The young men barely heard anything after mention of the inn. The idea of sleeping in an actual bed with a belly full of warm food, bathing in water actually warmed for that purpose, and inhaling the smell of anything other than raw sewage pushed aside all thought for purpose or the future. Creature comforts had appeared with increasing scarcity in their journeyings, and all intended to wring every last pleasure from whatever inn they stumbled upon.

The inn that fell across their path first was the Barrel Cork, more of a drinking establishment than an inn, raucous laughter and juvenile bantering flowing from slurring tongues and out into the street. Maewen scowled at the noise as they walked forward while Hardman daydreamed about a common room brawl.

Torbrand turned toward the rest. "Are you content with

225

this establishment, or would you prefer to chance looking further on? Gen?"

At first the party mistook Torbrand's meaning in addressing Gen, and only when he repeated it with more surprise did they turn to regard their companion who stood stock-still in the street, eyes unfocused, and fists clenched. Maewen crossed to him hurriedly and took his face in her hands, forcing his eyes to hers.

"Look at me, Gen," she intoned softly in Elvish.

Gen blinked several times, and breathed out sharply, face full of worry.

"She is in pain! Awful pain! Who would do that to her?"

"The Chalaine?" Maewen prodded. "What did you feel?"

"I've got to get to her! Something is wrong. It felt like she was burning in a fire! We must go to her!"

"Does she live? Is she still in pain?"

"She lives." He paused, a quizzical expression replacing the alarmed look of moments before. "She seems fine now."

Torbrand strode forward, eying several people who walked nearby, regarding them with curiosity. "We need to have this conversation in a more private place," he admonished.

He led them into a dark alley between the stable and the inn while he went to negotiate with the keeper. Master Rabin provided three empty rooms and promised plenty of food and drink for Torbrand's party. After slinking through the common area, they congregated in one of the plain rooms, closing the creaky door behind them and taking seats on two beds of dubious quality.

Maewen spoke first. "Have you felt anything further?"

"No, she seems perfectly fine now. There was no pain leading up to the burning sensation, either. It is strange."

"What do you want to do?" Maewen asked.

"I don't know. My instinct is to go to her, but I know it would not be wise."

"You should wait, Gen," Maewen opined. "Mirelle wanted you safe in Mikmir, and that really is the best course you could take. This may just be a fluke or an accident of some kind."

The others nodded and murmured in agreement. Gerand stood and placed his hand on Gen's shoulder. "If the Chalaine is in danger, I will gladly go with you to the Abyss and back to help her. But we should wait for a clearer sign before we undertake that journey."

Gen nodded and everyone relaxed, the arrival of hot food and ale stifling all conversation as they savored every bite, ordering a second helping of everything.

"You know," Volney commented as he leaned back and set his plate to the side, "I can still smell that sewer."

"It is still on some of our clothes and gear," Maewen lamented. "Torbrand, do you think Master Rabin could find someone to launder our clothes tomorrow?"

Torbrand rubbed his beard. "With enough money, I think Master Rabin could find a fish swimming in a sand dune. Since Tenswater seems to relish its own cleanliness, I think the request an easy one. We may want to wait to shave until later. Our unkempt appearance helps conceal our identity."

That settled, Torbrand called out and a serving girl nervously gathered their dinnerware and left them to themselves. Before long, the party broke up to sleep, rejoicing in the scant comfort provided by straw mattresses, which, by the smell, most often found use as places to "sleep it off."

The next day dawned cold, brooding clouds moving slowly and spitting flurries or drizzling coldly in fits. They met briefly to review what supplies they should gather for their trek to Mikmir.

"I'm afraid we'll likely have to contend with the snow around the lake," Maewen predicted, "so we'll need warmer clothes for the young men. We need a bow for Gen, as well. Do we have enough for horses?"

"Barely," Torbrand answered, "I am not sure if the prices have come back down since the lockdown was lifted. They had risen fairly high. If we can't afford them, we will be stealing them. I am *not* walking all the way to Mikmir. Those with scruples can return with payment later."

Torbrand, Volney, and Gerand left after taking the morning meal, and the day passed slowly. The boredom and inactivity wore on Hardman the worst. He paced, mumbled, and swung Destiny around listlessly, itching for an opportunity to go stir up trouble. Maewen sat against the door purposefully, throwing Hardman a withering look anytime "Just one drink downstairs?" passed his lips.

Ducking Destiny's careless trajectories in the cramped room provided Gen with a modicum of entertainment while they waited, watching the weather providing the rest. The storm worsened as the day wore on, and when Torbrand and his companions returned, they dripped all over the floor, the two young men shaking with the cold.

"We're all set," Torbrand announced. "Let's eat and hope Mikmir has better weather than this."

"What time of day will it be when we pass through?" Volney asked.

"Midday, I believe," Torbrand replied. "The Portal we will pass through leads to Lipgate, about a day east of the town of Portal Gate along the lake."

"Let's move then," Hardman grumbled. "I am tired of Tenswater."

Mena twisted her hands nervously. Her bold companion sat perfectly at ease, having replaced her more magnificent dress with the plain robes and veil of a servant. Mirelle had set her mind to play the Aughmerian serving woman today in hopes of speaking with her companions in the dungeon and finding some word about Gen. The Chalaine's message about Athan's baiting Gen by causing her fake pain set Mirelle to pacing and plotting.

"Surely he would not be so foolish as to come to Ironkeep!" Mena had suggested two weeks after delivering the Chalaine's message. She hoped as much to comfort the Chalaine's mother—who clearly cared for Gen a vast deal—as to deter the machinations of her plotting mind that so plainly manifested themselves in her troubled eyes.

"You are wrong," Mirelle had answered without deviating from the set course of her pacing. "When it comes to the Chalaine's safety, he will undertake anything, however foolhardy. He will come if Athan keeps at it, and even if he doesn't come, Athan's men are combing the world for him."

After three days, Mirelle had returned a message to the Chalaine that she had a plan to warn Gen to steer clear of Aughmere and Ironkeep, but she said nothing of how save that Mena was to find a way to her quarters on Seventh Day after next.

The time passed slowly, Mena fretting over her unknown role in the former Queen of Rhugoth's plans. The Chalaine expressed full confidence in her mother's abilities, but Mena felt strangely vulnerable under the scrutiny of the Church elite wandering the halls, and she was humbled by her close association with Mirelle and her Holy daughter. She almost missed her father, for no one dared glance at her with even a hint of malice under his obsessed gaze. With him gone, she felt unprotected.

While she was allowed to leave the Chalaine for short periods at a time, Mena could not stay away long without rousing suspicion. In order to help Mirelle, Mena had located another serving woman with Mirelle's height and complexion with which to switch places for the time she was gone. This, in itself, did not worry her, for one of the veil's only virtues was facilitating this kind of deception. The women of Aughmere had practiced it for years. Thoughts of what Mirelle had planned and what discovery would cost them both set loose the butterflies in her stomach and sapped the energy from her limbs.

On Seventh Day, she walked into Mirelle's quarters to find the former First Mother dressed in servant's garb. Mirelle, a prisoner, intended to walk the halls of Ironkeep right under the nose of Church Mages and soldiers. Mena wrung her hands as she approached, but Mirelle's carefree manner calmed her. Perhaps the First Mother only planned for a short visit to her daughter and it would all be over.

"When are our replacements to arrive?" Mena asked.

"Any time now," Mirelle replied, affixing the plain brown veil mesh over her head and smoothing the brown frock. "I asked for my breakfast late this morning."

"I don't know of any woman here as tall as you are," Mena warned. "I fear you will be conspicuous. You also walk the wrong way."

"Is there some other way to walk than one foot in front of the other?"

"Well, no," Mena returned nervously, "but you strut about as if you own the place. You must walk as if the place owns you. Hunch a little. And it would be best if I did the talking. I don't think you could come off as properly meek."

"As you wish. This is foreign to me, but my need is great and it will inspire my better efforts, I assure you."

A knock at the door signaled the start of their adventure as their replacements entered. The woman Mirelle was to mimic was fully four inches shorter than her counterpart and not as blonde. "I am the best they could do," she apologized. Mirelle waved off her concern and ate her breakfast calmly while everyone else engaged in an informal fidgeting contest.

"Where do you intend to go?" Mena inquired as Mirelle

finished up.

"Well, I need to get into Athan's head, but his quarters will have to do."

"What!"

"After that, I should like to get into the dungeon and speak with some of my people there. If we can manage it, I want to see my daughter."

Mena, flummoxed into muteness, could only follow dumbly along as Mirelle gathered the plates and strode for the door. The former First Mother was crazy.

"Ah, yes," Mirelle said, "the place owns me."

Stooping slightly at the shoulders, Mirelle put her hand on the door handle and turned back to Mena. "When I leave the room, do I go left or right?"

She pointed to the left and Mirelle yanked open the door without further delay. Mena rushed up behind her, not daring to look at the Eldephaere guards as they passed by, but feeling their icy stare, nonetheless.

"I will need you to lead, Mena," Mirelle whispered after they were safely away.

Mena gulped and struck out toward the kitchen.

"Tuck your veil into the neck of your dress," Mena instructed.

"Why?" Mirelle asked, complying.

"It signals to the others that you are up to no good, and the women in the keep will know not to hinder or engage you."

"Clever."

Mena gained confidence the farther they went, noticing that the Churchmen and soldiers barely spared them a passing glance despite Mirelle's utterly unconvincing attempt at ambulatory humility.

"Slower!" Mena admonished between the frequent "Hunch!" and "Eyes down!" Only the general thickheaded unobservant nature of men in general would spare them a cell. Every serving woman they passed gawked unobtrusively at the swan trying to pass for a chicken in the coop. Once they managed the kitchen, Mena breathed easier.

"How do we get to Athan's quarters?" Mirelle asked after setting the dishes on an already overflowing table and pulling Mena into a dank pantry.

"I know the wing where the Padras are quartered, but I cannot say which door is his. We will need to inquire. We also need a good reason for going there, and I personally would like assurances that he will *not* be there."

"He will not," Mirelle assured her. "I've already learned that he rarely visits his quarters during the day."

"And who did you learn all this from?" Mena whispered.

"Leda and Brince," Mirelle answered. "They serve the Padras during the day."

"Look," Mena implored. "You stay here while I go ask around. If you keep your veil inside your dress and if you stay inside this pantry, no one will bother you. You are too tall and too regal, no matter how you are dressed."

"As you wish, dear."

After Mena left the pantry, Mirelle leaned against the shelf and tried to conjure up a way to warn Gen to stay away from Ironkeep. When she had first arrived in the Aughmerian stronghold, she resigned herself to a dull winter and spring isolated from news and good company. Fortunately, the sisterhood of the repressed Aughmerian women surprised her with their ability to work around their restrictions and bring word of the world at large. Even so, there was little to tell until Mena managed to send Leda with news of Athan's plans to lure Gen to Ironkeep. Mirelle needed no other incentive to act.

Mirelle turned and squinted out a crack in the pantry door as Joselin, Shadan Khairn's first wife, entered. Mirelle knew Athan had requested that she and several other of Torbrand's wives and progeny come from the Ellenais shard to attend to the management of the household while Chertanne and the Padras lodged there. Joselin, while arrayed like all the other women, carried her stout frame with an unmistakable authority, and her voice cut through the din of the kitchen with a warlord's edge.

Mirelle remembered well Joselin's visit to her on the first day of her confinement, probably out of curiosity rather than necessity. While Mirelle could not fairly say that Joselin possessed a mean-spirited temperament, the way she profusely apologized for Athan forcing that "monster child" Mena on the Chalaine and the lengthy diatribe afterward about Torbrand's favorite daughter, men, and Ironkeep in general, Mirelle knew a bitter woman when she saw one.

"What's this I hear about some skulking business going on today?" she thundered, ending all conversation. The serving girls worked twice as quickly but silently while Joselin afflicted each one with a withering glare. Mirelle slunk back into the pantry and prayed that Mena had the good sense to stay away until Joselin cleared out.

"A flock of mute magpies, are ya?" Joselin grumbled. "Well. Hmmm. If I see any veils tucked in today, someone will be swimming in cauldron grease and chamber pots until Eldaloth says otherwise!"

Mirelle yanked the veil out of the neck of her dress and hoped that Joselin had no quarrel with the pantry. She breathed as quietly as she could while Joselin stalked around the kitchen taking time to personally criticize each woman there.

"And what a surprise," Joselin exclaimed, interrupting one of her more spirited attempts at demeaning her underlings, "Mena."

Mirelle cursed under her breath and chanced a peek out the crack, finding Mena rigid in the kitchen doorway facing Joselin like a deer trapped by the hunter. "I should have expected that with reports of an uppity woman with her veil tucked in roaming the halls that you would be involved."

The pudgy accuser sauntered closer, clearly relishing this opportunity to debase someone she truly hated rather than merely despised. She grabbed a wooden spoon from off of a nearby table and thrust it in Mena's direction.

"Don't think that just because the Padras have assigned you to the Chalaine that you can do whatever you please in *my* house. She won't be here forever, and your father is a fugitive now. When the time comes, I'll have my claws in you as deep as I can push 'em!"

"Yes, Mistress," Mena squeaked.

"So what are you up to? I see your veil is tucked in."

"Nothing, Mistress. The Chalaine. . ." A sharp whack of the spoon to the head brought Mena up short.

"Don't *nothing* me. You're never up to nothing, you spoiled, lazy wretch!"

"If I am lazy, then certainly I must be up to nothing sometimes."

Whack! "Don't sass me, smart mouth. What are you up to?"

"The Chalaine wanted more food! The baby grows, and she is hungry!"

Joselin raised the spoon reflexively but found no cause to strike. "So why is that a cause for tucking in the veil? Seems harmless."

"Padra Athan monitors her food closely. The Chalaine didn't want him to know."

From the pantry, Mirelle felt like applauding Mena's quick thinking.

"Is that so?"

"Yes."

"Well, the Chalaine shouldn't be snacking behind the Padra's back, and I am surprised you would go along with it! What if the Chalaine got hold of a rotten ham or old fish? Or maybe a rat's done his business in the wheat and the Chalaine got sick and lost the holy baby? How would you feel then?"

"I do not wish to undermine the Padra, but I cannot disobey the Chalaine! She is the Holy Mother of prophecy! Guide me, Joselin! Should I comply with the Chalaine's request or return and tell her that you say she is in the wrong and should stay hungry until Padra Athan's command?"

"Well," Joselin mumbled, stalling after Mena's unexpected transfer of the onus of the issue to her. "I *suppose* that you *should* do as the Chalaine requests, only you tell her to get permission from Padra Athan himself in the future."

"Yes, Mistress."

"Well, get on with you, then. Eldaloth knows the women in Ironkeep have seen you lollygagging around quite enough these past months."

Mirelle exhaled as Joselin marched from the room. Mena retrieved a serving platter, rubbing the bumps on her head with her other hand.

"The Chalaine will heal those for you, if we manage to see her," Mirelle said as Mena joined her in the pantry. "Did you find out what you need to know?"

"Yes. We are fortunate. The women who clean the Padras' quarters will let us join their party today. They await us in the Great Hall. I suppose I won't be needing this." Mena put the tray on one of the shelves. "Now remember. . ."

"I know," Mirelle stopped her. "Hunch. Eyes down. Slow. The place owns me. Let's go."

As they walked toward the Great Hall, the number of men and women they encountered increased. Mirelle had to remind her nervous companion to slow down and stop fidgeting as they crossed through the tall, dark doors that led into the immense room. Four other women in brown dresses awaited them there, having brought buckets, brooms, and cloths enough for the addition to their party. Wordlessly they set off through a side door, Mena grabbing a bucket and Mirelle a broom. They climbed a flight of slippery polished wooden stairs, the women ahead of them talking quickly in low tones.

"You're holding that like a scepter!" Mena whispered.

"There can't be two ways about it! How is one supposed to hold a broom?" Mirelle inquired with some irritation. The women in front of them snickered.

"Not so straight up and down," Mena counseled. "Haven't you ever swept before?"

"I can honestly say this is the first time I've ever handled this particular cleaning instrument."

"You would be worthless around here," Mena observed.

Mirelle smirked. "True, though I find the thought bothers me little."

All talking died as they ascended into a brightly lit hallway furnished with soft red rugs, lamp light beaming through the crystal glass that imprisoned the flame. An Eldephaere guard stood at post in front of every door. Mirelle's breath caught in her throat as Padra Nolan left his room, face somber, and regarded the group. Athan's lackey. Mirelle wanted to claw his face, too. Remembering their subterfuge, she hunched doubly as deep and tried to install as lowly an opinion of herself as she could while the Padra walked unwittingly by.

Mena's bucket stopped shaking as Padra Nolan's steps faded down the stairs. Taking Mirelle by the arm, she led her past the stoic guard and through the first door on the left, the other women breaking up and passing through other doors farther on. Mena shut the door and exhaled.

"Open the shutters," Mirelle ordered, leaning her broom against the wall. "I long to see the sunlight."

"It will be cold."

"I can live with the cold for a bit if I can just see the sun."

Mena complied, and both looked out over the snowy courtyard. The sunlight, while winter-weak, infused Mirelle with energy. The massive iron-banded gates of Ironkeep stood open as wagons, horses, and soldiers passed through. A couple of Padras wandered about, overseeing everything.

Mirelle sighed. "We'd best be about our business."

"What are we to do?" Mena asked.

"You clean. I'll look about."

Mena humphed. Mirelle regarded her with a smile. "Careful, or you'll risk appearing as useless as I am." Mena swept listlessly as Mirelle rifled through the papers on Padra Athan's table.

"Anything good?" Mena asked after a while.

"Not really, though it is humorous how he goes on about how Chertanne is deciding this and organizing that. Chertanne is much busier dead than he ever was alive. Being Pontiff has certainly invigorated his work ethic. Nothing I can use, unfortunately, but I think my best bet lies over there."

Mirelle crossed the room to where a simple chest sat on the floor.

"It's locked," Mena stated flatly, dipping the rag in the water to start some dusting. "And likely has spells on it."

Mirelle grinned. "Well, I hope you can keep a secret."

Mena dropped the rag on the floor and crossed to her. "What's that?"

"Well, I've a few skills of my own." The former First Mother removed a pin from her hair. "The spells I will have to risk, but my first Protector knew a few things he passed onto me."

Mirelle bent the end of the pin, and after she probed in the keyhole for several long moments, the lock clicked and opened. She lifted the lid easily and stared inside, eyes wide.

"How did you. . ."

"That son of a whore!" Mirelle exclaimed, face livid. There in Athan's chest sat the mirror Ethris had stolen from the Church, the Assassin's Glass. She plucked it out, holding it like a dagger. "I should have known!"

"Quietly, Highness," Mena admonished nervously.

"I should have known!" Mirelle repeated, voice subdued. "Chertanne would never have the brains or the guts to kill Ogbith. There will be a reckoning for this!"

"What are you talking about?" Mena asked, face inquisitive but apprehensive.

Mirelle walked to the window, needing fresh air. She told Mena the story of Regent Ogbith's murder, the young woman agape at the information.

"But wait!" Mirelle burst out. "This is it! This is all I need." She turned toward the window. "Show me Gen!"

Mena scooted close to her her, eyes wide as the mirror swirled blue, finally settling on a cloaked figure walking down a street in a breezy snow. Gen stopped suddenly, rubbing his chest and turning to the side, eyes searching. The face was unmistakable. His eyes peered directly through the small Portal at the two of them.

"Who are you?" he asked, eyes searching.

Mirelle ripped the veil from her head with her free hand, Mena following suit. Others crowded in around Gen.

"Father! Gerand!" Mena said, voice soft with wonder. Mirelle thought she detected a particular note of pleasure in her voice for the Prince of Tolnor.

"Mirelle," Gen said. "Are you all right? The Chalaine. . ."

"I am fine. Listen to me Gen, listen carefully. The Chalaine, well, the pain that you feel from the Chalaine is Padra Athan's doing. He is. . ."

Behind Mirelle, the door hinges creaked. Fire shot through her veins and she stumbled. Beside her, Mena gasped in pain. Mirelle gritted her teeth, turning. Padra Athan stood in the doorway, Joselin behind.

"You are done, Mirelle," he growled.

The agony intensified. Mirelle fell back against the desk,

the mirror spinning out of her hand and shattering on the corner of the table. Padra Athan released the spell, the pain subsiding. She felt like someone had twisted her into knots. Athan sprinted to inspect the shards of the mirror that lay scattered about the floor reflecting the brilliant light from the window.

His dark gaze fell on her. "It's ruined! You meddlesome woman! You have meddled your last!"

Mirelle struggled to her feet, rubbing the muscles in her neck. "How dare you accuse me of meddling when you slaughtered Regent Ogbith! You are a murderer and a coward!"

"Leave us, Joselin," Athan ordered, "and take Mena with you to the kitchens until I come for her. Not a word of this to anyone, or you'll regret it."

Joselin, properly cowed, grabbed Mena by the sleeve and fled. Athan closed the door and leaned heavily against it, rubbing his temples. "Yes, I had Regent Ogbith assassinated. His bungling command doomed the caravan, and you know it."

"And killing him was the only way to deal with the issue? He followed the plans meticulously drawn out and endorsed by the Church. How is he to blame for what happened? If Shadan Khairn had command, it would have ended just as badly. We should have followed Gen and Maewen's advice."

"I disagree, and I won't take the time to debate what has been. I have to deal with what is to be done. While I can't always see a clear path before me, I can see the one in front of you, and you should thank me. You and Mena will enjoy more difficult accommodations from now on, but I think you'll like your company better. Guard!"

"You'll pay for what you've done, Athan!" Mirelle warned him. "You cannot do Eldaloth's work with Mikkik's methods. You are the most faithless of us all!"

Athan appeared stung by her accusations, but anger

burned deep within his eyes. "Take her to her beloved Dark Guard," he ordered the sneering Eldephaere. "The First Mother will spend the rest of her stay in Ironkeep enjoying the squeaking of rats and madmen!"

The Portal to Kingsblood Lake and Mikmir awaited not one hundred yards down the road, but everyone in the group stood in befuddled amazement at what they had just witnessed. Mirelle's desperate and painfully terminated communication angered Gen and stoked his worries afresh. For several long moments they merely stared at each other or at nothing at all as thoughts and emotions wrangled with reason to form some sort of plan.

"I cannot go to Ironkeep," Maewen said first. "I have errands to accomplish for the First Mother and for Ethris, as do Hardman and Torbrand. Gen, I know what you will do, but it is exactly what Athan wants."

"We'll see if it's what he wants after I get there," Gen growled, mind set. "I cannot hide in Mikmir while Mirelle and the Chalaine are treated in such a manner."

Torbrand stepped in front of Gen and met his gaze. "Remember what I taught you. Athan knows you care for Mirelle and the Chalaine more than anyone. He is using them to get to you. They are bait. If you want to frustrate Athan, then get to Mikmir and do not go near the people you love." He dropped his voice to a whisper. "You know what I feel for Mena, and I would go to set her free from that place, but not on Athan's terms. All the sword training in Ki'Hal cannot overcome magic! Mirelle and the Chalaine would agree with me on this."

Gen was unmoved. "What you argue is wisdom. I know very well that this trap is set for me. But Mirelle's communication convinced me that their pain is real. If

Athan wants me badly enough to hurt the Chalaine—of all people!—then they cannot be safe while I live. An end to their suffering will only come by their escape or by my death. I will go to Ironkeep so that one or the other can happen."

"I will go with Gen," Gerand announced after a short silence. "If Mirelle and the Chalaine are being treated in such a fashion, then the Dark Guard must be dead or imprisoned. I go for my brothers and for my Queen."

"As do I," Volney joined in. "I will not let Aughmerians maltreat my countrymen and my Queen without answering for it, though the journey be hard and cold."

Hardman appeared torn, face scrunching and hand caressing Destiny's handle. "A rescue in Ironkeep does sound like more fun than I've had in years. . ."

"General, you cannot go back on your word to Mirelle!" Maewen reproached him. "Your part is critical! We need you in Mikmir, and there are no two ways about it. If Gen succeeds in Ironkeep, it will be through stealth and cunning, not a rousing fight against an entire fort full of soldiers."

"Yes, yes, I see," Hardman relented. "Stealth and cunning are rather dull. Oh well. We part ways here, lad."

"Thank you for coming for us," Gen said.

Maewen came forward and stared into his eyes with as much authority as she could muster. "What you are doing is a mistake, Gen. I cannot give you my blessing, but I do hope to see you again. You will be on your own. We do not dare say a word of what we just witnessed to any of the Rhugothian aristocracy, or there will be war."

"I understand."

"May Eldaloth bless your foolish heart."

"Thank you, Maewen."

"Gen," Torbrand said, "I am with Maewen on this, but if you insist on going, I can shorten your journey by a couple of weeks and get you inside Ironkeep more easily than you might think. Maewen, can we spare an hour so I can teach Gen a few things about Ironkeep and speed him on his journey?"

"Certainly."

"Very well, let's get inside for a little while."

"I'll just go to a tavern while. . ." Hardman began.

"No, you won't," Maewen insisted.

They started back along the street, searching for a suitable place to talk.

"I wonder who the gorgeous dark-haired girl was with Mirelle?" Volney asked.

"She was very pretty, but probably one of the slaves," Gerand speculated.

"She is not a slave. That was your wife," Gen informed Gerand, "Mena."

"What!?"

"You heard him," Volney laughed. "Perhaps your marriage doesn't seem quite as repugnant as it did a few months ago?"

Gerand glowered, but to Gen's eye, it did not seem as determined a glower as it was when Gen first handed him Torbrand's letter in Mikmir.

CHAPTER 63 – ELDEPHAERE

"I swear those two have been following us for at least two miles," Volney warned them again. "We need to lose them."

Bitterly cold winds had lashed Rhugoth from the time they had set foot on the shard cluster after parting ways with Torbrand, Maewen, and Hardman in Tenswater. As yet the wind had kept little company with snow or sleet, but the cold carried a moist weight that breached any fortification set against it. The chill in Tenswater, by comparison, was a whimpering mewling.

The road took Gen, Volney, and Gerand through a Portal that led to the less inhabited northern provinces of Rhugoth while their companions proceeded through a different one leading to Mikmir in the south. The Portal opened into the small and charming village of Aberlee set alongside a line of low hills of long grass. They passed the night in comfort in the Sweetberry Inn and set off early in the morning to follow a lightly used road that hugged the Deer River to their right. By riding hard, they hoped to reach Chale a little after nightfall and then Nowain, their intended destination, a day after that.

Gen glanced over his shoulder. "They've been with us

since this morning. We picked them up at the Sweetberry Inn last night. Didn't you notice them in the common room? Eldephaere."

"No," Volney answered. "Did you, Gerand?"

"I noticed one of them. Why do you think they are Eldephaere, Gen?"

"They all seem to have the same glassy look," Gen said. "It's as if they are somehow stripped of every desire except to serve the Church or the prophecy, so they sit blankly, tools waiting on the workbench for a hand to put them to use."

"Do you think they are following us?" Volney whispered.

"Most likely."

"How could they possibly have tracked us from Tenswater?" Gerand asked incredulously.

"I don't think they tracked us at all," Gen speculated. "I think the Church placed a few of them outside every Portal as soon as they shut down Tenswater. They probably did not expect us to come this way, which is why there are only two rather than twenty."

"Do you think that Maewen, Torbrand, and Hardman ran into trouble, then?" Volney questioned.

Gen smiled wryly. "Well, I think we could safely say that Maewen and her companions are the trouble. They do have one advantage. The Portal to Lipgate is heavily used and easier to sneak into."

"Sneaking Hardman anywhere is like trying to sneak Mikkik into a packed Church. The man is terrifying—especially those teeth and the disgusting pants."

Gerand smiled and turned to Gen. "What do you think the Eldephaere will do? Ambush us?"

"They would if they had greater numbers. But as it is, I think they will be content to watch and report. I don't know if they have members in Chale or Nowain, but we'll need to be on our guard." *And,* Gen thought, *if they believe*

I'm the Ilch, they'll fear my magic.

"Do you think they know where we're going?" Gerand followed.

"My guess is they'll assume we're heading to Mikmir or some hideout here in the north. According to Torbrand, a couple of Church lackeys shouldn't know about the existence of the Portal in Nowain. Chances are, however, that Ironkeep will be crawling with Eldephaere. You must be wary when you fight them. They have no thought for their own lives. They will take a blade to the gut if they can put one through your heart."

"That's nice," Volney commented after another troubled glance behind them.

During the day they tried to coax the persistent pair into passing them or into a situation where they might get a better look at them, but if Gen and his companions stopped, the two Eldephaere stopped. If they rode toward them, the Eldephaere would ride away.

"Maybe we should ambush them before we get to Chale," Gerand suggested. "If there are other Eldephaere there, we cannot risk them informing others about our whereabouts or growing in numbers to attack us."

"I've thought the same," Gen agreed. "I have tried to think of a way we could accomplish it, since they seem determined not to approach us. We could try galloping ahead and out of sight so we could lay the trap, or we could split up and force them to follow one of us while the other two double back." But then something Gen had read in the books about Trysmagic came to mind. "But let's ride on a while longer and see if we can't scout a place that might provide us with a tactical advantage."

They rode on, the Deer River flowing steadily by, the water cold and dark, but not frozen. Gen turned his head around briefly and used magic to break the saddle buckle of the rider closest to the river. As expected, the rider tipped, and in doing so pulled the reins to the right. The horse careened toward the river, stopping short of going in, but not before the Eldephaere landed unceremoniously in icy water along a shallow bank lined with brown grass.

Gen found grins on both his companions' faces. "Here's our chance!" he exclaimed. "Ride hard!"

Heels jabbed into horseflesh as they bolted down the road, wind numbing their faces. They raced around a low hill and slowed in shock. Along a low rock wall a handful of Church soldiers stared anxiously in their direction as they fumbled with equipment in an attempt to hastily remount their horses. These wore no disguise, white tabards with a sliver of a moon covering jangling chain mail.

"Cut through them!" Gen commanded, reasserting his heels into his mount's flanks. Their speedy flight and drawn swords prompted most of the soldiers to a scrambling retreat to the side of the road, the single brave soldier willing to accept the charge paying for his courage with Gen's sword taking his arm off at the elbow. The three pushed the horses until they lathered before slowing down and listening behind them for signs of pursuit.

"How many did you count, Gen?" Gerand asked.

"There were eight on the side of the road. The one in the middle will likely not be joining the pursuit. If we leave the road, the grass will make for easy tracking. If we can keep ahead of them, we may be able to turn down a side road for some of the farms and take a more indirect route to Norwain. Worse comes to worse, I think we can take them. The weather, however, I do not think we can overcome."

They rode on at a steady pace, necks sore from frequent twists to watch the road behind. Twice they caught sight of a single Eldephaere rider just behind a bend, but he would turn his horse and ride away before they could accost him. After a third occurrence, Gen grabbed his bow and quiver and hopped down.

"Take my horse ahead. Ride slow, and I'll catch up to

you soon."

Gerand and Volney required no explanation. Gen strung his bow and ducked into the thick grass and shrubs along the river. He blew on his hands to warm them, and, hearing the expected patter of horse hooves, strung an arrow and waited. The scout emerged a short time later, riding cautiously, eyes searching. Gen pulled back into the undergrowth, waiting until the back of the rider was toward him before stepping out and loosing the arrow in one fluid motion.

The rider's back arched, arms flailing, as the arrow struck the small of his back. Writhing in pain, he fell from the horse, screaming a warning. Gen sprinted forward, commandeering the horse and darting ahead to join Gerand and Volney.

"Did you kill him?" Volney asked.

"No," Gen reported, taking the reins of his original horse from his friend. "A wounded man is much more difficult to deal with than a dead one, provided they care about their men."

The three pressed forward at an even pace, the air chilling with each mile. They ate from horseback, eyes and ears wary for any sign of ambush or pursuit. During the afternoon, broad snowflakes drifted down from low dark clouds, their density slowly increasing as the sun dropped. An inch of fresh powder lay on the ground before they paused to rest the horses and take their supper.

"We'll be easy to track now," Gerand observed as he took a swig from the waterskin he kept near his body. The icy cold seeped through their clothing, the horses' breath shooting out in clouds from their nostrils as they stamped uncomfortably at the ground. Gerand asked, "Are we going to have to spend the night out here?"

Before Gen could answer the question, the sound of galloping hooves behind them brought them on guard. "They're coming for us," Gen announced. "The pursuit ends here. Mind what I told you about how they fight."

Gerand and Volney drew swords while Gen dropped to the ground and unlimbered his bow. He barely had time to nock an arrow before the first rider of the galloping charge came into view through the falling snow. The man stood in the stirrups, sword high. Upon seeing his prey he yelled fiercely. Gen's first shot took the soldier in the chest and off the horse backward, and Gen's second shot took another Eldephaere in the neck.

Snow flew from hooves as the remaining six Eldephaere pushed their horses and accelerated toward their victims. Gen dropped his bow and swung up onto his horse before drawing his sword.

"Take a defensive posture!" Gen yelled. "Let them pass through!" Gen doubted Volney and Gerand heard a word of his instructions over the roar of hooves and the battle yells of the Eldephaere. The charge tore through them like an ill wind, and, to their dismay, the Eldephaere struck at the horses rather than their riders, sending all three of the young men hard to the ground amid equine blood and the pained screams of wounded horses.

They gained their feet as the charging soldiers slowed and wheeled about. Desperately Gen and his companions hunted for some advantage in the terrain.

"Get into the scrub brush near the river!" Gen yelled sprinting toward the river's edge. Their pursuers urged their horses forward, anxious to trap their prey before they could reach the inconveniencing cover. Brittle branches snagged on clothing and broke as Gen dove in between two thick bushes, Gerand close behind. A grunt from Volney spun them around, their lumbering companion crashing into a bush, a gash across his shoulder bled through his clothes. The lead Eldephaere who had inflicted the wound nudged his horse closer for another strike.

Frantically, Gerand lunged forward, chopping down on the horse's foreleg. It screamed and fell, rider crushed beneath it. Gerand grabbed Volney, straining to drag him deeper into the undergrowth. Another Eledephaere took his companion's place, sword arcing toward Volney's exposed, bleeding back. The stroke never fell, and by the time Gerand turned, the horse had run off dragging its lifeless, fallen master down the road, boot stuck in the stirrup.

Gen hoped Gerand wouldn't ask about the mysterious death.

"Do not dismount!" one of the Eldephaere ordered. "They wish to take away our advantage. Do not get close. They cannot swim away. The cold will do the work for us. We need only wait."

Gen staunched Volney's bleeding while he groaned in pain, face paling. "It's not too bad," Gen whispered. "But we need to get to Chale so he can be properly looked after. There are only four left. What do you say?"

Gerand nodded. "I'll leave one for you."

"Volney, keep still," Gen instructed. "We'll be back for you."

As one, Gerand and Gen left the protective cover of the bushes, the Eldephaere sizing them up.

"Would you care to fight on equal terms like men, or like cowards from horseback?" Gen challenged.

An Eldephaere countered, "Hypocritical. Did I not find one of my men shot in the back? When fighting evil, an unfair advantage is no dishonor. Hyah!"

Four horses closed with them at a cautious pace. Gen and Volney stepped backward to put their backs to the brush.

"Drive them into the river!" the leader shouted, and the horses charged them. Gen swore, he and Gerand diving away from each other and into the snagging branches. Horses crashed into the undergrowth. Hooves pounded all around them, Gen trying to get his bearings as dead leaves, twigs, and horse legs fell around him in a swirling chaos. He crouched, desperately trying to find his way out of the morass, when an Eldephaere jumped from his saddle, dagger in hand, and knocked him to the ground.

Gen wasted no time, dissolving a vein in the man's head and killing him instantly. Grunts and groans cascaded in from everywhere, and he worked his way toward the closest sound. Finding himself behind a horse rearing and stamping down on the brush, he chopped down on its rear leg, severing ligaments and sending the horse screaming to the ground. A quick thrust finished the rider. Grunting sounds just ahead spurred him forward. Gerand wrestled with two dagger-wielding Eldephaere in a dense thicket, the protruding, rigid branches interfering with every grab and stroke.

Gen dropped his sword and drew a knife in a fluid moment, jamming it into the calf of the nearest Eldephaere. The man rolled over and Gen leaped on him, pinning his knife hand to the ground and losing his own in the process. The Eldephaere's companion kicked out, bruising Gen's ribs, but Gen retained his dominance while the man thrashed. Gerand recovered, hooking his arm around the throat of Gen's assailant, pulling him backward. The Eldephaere struck out wildly with his dagger, attempting to hit anything to release the choking grip.

Using the elven art of Kuri-tan, Gen pummeled his victim with bruising knee strikes and head-butts until he fell silent and unconscious while Gerand squeezed the life out of the remaining soldier a few moments later. Both young men slumped to the ground, exhausted and panting.

"Hello there?" Volney asked tentatively. "Gen? Gerand?"

"We're here," Gen reassured, taking stock of his bruised ribs. "Gerand, are you hurt?"

"They gashed me three times. Only one is bad. Give me a moment and I'll have it staunched."

"Where?"

"The bad one is on the shoulder. The other two in the leg."

Gen shook his head. They needed help. "I'll kill the wounded horses and see if I can't track down some that aren't injured."

Gen pursued the unpleasant work quickly. The heat of the battle was wearing off, the cold greedily returning to send a powerful chill down his sweating body. To his dismay, only one healthy horse remained, and Gen led it back to where Gerand, grimacing in pain, tried his best to rally Volney, whose ashen face revealed a resignation that clenched Gen's gut.

"I'm going to die," Volney mumbled blankly.

"Shut up," Gerand remonstrated him roughly. "You've got a scratch on your back that will easily heal. We just need to find you some warm inn and a beautiful wench to watch over you. You'll be smiling and saying stupid things in no time."

Gen checked Gerand's wounds. "Gerand, help me get Volney up into the saddle. Can you sit behind him and hold him up?"

"I think so. And just so you know, I can't move my arm well enough to fight with any effectiveness."

"I understand."

The snow picked up in earnest as Gen collected the essentials from their dead horses and helped his friends get set in the saddle. The Eldephaere horse stamped nervously at its unfamiliar riders, and Gen used some oats from a saddle bag to earn its trust and allay its nervousness. As he took the reins and led it down the road, the snow washed over them as evening deepened. The cold leeched their strength from them, and Gen found his thoughts drifting along with the snow. Memories of the brutal Whitewind shard he had traveled to with Torbrand resurfaced as snow collected on his cloak.

Nearly two miles from the battle, full dark had fallen

251

along with a few inches of fluffy powder. Gen checked on his companions, finding them unmoving and seemingly frozen together. They merely grunted in response to his inquiries about their welfare, and he couldn't help but think that at least *they* had the heat of the struggling horse and each other to help them push through. As he turned and considered his options, a flicker of light to his left caught his eye. Distant and weak, its orange color could only mean one thing.

With renewed energy he pushed forward in a direct line toward the scant illumination. A light was shining through a crack in a shutter. He stopped and turned to his shivering companions.

"We need a cover story. I am a bard—named Rafael— and you two are soldiers returning home to your families. Volney, you'll be Sans, and Gerand, you will be Loris. Brigands ambushed us on the road to Chale. Do you understand? Rafael, Sans, and Loris."

A positive sounding groan emanating from the dark lump on the horse was enough, and Gen resumed his trek forward. A small house—barely more than a hut—resolved out of the darkness, an occasional spark from the chimney spurting out into the falling snow. A fire. Gen pulled forward more eagerly. While he hoped the home's occupants would be of a friendly nature, he would force his way in if necessary. Barking from inside startled him as he stepped up to the door, and he knocked, a woman and child inside gasping at the unexpected noise.

"Quiet, Bolger," the woman ordered nervously. "One moment, if you please."

The door opened cautiously a few moments later, a slender young woman, bundled against the weather and holding a menacing stick, searched the face at her door in the darkness.

Gen executed a bow and tried his best to put on a pleasant demeanor. "My deepest apologies, good woman, for disturbing you this night, but my companions and I are in great need. I am Rafael, a bard, and I, with my two companions there, was traveling toward Chale when a band of brigands fell upon us. They are injured, and we are desperate and cold this evening. Would you kindly provide us with some assistance for the night? We can compensate you."

While he talked, a dark-haired boy, no older than five, came around the door and grabbed onto his mother's leg. The woman stared at Gen for such a long time that he started to feel awkward. At last, she seemed to relax.

"Get back inside, Tolliver, and put another log on the fire." To Gen she said, "I've a small place here, but I will help as I can. I am Lena."

"Our deepest thanks, Lena. Is there anywhere to stable the horse?"

"There is a mine entrance in the hill just to the right of the house. I've a few chickens I keep inside. Your horse can stay there."

"Eldaloth bless you, Lena." Gen helped his companions down and practically dragged them inside. The house was indeed small. A front room with a table and three chairs welcomed them with a cheery heat. Another room lay beyond a blanket hanging over a doorway, the fireplace open to the rooms on either side. A small kitchen to the right of the main room revealed evidence of a neat and orderly person. Dishes and bowls had been stacked evenly on rough wooden shelves. Most notable, however, were intricate carvings sitting on the fireplace mantel and lining a single shelf that ran all the way around the room.

The boy poked his head through the blanket that separated them from the other room as Lena pulled the table away from the fire and into the kitchen to allow room for the two injured men to lay on the floor. Bolger, a black and white mutt, reclined by the fire.

"This one has a cut to his back," Gen explained. "The

253

other has wounds to his shoulder and legs. I will see to the horse and return shortly. Again, my thanks."

"One moment, Rafael," Lena called. "Let me fetch the lantern. It is a dark night."

After the warmth of the house, the cold slapped Gen's face and watered his eyes. He saw to the horse as quickly as he could and ran back, knocking the snow off his boots before pushing the door open and plunging back into the welcome warmth. Lena had removed her winter clothing, and Gen studied her, noting her youth. A ragged brown dress spoke of her poverty, but her face, with thin, delicate features, reflected a kind aspect, especially the ice blue eyes that now carefully regarded the angry wound on Volney's back. She pushed her long brown hair behind an ear, and turned back to Gen, who removed his own cloak. She regarded him with an odd expression for a moment before snapping into action.

"Help your friend with his shirt so I can get a look at the shoulder. Tolliver, get the pot and fill it halfway with water from the barrel."

"Do you know some healing lore?" Gen asked hopefully as he crossed to Gerand.

"I do. My husband used to always hurt himself in that ridiculous mine of his."

"Where is he?"

"Harry? Dead."

"I'm sorry," Gen apologized.

"Collapsed on him this spring," Lena explained. "He thought he'd see us rich from that stupid hole. As it was, we could barely pay Grimson the rent for this place."

Gen pulled the shirt from a frowning Gerand. "And the carvings. His work, too? They are wonderful."

"No," she blushed. "Those are mine. I try to sell a few to pay for this place. Been a bit slow lately. Just returned from Chale yesterday. Sold enough for food for the winter. Not sure what I'll do for the rent."

254

Gen heard the indirect plea. He said, "I think my companions and I will help you along as reward for this service."

She blushed again, and Gen smiled to reassure her. After several minutes, Lena instructed Gen to clean Volney's wounds with the hot water while she continued to mash some sort of paste in the kitchen.

She eyed Gen while she worked the pestle. "I don't think I've ever heard of brigands bothering with anyone or anything this far north."

"Just unlucky, I guess," Gen answered evasively.

"A whole patrol of Church soldiers passed by earlier today, probably heading toward Aberlee."

"We passed them on the road," Gen said. "The brigands hit us soon after. They came out of the hills. Probably after my earnings. Fortunately, these two, Sans and Loris, are soldiers who were returning home for the winter. They fought them off."

"You've got yourself a sword, too."

"Yes. A necessity in the trade."

"Let's get to work," she said, handing him a cup. "Get them to swallow this. It will help them sleep while we do the more painful bits. You seem to be moving a bit stiffly, too."

"One of the blackguards caught me in the ribs during the scuffle. Bruised, not broken. There is no need to worry for me."

"You may feel differently in the morning," she said.

Gen thought she might be right. Before long, Volney and Gerand had passed out, and Gen assisted Lena as she expertly cleaned and applied a rough stitching to the more serious wounds. Next came the bitter paste and the tying of bandages.

"If it weren't for the draught," Lena said, "the paste would have them screaming and pulling up the floorboards. It will keep the cuts clean until they can heal. Are you sure you don't want me to look at those bruised ribs?"

"No, thank you."

Gen slumped against the wall, and Bolger sauntered over and put his head in Gen's lap. Gen scratched behind his ears as Lena went to the kitchen to tidy up. She regarded him questioningly a few times as she worked, and when finished she crossed into the adjacent room to put Tolliver to bed. Gen let his mind wander to the Chalaine and Mirelle, tiredness pushing the lids of his eyes down. He barely woke when Lena stoked the fire again, but vivid dreams took him down into the dark.

A blast of cold wind and Tolliver's excited shouting brought them all out of slumber early the next morning. Gen, surprised at how well he had slept, pushed himself away from a protesting Bolger and leaned against the wall. A sleepy Lena emerged from the other side of the hanging blanket and pulled Tolliver away from the door and closed it.

"The snow's as tall as Bolger, and it's still snowing!" he exclaimed. Bolger barked as if in reply. Gen frowned.

"It appears we may need to trespass a little longer on your kindness," Gen apologized.

"Well, I knew that after one look at Sans's wounds. He won't be fit to go anywhere for a good spell. He's young, though, so I think he could probably ride in a week."

Gen cursed inwardly. He needed to get to the Chalaine. Gerand's eyes slowly opened, and Volney, lying facedown, eventually worked up enough energy to grunt something unintelligible. Lena set herself to preparing a meal while Gen checked on his companions before wandering the room to inspect the carvings. Intricately detailed figures of rustic men and women engaged in everyday tasks evoked smiles from Gen's face. Another small shelf by the door held a variety of creatures. An Uyumaak Basher stood near a ferocious boar, and a majestic falcon appeared ready to devour a nearby toothy lizard.

"Those are mine," Tolliver stated possessively, both as an explanation and a warning. "Ma promised she won't sell them."

"Your mother is very skilled. I might buy a piece or two myself before I go."

"You can't buy these!" Tolliver exclaimed.

"He doesn't mean those, Tolliver dear," Lena piped in from the kitchen.

Gen chuckled and the little boy relaxed. Tolliver grabbed his hand. "I'll show you one you should buy," he said. Gen let Tolliver lead him around the room to a low shelf by the bedroom door just by the mantle. He pointed a finger upward. "Get that one."

Gen immediately picked out the one he meant and felt a surge of panic. There, staring back at him, was a perfect likeness of himself two hands high. Gen slowly lifted it down, marveling. Lena had carved the major scars of his face nearly perfectly, and his Dark Guard uniform had a notch where he wore his Defender of the Faith pin. Gen turned toward Lena, who grinned as she sliced an apple.

"I knew who *you* were the moment I saw your face peering at me from the dark," she explained. "Probably wouldn't have let you in, otherwise."

Gen shook his head, chagrined. "You must have seen me in person to have crafted this so well."

"Harry took us to Mikmir to see the Chalaine and the Ha'Ulrich ride out for Elde Luri Mora. I saw you on your horse next to the First Mother. Your face was . . . unforgettable. No offense."

"None taken," Gen said. "Has no news of what happened on the Shroud Lake shard reached this far?"

"If you mean that bit about you being the Ilch and being

dead, then yes, it has. Set your mind at ease. Most folks couldn't believe it, and when you showed up at my door alive and running around on a leg you aren't supposed to have, then I just figured I was right about you. I have an eye for people, Lord Blackshire, and even if I had never heard one of those astounding stories of your bravery, I would have known what kind of man you are."

"I thank you for your trust."

She nodded. "Your companions I do not remember, however."

"Let me introduce you. The one by the fire is Gerand Kildan, a prince of Tolnor and a Dark Guard. The one on the floor is Volney Torunne, a Rhugothian and son of General Torunne. He is also a Dark Guard. These two have supported me in my recent difficulties."

Lena wrung her hands. "Such distinguished company for a poor widow such as myself! I am sorry if you find my care a little more humble than you are used to."

To Gen's surprise, Volney spoke, voice thick with emotion, if a bit sleepy. "After what we have passed through, dear lady, you are Eldaloth's own daughter, and this is Erelinda. Your face will always be the most beautiful to me."

Lena blushed, and Gerand raised his eyebrows.

Tolliver pulled on Gen's leg and handed him the lizard carving. "You be the lizard. I'll be the falcon. You try to eat Bolger, and I'll stop you!"

CHAPTER 64 – VENGEANCE

After one week of healing and horrible weather, the sun finally broke through the oppressive gray wall and streamed down to the blinding, pure white snow. The air warmed slightly, snow melting gradually. Another week passed before Gen thought they could attempt to resume their trip.

During the long wait, Gen discovered another skill that Volney possessed besides swordfighting, one at which he was a complete master—entertaining children.

Gen's role as Tolliver's playmate ended almost as soon as Volney could sit upright again, at which point Gen found himself sitting with Gerand and Lena at the table laughing at Volney's antics. Under Volney's hand, the toothy lizard developed a hankering for boy-flesh, and Tolliver yelped and laughed so much that it became infectious. While Gen pitched in with the occasional song and practiced tales, he envied his companion's skill at inventing ridiculous, impromptu stories, using the carvings as props.

More than once Gen found Lena's eyes on Volney, glowing with appreciation, and often she would join Volney and Tolliver in their fun.

"You know," Gerand commented, "if Volney could be

as at ease with women as he is with children, he might do better."

"I think he has found a woman he is at ease with," Gen remarked, Gerand nodding thoughtfully.

When they announced their intention to go, Tolliver burst into tears and Lena's face darkened and fell, though she tried to hide it.

"How much is your rent for this place?" Volney asked as they donned their gear.

"One copper a month."

"How much do we have left, Gen?"

Gen had spent part of the idle days using Trysmagic to create silver coins, and he produced a coin pouch and set it on the table. "That should keep your landlord off your back—and hopefully off the premises—for some time."

Lena crossed to the table, face suspicious, and pulled open the coin purse.

"I wish you wouldn't. . ." Gen objected a little too late.

Lena's eyes bloomed with disbelief. "This is too much! I could *buy* this place with this and have enough left over to eat like a Queen for years!"

"Sounds like a worthy plan," Volney said, taking her hand and kissing it. "You have done us so much good, we could never truly repay what we owe."

"Will you come back?" Tolliver asked, face cloudy.

Volney stooped and smiled. "Of course! By the time I return, I'm sure Lizard will be starved and need a huge helping of Tolliver!" He playfully poked the boy's ribs and stood, eyes sad. "Farewell!" he said, leaving quickly to hide his emotion.

They retrieved the horse from the mine and set out on the snowy lane, Lena waving to them from the open door, Tolliver in her arms. Volney glanced back at the humble house several times before it disappeared from view.

"I think Volney might actually come back here someday. More than a toothy lizard has captured his interest, I'd wager," Gerand teased.

Volney's face turned uncharacteristically serious. "I will come back here, and I don't want to hear any teasing from you two about it. Do not ruin this for me. Just let me enjoy this little dream of mine before I get killed in Ironkeep."

Only the snow and mud complicated their journey to Nowain, and in two days' time they approached the small city Torbrand had directed them to. It was situated on a flat plain peppered by enormous oaks, and, like Tell, the city center itself consisted of a few buildings that serviced nearby farmsteads.

"Where did Torbrand say to go?" Gerand asked as they approached late on a cloudy afternoon.

"He told me to inquire after the rat catcher, who is, apparently, a Portal Mage on an Aughmerian payroll," Gen answered. "They sneak spies into Rhugoth through here."

"How does he get away with that?" Volney asked, outraged. "The Portal Guild would shut off access to all of Aughmere if they found out!"

"Just think of what Unification means to the Portal Guild, Volney," Gerand explained. "For now, they are a necessity. If Portals do still exist after Unification, they become a convenience. Portal Mages won't want to make enemies now for fear of offending potential future customers who will have other options."

As they neared town, they concealed their swords beneath their long cloaks to avoid suspicion. The road through town remained deserted as they passed a smithy's house, the forge cold. A meaty-faced man cracked a shutter as they walked by, closing it quickly.

"Someone's around. Should we inquire here?" Gerand asked.

"Yes," Gen replied. "I'll keep out of sight. If Lena recognized me, others might do the same."

Gerand took the lead, knocking softly. A behemoth of a man opened the door a sliver, eying them suspiciously.

"Excuse me," Gerand said, "but we are in search of a rat catcher that lives nearby. Could you direct us toward him?"

The smithy humphed in disdain. "If you mean Tory, then he's in the last building at the far side of town. If you have a rat problem, I'd take it up with the catcher in Chale. Tory'd rather keep a rat for a pet than kill it."

"Thank you. Our apologies for inconveniencing you on a cold day," Gerand said. The smithy shut the door as if the young man had the plague.

"Friendly town," Volney observed.

They walked in the direction the smith indicated, but before they reached their destination, Gerand stopped them in the middle of the street. "Look, we need some sort of a plan or we'll be slaughtered. Ironkeep is crawling with Eldephaere and Churchmen. I hardly need remind anyone here about what happened when we ran into Padra Nolan. I've never felt so worthless in all my life. Then there's the issue of your face, Gen. No offense. Even if we try some disguise, we can't conceal your face without arousing suspicion."

"Unless he dresses like a girl," Volney offered. "They have to wear those veils, right, like the Chalaine does?"

"Correct," Gen affirmed. "I think our best bet is to pose as servants. I will have to dress as a woman to hide my face, but I can also conceal our weapons that way, as well."

"Provided you can find the clothes of an Aughmerian servant girl who is tall and fat enough to accommodate your height and all the extra baggage," Gerand added.

"So Gen will steal the clothes off some poor slave girl and invade Ironkeep in a dress. So much for Tolnorian honor and dignity!" Volney quipped.

Gerand laughed. "He's been Rhugothian for over a year

now, so he's willing to sink to whatever depths necessary to get the job done."

The Portal Mage's home was a simple log cabin lined on both sides with orderly stacks of wood. A healthy cloud of smoke puffed from the chimney, someone singing and airy tune inside.

"I'll remain outside until it is time to go so I don't raise an alarm with Tory," Gen informed them. "If we wait two hours, it should be the dead of night on the Menegothian shard, and we'll have the night in Aughmere to come up with a plan. See if Tory has anything to help us. If he wants a password, use *cloven hoof*."

Gen walked over to one of the woodpiles to get out of sight, and then Gerand rapped on the door. A gangly, youthful man answered, face happy but curious.

"Are you Tory the rat catcher?" Gerand asked.

"Yes," he answered, face unsure. "Is the snow and cold driving the beasties indoors?"

"Actually," said Gerand, "we are here on a mission from Torbrand Khairn."

"He's no longer in charge of the Black Vine," Tory said. "High King Khairn now directly oversees the operations into Rhugoth. What password were you given?"

"Cloven hoof."

Tory's face registered shock for a moment, but he quickly covered it up. "Well, I suppose you are welcome, then. Come in."

Gerand and Volney crossed the threshold into a wide room, wooden planks squealing beneath their feet. A fire burned hot in an expansive fireplace. A narrow table with high backed chairs waited in front of the flames. Tory closed the door and invited them to sit.

"Will you take some refreshment, or were you looking to cross immediately?"

"We want to cross in two hours," Gerand replied. "Where is the Portal?"

Tory said, "In my bedroom, as it turns out. Let me warm some spiced cider for you."

Tory disappeared into a room that ran behind the double-sided fireplace, returning with two clay mugs a short while later and placing the drinks in front of them.

"I apologize for the darkness of the room. It is simply too cold to open the shutters, and the Black Vine does not see fit to provide me with the means to buy some of those wonderful Rhugothian windows."

"The fire and the warm drink are comforts enough," Gerand thanked him.

"Very well. I'll prepare some supper. Are you expecting anyone else?"

"In a couple of hours, yes. Just one more."

"I will plan accordingly. If you should need anything, please don't hesitate to ask."

Tory disappeared into the kitchen again, bowls and utensils clanking and scuffling as he worked.

"That has to be the most accommodating Portal Mage I have ever run across," Volney commented quietly. "Most I've run into seemed a little arrogant or mightily irritated."

"Like I said," Gerand yawned. "They'll actually have to sell their services after Unification, if they have any services to sell at all. I imagine they're all being much nicer these day. I am so tired. Trudging through the snow really takes it out of me."

"Me too," Volney agreed. The warm fire crackled and popped pleasantly, as Tory hummed a tune. The warmth caressed their tired bodies as they leaned back comfortably and drank.

Tory, sentry of the Black Vine, chopped a carrot precisely and patiently as he waited. Cooking always calmed him, and the singing helped him to drive distractions out of his head so he could think more quickly. Of all the Black Vine jobs, sentry was almost as unglamorous as scribe. Sitting around waiting for people to come and go provided few opportunities for distinction. He'd learned the art of hospitality in hopes of setting himself apart. His hospitality did that, but he found out that his unusual skill had, instead, cemented him in his position.

Doubly worse, playing nursemaid to a spoiled Portal Mage ground on his patience, and he considered his patience above average. The only satisfaction he could derive from the unfortunate responsibility was reporting throughout the pathetic town that the Portal Mage was his retarded brother. Judin's antisocial personality and disdain for small rural towns kept him close to the cabin and out of trouble, while Tory only had to leave to keep up appearances as a rat catcher, a job he executed as ineptly as possible to keep business down.

The first young man's head hit the table with a thunk, and Tory raised his head and started counting. His companion's head hit four seconds afterward. The sentry shook his head. He had tried to measure the drug precisely for their respective body weights so they would fall at the same time. A four second differential, while satisfactory, would not do to help him advance his hopes of acquiring the rank of spy.

Calmly, he pushed the diced carrots into the stew pot and swung it over the fire. Wiping his hands, he crossed back into the main room to find his two victims resting awkwardly on the table.

At least they didn't spill the drinks, Tory thought as he opened the bedroom door. A blast of cold hit him. Judin, still in his bedclothes, huddled under several blankets, book in hand. He had opened the shutters wide.

"Is someone here?" Judin asked, displeased at the interruption.

"I'm afraid so. I need to speak with Padra Athan, if you would open the Portal, please."

"Let me finish this chapter. . ."

"Now, Judin, or tonight's meal will burn."

As the sun fell, Gen started to regret his decision to stay outdoors. The departure of the clouds and the arrival of evening ushered in a bitter cold. While mentally he could ignore it, his body wasn't so silent on the matter. The smoke from the chimney smelled invitingly of warmth, and the woodpile dug unpleasantly into his back. He'd already created a small oval track in the snow from pacing listlessly when he abandoned the uncomfortable touch of the woodpile.

When did I become so soft? he wondered.

That thought and the faint buzz in his head that signaled the nearness of the Portal reminded him of the enormity and even preposterousness of the mission ahead, and he returned to stand to the side of the house, closing his eyes and disciplining his mind and feelings. He could not fail. He needed to return to the emptiness that had propelled him in his first few months at Rhugoth.

The severity and depth of his guilt and the power of his love for Mirelle, the Chalaine, and his friends had driven clarity from his mind, and he sought it now for their sake. A need to escape pain had motivated him before. Now he needed discipline to help others escape it. He closed his eyes briefly, breathing in and out and emptying his mind.

The sun had nearly set when the front door around the corner opened, and the sound of several heavy footsteps hinted that soldiers had come out of the structure and roughly closed the door behind themselves. The sound of the footfalls was not right, and Gen held up, listening. Gruff voices joked about the cold briefly, the tenor of one sending a chill up Gen's spine. Inching quietly to the edge of the building, he poked his head around the corner, pulling back quickly. Captain Omar and two Aughmerian soldiers stood guard at the door.

Gen froze. The calm he had invited before dissolved at the sight of the brutish guard that had tormented him in Tell and hurt Regina. Reason told him that Gerand and Volney were captives and that he should flee back to Mikmir, but those voices of wisdom again failed to shout above Gen's noisy, resurgent emotions. Knowing what strength it would cost him, he turned the corner, striding evenly as he killed Captain Omar's two companions by unmaking a portion of their brains while simultaneously clogging Omar's throat. While surprise still held Omar, Gen created a band of stone around the Captain's arms.

Gen crossed to the ailing brute, the vulgar looks and massive, neckless head queuing unwanted memories in Gen's mind. Roughly, Gen grabbed him by the top of the breastplate and yanked him forward.

"Remember me, Omar?" Gen asked as Omar's eyes widened from shock, face purpling. Gen removed the obstruction in his throat. "Quietly now, Omar. Quietly."

"You are dead!"

"Do you think the Ilch could be killed so easily, Omar?" Omar's eyes widened. "Spare me!"

"Oh, I'll spare you, Omar, if you can remember something."

"What"

"Her name, Omar. Do you even remember her name?"

Omar's eyes darted about as if searching different cubbyholes in his mind. Gen reached down for his sword when Omar rammed his forehead into Gen's face. Gen rocked backward.

"Help!" Omar yelled frantically. Gen stepped forward,

pulled Omar's sword from its scabbard, and punched it through his heart and into the door behind. Omar's cry and the sword sticking through the door set footsteps inside the house to sprinting. Gen leaped away back to the woodpile, jumping on top as people in the house worked to push Omar's corpse away from the door.

Gen pulled himself up onto the snowy roof, hands pushing through the snow to clutch the thatch beneath. He could sense the Portal almost directly beneath him. Scooting forward, he dissolved part of the roof with Trysmagic, finding a bedroom below with a dark-haired man standing near the active Portal in his bedclothes, eyes closed in concentration.

I hope that's the Portal Mage, Gen thought as he stood, opening a hole in the roof beneath his own feet. The Portal Mage yelped as Gen hit the floor hard, cracking the wooden planks. The Portal winked out. In a moment, Gen's blade flashed up under the chin of the frightened man.

"Where are the two soldiers that were here?"

The Mage swallowed hard. "Taken. Taken through."

"The Portal. Open it," Gen commanded with a slight prod of the sword. The Portal flared to life, and Gen grabbed the shrieking Mage by the arm and pulled him into the Portal with him. Once they were through, he knocked him unconscious with the hilt of his blade. The Portal closed just as Gen noticed two Eldephaere. As Torbrand had told him, the Portal opened into a small storeroom. A weak lamp behind his opponents turned them to advancing shadows.

They yelled a warning and took a step toward him. Gen surged forward, lengthening his body and thrusting his sword through the neck of the first. Pulling back into a more compact stance, he flicked his blade to the left to decapitate the other before his raised stroke could fall.

All planning voided, Gen kicked open the storeroom

door and waded into a kitchen full of Eldephaere. Two he blasted to the floor with the force of his kick, and, with a combination of killing Trysmagic, Kuri-tan, and quick strikes, he cut down eight vacant-eyed Church soldiers and sprinted out into the hall. His magic was nearly spent, but the Im'Tith brand on his chest let him know the Chalaine was somewhere close by, and this infused him with drive. While he could sense her, he had no way of knowing which way would lead to her in the maze of doors and side corridors around him.

This isn't going to work! a voice that sounded like Samian shouted in his head. *You have done exactly what they wanted. Get back to the Portal and retreat!*

Gen weighed his options. He could try to hide in the keep or awaken the Portal Mage and return to his friends. Even as his will wavered, a flood of pain from the Chalaine poured over him as it had almost every day since they left Tenswater.

They are doing this to get to you! Run!

Gen could not obey the wiser voices in his mind. To use the Chalaine so abominably just to get to him was unforgivable. It would stop, either by her departure or his death.

Decided, he sprinted through the halls, one way as good as another, trying to narrow his choices by attrition. Guards popped up in front of doors and around corners with alarming regularity, and he dispatched them all with as much rapidity and stealth as he could manage. The bodies he could not hide, and, as his frustration mounted, a hue and cry was raised in the keep, servants and soldiers pouring from doorways.

Gen ducked into a room from which several female servants emerged, finding what he had hoped—loose servant dresses and veils. Finding the largest he could, he slipped it over his head and affixed the headdress and veil. The sword's scabbard poked the brown cloth out a bit in the back, and it was shorter than he liked, but he didn't take the time to feel foolish, stepping out into the hall and resuming his quest in the midst of a chaotic search. None of the men seemed to spare him a second glance, though some of the women regarded him strangely. He pressed on.

After several minutes of wrong turns and avoiding patrols, he found a long, well-lit hallway bedecked with trophies of war and fine tapestries. He walked as inconspicuously as he could until the hall terminated at two darkly stained oaken doors with two Eldephaere standing guard in front. The Chalaine was somewhere in a straight line behind those doors. The two Eldephaere regarded him quizzically for a moment before he used Trysmagic to stop their hearts and send them to the floor. He dragged them away from the door to clear room to open it, listening carefully but hearing no sound from the other side.

Breathing deeply, he grabbed the two iron rings bolted into the doors and pushed. The hallway behind was empty save for a single figure who Gen scarce had time to recognize before a crushing scream only he could hear tore through his mind, ruining the spell he had ready. His attacker smirked at him as he fell to his knees in pain.

"Cute," Padra Athan mocked, and Gen knew no more.

CHAPTER 65 - BLOOD MAGIC

"Are you sure you broke all the seals?" Athan asked a drawn Padra Nolan. Padra Nolan removed his hands from Gen's head and walked unsteadily toward a pitcher of wine and a goblet laid out on a small, darkly stained table.

"I believe so. It is amazing the amount of information Mikkik packed away in his mind. The blood magic that Aldemar alluded to in his documents was gifted to Gen, as well. It is an odd form of magic, and corrupt, but what Gen needs to know for bringing Chertanne back is there. In fact, *you* could perform the ritual if you had time to learn it. I am shaken, Athan, shaken and scared."

"What frightens you, Nolan?"

"The learning Mikkik bestowed upon Gen has revealed to me more plainly than any other study I have done the dark and devious nature of our common foe. But more particularly, by having the seals broken, Gen now possesses terrible knowledge to accompany his power, spells that far eclipse anything Chertanne was ever taught. I am scared to awaken this young man. If it weren't for the necessity of Chertanne's revival, I would kill him now."

Athan nodded gravely, rubbing his chin. "Fortunately, Trys will not wax full for a few more months, and his power will be limited. The Chalaine will act as our check against whatever retribution he wishes to exact upon us."

Nolan rubbed his eyes. "He does possess strong feelings for her, but are you sure it is safe to put her and the Child in her belly in the same room with him? What if there was something I missed? Some hidden command?"

"It is a risk we must take," Athan said. "For the magic to work, the one bled must be willing, and she is the only one he will listen to. Do not fear. He prizes and honors her above all and surely would have killed her long before now if Mikkik controlled him. But I agree that he should be destroyed. If what you say is true, I cannot honor my bargain with the Chalaine. Once the ceremony is done, we will rake his mind thoroughly one last time and kill him."

"That is wise," Padra Nolan agreed. "I would like to write down what I have learned while it is fresh." He turned to leave.

"Yes, but one last question," Athan said. "Are you sure that Millim Eri sealed Mikkik's training from him?"

"I am positive. There were two—a male and a female— that watched over him during his youth and adolescence. They appeared directly after every one of Joranne's sessions and blacked them out of his mind. With the Chalaine's revelation about Aldemar still walking Ki'Hal, it is time to rewrite some doctrine as it concerns the Millim Eri surviving the Shattering."

"Indeed. You may go. Send in the Chalaine."

Padra Nolan cracked the door, revealing the Chalaine pacing in the hallway outside. As soon as the door swung open, she stepped past the genuflecting Padra Nolan before he could straighten and invite her to step inside the small room. Gen lay unconscious on a small pallet, and the Chalaine inspected him carefully, filling her eyes with his familiar form. She could find no injury upon him, and she tried to be as clinical and calm as she could, not wanting to show Padra Athan how desperately excited she was.

Gen breathed in and out comfortably. He wore traveling clothes, his face shaven and hair cropped neatly. The Chalaine choked back tears, and, noticing Athan's watchful stare, steeled herself quickly.

She cleared her throat. "You cleaned him up."

"Yes," Athan confirmed, stepping forward to shut the door. "He and his companions arrived looking little better than slave beggars. "

"What did you do with Volney and Gerand?"

"They are resting comfortably in a cell with their fellow Dark Guard."

"Then if you would kindly wake him and step out," the Chalaine said, "I will be true to my commitment to convince him to aid us."

"I will not leave, Chalaine."

"But I said. . ."

Athan stepped forward. "I know what you said, Highness, and I did not agree to it. I must remain here and addle his mind sufficiently so that he cannot work his magic again, lest he conjure a way to escape and start another bloodbath in the Keep. I don't expect you to like it, but those are my conditions."

"He is strong-minded, Athan. He thinks you've tortured me these past weeks. Are you sure you want to risk it?"

She knew it a desperate argument, but she had to confess her love to him before the secrecy drove her mad. With Chertanne dead, the guilt she felt over her feelings for her Protector had dissolved into the winter wind. He had to know, but she would not speak of it with Athan in the room.

"I am confident in my skill, my Queen," Athan pronounced expressionlessly. "Please prepare your arguments well. His mind will be impaired, so keep your speech and questions simple. Remember, he must accept with an oath."

Athan stepped to a corner outside Gen's field of vision

and incanted. Gen's eyes popped open. Immediately the Chalaine could discern the effects of the spell. His green eyes that had always shone with nobility and intelligence were dimmed and cloudy. It required several seconds for him to recognize his companion, and when he did, he smiled drunkenly, his hand flopping tentatively for hers.

"Chalaine," he intoned pleasantly. "Did you bring the cards? I've come all this way for a game."

Her tears came freely now, and she rubbed his hand and arm briskly, hoping the friction would polish some clarity into his eyes. "No cards today, Gen. Listen carefully. Do you know about Chertanne?"

"Yes. Good old Jaron. Good man, that one. Happier days for you, then? I bet Dason is pleased, eh?"

The Chalaine bit her lip at his implication and tumbled on. "Gen, the Padras say you can bring Chertanne back to life."

He laughed, and when he talked, the words came slowly and a little slurred. "Like anyone wants to. No one knows how to do that. . . Do they?"

His eyes widened and rolled about questioningly for several long moments. "I . . . I know how to do it. . . I know. . . horror upon horror!"

He pulled his arm away and convulsed, falling from the palette. Padra Athan incanted again, and Gen fell back into a sleep. The Chalaine knelt beside him as he twitched uncomfortably.

"What is he talking about?" the Chalaine demanded, noticing Athan's troubled look.

"He is coming to grips with Mikkik's training. I underestimated the effect it would have upon him. I will try to calm him."

The Chalaine watched Gen's face, his eyes convulsing behind his eyelids. "Mikkik's training?"

"Mikkik taught Gen many things that the Millim Eri hid from him. Of a necessity, we had to reveal them to him."

"So you admit, then, that Gen was not complicit with Mikkik when he attempted to kill Chertanne in Elde Luri Mora?"

Athan shrugged. "Perhaps not consciously. But we've no time to be pedantic about this. One moment and I will wake him again."

When Gen opened his eyes again, he lay perfectly still, eyes open, face bewildered, ashen, and lost, like a drowned man staring up out of the water. The Chalaine stroked his face gently, trying to comfort him, but his terror and stupor diverted his attention inward, and several minutes passed before his eyes finally found hers, now filled with sadness and concern.

"Gen. . ."

"Do you want me to do this, Chalaine?" he groaned. "Do you want me to help you bring Chertanne back to this world, to be its King and your husband?"

She couldn't tell the truth, and she didn't have the heart to say yes, so she chose something in between. "It must be done, for the sake of the prophecy. You must swear to it. The lives of us all are at stake."

"Then I will do it, for your sake. I swear."

Before she could utter another word, Athan incanted and Gen fell back into slumber. She grabbed his hand fiercely and pressed it to her cheek as the tears ran unseen down her veiled face. Frustration and self-loathing smothered her, and she fought to breathe.

"Well done, your Highness," Athan complimented her smoothly. "We will begin immediately. I will keep him asleep during the bleeding. When it comes time, I will of necessity need to allow Gen his full faculties. When he performs the ceremony, no one is to be in the room with him save Chertanne. Wait here a moment while we clear a section of the lower prison. Guards! Take Gen below. I will retrieve the Chalaine personally in a few minutes."

Two burly Eldephaere grabbed Gen under the armpits

and dragged him indecorously from the room. The Chalaine sat on the palette where Gen had lain and put her head in her hands. Gen had no future now, and for all her thinking she could find no scheme or leverage to employ to win his freedom or even his life. Athan held complete control, and with her mother imprisoned and herself restricted to her room, there was no influence she could bring to bear to manipulate the inevitable path before her. She prayed to her God and hoped he would find some way to see Gen through whatever Athan held in store.

The Padra did not tarry for long, opening the chamber door and signaling for her to follow. She smoothed her dress as she crossed through the open door and down a gray spiraling stairway discolored black and green by moisture and mold. The scent of mildew and uncleanness spun her head, the enclosed space upsetting her frayed nerves. Rats screeched as soldiers ahead of her kicked them down the stairs or crushed them outright.

After several turns, the stairs terminated on a small landing. Directly in front of them was a heavy wooden door with a set of small bars affixed in a square at head height. To their left, another stairway, even narrower than the one they had just descended, dropped off into the dark, moans and sobs ascending from it as if the prison below were the belly of some beast slowly digesting its victims.

"This place is not humane!" the Chalaine exclaimed as a whimper of terror greeted them from below. "Please tell me you do not have my mother in this place!"

"Open the door," Athan commanded the Eldephaere, ignoring the Chalaine's question. The door shrieked open, and Athan followed her inside. From appearances, the room was used for storage. Barrels and sacks had been shoved to the side to make room for a massive cauldron. A single lantern atop a pile of grain sacks glowed dimly, and the Chalaine felt like a thief meeting someone surreptitiously in some dark place to divide ill-gotten spoils.

Gen lay in a heap on the floor, guarded by two Eldephaere.

"Take three of the barrels and place them in a line next to the cauldron," Athan commanded. "Lay Gen on them and hang his arm over the cauldron." This was done quickly. Two other Padras joined Athan as he removed a thin-bladed knife from his robes. The Chalaine swallowed hard.

"Come near him, Chalaine. Whatever the cost, do not let him die. Do you understand?"

She nodded her head in acknowledgment but felt fearful. Usually, she could tell when someone neared death by touching them, but touching Gen would heal him prematurely. She had to rely on sight and sound, and she feared her own inexperience might kill him. Before she could think about it, Athan slashed Gen's wrist, blood spurting into the cauldron. Thanks to Athan's magic, Gen did not twitch or cry out, though she knew even awake he would have shown no reaction. As for herself, her stomach lurched, and it felt as if her knees might buckle at any moment.

Walking carefully forward, she put her face close to his so she could see it more clearly and watch the rise and fall of his chest. Time crawled by haltingly on broken legs, discomfort and disgust apparent on every face. Slowly Gen's face paled. His breathing slowed, and the blood pulsed more and more weakly from his wrist. As his breath grew ragged, she healed him, health and color returning a warmth to his marble white features.

"Six more,"Athan announced gravely, slashing Gen again. The Chalaine closed her eyes and groaned inwardly as the blood ran into the cauldron, the drips echoing uncomfortably in the small room. By the time they finished the fourth bleeding, the Chalaine's head throbbed from the intense concentration.

"I need rest before I can continue," she complained. "I need fresh air and some refreshment." Athan measured her up for a moment and then acquiesced.

"Take her to her quarters for half an hour. I will stay with the blood."

Emerging from the dismal pit of the dungeon and into the comparatively well-lit confines of her room eased the constriction squeezing her chest and mellowed the headache. She threw herself down on her bed and exhaled to expel the tension.

She did not want to brood anymore on the impossibility of freeing Gen, and she quashed the tears threatening to well in her eyes. Flutterings in her belly, growing stronger by the day, distracted her, and she was reminded that within the confines of her womb grew the object worthy of sacrifice. She had hoped that if any sacrifice were needed, it would be her own life and not those whom she counted so dear.

A timid knock at the door brought her to her elbows. "Come in."

A waif of a girl, no older than twelve, entered, carrying a plate of dried apples and cheese in one hand and in the other a goblet of wine. The door shut behind her and the Chalaine waived her over, signaling for the girl to place the tray on the small table near the bed.

"What is your name?"

"Rena," she answered with a curtsy, voice nasal and high.

"Thank you, Rena."

"You are welcome, Lady Khairn," she replied, and the Chalaine paused. *Am I still Lady Khairn?* She rarely saw anyone, and everyone she did see called her Chalaine, even Athan. It was as if even those committed to the idea of her marriage could not, deep down, think of her as Chertanne's wife. And yet this very day she was taking part in a scheme that risked the life of the man whose name she would wear proudly for the sake of one whose name had already worn off.

"Are you well, Milady?"

"Yes, yes," the Chalaine answered, emerging from her stupor. "I am sorry. Thank you again for the food. I will be finished and gone in half an hour. You can return for everything then."

The Chalaine wanted to remove her veil to eat, but her young servant stood fidgeting nervously. "Are you sure there is nothing else you require?" Rena inquired, voice desperate.

"I do not. . ." Then the Chalaine saw it, the servant's veil pitched slightly to the left. Rena had a message. "Now that you mention it, I wonder if you might brush my hair? It is a bit tangled, and I find it soothing."

Rena relaxed. "I would happy to, Lady Khairn."

"Please, call me Chalaine."

"As you wish," Rena said, pleased. The Chalaine removed her veil and chewed on a leathery apple slice while she waited for Rena to stop gawking. Once Rena began, the Chalaine focused, waiting for the girl to begin the conversation that would contain the indirect message.

"Do you and your mother look much alike?" she asked.

So the message is from my mother.

"I believe so, though I have always thought she had an elegance that I do not."

The girl said, "I am sure she is thinking about you, wherever she is. She did arrive with you, did she not, along with several of your guards?"

"Yes, though I have not seen her or them since. I wish I could see them."

"I imagine so."

"I fear for their health and safety," the Chalaine said. "I think the Padras locked them up in the miserable dungeon they have in the bottom of this place."

"Well, if they did, then they *all* probably sit around and wonder if you're being treated well, since they wouldn't get any news of you down there."

Does that mean they are all in the same place? the Chalaine wondered. If true, it would be good news.

"I think they know that I have to be well taken care of. I am carrying Eldaloth within me, after all."

"Of course," Rena agreed. The Chalaine ate quickly as Rena remained silent. Was that the extent of the message? Was there no more?

Rena alleviated her worry and spoke again. "I do not wish to offend you, Chalaine, but I have heard so many stories about the man Gen. Are they true?"

"I would have to know what stories you refer to."

Rena swallowed. The Chalaine could sense the confusion and difficulty in her voice. "Is it true he came here looking for you?"

"Yes."

"Were your frightened? He is the Ilch."

"I would never be frightened of Gen. He is not the Ilch. He is my loyal servant, and I care for him deeply. He would no more harm me than he would harm you or any other innocent creature. He has saved me so many times and in so many ways, I could never repay the debt."

Rena breathed more easily, though the Chalaine could not tell if her next question was part of the message or part of her curiosity.

"Well, I heard that your mother is very fond of him and worries about him continually."

"That is true. She loves him as much as I do."

"I apologize for asking such sensitive questions. It is not my business."

"No need to apologize."

More silence ensued. Rena continued working at the Chalaine's hair, using the pause in the conversation as a transition.

"Did you know that Ironkeep has many Portals within it?" Rena asked a couple of minutes later.

"I had heard that."

"They are all over. There are some that haven't even been discovered. I've never been through a Portal. Is it really as sickening as they say?"

"The first few times, yes," the Chalaine explained, wondering where this was going. "Though you get used to it."

"There are many Portal Mages here. There was one that Shadan Khairn—well, Chertanne's father—kept around that wasn't part of the Guild. He was funny. I didn't see him much after the Shadan invaded Tolnor. I wonder what became of him?"

The Chalaine began to understand. "Using a Portal Mage that is not part of the Guild would bring the wrath of the Guild down upon the Shadan! Surely he didn't want it known."

"Probably not," Rena agreed. "Torbrand probably had him killed when the war was over, or maybe he locked him up in that miserable dungeon. At least he would be in good company in the dungeon, if your mother and your guards are there."

The Chalaine's heart leapt within her. She knew exactly where this was going now and laughed casually. "I would agree with that and envy him for it."

Rena stopped combing. The message was over. "I have forgotten to take the chamber pot from the Padras' quarters. Forgive me, Chalaine, but I must go."

"I release you. Thank you for your conversation. It has calmed my mind considerably."

"You are most welcome. Fare thee well, Milady."

Time passed too quickly as the Chalaine thought and schemed, wondering what use she could make of the message implied in Rena's conversation. Gen's safety depended on somehow maneuvering him near the others in the prison, and while she hoped that Padra Athan would imprison him in the dungeon, she doubted they would send him so far out of their control or so near his allies. At worst, she suspected that Padra Athan would betray her and kill Gen once Chertanne lived. The Padras most likely scenario, as she figured it, was to send Gen away to Mur Eldaloth, as they had originally planned, and she could see no way to prevent it. Even worse, Chertanne might seek Gen's life out of revenge, whatever her Protector's part in his return to life.

She racked her brain as she returned to the dark chamber in the dungeon, but she could come to no conclusions. Blood pumping from Gen's arm and the task of keeping him alive ended her vain machinations, and once again she found herself relying on faith.

The last three bleedings passed quickly compared to the first four, Athan shooing everyone from the room and back out into the hallway once the last bleeding ended. The Chalaine gazed at Gen one last time as the Eldephaere shut the door, turning to find all the Padras lined up on the stairs.

"Only Padras will remain here. Everyone else, go up," Athan ordered. The Chalaine walked toward the stairs when a thought came to her.

"May I descend to visit my Mother and her companions? I should be nearby if Chertanne awakens."

Athan, conversing in hushed tones with his fellow Churchmen, stopped abruptly and turned in her direction. "No. You will wait here in the event I need you to remind Gen of his oath. Guard, bring Chertanne."

Athan turned away again and, after issuing commands, the rest of the Padras filed onto the small landing, pushing her partway down the stairs to the dungeon. In a few minutes, a group of Eldephaere struggled to bring Chertanne's corpse, covered in a white shroud, down the winding steps. A bier simply couldn't squeeze around the corners, so they transported the body unceremoniously with hands on ankles and under armpits.

"Place him directly into the vat of blood," Athan

instructed, removing a folded document from his robe. "Leave this document by Gen."

The Chalaine wondered what Athan had written, but she found all thoughts driven from her mind as the men entered, and, after a great slosh, returned again, locking the door behind them with a rusted set of keys.

"Create the wards," Athan commanded, "and then stand away. Make sure you are not visible to Gen through the bars of the door."

The hair on the Chalaine's arms stood up as magical energy filled the room, the Padras incanting. Once done, Athan and half of the Padras pushed her farther down the steps as the other half ascended to get out of sight of the door. Athan exhaled and concentrated.

"Pray this works, Chalaine," he whispered. "Everything depends upon him."

The Chalaine wondered which of the two men in the room behind the wall that Athan meant.

Gen's eyes fluttered open. He sat up quickly, intending to assess his environment, but a power in the room burned like a bonfire in the dark, drawing his attention immediately. Next to him sat a vat of his own blood, energy emanating from it and suffusing him with strength. He reached out a hand to touch the black iron of the pot, a nearly drunk feeling overcoming him.

With the vat's contents, he could raze Ironkeep, turning its walls into dust for the wind to carry off. His head swam with the new training now open to him, and in horror he knew he could just as easily use the virtue of the blood to create weapons of such power they could annihilate the very soul of a living creature, as Mikkik sought to do to Eldaloth.

Only when he stood did he notice the note as it fell from his lap onto the floor. He stooped to retrieve and open, finding Athan's practiced, practical script.

Gen,

We have placed Chertanne in the vat and into the blood. Remember your vow to the Chalaine to use your power to raise him. Remember that he is key to the unfolding of prophecy, whatever your personal feelings. I pledge that I will see that the Chalaine is treated with honor and respect at all times when Chertanne returns and that I will not harm those you care for. I have done what I have done for the sake of the world. The Chalaine understands that this must be done. Honor your promise to her.

You should open a Portal to Erelinda, for it is there that Eldaloth's servant surely resides.

If, however, you hurt Chertanne in any way, there will be retribution against those you care for. While this is, perhaps, beneath me, it is the only reason that you listen to. When you are finished, have Chertanne call for us, and we will come for him.

Padra Athan

Gen refolded the note and set it next to the lantern, peering into the oversized cauldron. Chertanne's corpse lay on its side half covered in the blood. Gen stepped back, repulsed and uncertain. He could feel the Chalaine just beneath and behind him and remembered agreeing to perform the spell to return her husband to life, but something had clouded his mind then. With his judgment now unencumbered by potion or magic, his heart struggled.

Surely the Chalaine has been and would be happier without him. With the knowledge available to Gen now, he had no doubt he could leave Chertanne dead and take her back to

284

Rhugoth.

But as the thought ran through his mind, so did his mistake in Elde Luri Mora; he had tried to kill Chertanne out of pride and vengeance. He had ignored the Chalaine's wishes and orders and turned his life to ruin. If she believed that reviving Chertanne was the right course, then he felt he should honor his commitment to her and perform the ritual as she asked. He no longer trusted his own feelings and reasoning.

Gen closed his eyes and enveloped himself in the essence radiating from his collected blood, pulling it within him. In the training the Millim Eri had concealed from him he found the knowledge to create a Portal into the Abyss and to Erelinda, though Mikkik would never attempt the latter. Chertanne's body would act as a lodestone to the spirit, and—once connected—he would use blood magic to re-forge the link between body and soul to bind them again. It was the ultimate power of blood.

While Athan assumed that Chertanne rested peacefully in the light of Erelinda, Gen thought this wishful thinking, concentrating instead on the location Chertanne's actions merited. In a thought he accomplished it, the Portal into a palpable blackness coalescing just above the cauldron. A dread chill filled the room, reminding him of the hole from which had risen the demon at the betrothal.

As soon as the gateway solidified, a horrifying, discordant chorus of suffering filled the room at a suffocating volume. Opening his eyes, Gen watched as the vision in the Portal swirled and spun about a wasted, benighted landscape. Sooty smoke and orange sparks obscured the denizens of that world.

In the obscurity walked the dead, but not alone. Billowing, shifting shadows with red eyes stalked the pale, ghostly bodies of dead spirits they tormented. Without warning, their ethereal vapors would encase their victims, red eyes replacing the sufferer's in their sockets while the smoky shape coalesced around them. Howls of pain and fright ripped from raw throats, the dark beings swelling in size until the sufferer was released to collapse upon a floor of sharp volcanic rock. Red eyes would return into the swirling form of a shadow as it hunted another prey, leaving the sufferer's eyes all the more sunken and hollow.

Gen shuddered, wondering how much of that world he would be forced to witness, but at last the Portal settled on Chertanne, weak and crawling on the floor, a nightmare apparition hovering above him, waiting. As the Portal settled, the red eyes turned upward and regarded Gen.

"What are your sins?" it rasped. A tendril of dark mist passed through the Portal toward Gen's face, but before it touched him, it withdrew. It said, "Rejoice. For you shall never know the torture of the Abyss. Weep, for you shall never know the joy of Erelinda. There is no traveler within your shell to take the journey."

Gen's heart sank. Here at last was confirmed what he had long suspected. The Ilch was no more than a construct, a *thing* with no soul of its own, created to live, to die, and to know no more.

"I shall feed on this one then, for he has much to answer for," the creature swooped in to envelop the struggling Chertanne. Gen acted, pulling power from the blood and creating the binding link between body and soul that Jaron had severed. Chertanne's spirit broke through the swirling dark of the apparition's body.

"You cannot rob me!" it howled. "I must feed!"

Gen shuddered and shut the Portal, Chertanne coughing and sputtering inside the cauldron. The blood remained, and not all of its power was exhausted. Tentatively, Chertanne's red-soaked head peeked above the rim of the cauldron, bright eyes wide with fear. Upon seeing Gen, he shrieked.

"I knew you would join me here! Even in the Abyss you must torment me!"

He shrank back into the vat, sloshing about and mumbling incoherently. Shuffling sounds outside reminded Gen that Athan would cast a stupor upon him, and with a quick spell, he covered the grate in the door in metal. The Padras would get him sooner or later, but he had to speak to the Chalaine one last time. He could sense her just a little behind and down from where he stood. With a thought, stone evaporated into air, and he saw her, an Eldephaere guard nearby ready to raise an alarm. Using the remaining power of Trys, Gen walled off the stairway from the upper landing and encased the guard in a hollow prison of rock.

Darkness overtook them as the new wall blocked out the massed lamps above, but a guttering torch farther down the stairs provided enough light for him to feel his way forward and into the Chalaine's fervent embrace. Tears flowed silently in the dank prison, and for a moment his hurts and his cares abated.

"Forgive me, Chalaine. I have made a mess of everything."

"Quietly now, Gen," she consoled, burying her head in his shoulder. "It's not your fault. It never was your fault. Is he alive?"

"Chertanne? Yes. I only did it because you wished it."

"It was the right thing to do, but you must leave here," she begged

"I haven't the strength to tunnel out of here with magic. It is you who should leave after all the pain they've caused."

The Chalaine pulled away from him and took his hand, pulling him down the stairs. "It was all a fraud to pull you here, Gen," she explained. "I never felt any hurt and was in no danger. I was only bait. You must believe I would never have willingly submitted. They gave me no choice."

"I know. They should still pay for using you so."

"That is of no consequence now, Gen."

"Where are we going?" he asked.

"To see my mother . . . I hope."

"They have her locked up down *here*?" Gen thundered.

"Quietly, Gen! We have to hurry. The Padras will be here any moment."

But as they rounded a corner they found three Eldephaere waiting in a dingy, straw-covered anteroom with swords drawn. Of all Mikkik's restored teachings, Gen still found the ease with which Trysmagic could kill living creatures the most sinister. With barely a thought and hardly any power, the three soldiers crumpled to the floor, dead in an instant. Quickly, Gen gathered the key from one of the bodies and inserted it into the heavy iron door.

"Grab the lantern, Chalaine."

Hinges whined and screeched as the door to the lower dungeon scraped open. The howls and pitiful pleas for food or freedom from half naked and half sane denizens immersed them in a scene little better than what Gen had witnessed in the Abyss. Emaciated, pale limbs with knobby fingers and ridged, dirty nails clutched at them through iron bars, and the stench of their bodies and breath set the Chalaine's stomach to churning.

"Mother!" the Chalaine called queasily.

"In the back, dear child. What are you doing here?"

"I've brought Gen! It's time."

"You work quickly, dearest."

They found them at the rear of the dungeon. Unlike the freestanding cells at the entrance, these were hollowed into the rock and sealed with heavy wooden doors. Mirelle guided them in by yelling through the bars in the doors. Gen made quick work with the key, familiar faces spilling out of dark holes and into the warmth of the lantern light. Dason knelt before the Chalaine, kissing her hand, a litany of warm sentiments gushing from a full heart. Mirelle fairly leapt into Gen's arms, smiles popping up on worn faces at the spectacle.

"Thank you Eldaloth," she whispered as they embraced, "for bringing him back to me." Wiping her eyes, she disentangled herself from Gen and turned her gaze upon the Portal Mage. "Udan, it's your turn. Where is this Portal?"

"This way." He nodded. "Follow me."

Gen moved away from the company. "I'll bar the door and grab the Eldephaeres' swords. I'll catch up with you."

"I'll help," Tolbrook offered, following.

After relocking the door and piling as much as they could in front of it, Gen and Tolbrook undid the sword belts and ran back to the company that stood in front of an empty cell. Udan turned. "It is in here. One moment."

"Do you know where the Portal goes, Udan?" Mirelle inquired.

"No. This Portal was never discovered. We'll want to send someone through for a look."

"I will do it," Gen volunteered from the back. "I'll be going through whatever the place may be like."

Udan nodded in acknowledgment and concentrated, a brilliant blue light blazing in the darkness. The illumination's significance was not lost on the other prisoners, renewed pleas for freedom clamoring for their consideration. Gen wasted no time, crossing into the Portal and returning, face grim.

"I'm afraid it isn't pleasant," he reported. "It is a desert of black sand and vapors of smoke. I saw few plants and no water. I must take the chance. The rest can choose."

"I go with Gen," Mirelle announced firmly.

"As do I," Gerand and Volney followed.

"I go where Mirelle goes," Cadaen added.

"I will go with Mirelle," Mena said meekly.

"Are you staying behind, Chalaine?" Mirelle asked.

"I must, for the prophecy's sake."

"No!" Dason said. "You should flee! Anywhere is better than this place."

"Not for me, Dason. They have treated me well, and I need to be with Chertanne. I must stay."

"Then I stay, as well," Dason said, throwing Gen a challenging look. "*I* will not leave you." Captain Tolbrook and the rest of the Dark Guard echoed the same sentiment.

Mirelle crossed to her daughter and embraced her. "It is settled, then. May Eldaloth see us together again in brighter places and happier times."

The Chalaine crossed to Gen and let him enfold her in his arms. She kissed his cheek and whispered, "I love you more than you can know. Take care of yourself and my mother."

"I will."

Shouting and clanging at the prison door reminded them to hurry, and the Chalaine smiled as the people she had fretted over for so long disappeared from the dungeon. Udan crossed through his own Portal, and the blue light winked out.

When the Chalaine emerged from the dungeon, she would again find herself the wife of a wretch, but no longer would she worry for those she loved best. Eldaloth had heard her prayer and provided an escape, and she found this merciful gift had propped up her flagging faith. Surrounded by the Dark Guard, she walked calmly back to the prison door, arriving just as Athan stormed through, soldiers and Padras streaming in behind.

"Where is he?" he thundered, eyes darting everywhere.

To spare his feelings, the Chalaine stripped her voice of as much joy as she could before answering.

"Gone."

CHAPTER 66 - TREES OF STONE

Mirelle, Cadaen, Mena, Gen, Udan, Volney, and Gerand stood on a sea of black sand. Sulfurous vapors wafted by on the wind, puckering faces. A constant layer of low-flying clouds sped by above, the light dim and uneven, the sun thrusting through at unpredictable intervals and disappearing just as unexpectedly. Small, leathery plants poked up from the sand, providing the only vegetation for a wasted terrain. Sharp, porous rocks rose up in crumbling heaps in every direction, and no vista provided a fairer prospect than another. Despite the season, the air was stifling, dry, and hot, and the combination of the sickening smell and the heat engendered a general malaise in every mind and stomach.

Volney exhaled sharply after a period of aimless and disappointed wandering around. "Eldaloth obviously hid the Portal to this place out of mercy for his creatures. Leave it to our luck to escape to a place *less* desirable than a dungeon. First a wagon, then a sewer, then a dungeon, and now a desert, and not just any desert, a rotten, foul, reeking, stink-hole of a desert! And if we escape this place, no doubt we'll find ourselves on the Uyumaak latrine shard and forced to wipe their scaly. . ."

"Believe it or not," Udan cut in loudly in an attempt to head Volney off, "there are shards worse than this one. Gen knows about one of them. It's so cold your face falls right off after a few moments."

"You know," Volney ranted, "I'll never understand why it is that other people try to make you feel at peace with your situation by telling you there's a worse one. Is that supposed to make me feel better? It's like stabbing me in the leg, twisting the blade around, and then telling me I should be grateful it's not in my eye! For Erelinda's sake, can someone conjure me up a warm bed and a decent meal? It's been so long!"

Gerand crossed to his friend and put his arm around his shoulders. "We all feel the same, Volney. Udan was merely pointing out that we at least have a chance to survive here. Have faith, friend. Better sand than snow."

"I am sorry," Gen apologized to everyone after letting the red fade from Volney's cheeks. "I wish there had been time to prepare or some other path we could have followed."

Mirelle latched onto his arm as if preparing for a summer stroll in a pleasant garden. "We all had the choice, Gen. You didn't force anyone here. What do we do now?"

"Shelter first, then I'll scout around for signs of food or water. We need to find protection from the sun and the wind. These pitted black rocks should hold a myriad of caves we can avail ourselves of if we can find an outcropping big enough. We'll go slowly. Try not to exert yourselves overmuch."

For the next two hours they wandered about in the dreary wasteland. Seething pools of boiling mud radiated a foul smell, and they steered clear of them when they could. The pools increased in size and frequency the further they pressed on, and Gen finally called for them to reverse course, Volney murmuring under his breath.

The rest bore up well, but as darkness started to fall

without their finding any outcropping of significant size, they had to settle for the lee side of a rounded hump of a boulder that had a smoother, solider aspect than the jagged black ones they had searched during the day. Wind had scooped out a small bowl around it, and they descended the slight incline and sat heavily against the stone in complete exhaustion, all except Mena, who knelt by Gerand.

"Is there any comfort I can give you, Milord?" Mena offered. Gerand's face contorted in surprise.

"What?"

"I could rub your shoulders or your feet, or you could lay your head on my lap for comfort while you rest. I could sing you something to take your mind off of a difficult day."

"No," Gerand declined, fumbling to sort his thoughts and feelings out. "No. I mean, thank you, but no."

"I'll take any of those, Mena," Udan said hopefully. "My feet are killing me."

Volney laughed. "That won't do, Udan. She is his wife."

"You two are married?" Udan asked incredulously. "Since when? Torbrand let you marry his daughter? How in all of Ki'Hal did you manage. . ."

"Shhhh," Volney warned him. "We don't talk about it."

"No, really, I must hear the. . ." Gen's shook his head, and Udan let the subject drop.

Mena, disappointed, rose to go.

"I apologize," Gerand blurted out quickly, "if I've offended you, Mena. I don't wish you to think that anything you have to offer me is somehow undesirable. Rather, that in circumstances such as these it would be ungentlemanly of me to accept comfort when it should be my place to provide it. If there is something I can do for you to ease your burden, then name it."

She returned to his side. "Then let me serve you. Please. Let me stand by your side. I know my father bequeathing me to you was a deep insult to your honor and to your nation. I can't imagine how much I must disgust you or what loves or friends you lost when I was thrust upon you. I cannot undo what it is done, but at least give me the chance to show you my worth. I will not hope that you can love me as I do you, but if anything I can do will blunt the bitterness in your eyes every time you look at me, let me perform it."

Awkwardness pervaded the party as they witnessed this private moment, Mena's heartfelt intensity momentarily distracting them from hunger, thirst, and fatigue. Gerand, stunned to silence by this sudden vehemence, regarded his estranged bride and took her hand tenderly, signaling for her to sit by her side.

"Mena, what was done to us was wrong. . ."

"I know, but. . ."

"Listen for a moment. I will not use you or have you serve me like a slave."

"I don't want to be your slave!"

"Please, let me finish. I cannot love or even like someone I do not know, and I cannot trust your regard for me until I am sure you know me, and not just some ideal you may have conjured up of Tolnorian nobility. I have faults enough to sour any good woman's opinion. The best I can offer you—and all I can accept from you now—is your company and your conversation. Let us plant that seed and see what grows."

"Bloody well said!" Udan interjected inappropriately. "Though you're a fool to turn down the foot rub."

Gerand shot an angry look at Udan before turning back to Mena, who smiled gratefully at her husband. "Thank you for your concession. I will make the most of it."

She put her hand on Gerand's bearded cheek and kissed him lightly on the lips before settling in next to him. Gerand's face couldn't quite settle on an emotion, though he offered no protest at Mena having taken a little more liberty than they had agreed upon.

"Can I speak with you privately for a moment, Gen?" Mirelle requested.

"Certainly."

The others watched as the two disappeared around the rock and walked out into a stiff wind, Gen reflexively assuring Cadaen that he would keep Mirelle safe. The clouds had cleared up, allowing a chill to goosebump Mirelle's arms. The shards intermixed with the stars, coalescing into even bands, evidencing their gradual journey toward the day of Unification. Trys now waxed half full. Mirelle led Gen toward a smaller boulder nearby before addressing him in low tones.

"Did Athan's plan work? Is Chertanne alive?"

"He is. I did it myself."

Mirelle shook her head in acceptance and paced in a slow turn, thinking. "I had no qualms with Chertanne dead, and I doubt you did either. While it complicated the prophecy, I was happy that the Chalaine was free."

"The Chalaine made me swear to do it, or I would have declined."

"No doubt Athan hung you over her head as leverage."

It was Gen's turn to pace, running his hands through his hair. "Nothing I have done since Elde Luri Mora has felt right. Now I've led everyone to this cursed place. We'll die here if we don't find water soon."

"I've learned a bit about faith lately, Gen," Mirelle said. "Maybe it's time you rely on that. How are you going to explain to everyone that Chertanne is alive?"

"How can I without exposing myself?"

"You need only say that the Chalaine told you that the Church managed to resurrect him somehow. That is all that need be said. As for our escape, your fighting prowess will suffice as explanation."

A shout from Cadaen sent the two sprinting back to the boulder where they found everyone standing and staring into the darkness. On a hill to the east, a single figure, shrouded and unknowable, stood perfectly still. Tendrils of thin fabric from its cloak whipped in the wind, the immobility of the apparition suggesting a statue beneath the clothing. Gen raised his arms in a placating gesture and took a step forward, but a sudden wind kicked up dust and sand, and when it had passed, the phantom had gone.

"Haunting," Udan said.

"But it is a good sign for us," Gen offered, voice hopeful. "Someone is on this shard and has survived here. I'm going to go look around."

Gen searched for signs of civilization until midnight but found nothing promising. The next day bloomed as hot and miserable as the last. The farther they traveled east, the fewer outcroppings of stone they encountered. The dunes piled higher, and the black sand intermingled with a fine dust that clung to their teeth and lips and settled in their ears and boots. Near midafternoon, Mena abruptly stumbled and fell face first to the ground. Everyone gathered around the stricken woman quickly, Gerand pulling her over onto his lap and wiping her sweating face with the inside of his cloak.

"I'm glad she fell first," Udan panted. "I won't be far behind."

Gen, sick with worry, turned toward them. "We shouldn't travel during the day. After our encounter last night I had hoped we would find signs of civilization by now. Everyone stay here and rest. I'll try to find somewhere for us to hole up."

After an hour of searching, Gen found a dry river bed running north and south, providing some shade against the punitive sun. By the time he had collected everyone and marched them there, both Mirelle and Udan needed support, and Gerand sweated profusely as he practically carried Mena down the sharp incline and into the shade.

"Is anyone hiding any food?" Volney petitioned. "My cloak is starting to smell like roast pork for some reason."

"I'm afraid the prison guards neglected to portion out enough porridge to us to stuff any in our pockets before we left," Udan answered. "Remember? You were there."

Volney beat the back of his head against the rock before resting the front on his knees and dozing off in the sweltering heat. The rest of the party followed suit save Gen, who regarded them with sadness. He couldn't let it end this way if he could help it. While he couldn't conjure up food without suspicion, water, he thought, he could manage.

As evening came on, he left the others behind and scouted out a small cave worn out of the side of the riverbed wall. It was dark, low, and dusty and he hoped that no one in the party had enough lore to tell that water had not graced the small chamber in decades. He rested for a moment in the cooling air, for despite his conditioning, the exertion and worry wore upon him more than he let on.

At last, he straightened and knelt, placing his hands on the spot. Digging deep, he pulled in every ounce of power he could and willed the rock to transform into water. As he finished, his head spun with weakness and his limbs refused his command. He toppled over into the pool that he had created, helplessly bobbing facedown on the surface. His exhausted mind screamed danger, but nothing could motivate his muscles to move. Dimly, he enjoyed the cool caress of the water and its feel upon his sunburned face. The woozy calm of fading consciousness and undulating caress of the water felt more like home than any place had for months.

The sheltered riverbed protected Gen's footprints and allowed Cadaen to find them easily, even in the fading light. He warned the rest of the party to stay clear of them as they proceeded worriedly, calling out the lost Protector's name. They had not gone far when they encountered the low cave and the pool of water, and only Cadaen and Mirelle waited to satiate their thirst as they cast around for more clues of Gen's whereabouts.

"The trail leads to the water and no further," Cadaen reported as he and Mirelle took their turn to drink amid the grateful tones of their companions. "Look at the shape of this pool," Cadaen continued. "It is regular, more like a carved cistern. Perhaps fed by an underground spring. The water is very clean."

Mirelle pulled everyone together, face thoughtful and lined with worry. "We cannot continue to search tonight, but we must be careful at this place. The pool here is not natural, and, since this is the only water we have found, it is likely that whoever lives here knows about it. My guess is that Gen encountered the owners of this well. Whether he speaks with them now or was killed or taken captive, I cannot guess. We have but two swords now, and we keep watch. There is enough water here for days, but we must find food or perish."

"There is no need for worry." A strangely accented but beautiful voice from the outcropping above them startled them all. The robed figure they had seen the night before stood above them. The gray cloak enclosed her completely, only a hint of her face visible in the late evening. Long pieces of diaphanous cloth sown into the sleeves and sides of the cloak fluttered about in the breeze. She held a small sack in one hand. Everyone's eyes shot wide as she stepped off the outcropping with easy grace and dropped fifteen feet to the riverbed, landing softly.

Everyone regarded their guest with wonder as she lowered her hood, her elven face and glorious dark hair stunning them with their majesty. Her cool blue eyes were tinged with sadness and reflected an innate pride as she crossed to Mirelle.

"Eat," she commanded, placing a ripe peach in Mirelle's hand and then continuing on to the rest. "I have only one for each of you, but there are certainly more to be had. Eat first, questions later. I am Al'Handra."

"I am. . ."

"Mirelle," Al'Handra interjected. "I know your names. Your reckless companion provided me with those."

"Then Gen found you?"

"Rather, the reverse." Al'Handra smirked, an odd expression for a face such as hers. "He is safe and in good condition. Many of my people would have left you out here to perish, despite his information, but I have always had a weakness for the race of men, and he provided me the best news that I have had in centuries. You find me magnanimous, and thus, you will not die here in the waste."

"What did he tell you?" Mirelle asked, licking the juice off of her lips.

"That my daughter yet lives. You know her by her human name, Maewen." Mirelle's eyes widened and her lips parted to say something, but Al'Handra continued. "There are some other pieces of information about himself, the Chalaine, and the Ha'Ulrich that my master, Devlis, would speak with you about in private. We journey tonight. We shall commence when you are ready."

They ate with delight, juice dripping through their fingers and down their chins, the peaches unusually sweet, almost decadent. The unexpected delicacy filled them, weary limbs forgetting their exhaustion. Al'Handra watched them stoically, their delighted reactions bringing her no pleasure or surprise, even their rather inelegant attempts to suck the juice off their sticky fingers. Shortly, Mirelle thanked her and signaled their readiness to travel.

Al'Handra nodded and walked forward at a steady pace, not looking back to monitor their progress or engage them in conversation. While her cold manner troubled them, if she could provide more food and somewhere better to rest, no one would feel compelled to complain about her manners. She led them down the dry riverbed, the night again clear and cold. After a two hour march, the shard edge approached. Al'Handra did not deviate, striding up to the precipice and stopping at the brink of the empty vastness.

"The stair is narrow and unprotected. If your legs are weak, wait until they recover strength before attempting them. I will go before you into Ras'Ael and announce your coming."

With no further explanation she stepped off the edge and turned, descending down the stairs they could not see until they stood where she had, and when they did, their heads spun. Some two hundred steps had been carved into the shard edge, and—while appearing sturdy—they stretched no more than three feet wide with no rail between the stair and a plummet into blackness. Al'Handra walked down them confidently and evenly.

"I will need a moment before I try that," Udan admitted, face pale. "Maybe more than a moment."

"Shouldn't we tie ourselves together or something?" Volney asked, voice queasy.

"No," Gerand corrected. "That is for traveling through snow storms and fog. Here it would mean that if one person fell, he would drag everyone with him. We go one at a time with several feet between us. That way, when you stumble and fall, you won't take me with you."

Volney peeked over the edge and frowned, backing away. "I'll say it again. I grew up on a plain."

"I'm going," Mirelle announced, and before anyone, including herself, could dissuade her, she stepped off the edge and onto the stair. Cadaen came after, and the rest trickled down at irregular intervals, Udan and Volney bringing up the distant rear. The stair emptied onto a platform in the middle of a broad opening stretching nearly a quarter of a mile across the shard face, the entrance into an immense cavity in the shard's bowels. The smell of fruit and blossoms flirted with the air. Inside the cave an orchard was bathed in soft moonlight that flooded through the hole, the occasional winks of fireflies punctuating the darkness. Beyond the orchard, the light reflected off of something that gave the impression of a field full of sparkling, emerald stars.

Al'Handra awaited them on the platform, hands behind her back. After Volney gratefully joined the rest of the group on less treacherous ground, the austere elf spoke.

"Welcome to Ras'Ael, or in your tongue, the Grave of Light. Here you will find fifty-two elves and fourteen dwarves. There were more of us once, but thirty-two elves have journeyed to Erelinda after the manner of my people, and time has claimed thirty-eight of the dwarves that survived the Shattering. Among those here is our leader, Devlis, an elf mighty in the magic arts and steeped in lore. He will speak with Mirelle now and instructs me to see the rest of you quartered. Follow."

She led them off the platform and down a grassy embankment onto a stone path that led around the orchard. Just as a complaint about the darkness formed on Mirelle's lips, the fireflies of the orchard grouped around them, providing a weak but ample light to tread by. The path led to a railed stair carved in dark stone that led up to a shelf smoothed and shaped so that no crack or edge would catch a boot tip. The fireflies deserted them here, but as they walked on, the green stones they had seen sparkling in the distance flared to life and they stopped in wonderment.

Around them, massive trees rose from the rock at their feet and stretched into the air to where they supported the ceiling of the cave. While the intricate detail of the bark tricked the eye into seeing wood, a more careful examination by the light of the glowing green leaves carved in jade crystals revealed that the trees were indeed the work of art and not of nature.

Every detail, from root to stem, had been meticulously shaped from the dark rock, though Mirelle's party found themselves hurrying by as Al'Handra strode forward unabated by their expressions of delight. As they passed, the green gem leaves winked out behind them and lit before, and in that light they caught glimpses of doorways and windows carved out of the stony tree trunks. Most yawned empty and black, but from time to time a curious dwarf or elf would stare out at them expressionlessly, faces bathed in the green light.

Al'Handra abruptly stopped at the entrance to one of the massive stone trees. "You will stay here tonight. When it is light, we will proportion you among the vacant trees more comfortably. Come, Mirelle. Devlis waits."

Mirelle followed, Cadaen shadowing her, as Al'Handra proceeded up a small incline. The trees occluded the view of the orchard and the opening of the shard beyond, and despite the magic and awe she felt from the trees, the farther they passed into the cave, the more the city resembled the grave suggested by its name. They passed out of the main cluster of trees and into a flat open space. One immense tree, larger and more grand than the rest, hulked fifty yards ahead.

"I will retire now," Al'Handra informed them. "Proceed to the tree there and enter. You are expected. I will probably see you again tomorrow. Farewell."

"Thank you," Mirelle said with sincere gratitude, though Al'Handra didn't acknowledge it.

"A queer place," Cadaen whispered as Mirelle proceeded on tentatively. "Wondrous, but. . ."

"Stale," she finished for him. "Grave of Light, she called it. That is what it feels like, especially here in the dark. Just think, Cadaen. These elves and dwarves have lived here for centuries with nothing but this and the harsh desert above. Hopefully Devlis is a little more forthcoming than Al'Handra. I wonder how Maewen's father ever loved such a cold creature."

"She was not always so," a voice from behind them said, startling them out of their wits. Cadaen went for his sword but could not pull it out. They faced an older elf, dressed in plain black robe tied with a knotted rope. The only color about him was a green feather pin above his left breast. A white, thin beard fell from his chin like a waterfall to his chest. His snowy hair he wore long, and above his upswept ears, absorbing green eyes stood out youthfully on a face carved rough by age.

"Relax, Master Cadaen," he said. "I mean no harm. I am Devlis, whom you seek."

"What have you done to my. . ." The sword suddenly came loose of the scabbard.

"There," Devlis apologized. "I simply did not want to find myself split in two by accident."

"You elves seem to have a talent for sneaking up on people," Cadaen complained, resheathing his sword.

"We are silent by nature and do not startle easily, so we have not developed those little habits of politely announcing ourselves by coughing or sniffing as you do. Come. I live in the tree just ahead there."

"The craftsmanship of the trees is marvelous," Mirelle expressed as the older elf passed by her and started toward the solitary tree at the back of the cave.

"Yes, it is a fine work," Devlis said, "but I still wonder at times if they are too real. Sometimes I find myself believing I walk in a real grove of great oaks, only to place my hand on the rocky trunk to disappoint myself over and over. Here we are."

They passed through the archway into a circular room with a polished floor of dark brown rock. He spoke a word in Elvish, and a diamond the size of one of the peaches they had just eaten glowed with a comforting white light. It rested on a small black metal sconce over an intricate throne hewn from the walls. Green jade ran in an arch around back of the throne. A stairway rose off to their right, leading to rooms higher up in the trunk. The dwarves had carved seats into the wall circling away from the throne, and a circular section of the middle of the floor was raised to form a table of sorts, or perhaps a platform from which to perform or speak.

"That is a treasure, indeed," Mirelle commented about the diamond.

Devlis smiled and sat in on the throne. "Here it is worth precisely nothing, save as a focus for light. I would not keep you long, for I know of your travails, and you need not feel as if you have to explain anything. Gen's mind provided more information than we have, in our own limited way, been able to gather over the centuries. I am gratified to know the race of men still thrives. I worked with your ancestors much during the Mikkikian Wars. You are an impatient, unwise race, but the Millim Eri gifted you magic, and Eldaloth gifted you with many children. I suppose it natural that. . ."

"Devlis," Mirelle interrupted. "I mean no disrespect, but I am concerned for Gen. Where is he, and is he well?"

"I do apologize, Mirelle. It has been so long since I have had someone new to speak with. I have always supposed your impatience born of short lives. I doubt I could tolerate waiting for anything, either, if I knew death lingered a few years off. Your man is well. He is resting in a chamber above. I will send him to you tomorrow, though I do wish to speak with him more."

"I thought you had all you needed from his mind, already."

"I don't wish to glean anything more from him. It is some wisdom I wish to impart. He is a unique creature with powerful gifts, who is, nonetheless, angry with himself and not seeing clearly. If I can set him upon a more useful path, then I think I would be helping my masters, the Millim Eri—and you, I should think."

"Yes, thank you. And what of the elves and dwarves here? How came you here?"

Devlis leaned back, eyes unfocusing and retreating into the past. "When the dwarves of Khore-Thaka-Tnahk and the men from Echo Hold did not come to the alliance at Emerald Lake, some of us returned to learn their fate. Deep in the holds of the Far Reach Mountains, we sought them out and found a few alive with their young ones. Ghama Dhron, the abomination of snakes Gen used on the Shroud Lake shard, had slaughtered nearly the entire race of dwarves.

"Ki'Hal shattered soon after, and we found ourselves here in this dwarf cave. The dwarves carved and ensorcelled these trees in gratitude for us seeking them out. Only fourteen of that race remain, and they are old and near death. Many elves have passed on, throwing themselves into the swirling nothingness where the shards sail. We have only managed one child in our time here—Falael, my son. We have grown forlorn and cold in this place, so you must forgive our severity."

"Unification will come soon," Mirelle said, "and you can walk forests of wood again."

"Yes, yes, it is true. But we shall leave much sooner so we don't have to tunnel our way out."

"Through a Portal?" she asked.

"No. The same way you will in four weeks"

"What way is that?"

"By jumping."

CHAPTER 67 – BLOSSOM

A full week had passed after Chertanne's revivification before Padra Athan arrived at the Chalaine's door and announced that the time had at last arrived for the wife to see her husband. The Chalaine had spent the week pacing, wondering at the delay. Athan's appearance added to the clues she had already gathered. The Padra's face bespoke neither relief nor victory, but exhaustion and anxiety. Even during their slog through the Shroud Lake shard he had carried confidence and drive, but uncertainty smoldered where once passion burned.

"Is something amiss, your Grace?" the Chalaine asked tentatively as he entered her room. Athan signaled for her Eldephaere guards to shut the door and then fidgeted until the Chalaine asked him to sit.

"I . . . I don't know where to begin, so I will just say it. As you know, when the soul departs the body, there are two paths. One's character determines in which state the soul will find itself, either to wander the sunny fields of Erelinda or to suffer in the dark torture of the Abyss. Chertanne, I am afraid, dwelt in the latter during his separation from his body."

The Chalaine never had doubted that Chertanne would

end up in the Abyss, but for the Padra, it appeared to have come as an unwelcome revelation.

"I expected as much," she stated honestly.

"He is a changed man, Chalaine, and I cannot decide if it is for the better."

"What is he like, now, your Grace?" A long time had passed since she had cared to know anything about Chertanne at all, but Athan's haunted gravity sparked her curiosity.

The Padra swallowed before answering. "He is terrified."

"Cowardice has always dogged him, Padra."

"I don't think you understand, Chalaine. He hides from everyone. He shrieks in terror at the slightest noise and jumps at shadows. He sees apparitions of horrors that are not there. He whimpers in corners, refuses to eat, and acts at all times as if something horrible is waiting just outside the door to torment and devour him. We have had to sedate him with potions or use magic just to get food down his mouth. I had hoped to show him publicly to assuage the doubters, but his rational capacity is gone. Half the time, he still believes he is in the Abyss, and all of this is just some trick."

The Chalaine's eyebrows rose in astonishment. "What am I to do?"

Athan stood and resumed pacing. "I don't know that you can do anything, but you must see him, for good or ill."

"Has he mentioned me at all?"

"No, but he rarely talks coherently. He mutters under his breath a great deal."

"Can't you block his memories, like the Millim Eri did with Gen?"

"We thought of that and tried, but in doing so we learned an awful truth about the way the Abyss works. The memories that it brands upon the mind cannot be forgotten or undone. They are not dulled by time. They cannot be replaced or reinterpreted. It is a powerful magic that we cannot overcome. There is a dagger in Chertanne's mind, and the Abyss will never stop twisting it."

The Chalaine shuddered, feeling suddenly reluctant. "Are you sure it is such a good idea that I see him? He did not like me."

"I do not know if it is a good idea, Chalaine," he answered frankly. "You'll be fortunate if he even recognizes you. But I need you to see him so you can at least bear witness that he lives. If he cannot be seen and heard, then *you* need to be."

The Chalaine nodded her acceptance and followed Athan out the door. The dark wood and trophy-laden hallways still seemed as foreign as the day she arrived. Ironkeep creaked with every step, unlike the solid foundations of her castle in Mikmir. Servant girls stared at her as they passed through wide hallways. A thickening of the guard indicated that they neared their destination, but the location was wrong.

"We had to move him from his quarters to something a little more plain," Athan explained, noting her perplexity. "There were too many places for him to hide and too many objects to stoke his imagination in his extensive suite."

While perhaps a trick of her own thoughts, the Eldephaere in the hallway and the two Padras at the door appeared profoundly uncomfortable. Athan nodded to the Eldephaere at the door who undid a large lock before swinging the door inward.

"Go away!" Chertanne screamed, and the Chalaine strained to see inside.

"It is only I, Highness," Athan soothed as they entered. "I have brought the Chalaine."

"Shut the door, you fools! Shut it!" Athan nodded and it was done.

The room was little bigger than a servant's quarters and was sparsely furnished. A single wooden chair lay on its side near a lantern. A muttering, whining Chertanne had crawled under a mattress that stank of urine and sweat.

"It may take a moment," Athan whispered to the Chalaine. "He always has to make sure that nothing gets in when the door is opened."

"Wouldn't a room with a window and sunlight be better for him?" the Chalaine asked. "This room is as dark as the Abyss."

"No! It is not!" Chertanne yelled, sticking his head out from under the mattress. "It is not! Oh, mercy! You're some devil, aren't you? Take it away, Athan! You're all devils and demons come to tear my insides out and chew my bones!"

"We tried taking him outside," Athan said, "hoping that would convince him he was no longer in the Abyss, but he could not bear the light. He howled and howled until we brought him back inside." The Padra turned back to the mattress. "Chertanne! Come out. Let's talk. You must greet your wife. She is anxious for your wellbeing!"

"No! It's a trick. I am dead. I have no wife." Chertanne burst into tears, crawling completely beneath the mattress and into a corner. The Chalaine felt dizzy. Chertanne was completely mad.

"Believe it or not, he is better than he was," Athan offered with enough resignation to strangle any hope the statement was meant to convey. "We can go, if you wish."

The Chalaine teetered on the brink of indecision. She *wanted* to go more than anything, but her husband's pathetic indisposition inspired the healer within her and she stepped closer, grabbing the mattress.

"Chalaine, I wouldn't. . ."

The Chalaine yanked the mattress away, and Chertanne howled in horror, turning toward the wall and curling into a ball. They had tried to dress him in kingly fashion, but his scraping and hiding had shredded and sullied his fine clothing. What fat had remained after the draining march to and from Elde Luri Mora had melted completely away, leaving a gaunt, bony face and frame.

Crouching down, she touched his arm and he shrank back. "Chertanne, look at me."

"No!"

"Look at me and remember." Gradually he turned his head until one tortured eye regarded her. Ensuring that Athan stood directly behind her, she lifted her veil and showed Chertanne her face. Slowly, he turned until both of his black-rimmed eyes stared at her in wonderment and relief, a hint of recognition sparking within his dark mind. A trembling, pale hand stretched out and probed her face as if to prove it solid and not some illusion. Tears ran down his cheeks, and he removed his hand, the veil falling.

"Then I am not in the Abyss," he said quietly, eyes fixed on the Chalaine. Suddenly, he lurched from his corner and threw his arms around his wife like a drowning sailor clutching for a plank to float on in the stormy water.

"Please save me," he wept. "There is a fire in my mind, and I cannot put it out!" His body shook as he cried, and the Chalaine rubbed his back as he trembled, assuring him he was safe. Somewhere amid the tangle of the black thorns of her hatred and disgust for Chertanne bloomed a tender flower of feeling, and its name was pity.

Gen approached Mirelle quietly, wanting to watch her unnoticed. She sat on a raised stone slab overlooking a blossoming orchard of apple and peach trees bathed in the warm light streaming through the massive opening into the shard cave. Her hair hung loose about her shoulders, and she sat with her arms around her legs, her head resting on her knees and her face toward the light. Cadaen was nowhere to be found, and Gen wondered how she had evaded him.

Gen had noticed the change in her from the moment he had embraced her as she emerged from the prison cell in Ironkeep. Unlike when he found her crippled by uncertainty and fear on the barge across Shroud Lake, the dampening of her spirit that he now sensed did not stem from ephemeral external circumstances, but from a profound change to her personality. In her glory in Mikmir, she had accepted nothing contrary to her will, using her substantial gifts to mold and bend every situation to her liking and advantage. While strength still exuded from her, her eyes bespoke resignation and sadness, and Gen took no pleasure in seeing it.

Since the time that she confessed her love for him so memorably on the trail to Elde Luri Mora, Gen had little time to sort out the confused feelings the First Mother conjured within him. While in the castle, her flirtations and affection had both terrified and delighted him, and to keep the delighted part from hammering good sense into oblivion, he had convinced himself that she merely sported with him for her own amusement.

Since the disaster at Elde Luri Mora, however, he tried to bury his love for the Chalaine and whatever he felt for Mirelle. The Chalaine's stinging words at the waterfall had chased from his heart every other desire save to make restitution for his mistakes, and he had used the dense metal of purpose to shield himself from unwanted and inappropriate emotion.

But seeing Mirelle sitting in the sunlight, an icon of loneliness against a backdrop of vibrant, blooming life, beat against the walls of his own emotional seclusion. As he stopped and considered the woman, he wished he could will her to stand and face him, eyes playful, face radiant, and greet him with that particular note of pleasure in her voice as she always had. Of course, a world of change had

311

passed since those first carefree days in the Chambers of the Chalaine, and to expect them to return was folly.

Gen ended his observations and strode forward. She did not acknowledge his coming at first, and he sat beside her, watching a gentle breeze tease fallen blossoms about in the midst of rows of festive branches.

"I wondered when you would come," she finally said. "How do you feel?"

"I am well enough. There is something I must do, however."

"And what is that?"

"I have not yet apologized and asked for your forgiveness for not heeding the warnings you and the Chalaine gave that night in Elde Luri Mora."

Mirelle turned her face toward him, expression incredulous and bemused, and started to laugh. "More apologies? Haven't we gone over this before? Really, Gen, after all we've been through. . ."

"I must because of what I put you through, Mirelle. You have always been a loyal friend, and I betrayed you and your daughter with my reckless pride. When Ethris told you I was the Ilch, you should have ordered him to kill me. Everything would be better if you had."

She shook her head. "I do not believe so."

"How can you? I can see now that I have, however unintentionally, done Mikkik's work for him. I created division by affronting Chertanne, caused pain to the last two people in the world I should ever hope to cause any distress, and now the people of Ki'Hal have to live with the horror of knowing that one they regarded as a hero was instead an incarnation of evil."

Mirelle regarded him, eyes hard. "Gen, Chertanne would have caused plenty of division of his own accord without your help. If it weren't for your efforts, quite frankly, there might not be a Chalaine or a Ha'Ulrich for us to debate upon. It is Chertanne that distresses both the Chalaine and me. Our only concern for you is our worry for your health and safety. As for the people, what is the real horror? The Ilch who never harmed anyone, or the Ha'Ulrich, who will sunder their hopes and probably get my daughter killed in the process?"

"I thank you for your good opinion," Gen replied, "but I think even you will have to admit that I became so drunken with my own pretensions and pride that I destroyed my opportunity to be of service to the Chalaine, and to you."

"Yes, that I can blame you for, though I felt some gratification in seeing you start to realize your own power. Your application of that realization was tragically mistimed."

"I am glad we can agree on that point. I suppose it is time for the gratitude," Gen said, turning to look her in the eyes.

"There is no need," she said in her best imitation of Gen's voice, a playful spark springing to her eyes.

"But there must be some reward for saving the evil creature of prophecy. Honor demands that something be done."

"You have already given me my honor, my daughter's life, and someone to love. No more is needed or required. It is my pleasure to help you, however I can."

They laughed quietly for a moment.

Gen brushed away a fallen blossom that had alighted on his pants. "So do you remember everything I have said?"

"Most of it," she answered, stretching. "So are you going invite me to walk with you through the orchard? It seems that it would be the thing to do, or perhaps the *only* thing to do here."

Mirelle took Gen's arm and they walked in silence for over an hour, taking solace in one another's presence. They meandered without purpose or direction through the long rows of trees, finally arriving at the mouth of the shard. The elves had constructed a low wall across its length, though it provided little aid against the surge of vertigo at the sight of the shards swirling below in the emptiness of space. The massive chunks of the world had nearly realigned, rotating now in a rough sphere, approaching the prophetic day of Unification.

"I hope my daughter is well," Mirelle expressed sadly, eyes on the shards as if to divine the Chalaine's location. "I wish I could be with her. Who knows what Athan and Chertanne will put her through. Now she doesn't even have Mena to keep her company."

"I think about that often," Gen replied in kind. "If they truly believe the prophecy, then her swollen belly will act as a reminder to treat her with respect. Where she goes, there goes God."

"I hope you are right, though she is no doubt as lonely as she has ever been."

They left the opening and returned through the trees. Gen glanced up to the rock where he and Mirelle had lately spoken and found Gerand and Mena there with feet dangling over the edge. "Wait a minute, Mirelle," Gen requested.

"What? Oh, I see. What are we waiting for?"

"To see how this turns out." Gen briefly recounted his history with Mena and Gerand's bitter rejection of the idea that Shadan Khairn had forced his daughter upon him as a wife. They sat inconspicuously underneath a flowering apple tree, pink blossoms littering the grass beneath them as they watched the couple talk with each other in the distance.

"I will never get all these blossoms out of my hair," Mirelle complained quietly as she shook her blonde locks. "Are there any left?"

"A few."

"Could you lend assistance to a lady?"

"Mirelle, please."

"This is not some pathetic attempt to trick you into touching me. I am sorry if it seemed that way. Forget the request. I am perfectly aware of your feelings and don't want to discomfort you."

"It is I who am sorry, Mirelle. Hold still. This won't take a moment."

As Gen worked through her hair, he found it more difficult than he thought to remove the tiny particles and elusive petals. The sweet smell of the blossoms and the pleasure of the touch of her hair sickened him with guilt, and seeing her head bent back, eyes closed, face peaceful but sad, he stopped.

"I think that is most of it," he lied. "Do the elven women have brushes for their hair?"

"How would I know? Are you well?" she asked.

"Just a little tired. I don't think I have my full strength, yet."

"What will you do if you can see the Chalaine again?"

"Beg her forgiveness," he said. "I failed her badly. She has so many trials, and I. . ."

"No more stupid speeches of that sort, Gen. The Chalaine will want none of that blubbering. Will you tell her how you feel?"

Gen's face contracted. "That she knows too well and would as soon forget, I think. It is no boon to her. From what I understand now, she and the Ha'Ulrich must come to some good feeling toward each other or we are all doomed, and I certainly stood in the way of that."

"They will never love each other," Mirelle stated, voice sure. "He is incapable of love, and he has wronged the Chalaine too deeply for her to forgive. To own the truth, Ethris and I had intended to supplant Chertanne with you once we learned you held the power of Trys. So you see, I hoped that you would love my daughter while desperately loving you myself. When I kissed you, I told myself it was to keep you from marrying Fenna so you would be free to wed my daughter."

He was stunned. "And how were you to get rid of Chertanne?"

"Assassinate him. Don't give me that look! You actually tried to do it; I had only planned to do so. Jaron ultimately had the satisfaction. One of Chertanne's only redeeming virtues is that he is alive again, so hopefully someone else can have the pleasure. We were going to use the Assassin's Glass to do it after we were sure the Chalaine was pregnant. Of course, we had no idea the Church had ways of returning the dead to life. Please don't tell the Chalaine about our plan if we chance to see her again, if you would be so kind. Oh, look, he's finally done it. It's about time."

Gen, mind spinning, turned toward the slab, finding Mena and Gerand kissing ardently. He smiled and turned to Mirelle, finding her gaze riveted on them as well, and while her lips turned up softly, her eyes were flint.

She sighed. "It is no good for the beggar to watch the feast, so if you aren't planning on grabbing me and kissing me until I can't see straight, I must bid you farewell. Those two could use a good example, you know."

Gen could not think of a single reply, and Mirelle squeezed his arm and left, face disappointed. Gen exhaled and ran his fingers through his hair, a shower of blossom petals falling about him.

He turned away from Gerand and Mena, comprehending perfectly Mirelle's comment about beggars and feasts. The sunshine attracted him, and he returned to the low wall in front of the opening in the shard, flipping his legs over the edge to dangle them into the void. The shards drifted in orderly patterns, covered in the white of winter. So small they seemed that he felt he could extend his hand and pluck one up and examine it closely. The Chalaine, pregnant and defenseless against Chertanne's barbarity, walked somewhere below, and Gen could do nothing to help her.

The approach of Devlis, a jade staff in hand, distracted him from his thoughts. The ancient elf regarded him with curiosity, standing just to his side and gazing into the expanse below.

"You do not fear the fall?" he asked in Elvish.

"No."

"Do you have such confidence in your own control, then?"

Gen chuckled. "In matters of physical balance and strength, yes. My temperament I cannot vouch for."

Devlis leaned on his staff. "It is always so with your kind. There simply isn't time in your short lives to develop the steadiness that would help you rule your natures, or if it is developed, then much of the power you could wield with your wisdom has faded with age and infirmity. So you are left vainly trying to convince the heady generations of the unheeding young to hearken to you and obey your counsel. And so the cycle has gone, century after century, and the entire race is unable to progress simply because they cannot live long enough to reap the benefits of the lessons they learn in life."

Gen nodded. "And your people live so long they can no longer take pleasure in or feel sadness for anything because every experience is too familiar and every feeling a repeat of something felt a hundred times before."

Devlis rubbed is chin in thought. "A fair assessment, perhaps, but your arrival has certainly stirred some sentiment within us. But I want to return to my initial comment, for I did not offer it to give you insult or make light of your race. You see, you are unique among your kind. You have the benefit of long wisdom, given you by the men and elf who inhabited your mind for a time after they released themselves from the stones. The Millim Eri did not foresee this."

"If you know that much, then you have no doubt also seen how the additional endowment of wisdom has profited me little, for I leaned on my own instead."

"In some things yes," Devlis said, "but in others you acted with a wisdom and courage beyond your years. Your challenge of Chertanne is an example. If left to your own wisdom, I doubt you would have had the sense of moral courage or the disregard for titles and station it required to act when you saw indecency. It seems so natural to you that you acted as you did that you can scarce understand why it should seem remarkable. Take the chance to ask your woman about how she perceived those events, and you may start to understand."

"My woman?"

"Mirelle."

Gen turned away from his gaze. "She is not *my* woman."

"She is. You simply aren't her man. But to the point. I come to encourage you. You are wrapped up in a mission you see as noble, but which is, in fact, short sighted. You have shut away the wisdom in your head so you can wallow in your failures in an attempt to justify your own inaction."

"My inaction?" Gen exclaimed, irritated at Devlis's assumptions. "I would like nothing more than to cross to the world below and act. The Chalaine needs my help, and I desperately wish to give it."

"That isn't the inaction I am referring to," Devlis said, stepping closer. "Your idea of action is to present her a pile of the bodies of her enemies, whisk her away to some stronghold, and then guard her like a starved dog guards its last bone."

"And you say that such an action isn't necessary?"

"What I am saying is that your goal is only to spare her pain, but not to *help* her. Do you think the Chalaine sits and thinks all day of her own comfort and safety? That she wants nothing more than to be loved and happy? Certainly, these are desirable to her, but her teachers raised her to respect her duty and to strive to fulfill it. You understand this. I saw it in your mind. What I am suggesting is that you help the Chalaine by helping her purpose, by lending your wisdom to her duty, and not just by cutting up everything that threatens her."

Gen thought for a moment. "But her only duty is to bear a child, and to bear a child requires nothing but her survival. Cutting up everything that threatens her seems to be a wise course in helping her."

Devlis leaned heavily on his staff. "Let me explain this differently. Your problem is that you treat the Chalaine's problems as if you were both standing alone in a room. If a monster comes in, you kill it and are done, not caring where it came from or the forces that set it in motion. From what I have gleaned from your mind and from your companions is that there are many forces—political, magical, and sinister—that strive to turn the Ki'Hal that men have fashioned into chaos. What I am suggesting is that you are possessed of unique gifts that can help the Chalaine by shaping and manipulating the forces that are sending the world to its destruction. Your woman has an excellent sense of this and can help find places you can be of use and apply what is already in your head."

"Please don't call Mirelle *my woman*. She would be very offended."

"She most certainly would not," Devlis stated flatly. "But let me offer this. When you return to Rhugoth, your inclination is to return to the Chalaine. Do not give way so easily to your first impulse. Tap into your mind. Talk with Mirelle. You might be surprised what two clever people can do, even if human."

Devlis left, and for several moments the thought of getting off the shard and returning to Ki'Hal drove away all of Devlis' instruction. But as Gen rose and walked the orchard, the ancient elf's words sank into his heart, and a memory from Telmerran surfaced. During the First Mikkikian war, an Uyumaak horde had streamed toward the Castle Mekhower, the stronghold of Telmerran's Lord.

Telmerran and his men, having campaigned much in the warm summer, heard of the danger and tried to return to aid their Lord. They arrived too late, finding the castle besieged. Throughout the winter, Telmerran and his intrepid men cut off supply lines, raided camps, and assassinated leaders until the siege collapsed in chaos.

The memory gave weight to Devlis' words. If he could not be with the Chalaine within her stronghold, then he could weaken the enemies that beset her and perhaps save her from a certain doom when she stood with Chertanne before Mikkik's armies.

Invigorated by these thoughts, he sprang up the stairs, interrupting an embarrassed Gerand and Mena. He grinned and waved, jogging toward the stone tree the elves had provided to Mirelle for her residence.

"First, I think," Gen said, sitting with Mirelle on a balcony carved into a limb, "I must know what you have already set in motion."

Mirelle, a little bewildered though not displeased by Gen's sudden change of spirit, leaned back and thought for a moment.

"Quite frankly, you ruined most of what I had planned as a contingency by running off to Aughmere. After Athan had captured you, my plan, of course, was to recover you and see you safely to Rhugoth. You were to winter there. When the time came to march, we were going to contrive some way to have you close to the Chalaine and Chertanne so that when they faced Mikkik, you could interfere and, with any luck, save my daughter and her Child."

"What of Ethris?" Gen asked. "Maewen said you had sent him to Rhugoth."

"Ethris has two important missions. First is to sow

doubt about the tales the Church is spreading about Chertanne and to prepare the people to accept you when you return. General Harband is to secretly gather and inform the Regents that they are to assume power again at the start of spring."

"That will break the Fidelium!"

She smiled. "Absolutely. I might add that when Rhugothians and Tolnorians find out that Chertanne has assumed leadership of the Church of the One, there very well may follow some religious and political turmoil, regardless of anyone's dedication to the Fidelium. I still cannot believe Beliarmus could do something so idiotic. I know my people. They will readily believe your innocence, and I want just enough ill will toward Chertanne percolating in their hearts that they will abandon him and follow some other lead—your lead, for instance—when the time comes to do so.

"Of course," she continued, "while Ethris works for me on the one hand, he will offer his services of protection and counsel to the Warlord that Chertanne assigned to govern Rhugoth. Ethris is, of course, spying and manipulating instead. So you see, the idea is that Rhugoth can be taken out of Chertanne's control at our convenience with a minimum of fuss or bloodshed. I don't know how many Aughmerian soldiers are sleeping in Mikmir right now, but they will find themselves dead or walking home if I say so."

Gen leaned back and grinned. "You don't know how good it is to hear you talk so. I feel like I am back in Mikmir already. What of Torbrand and Maewen?"

"Maewen, after saving you and reporting back to Ethris, was to lay low for the winter until she could get back onto the Shroud Lake shard. Before Athan had me bundled up and shipped off to Ironkeep, a new alliance of mine informed me that the Church was interested in scouting out Echo Hold as well as assessing Mikkik's activities there. Maewen will shadow them and bring word to Ethris since we can't be sure how much the Church will want to share, or—if they do—how much they will distort.

"As for Torbrand, I am still amazed that monster is on our side. You changed him, somehow, Gen. I never thought I could count on his service, but he seemed eager to help. He was to return to Tolnor and seek out Gerand and Dason's father, Lord Kildan, and find out how many Aughmerian soldiers still quarter in your former nation. I'm hoping Lord Kildan knows the hiding place of King Filingrail. I'd planned to reinstate him, but chances were always slim, at best."

"You are very ambitious."

Mirelle smiled weakly. "So, what is it that you want to do?"

"I wanted to understand, first."

"May I ask why you are suddenly so interested?" Mirelle said, eyes curious.

"Master Devlis reminded me of a few lessons I have lying around in my head. I want to throw off this darkness of spirit and be of use. I have other ways I can help the Chalaine besides sticking a sword in every enemy I come across."

"And this has brought you bounding to my door?"

"Mostly. Neither one of us weathers idleness very well. I am ready to be obedient to you—as I should have been all along—and do whatever you suggest to aid the Chalaine. You are as clever a person as I have ever known, and I need someone with your experience to help channel whatever influence or power I have left to give."

Mirelle nodded, eyes bright. "Devlis must have given you some speech."

Gen recounted Devlis's instruction to him, leaving out his comments about *Gen's woman*.

Mirelle nodded her agreement with his words. "He is right, you know. But let me be clear. I don't want you as a servant or an obedient subject. I want you to stand beside me, and not behind me. You have a great deal of knowledge and wisdom packed away in that head of yours, and if you are quite done with your pointless self-deprecation and crippling guilt, then I think I can help you make use of them. In other words, if I even think I'm about to hear the words 'I am sorry' come out of your mouth, I'll belt you as hard as I can. Understood?"

Gen laughed, grabbing her hand and kissing it. This felt more like old times. "I understand. Where do we begin?"

Time passed surprisingly quickly for Gen as he and Mirelle spent almost every hour together plotting and planning or speaking of their mutual concern for the Chalaine. Cadaen kept busy following them around the strange confines of the cave, and Gerand and Mena passed the time quite pleasurably, as well. Only Volney and Udan suffered from a persistent case of boredom after the initial infatuation with their unusual surroundings wore off.

The elves and dwarves remained aloof of them, all save Falael who found Gen often and conversed with him in Elvish. He had never seen humans or the wonders of Ki'Hal, and only he and his father seemed possessed of some life among the dull stares of his race. The few dwarves they saw walked bent over, ancient beards dragging upon the ground.

One morning, while Gen and Mirelle walked among the fruit trees, an excited Volney sprinted up to them. "I think it is time. They are all marching this way."

"Gather everyone," Mirelled ordered.

"There's no need," Gen told her. "It looks as if Devlis has brought them."

Moments later, the elves descended with the humans in

tow. All wore cloaks, and Devlis and Al'Handra carried others, offering them to Mirelle and Gen.

"Give these to your people. It is time to leave this place."

"What of the dwarves?" Gen asked.

"They wish to remain. Come."

Devlis led them to the shard edge. "Al'Handra, if you will?"

She spoke a word, and a section of the low wall crumbled and fell into space.

"Each of you put your cloak on," Devlis continued. "They are imbued with a power that will let you fall from any height and land unharmed. Simply follow our lead. What you know as the Rhugothian shard cluster will pass below us soon. My people and I will await there for Unification and seek out our masters, the Millim Eri. We may yet cross paths. I leave Falael with you. He is curious about your kind, and his lore will serve you well. Ah, here it comes."

They leaned close to the edge, watching as the large shards that formed Rhugoth appeared a dizzying distance below, sliding slowly beneath them.

"He can't be serious," Volney and Udan said in unison, but in that moment, Devlis jumped, and his people streamed through the gap, falling in a pack to the distant ground below. Gen swallowed hard. Heights did not frighten him, but falling great distances did.

"Is there any way to tell if they all just died?" Volney asked.

"No, it's too far down," Gerand answered.

"Faith, gentlemen," Gen encouraged them. Mirelle shrieked as Gen grabbed her by the waist and pulled her over with him, Falael close behind. The rest followed suit.

Wind howled in their ears as they fell, the shard below rushing up to greet them. Gen glanced at Mirelle, whose eyes were wide and face pale. The closer they came to the ground, the greater the sensation of danger and speed. Swiftly, individual trees and houses resolved into view, hurtling toward them. The sight of the elves already milling around on the ground gave them confidence that a deadly impact was not to be the end of their journey, but Volney yelled in terror anyway.

The magic worked. A few yards before impact, their descent slowed and they touched lightly on the grass of a verdant field bracketed by sun-bathed hills.

"That was exciting," Mirelle commented, face flushed.

Volney wiped the vomit from his mouth and grumbled something unintelligible that sounded a lot like he disagreed.

CHAPTER 68 – REUNIFICATION

The Church's augurs predicted that the beginning of the fifth watch on the first day of spring would be Unification, the day when all the shards that now swirled close and in unfamiliar patterns would lock together like puzzle pieces and bring wholeness to a world whose parts had long been estranged from one another. That day, Trys would throw off its cloak completely and shine down upon them as a sign of hope and looming trouble. The Chalaine stole glimpses of the sky whenever she could, the movements in the sky and within her belly connected and purposeful.

She reclined in a rocking chair next to her still-sleeping husband with her hand on her protruding abdomen. The small kicks and jabs within her always elicited a smile from her lips, although in those moments she missed her mother the most and wished more than anything for at least one of her beloved companions with whom she could share her wonder.

She could easily imagine Fenna's delight, Mena's instructive comments, and her mother's comforting wisdom. In her mind's eye Jaron stood behind her like an expectant grandfather, proud and protective, and she often thought of Gen's hand on her swollen belly, patiently waiting for an unpredictable and barely perceptible movement to provide tactile evidence of the tiny inhabitant's burgeoning life.

But what would Gen's reaction be? She often wondered. Would one so learned and unsurprisable simply nod in stoic confirmation? Would he raise his eyebrow and smile? Act giddy? Embrace her in congratulations? Kiss her cheek or perhaps her pregnant belly? And there she had to stop herself before she carelessly trod the well-worn path to guilt and self-recrimination. Chertanne needed her desperately, and in his desperation she had hoped that love—both from him and for him—might find a chance to sneak past the black specter of their unpleasant history that haunted every attempt at mutual trust and civility.

True, Chertanne had changed, but he was not entirely transformed. His experience in the Abyss had taught him consequence and accountability, but also terror and insecurity. His stupid, ill-founded confidence had gone. His selfishness, now colored by paranoia and fear rather than arrogance, sometimes came across as a strange blend of surliness and neediness, an obsequious peevishness. But his low condition, his dependence upon her for security and sanity, and his attempts at making amends had inspired her tenderness and pity and reminded her of Aldemar's counsel to try to heal her husband's diseased soul. Such a healing, which had been set as far out of reach as the moons before his death, hung closer after his revival, close enough for her to attempt it.

And so she threw herself into his service. He still needed to see her unveiled face regularly to stave off nightmares and the sudden fits of anxiety and panic during the day. Even three months after his revival, sudden noises or movements unnerved him, and it required two solid months of persuasion to convince him that nothing but sunshine or starlight awaited him on the other side of the window shutters. The Chalaine read to him daily, insisted on serving him all his meals, and held his hand unveiled in the evenings to help him sleep. She calmed his night terrors, sang songs to soothe his nervousness, and rose early so that her face might be the first he saw when he awoke.

Of course, Athan rejoiced to see these services done, often remarking to her privately that he saw Eldaloth's hand in all the events that had transpired, even Jaron's regicide. The Chalaine could agree, though one thing still eluded her—love for her husband. Thoughts of Gen plagued her constantly. Her pregnancy amplified the vividness of her dreams, whether scary, pleasant, or passionate, and Chertanne never figured as a player in the latter two. At times she wished she would receive a letter from her mother announcing that she had used her considerable feminine arts to convince Gen to marry her. At least then, the Chalaine thought, she and Chertanne could coexist with some parity as utter wretches.

But to her heart, Gen's love was as omnipresent and inescapable as water in the sea or sand in the desert, a golden gift always before her emotional eyes that she could not open but that still warmed her heart for having been given. It didn't help that the Training Stones and his Ial stone hung against her chest, both evidences of his thoughtful care, and the animon in her pocket never wanted for her touch. While she knew she should at least put the Ial stone aside—for she suspected its calming, enticing scent was the source of her more inappropriate dreams—she absolutely could not bring herself to do it. Samian's rigorous training helped calm her and provide a sane shelter from her guilty dreaming.

Chertanne stirred, and the Chalaine looked up, noticing the sweat on his forehead and the uneasy expression on his sleeping face. She hauled herself out of the rocking chair and sat on the bed at his side, grasping his slowly clenched hand and rubbing his arm until his indisposition passed. A soft tapping at the door pulled her away. She cracked the door, finding Athan waiting for her, and she stepped out and closed the door quietly behind her. Seeing the man who had imprisoned her mother and Mena in the horrible dungeons of Mikmir brought her pain and disgust, but she worked up her most tolerable demeanor before conversing with him.

"How fare you, Chalaine?" he asked, face kind.

"I am well, as always."

"I have come to ask your opinion. I have had it circulated that Chertanne will show himself this evening just after Unification. I have stressed that he will not linger or celebrate, but simply be seen and leave. Do you think he can manage that much on his own if you are with him? I can be there to help with magic, but I would like for him and you to stand alone to help the assembly view you as in power and in charge."

"I think it best if you are nearby," the Chalaine opined. "He is not strong, and I cannot guess how he will react to the noise and celebration. If we aren't careful you will achieve the exact opposite of what you want."

"Very well," Athan accepted. "We should get word back from our eastern scouts before much longer to see if Mikkik indeed already prepares some horde for battle. When Chertanne wakes, I need you to bring him to me. There is a mystery which we have withheld until this moment that he needs to know. I realize he is worthless for war planning, but there is one strike we must prepare him to make on his own."

"If you mean swordplay," the Chalaine said, "he knows nothing of it! You have kept it from him. I should have been pleased if you had done so well with the brothels and concubines."

"We have long understood that he would wage war with magic," Athan explained, brushing aside her barb. "He will have allies for the mundane. What he needs to know, we can teach him in a few weeks' time, and I have hope it will help him to gain some sense of his own strength."

"As you wish. I will bring him."

"Thank you, your Grace. A pleasure, as always." Athan bowed and left, two Eldephaere in tow.

The Chalaine bit her lip. From the vision that Aldemar had shared with her, she knew that Mikkik's physical appearance was far from the terrifying monster she had conjured up for herself, but anything out of the ordinary spooked Chertanne. How could he stand in the same arena as Mikkik, companies of Uyumaak, and whatever monstrosities Mikkik had invented in the meantime when a metal goblet inadvertently dropped to the stones unmanned him?

"Chalaine!" Chertanne's terrified voice called from within. She entered and walked as quickly as she could to his bedside where he had risen to his elbows. His eyes flashed fear and anger. "How could you leave me? You know I need you! Veil off, so I know it is you and not some impostor." She complied, and his face relaxed. "What were you doing out there? What's out there that would take you from me?"

"Athan called and wished for a word with me. He has a request he wished me to pass on to you."

"Hang Athan! Do not leave me when I sleep! The only way I know whether I am dreaming or not is if you are here. You are never in my dreams of that . . . place."

She came to his side. "Do forgive me, Chertanne. I thought you would sleep for some time yet. I promise I will not leave you here alone again. Do you wish to hear his request?"

"Later. I must eat. Tell me while I eat. Where is the food?"

"You have arisen early, Chertanne. The food is not ready, but it should come soon."

"The request, then," he said, stepping out of the bed and

moving to a chair by the fire, "to pass the time."

Coaxing Chertanne to sit by the fire was another of the Chalaine's hard won victories. He had shunned the flames for weeks, regardless of the temperature of the room.

"Athan wished to speak with you about some part of the prophecy that they have kept in secret," she explained. "It is vital for you to know, he said. He also suggested that you may start to learn a bit of the sword."

"Oh, so now they let me learn it. Ridiculous. I face Mikkik in three months. Oh, help me! Three months! I will be killed and end up back in the Abyss! I'll be back, and they'll wait for me and tear my soul to shreds and spit the pieces into the fire!"

The Chalaine knelt by him as he clawed the chair with rigid fingers. "Be at peace, Chertanne. Do not forget your faith! You have a chance for redemption from that fate! Do you think Eldaloth would consign you to the Abyss, win or lose, if you stand against Mikkik for his sake? Facing Mikkik is the very act that will free you from the Abyss."

The Chalaine had told him this many times before, but she had yet to convince him of it. He relaxed, however, and stared at the coals, face uncertain.

"You always make it sound so easy. It can't be so simple."

"Perhaps our visit to Athan will give us more information and more cause for hope. You *can* find your strength, Chertanne."

The food arrived, and they talked a little as they ate. Afterward, serving women attended them to prepare them for the day. The Chalaine dressed simply to lend the preeminence to Chertanne, who, thanks to Athan, was attired as a mighty king in deep reds, golds, and blacks.

Athan waited for them in his study, a scroll of ancient appearance sprawled across his desk. He stood and bowed as they entered, waving his hand toward two comfortable chairs scooted close to the parchment. The Chalaine sat, and to her surprise spied Gen's sword, the sword of Alradan Mikmir, laying across the mantle of the fireplace. She felt like exclaiming, but fought down the urge.

"May I open the shutters, your Grace?" Athan offered. "It is yet cool, but the day is bright and pleasant."

Chertanne gripped his chair and nodded in the affirmative, unable to watch as Athan unbarred the shutters and threw them open to invite in the brilliant light and fresh scent of approaching of spring. After Chertanne was sure something horrible would not burst through the opening, he relaxed. The sky, now clear of shards, seemed foreign save for the moons, and the Chalaine wished she could go bask in the tender, emergent life outside. But Athan, plopping into his seat with an anticipatory smile on his face, drew her attention. If he could smile, then perhaps the secret would be a positive one after all.

"Chertanne," he began, "I have something to reveal to you that you may find shocking, but it should bolster you confidence. There is a portion of the prophecy that the Church has kept hidden for centuries, as instructed by the Ministrant, hidden from the enemy so that he could not use it or prepare for it. It is merely one stanza, but it— combined with the information given us by the Mikkik Dun Aldemar—reveals more about your nature and the way in which you will annihilate Mikkik forever. Chalaine, if you would care to read this part just before the last stanza."

The Chalaine scooted forward, text clear in the pure sunshine.

In his veins burns the blood
of him whom Mikkik slew,
and the sword bathed
from red to white blazes
stokes the assassin's terror,
His magic now his end.

The Chalaine read the words again at Athan's request before returning to her seat. Chertanne, forehead creased, appeared nonplussed while Athan waited expectantly for a student to work through a problem and emerge with a glorious answer. His patience, however, lost out to his eagerness.

"So you see, Chertanne, in some way we do not understand, within you flows the blood of Eldaloth himself! Now, you were taught that Mikkik used the 'Great Secret' to slay Eldaloth. You know that the three moons hold the key to power in their individual domains of magic. The power in blood can be used to create and destroy, and Mikkik knew this secret magic could bring the utter annihilation, body and soul, of another creature. Mikkik infused a sword with the power of sixty-nine Mikkik Dun and slew Eldaloth with it, and I believe Aldemar's last minute defection saved our God from complete destruction.

"Now, understand that the power of human blood is weak, the blood of elves stronger, and that of the Millim Eri—or Mikkik Dun—stronger still. Within you is Eldaloth's blood, the strongest of all, more powerful than Mikkik's, we believe. This fact alone is why we hid this section of the prophecy for centuries. We think that our common enemy is completely unaware of the nature of your blood."

The Chalaine saw where this was going. "So you want to bathe Aldradan Mikmir's sword in Chertanne's blood to create a weapon to kill Mikkik?"

"Yes, though there is more to it than that. It requires Trysmagic and Mikkik's 'secret,' and—thanks to Aldemar's writings—we have it. We have kept it hidden, even from ourselves, for Eldaloth prohibited the use of blood as a source of magic. As for Aldradan's sword, we found it fitting and appropriate for the task."

"But first Chertanne has to survive long enough to get close to Mikkik to use the sword," the Chalaine pointed out. "That task is the hardest."

That was the task that her love was supposed to provide for, she remembered bitterly. From her heart to his hand protective healing was to flow.

"Are you well, Ha'Ulrich?" Athan asked concernedly. The Chalaine turned to find her husband pale and crushing the arm rests of the chair again.

"Bathed in *my* blood?" he choked. You both seem to have wandered past that part as if it were as easy as picking daises."

Athan smiled. "Be at ease. It is rather the easy part. Only a single bleeding is needed. With my magic you will not feel a thing, and with the Chalaine's, you will bear no injury for it. You will perform the magic to turn the blade into a weapon when the time is close to confront Mikkik. We cannot risk a weapon of such power to fall into anyone else's hands."

Chertanne relaxed. "But how am I to face him? How will it all play out?"

"We simply don't know, Milord. We have long assumed that Mikkik would, as in times past, gather an army in the east and strike at the west."

"But, as I recall from my history lessons," the Chalaine interjected, "Mikkik was rarely seen with his armies. He preferred to remain in Goreth Forest, conjuring up his monstrosities and sending them forth. What makes you think he won't behave in the same fashion, especially since he knows what I carry in my belly just as well as you and I do?"

"It is true that he rarely commanded any battles personally," Athan confirmed. "But the return of Eldaloth will not provide an incentive for him to stay hidden. He simply cannot hide from a god. We feel—though acknowledging the unpredictability of our foe—that his best chance is to kill you both so that he need not fear. The failure of the Ilch to perform his mission will, we feel, increase the likelihood of Mikkik's personal appearance. He knows that the two of you must attend the battle by prophetic dictum. The failure of the Ilch will ensure that he must appear, as well, to personally finish you both."

Chertanne groaned. "Which he will do! I cannot fight him! He is simply too powerful for me to stand toe to toe with!"

"Have you not heard what I said, Chertanne!" Athan exclaimed. "It is your blood, the blood of Eldaloth himself, that will lend us the victory. I do not believe you were ever meant to be as strong as Mikkik, and you will not strike out into this fray upon your own. Armies and Magicians and Churchmen will stand ready to protect and help you. You do not bear this burden alone."

Silence prevailed as Chertanne thought things over. The Chalaine stared out the window, imagining a nice walk along a country lane, arm wrapped in Gen's. He had a picnic basket full of apples, cheese, and wine. He smiled at her and she at him. Birds sang everywhere. . .

"Chalaine!" Chertanne called.

"Hmmm?" she replied dreamily. Only then did she realize her husband and Athan had both stood.

"We need to go, Chalaine," Chertanne said, face still a little pale. "We must prepare for the ceremony this evening."

"Oh, yes, of course. I am sorry. I am a little tired this morning."

"Come on."

"Yes, Milord. I am with you."

Mirelle, while nervous, had rarely felt so ecstatic before addressing a crowd. Usually such occasions relied on pomp, ceremony, and stock phrases of patriotic fluff. But for this speech, she required no more than her heart, a heart which had filled to overflowing in the days since her return. Walking the halls of her own castle, sending Warlord Jarius and the Church ambassadors packing, and convening the Council of Regents again all inspired the return of the strength and security she had once felt. For the first time in months she knew what she was about, and it *felt* right.

Even better, she had Gen to share everything with. While she admitted her own bias, she had never found anyone with whom she felt such a commonality of spirit or whose knowledge and personality she respected and admired to such a high degree. He seemed freed of the dark moods that had afflicted him since his failure at Elde Luri Mora, and their mutual scheming and planning helped him feel useful to the cause of aiding the Chalaine, even if not in the way he would like.

Mirelle did not conceal her and Gen's return in the least, letting every scullery maid, guard, and scribe get a good glimpse of them to fuel the rumors in the street. Prior to their return, everyone in Rhugoth had heard Gen was a traitorous, dead Ilch and that she was safely ensconced in Ironkeep. By letting word of Gen's presence spread unofficially, she hoped to pique interest and render her official story more palatable when it came time to tell it. Today, Unification Day, would see it told.

She exited the maze to her quarters, a sharply dressed Cadaen behind, to find Gen waiting for her. She had wanted him to wear courtly rather than military regalia after their return, but for today's purposes she felt it important for everyone to see him as he had looked when he marched out of Mikmir nearly a year ago as a Dark Guard. And, Mirelle had to confess, seeing him dressed in his black uniform brought back many treasured memories of their past association.

She dressed for authority, not for beauty, pulling back her hair so that the circlet of silver would stand out and wearing a deep purple dress embroidered in gold so that no one would ever forget who ruled in Rhugoth. And she meant that. She would not leave her city and her country in other hands as long as she had the means to prevent it.

She beamed at Gen, embracing him affectionately and kissing his cheek. "How do I look?"

"Like today is not the day to cross you."

"Indeed, it is not," she said, taking his proffered arm. "I cannot tell you how happy I am to see this done."

"It needs doing now," Gen said as they began their journey to the Great Hall. "I just got word back from Maewen and General Harband this morning. The city is fit to boil over, and the countryside is full of tales about Aughmerian soldiers and high ranking Church officials being marched into boats and through Portals. Everyone knows you have broken the Fidelium and are now asking why. Fortunately, your people trust you and believe that if you did it, it was for a good reason. There are exceptions, of course, but after today, I think you will have to fight harder to keep the people from storming to Ironkeep and pulling the Chalaine out."

"Yes. I will have to be careful how I approach that, but I think I have it worked out. Did Ethris manage to take care of your little problem?"

"Yes," Gen replied. They needed his foot to look like any other.

"How?"

"Another branding."

"You're sporting quite the collection of brandings now, aren't you? You'll have to show them to me later."

"That would be most unseemly." Gen smiled.

Ethris awaited them at the gate into the Great Hall proper, dressed in white as always. He greeted them both.

"This will truly be a momentous day," he said. "The prophecy is falling apart, but I am more confident in its success than ever. I am not sure if I am a crusader or a faithless wretch."

"The faithless, incompetent wretch is Athan," Mirelle commented, tone angry. "We don't have a dungeon to match that of Aughmere's, but I might just have one built so I can throw him in it if I ever find him and can overcome my desire to throttle him on the spot."

Ethris frowned. "You are more in danger from the Church than they are from you, at this point. I'll put up a ward today, but please keep your words to a minimum, if you would, so we can get you safely back inside."

"No promises."

Ethris humphed. "Are you ready for your new title, young man?"

"Of course not," Gen said. "Will we see Maewen and General Harband tonight after the ceremony?"

"I believe so."

"Any word from Torbrand?" Mirelle asked.

"Not as yet. I fear that after our recent actions the Church has been watching the Portals doubly closely. It may be difficult for him to return. After today, however, there is no guarantee the Portals will work at all, though he could choose any road to get here he liked. Well, we're here."

They had arrived at the ornate front doors. Chamberlain Fedrick was bedecked in his finest robes and was alertly awaiting an opportunity to perform his office again. He winked at Mirelle as she entered, and she squeezed his arm as she took her place behind him. Soldiers filled in around them.

"Wait out of sight until I call you, Gen," Mirelle ordered. "You won't have to wait long."

"As you wish, First Mother."

Gen retreated to the side of the antechamber, and, once

he was safely out of the way, the Chamberlain tapped of his ceremonial staff on the ground. The doors swung open, revealing a massive tumult of people in the courtyard around the steps. A huge cheer burst forth as Mirelle strode out, and she could not help but smile. Behind her, Ethris chanted to create his ward and to amplify her voice. She stood at the top of the stairs and raised her arms to silence the crowd.

"Good people of Rhugoth, you cannot imagine my pleasure at seeing you once again and hearing your welcoming voices. I wish the news I had to bear you were all good, but as with all things, that which is good rarely comes as purely as we might hope, and the dark, it seems, must always find a way to besmirch the day.

"First, I bring you word that my daughter is in good health and that the Holy Child grows within her, as prophecy has dictated. She sends you her love and her good wishes. Alas, she is not here with us as some rumors would have it, but if all goes well, I am sure you will see her ere the year is out in the company of our God. Secondly, as most of you have guessed, I have reasserted my rule over this nation and reconvened the Council of Regents.

"With this news, however, I leave what is simple and must set straight the record concerning more complex matters, one of which concerns someone I trust completely and love dearly but who has been unforgivably slandered. You know of whom I speak. For you to understand this matter, I need you to listen carefully and to accept that I, your First Mother, have never and will never lie to you.

"You have heard that Gen attempted to kill Chertanne in Elde Luri Mora after the Chalaine's wedding. This is true." The crowd gasped, and a wave of murmurs rippled through the courtyard. Mirelle waited patiently for it to subside. "You have also heard that Gen did this because he is the Ilch, that Chertanne then slew him, and that a leg has been paraded about the countryside as proof. All of this, my good people, is a lie. Chertanne, as he did in my very own Hall two years ago, behaved toward the Chalaine, Rhugothians, and Gen in such an infamous and insupportable manner that Gen, due to his oath, had no other choice but to confront Chertanne, who then attacked Gen and failed. The good Pontiff, now dead, protected Chertanne from Gen's killing stroke, and from that moment on some of the Church invented the abominable and dishonorable tale which you all know, and Gen became a fugitive.

"I am here to assure you of these facts: Gen is still alive; he is not the Ilch; he is in full possession of both his legs; and he still serves the Chalaine and me. He is the same noble, courageous man you knew. I imagine most of you, to your credit, did not believe what you were told, that you could not reconcile Gen's heroic actions in our service with the notion that he was somehow the embodiment of evil. And well you could not, for this falsehood, fomented by certain of the Church, was created merely to strengthen your faith in Chertanne's power and help you feel more secure. But to put your minds at ease and to confirm what many of you believe, I give you Gen, once Lord Blackshire, now Lord Protector of Mikmir and my faithful counselor."

Nothing but birds made a sound as Gen strode out the door and walked to Mirelle's side, everyone agape. She took his hand and the crowd roared with applause. Gen turned to Mirelle and smiled, her face full of pleasure and the hint of a tear in her eye. She squeezed his hand and waited until the jubilation died down.

"Now, there are many tales I could tell of Gen's bravery on the Shroud Lake shard and during his imprisonment by the Church. I could, though I would shrink to do it, tell you of the sufferings and injustice he has faced. But may this suffice and explain my actions since my return. Because I refused to go along with the Church's story about Chertanne and Gen, I was kept as a prisoner in Ironkeep along with others who would not support such treachery. Gen, fearing that I and the Chalaine were in danger, escaped from his own imprisonment with the help of others and came all the way to Ironkeep to ensure our safety. There, he was captured again, but through good fortune and the grace of God, we escaped and come to you now having traveled many long and difficult miles.

"I say this. If Chertanne is to be revered and respected, and if Chertanne wishes to obtain the governance of this nation, it will not be through deceit or dictum, but by a clear demonstration of his own competence and good virtues. I have withdrawn from the Fidelium until such time as the Ha'Ulrich can honestly earn his title. Rhugoth will certainly aid Chertanne in any battle against Mikkik and his host, but the soldiers of this nation will not live and die at his command until I am sure he loves them as I do and until I am sure he can command them with more skill than he has hitherto shown.

"Most of all, I wish everyone to rest at ease. The Chalaine has always been well cared for and is happy and content. The prophecy will be fulfilled, and our nation is more secure and better able to face Mikkik's threat than it ever has been. Please say your morning oblations. Please attend Church and worship there. The falsehoods you were told are the work of a very few within the Church. Please rest secure in my love and in the knowledge that Rhugoth is again ours—proud, mighty, and the envy of the world!"

Peals of praise and applause rolled through the courtyard, and Mirelle smiled warmly, waving and applauding with her people. Gen smiled along with her, finally taking her arm and leading her back into the Great Hall.

"I think that went well," Ethris opined as they started toward Mirelle's throne.

"As do I," she agreed.

"I'll be about the wards," Ethris assured them. "Are you

sure you want to go forward with the celebration tonight? It is an awful risk."

"Those who are invited I know well and trust," Mirelle explained. "Besides, I have you and Gen with me. That is all I require. Do join us for lunch. I have a mountain of people clamoring for my attention today, but after lunch I have sworn to do nothing but celebrate and enjoy myself."

"And you have earned it," Ethris said affectionately. "Until lunch then."

Mirelle slid comfortably into her throne, rubbing the arm rests familiarly as Cadaen and Gen took up positions behind her. "You know, Gen, we've only been back a few days and I have a stack of letters from those wishing to court me. Do you know what that means?"

"That I'll be dancing with you the entire evening?"

She laughed. "You're beginning to understand. I hope that isn't too much of a punishment."

"Well, if you wear your hair down, I might get by. The way you look right now reminds me too much of all those filthy names you called me after Maewen and I had that unfortunate incident with the Uyumaak."

"Unfortunate incident? So that's what you call it now. I still call it a 'moronic debacle,' just so you know. But yes, my hair will be down, and I have just the gown picked out to make all my poor would-be suitors envious of you to the point of incapacitation. I can hardly wait. But first, we must press on with a few doldrums. Chamberlain Fedrick! Let the first one in!"

A mother and daughter joined all of Ki'Hal, who stood outdoors or on balconies or at windows staring into a perfectly clear night sky. No one knew quite what to expect when all the pieces of Ki'Hal knit back together. The sky, alien and lonely without the constant traffic of shards, bathed them in the weak nocturnal lights, Trys nearly full.

The mother and daughter stood miles apart, their thoughts of one another binding them together. While celebration and joy coursed all about them, each could not escape a longing for the other. The mother fretted for the happiness of her child, and the child needed the comfort of the mother. The absence of shards magnified the distance they felt, depriving them of the pleasant imagination that the other might be in sight on one of the flying pieces of the world.

In the end, only a tremor strong enough to knock down the truly inebriated marked the momentous occasion. Cheers rose and music broke out into the night. The dark circle finished its slide off of Trys's shining, full face. The prophecy marched on, fulfillment of a hoped for joy ever nearing. The mother and daughter both smiled and turned to the man near her, but only one received a proper kiss.

Chapter 69 - A March At Evening

"Oh, dear," Mirelle lamented with mock gravity, eyes running over the first page of a thick parcel that had recently arrived from Ironkeep. "I've been excommunicated. There is no mention of you, Gen, however. Of course, you have already been excommunicated and killed, so why bother re-excommunicating a dead person? Ah, but look. You are alive again. The Church has authorized its leaders to inform the people that the Ilch, while indeed dead, presented himself to Chertanne in your form, in the which he killed you, meaning the Ilch in your form. No apologies to you, of course."

They were taking lunch as they often did on the balcony of the Great Hall. The sun gained in strength with each day, and an air of life filled their lungs while strength of purpose reflected in their eyes. Mirelle continued her perusal. "It confirms that their scouts to the Shroud Lake shard did indeed find a Portal near Echo Hold, to which the Chalaine, Chertanne, and the faithful—which they underlined—armies of men will retreat to mount a defense against Mikkik's eastern horde and await the birth of God."

"Where does the Portal to Echo Hold lead?" Gen asked.

"To an underground cave in Tenswater, apparently. They've furiously mined it to clear a path. My spies brought word of that two weeks ago."

"I don't suppose Rhugothians are invited inside the walls."

"I'm getting to that. Let's see. No. Correction. Only those Rhugothians who will take an oath to obey the High King. Good. I want a solid contingent of our soldiers inside Echo Hold. I'll send General Torunne and his men. Now that 'Chertanne' has been so gracious as to return our imprisoned Dark Guard, I'll send some in disguise as Tolnorians, Captain Tolbrook included. I have graduated the surviving apprentices to full Dark Guard, so the good Captain needs something new to do. Echo Hold sounded like an adventure for him."

"The army will spend the first three weeks just cleaning the place," Gen speculated. "I should write and warn them about Sir Tornus."

"Please do. It appears they have already started moving men and supplies to the fortress. The Portal is a scant two days ride from the mountain road. Let's see. . . 'We must all be vigilant'. . . Blah, blah, blah. . . Here we go. 'The Chalaine and the Ha'Ulrich are well and anxious for the journey to begin. They send their love to all nations and peoples.'"

"Did the Chalaine manage to send any personal correspondence?"

"Alas, no. I think she realizes that no correspondence between us will be personal. Athan would read every word. Soon we shall see her. At least we are spared a month-long trek across the Shroud Lake shard. I don't think I could bear to pass that miserable copse of trees where I sincerely thought I would freeze or starve to death. As it is, we can leave comfortably in a few weeks."

Mirelle put the letter down and returned to her roast pork and strawberries. Gen admired her. Surely the world held no other woman like her. Just as with the Chalaine during their journey through the canyon, the days of close association with the First Mother had instilled a comfortable enjoyment, trust, and happiness with her that he now identified as the best parts of love. She and her daughter shared some traits, but in many ways differed from each other to such a degree that Gen wondered how he could love them both.

Mirelle met his eye, and a smile bloomed on her face that set his heart to pounding. "Cadaen, please go ask the door warden if Torbrand has arrived," she commanded. He complied, and moments later she sent the servant away. Once they were alone, she leaned forward and kissed Gen lightly. "I have waited a long time to see that look on your face."

Gen swallowed as she stared at him invitingly. Since his comment about pulling back her hair making her look severe, she always wore it down. A breeze teased it about her face as they sat together.

"I wasn't aware I was making any sort of look," Gen responded.

"I know. That's the best part." She kissed him again with more fervor. Gen's mind spun. *How could a woman who has never had a suitor do this so well?* he thought after the capability to think grudgingly returned.

"Gen, I know you love the Chalaine, but she is a married woman. I am not. While you may not love me in the same way or to the same degree, I think those feelings live inside you, though you have never said it. My feelings for you I have made abundantly plain in word and deed. Pledge yourself to me, and I promise you will not regret it. Whether Mikkik or Eldaloth rules at the end of the summer, if I am yours you will never lack for love, or companionship, or pleasure.

"Some time before we march, Gerand and Mena will wed after the Tolnorian fashion within these walls. I will invite a single Pureman here to perform the ritual. He can do the same for us, in secret, with only Ethris as witness. When the drama of the Apocraphon has run its course for good or ill, you and I can announce our love to the world."

Gen opened his mouth to speak, emotions and thoughts a tumult, but Mirelle put a finger to his lips and shushed him. "Think first, Gen, about what I have said. Sort your feelings out and then do what you think is best. Whatever you decide, I will always love you and be as close to you as you will let me be." Gen smiled and rubbed a strand of her hair between his fingers. "Think first, Gen," she admonished. "I know I can be a bit heavy-handed with my flirtations. Make sure you know where your heart and your head are. I know how difficult that can be."

"First Mother," Cadaen announced himself, startling them both. "Torbrand has arrived."

When did Cadaen become so stealthy? Gen wondered.

Mirelle held Gen's eyes a moment longer. "Excellent. Please bring him here and have the servants send up some refreshment for him."

"The news is not all good," Torbrand informed them, travel stained but chipper. "I'm afraid that Chertanne, by which I mean Athan, has increased the number of Aughmerian troops in Tolnor above what I had left there since you announced your split from the Fidelium. Apparently Chertanne—or rather Athan—is keen not to have another defection on his hands."

"And no sign of King Filingrail?"

"I contacted Lord Kildan as you suggested. As you can imagine, he has no kind feelings for me. Even after I firmly

. . . suggested . . . his servant deliver your letter explaining the situation, Duke Kildan refused to see me until the Church issued its revision of the events surrounding the death of the Ilch."

"We just heard of it today," Mirelle told him.

"It hit Tolnor two weeks ago. After that, his Lordship tracked me down, and we met in secret. He flat out refused to give up Filingrail's hiding place, stating it was a matter of that detestable Tolnorian honor. Given the disposition of Aughmerian troops, he also felt an uprising would do more harm than good."

"You said the news was not all good. It appears there is no good at all," Mirelle commented.

"To the good part, then," said Torbrand. "While Duke Kildan has not staged an uprising, he did manage to leave the country with around five hundred of his best soldiers and his Duchess, Missa. There was a tiny bit of bloodshed to which I was able to render my service."

"Where did they go?" Mirelle asked, astonished.

"That's the good news. To Rhugoth! They crossed into Tenswater but had to leave quickly before the Church got wind of what we were doing. We convinced the Portal Mage in Tolnor that we were on our way to Aughmere, and the then told the Portal Mage in Tenswater that the troops were Rhugothian. Word of your excommunication hadn't circulated too widely yet, so we slipped them through before the Church isolated your little shard cluster here."

Mirelle grinned. "Excellent. I wish to see Lord Kildan as soon as it can be arranged. We have some planning to do."

Torbrand leaned back and folded his arms. "I thought you might, and he will arrive in a few days. We need to have some arrangement for quartering his men, and you might be receiving some complaints from various of your subjects, both low and high, upon whom I have called for aid or otherwise inconvenienced . . . or offended."

"Very well. Will you take some refreshment?"

"No. I would like to see Mena."

"She is likely wandering the grounds somewhere with her husband."

"Then I shall look for them. I have some instructions to pass onto him concerning how my daughter is to be treated. Good day."

Mirelle though for a moment. "What do you make of Lord Kildan's move, Gen?"

"Chertanne, by which I mean Athan, will turn purple with fury. All the good generals outside of Aughmere—Torbrand, Torunne, Kildan, and Harband—are now on your side of the fence."

"And let's not forget to put you on the list," Mirelle said. "But what motivated Lord Kildan to act as he did?"

"Honor is the key. I can only guess, but the only way Duke Kildan could stomach Aughmerian occupation was by believing he would, in the end, serve the prophecy through complying with the commands of the Ha'Ulrich. Your dispatch no doubt opened his eyes to Athan's duplicitous—and thus dishonorable—machinations. For him, your cause is the only purely honorable one left."

She wiped her mouth and stood. "An interesting assessment. I am quite pleased he has come, whatever the reason."

Gen, High Protector of Rhugoth, sat alone in the library. Two weeks had passed since Torbrand's return, and the time had come at last to march. The Church had sent detailed instructions about where and when the armies of Rhugoth would be permitted to cross into Tenswater and through the Portal—long after the main bodies of Tolnorians and Aughmerians. They had a week long march around the Kingsblood Lake ahead of them, and the steady stream of arrangements and details and complaints had kept a good night's sleep just out of reach for the better part of the week. The title of Lord Protector held a heavy price, and Gen wondered where Regent Ogbith had ever found the time to go for a drink at the Quickblade Inn.

Luckily, he learned to rely on the experience of Telmerran. Lesson one was to delegate everything possible. Lesson two, the people you delegate to will most likely do it wrong. Lesson three, when they do mess up, get angry but be sure not to dismiss your best people over trivial matters. As for squabbling and complaints, a good leader must know that there is rarely a satisfactory answer for a whining soldier, so find a way to reward all complaints with extra work for the aggrieved. So far, it had worked fairly well, though he admitted that much of his success he could attribute to his mystique and the general knowledge that Mirelle favored him excessively.

An hour before Gerand's wedding, Gen had escaped all his duties and fled to the confines of the library, hoping to find some way to settle his mind and come up with a response to Mirelle's proposal. His love for the Chalaine filled every thought of acceptance with guilt; his love for Mirelle and his general awe of her intelligence and beauty made every argument to decline seem idiotic. All the broken pieces of shattered arguments bobbed and floated on a confused sea of emotion and reason.

I am the Ilch. The Chalaine is married. There is a war brewing. I love the Chalaine. I love Mirelle. We might all be dead in a month. I don't deserve either one. They would be happier with someone else. I would be miserable without them.

Nothing stuck. One thought could not claw its way to preeminence over the others. Mirelle, politely, had not pressed him further for an answer, though she certainly had not retired her affectionate attentions from him. While he knew she did this out of love and a need for companionship, he doubted she realized how addicted he had become to stolen kisses and warm embraces. The need for them ran through him like a sickly sweet drink that he hadn't quite identified as a poison or an elixir. Perhaps it was both, but he knew the difference between love of the heart and pleasures of passion, and he would not let the pleasures have a voice in his decision.

Frustrated, he went in search of a book that held a poem that had teased his memory all day with the ending stanza. At length he found it in a collection of writings preserved from the Second Mikkikian War, author unknown.

A black tower rises into the night,
And there sit I, gazing down on your dance,
The torches, like flowers of flickering light,
Unveil to my mind the tombs of the past.
I see the smiles of those who danced before
And lost in lovers' arms laughed to cheer
Who but for looking in eyes they adore
Would have seen the darkness circling near.
But blind to the threat, cares smothered by lips,
They dance in the torchlight, by distraction brave.
From behind comes death; from the dance they trip,
Ears for the music stopped up by the grave.
So decide to dance, but choose not to love,
For the torches burn out, and the shadows come.

He snapped the book shut and leaned back. *Choose not to love.* If love was a choice, he could not remember consciously making it. Vainly he willed the sun to halt in the sky to give him more time, but time skipped along, heedless of his wishes.

A servant entered the room. "Milord, it is time. Mirelle awaits you outside her apartments."

"Thank you. I will come shortly."

The servant left and Gen rose. From this day forward he

would live with regret, and all of his supposed wisdom only stared back at him with a silly grin and shrugged its shoulders. Replacing the book, he put on the coat of his dress uniform and left.

Mirelle waited patiently for him, dressed, as always, to erase any thoughts but those of her. She smiled, but noting the gravity in Gen's countenance, tempered her affectionate greeting. Gen extended his arm to her and she took it.

"Cadaen, would you mind walking ahead?" Gen requested. "I wish to speak to the First Mother privately."

Cadaen said, "If she wills it."

"I do, Cadaen. We shall be along by and by."

Cadaen bowed and left, and Gen walked forward slowly, breathing in Mirelle's inebriating scent. They crossed from the antechamber of the Chalaine and into the hallways beneath the Great Hall.

"Is all in order for the march tomorrow?" Mirelle asked tentatively.

"Hmm? Oh yes. Yes, it is. Will you please demote me?"

Mirelle laughed, breaking the tension. "Of course not! You have done too well, as I knew you would. The generals are astonished at how expertly you have handled your new position. I think Tern Kildan would claim you for a son if he could."

"He has been very helpful." Gen pulled her to a halt. "Listen to me. When you split with General Torunne at Echo Road, please take Kildan's counsel over Harband's. Harband is a capable commander, I'm sure, but he enjoys the killing a little too much. Also, do not ride at the front of your army or dress in a remarkable way. Uyumaak archers are trained to search out leadership and strike there first. Keep close to Cadaen, and keep capable soldiers with you at all times. If you're forced to run, do not wait for cover of night. Dark is more of a disadvantage to you than to Uyumaak. I should have taken time to teach you the knife. . ."

She smiled and put her hand on his cheek. "Gen, I will be fine. You're the one taking the most risk. Does that mind of yours ever stop turning? You looked so preoccupied and severe just now." Gen smoothed his features. "Oh, no you don't!" Mirelle objected. "None of Torbrand Khairn's soul-smothering training today, Lord Gen."

Gen grinned and kissed her.

"That was nice," she complimented him, smiling. "At last you kiss me. Things have been feeling a bit one-sided."

"I am sorry," Gen apologized.

"For the kiss?"

"Of course not. How could I regret that? How could anyone? I apologize for the seeming one-sided nature of things. I do love you, Mirelle."

Before he could say more, she put her arms around him and buried her head in his shoulder. He pulled her close as she trembled, tears sliding down her cheeks. "You have no idea how long I have waited to be loved, and how long I have hoped you would love me. While any man's sincere love would be a blessing, to have yours, the best man that I know, is a joy beyond any dream or hope I could ever have."

"Surely you must see that loving me is utter recklessness."

"No more than loving me," she returned, pulling herself away and wiping her eyes. "You must know that you will never get your way."

"Please, Mirelle. Be serious. You know what I am. You know what we face."

Mirelle ignored him, pulling him around and resuming their course down the hall.

"You know, I have called you 'Lord Gen' for weeks now, and it simply does not seem right. It has no weight."

"I need one of those impressive last names all those aristocrats seem to have. Alas, I have no family line I wish to claim, and, tragically, I am no longer Lord of Blackshire."

"What a coincidence. I need a last name, too! This whole First Mother business is nearly at an end, and Queen Mirelle won't do. What do you say we invent a last name together, and we can share it?"

"That was a clever segue," he chuckled.

"And you fell for it. I've always thought names that end in 'dor' carried a certain weight, like Erindor or Fillindor. What do you think?"

"You can't be serious. 'Mirelle Fillindor'? Ridiculous."

"Come up with a better one, then!"

"Short names carry more power, like 'Black', or 'Stone' or 'Loris'."

"*Black* and *Stone*?" she mocked. "How unoriginal. And really, would you want to be called Lord Loris for the rest of your life? Lord Fillindor is clearly better, whatever you may say."

"Come now. Who would ever cross a Lord and Lady Black?"

Mirelle's laugh mingled with the happy sounds of celebration that crescendoed as they neared the Great Hall. "I do look forward to watching Torbrand Khairn lead his daughter to the marriage altar. The dead collection of Shadans may just rise up from the grave to prevent it. This will be a spectacle."

As they neared the doors, the Chamberlain bowed and turned to announce them, but Mirelle held him back. "Not tonight, Hurney."

They slipped in unannounced, but not unnoticed, and in moments they enjoyed the warmth and cheer of friends, old and new. Leaving Mirelle with Lord Kildan, Gen crossed to Mena and Gerand, who were all smiles. Gen hugged them both warmly.

"I see that Volney's surprise has not arrived yet," Gen commented to his Tolnorian friend upon noticing their young companion sitting quietly in a corner.

Gerand glanced at their mutual friend. "I believe the steward is busy finding some piece of finery for Lena to wear that is fit for a company such as this. I hope Volney doesn't kill us. He will be mightily embarrassed."

"Probably," Gen said, "but he'll get over it rather quickly, I think. Look, there she is."

"Ahh!" Gerand exclaimed. "Yes, he will get over it. He might actually thank us before the year is out."

"She's adorable," Mena agreed. "But we're all rather plain compared to the First Mother. Perhaps, Gen, you could tell her she is quite beautiful enough and need not outshine us all so thoroughly. But I mean no disrespect, of course. I was only jesting. Please don't tell her I said anything. Why did my father let me grow up so outspoken? I suppose it is time she could look for a suitor."

"I think the search is over," Gerand smirked, nudging Gen.

"Really?" Mena said.

"Oh, yes. But watch. Lena is nearly upon him."

Lena, clearly nervous, had wound her way toward the unsuspecting Volney, touching him lightly on the arm. At first he didn't seem to recognize the young woman, but after a few moments he shot to his feet, face turning several shades of red before settling on sanguine. They chuckled as he desperately searched for some proper way to show his delight, resolving at last to kiss her hand.

Mirelle arrived at Gen's side. "I see all went according to plan. Gerand, Mena, are you ready to begin?"

Both bowed. Gerand said, "Yes, First Mother. Again we thank you. . ."

"None of that, Gerand. Go speak with your respective fathers, and all of you meet with the Chamberlain. I'll find the Pureman and send him over so he can dispense with his wisdom and final instructions."

"Yes, First Mother."

Mirelle said to Gen, "Now come, Lord Fillindor, we must find that Pureman."

"As you wish, Lady Black."

"And will he be leaving early this evening or very late?"

The scales in Gen's mind teetered both ways. Reason, wisdom, passion, and emotion collided so violently within his heart that he scarcely knew what came out of his own mouth. But when the repressed words finally found the freedom of the open air, they sounded right, and he knew it was the answer he had intended to give all along.

Be sure to catch the entire Trysmoon Saga!

Trysmoon Book One: Ascension
Trysmoon Book Two: Duty
Trysmoon Book Three: Hunted
Trysmoon Book Four: Sacrifice

Get more information at briankfullerbooks.com

41885305R00199

Made in the USA
Lexington, KY
31 May 2015